GAME MISCONDUCT

The Dartmouth Cobras

By
Bianca Sommerland

Copyright 2012, Bianca Sommerland

ALL RIGHTS RESERVED
Edited by Lisa Hollett
Cover art by Reese Dante

D1713712

Dedications

Les Canadiens. Je me souviens 24, J'espere pour 25.

Acknowledgements

A BIG thank you to my fabulous crit partners Cherise Sinclair and Cari Silverwood. You saw the potential for this book when it was just a dream of sexy bodies and hockey sticks and let me know loud and clear when it became more. To Sonya Grady, who knows the sport and nudged me away from spoon-feeding jargon—her only fault is rooting for the wrong team!

To my beta-readers: Ebony Mckennie, who's always ready to kick my butt when my confidence falters, Stacey Price, who gave me whiplash with her quick and decisive response, and Genevieve Trahan, who shares my love for the *right* team. Without you, I wouldn't have had the guts to hand my baby off to the public. Rosie Moewe, thank you for making sure my baby didn't go out there all dirty!

To Riane Holt for reading, rereading, getting on my case, threatening not to take out the whip . . . you are a great friend, and I couldn't have done this without you!

Most importantly, to my family, who puts up with my obsession for writing and hockey and dusts me off every so often when I've been immobile for too long.

~~~

Prologue

The players on the flat screen above the hard liquor skated in reverse as the bartender rewound the game. *Again.* Piss-drunk fans crowded around the bar cheered as though watching the winning goal live and thrust their empty glass mugs out for refills. Tap beer was on the house whenever the home team won. First time in a while the *generous* policy would cost the Red Claw's owner a dime.

"Perron passes to Vanek. Vanek winds up, shoots . . . Scores!" the announcer shouted as cheers erupted from the stadium crowd. "The Cobras win!"

Max Perron lifted his beer in acknowledgment as strangers slapped his shoulders and yapped about his wicked setup. Finally, they backed off him to surround Tyler Vanek, rookie extraordinaire.

"Naw, Thornton don't scare me!" Vanek laughed and thumped his chest with his fist, his tone dropping as he aped the Wild's enforcer. "'You wanna go? You wanna go?'" He paused to accept a beer from the pretty young waitress who'd been hovering and took a swig. "Sure, man, just let me drop this off in your net."

Freakin' mouthpiece. One corner of Max's mouth crept up. Maybe he should remind the kid he'd be gumming his buffalo wings if their good buddy Dominik Mason hadn't dropped the brute like a bag of manure.

He's got their attention. Why ruin a good thing? Max fished in his pocket for his cell phone to check for missed calls. *Maybe I'll have a reason to slip out early.*

The scuffing of shoes at his side brought his head up.

"She won't call, Perron." His captain and best friend, Sloan Callahan, gave him a grim smile. "Her and Coach have been together for three months—they won't be breaking up any time soon."

"Coach Stanton's a dick. Oriana will figure it out eventually." Max gulped some beer to wash down the bitterness clogging up his throat. "We talked before the game. She didn't sound happy."

1

Sloan sighed and rested his forearms on the shiny, black bar top. "Paul's good at smoothing things over with her. They're probably having make-up sex as we speak."

Make-up . . . his stomach clenched like he'd gotten a good gut-check. He groaned as he pictured her soft body laid out on the bed she shared with Coach, her beautiful eyes squeezed shut as she rose to each hard thrust.

"Fuck, man!" He slammed his bottle on the bar and stood. "*Seriously?* You really think I need to hear that?"

"Yeah, I do." Sloan nodded toward the back door of the bar. "I got Roxy for the night. Why don't you join us—have a bit of fun? You haven't had any since you got hung up on that girl."

Rolling his eyes, Max finished his beer. He had plenty of fun—just the other night he'd swapped Vanek's equipment with the goaltender's. Pranking the rookie was worth a couple of laughs.

You fixin' to tell Callahan messing with the kid is enough for you? He smirked and considered. Might throw the man off for a second . . . His lips tightened. *The man's dealt with all my kinks so far. I doubt that would faze him.*

Across the packed bar, he spotted Roxy, illuminated by the bright red exit sign. Her pouty, crimson lips curved when she caught him looking. She flipped her sleek, blond hair over one shoulder and tipped her head toward the door. The invitation alone was enough to make his dick swell against his thigh. He adjusted his jeans to give it some space.

Roxy slipped two fingers in her mouth. Her cheeks drew in as she sucked hard.

Naughty little whore—and damn proud of it too.

"Turning tricks just does it for me," she'd told him once. "Being with different guys every night, sneaking around . . . I'm careful, I'm clean, and I'm expensive enough to be picky. I don't see nothin' wrong with it. Do you think I'm a freak?"

"No, I don't think you're a freak." He'd indulged in a rare moment of postcoital cuddling with the hooker in the backseat of Sloan's classic 'stang. Inhaling the hot scent of sex mixed with Roxy's spicy perfume, he'd felt so at ease, he'd made a confession of his own. "I just wish I could find a girl like you who'd be mine—a girl who'd be okay with *my* freakiness."

"You'll find her, Max," she'd said. "But until you do, I'm perfectly happy giving you everything you need."

And she really was. So, after their intimate little chat, Max gave up looking for "that girl" and decided to enjoy all Roxy had to offer.

Then he met Oriana Delgado.

Beautiful, sweet, easy to talk to—hell, he'd started falling for her the moment she'd stuttered his name. He had a feeling she'd *get* him . . . only Coach got to her first. And the bastard had her daddy's stamp of approval, which mattered way too much. From what she'd let slip, Coach didn't treat her good.

I would treat her like a queen. I could give her so much more . . .

But not tonight. Tonight, she was in the arms of another man. A man she'd made it clear she wanted to be with. Nothing Max could say would change her mind. He couldn't force her to leave the man, and pining over her made him look like a fool.

The skin over his biceps tightened as he clenched his fists. He turned to Sloan. "Motel or parking lot?"

Sloan grinned and gestured for Max to lead the way out. "How 'bout the alley behind the bar? Someone might see us, but the thrill is worth the risk."

Max shuddered and nodded. He weaved through the throng of drunks, then paused beside Roxy. In a black fishnet shirt and a leather micro-mini, Roxy looked ready to be fucked. Nothing new; she always did. But this time was different. Something in her blazing, blue eyes was almost tender. Sloan must have told her about his . . . predicament.

A pity fuck. He snorted and rolled his shoulders. Not that it mattered—unless sympathy came with a discount?

Roxy frowned at his snort and reached for the metal door handle. "Shall we?"

"Yeah, we shall." Max put his hand on the door and held it open for her. "After you, ma'am."

"Uh—" She blushed and ducked out. "Thanks."

Once they'd cleared the door, he shoved her against the brick wall and braced an arm across her throat.

She let out a surprised squeak.

"Last time we were all together, you mentioned a scene you wanted to try." He bared his teeth in a ruthless smile. "Still game, babe?"

Her eyes widened, and she shivered. Her gaze flicked from him to Sloan. Then she closed her eyes and nodded.

Sloan snarled and lurched to grab a fistful of Roxy's hair. "Say it, Roxy. The money ain't worth the pain if you're not enjoying yourself. You know how rough I can be."

"Yes, Sloan." Roxy whimpered when Sloan released her. "I've been fantasizing about this for so long—I wouldn't have told you otherwise."

"Good girl." Sloan gave her a tender smile and plucked a switchblade from his pocket.

Heart hammering in his chest, Max inhaled deeply as Sloan opened the knife. He'd seen Sloan scene with knives before, knew the edge was dull, but he still felt an instinctive rush of adrenaline. Logic insisted he protect the defenseless woman from the psycho with the knife. But something deep and dark reveled in Roxy's reaction to the threat. As Sloan touched the blade to her throat, her thighs shifted. The sweet musk of her arousal mingled with her floral perfume and Sloan's cologne. Under pale flesh, a thick blue pulsed against the blade.

"What do you say if you want me to stop, Roxy?" Sloan's tone was dead calm.

The tip of Roxy's tongue flicked over her bottom lip. "Pay up."

"That's right." Sloan's expression changed, warping to one of pure insanity. "Listen to me, bitch. I had every intention of slicing you up and stuffing all your pretty pieces in that big trash bin over there." He pointed to a massive black bin across the alley from them. "But the way you moved in the bar got me all hard. I watched you all night and started thinking there might be better uses for this pretty body. Was I right?"

Roxy started to nod, then whimpered when the blade dented her flesh. "Please don't hurt me. I'll do whatever you want!"

Damn. Max rubbed his dick through his jeans and gave Roxy a heavy-lidded look as he watched for any sign that she was more scared than turned-on. She lowered one hand to the hem of her skirt and curled her fingers under the leather as though tempted to touch herself.

"Max, check if the slut's wet." Sloan's lips twitched as he glanced down. He'd noticed too. "I'm not in the mood for dry pussy tonight."

Kneeling beside Roxy, Max slid his hand up between her thighs. Her flesh quivered as he stroked her with his fingers. When he touched the crotch of her panties, she gasped.

The silken material was soaked. He pushed the fabric into her with two fingertips and grinned up at Sloan.

"She's drenched." He shoved in deeper and felt her pussy spasm. His cock twitched, and a bead of pre-cum seeped out. "I'm thinkin' she needs to be fucked."

"She will be." Sloan wrapped his hand around the nape of Roxy's neck. "But, first, she's gonna earn me sparing her life. Get on your knees, whore."

Roxy carefully eased down to her knees, hissing in each breath, eyes crossing as she tried to watch the knife, which Sloan kept pressed against her throat. The tips of her red stilettos scraped the pavement as she shifted from knee to knee.

"Stop moving," Sloan said.

"There's gravel digging into my knees." Roxy's color dropped as Sloan slid the knife across her throat like he fully intended to slice her flesh. "Please, it hurts!"

"It'll hurt more if I cut your neck, don't you think?" Sloan smiled when she nodded. "Now take out my dick and suck it. If you're good, me and my friend will fuck you and let you go."

"O-okay." Roxy brought her trembling fingers to the zipper of Sloan's black jeans and deftly freed his cock. She closed her eyes when Sloan traced her cheek with the tip of the knife. As soon as Sloan moved the knife, she swallowed his dick whole.

In the shadows of the bar, with the far-off streetlights glinting off the knife and the beads of sweat on Roxy's temples, with the black tears slipping down her cheeks, the whole scene reminded Max of a horror flick. Only, in the movies, the girl wouldn't leave the dark alley alive—no matter what she did. He stood, then took a step back to enjoy the show. Pussy juice cooled on his fingers as the wind picked up, and he brought them to his mouth to suck them clean.

Sloan groaned as Roxy deep-throated him, and Max gulped back a moan. Roxy sucking Sloan's dick with a knife held so close to her face was one of the most erotic things he'd ever seen. Not a scene he would have thought of on his own, but he couldn't deny how it affected him. His balls tightened with each wet thrust of his friend's cock between those soft, glossy lips, with the thrill of seeing things he shouldn't be seeing. The very atmosphere around them thickened with fear and arousal. Their emotions and desires wound so tight with his, he couldn't tell them apart. He felt like he'd swallowed a bottle of Viagra or something. Like jerking off for hours wouldn't be enough. Like his dick would be hard forever.

"Enjoying the show, Perron?" Sloan asked between grunts.

Max ground his teeth and nodded. He stuffed his hand in his jeans and gave his dick a hard tug. "You know I am."

"We sharing or are you just gonna watch?" Sloan raked his fingers into Roxy's hair and jerked her to her feet. "Because I need to pound this bitch's pussy."

"Do it," Max said.

"Please." Roxy's hands slapped the brick wall when Sloan shoved her away from him. "I want—"

Sloan flipped up her skirt and slapped her ass. "Shut up."

"Hey!" Roxy scowled over her shoulder at Sloan. "Careful, someone might hear."

Now she's worried? Max sighed. Much as being watched appealed to him, he had to admit, Roxy had a point. "If you're gonna play that way, maybe we should go somewhere private. She hollered so loud last time, you freaked *me* out."

"Don't worry." Sloan laughed and pulled a condom out of his pocket. Once covered, he positioned himself between Roxy's spread thighs. "No one's—"

Sloan froze and stared at the mouth of the alley. Max frowned and followed his friend's gaze.

His blood ran cold when he saw who stood there, wide-eyed and pale with shock.

She turned and ran.

"Oriana!" Max bolted after her. "Oriana!"

✳ ✳ ✳ ✳

Oriana's throat felt scored, like she'd swallowed sand and ground-up glass. She imagined blood rising with the bile in her throat; the pain was that deep. Her soft place to land wasn't there. Wasn't soft. Wasn't . . . she didn't know what it was. What *he* was. How could he?

A horn blared, then another. Bright white headlights flashed. She stumbled back from the edge of the curb. Arms wrapped around her waist and held her tight.

"Oriana!" Max hauled her farther away from the intersection. Golden strands of hair stuck to the beads of sweat on his temples. "Hell! Why didn't you stop?"

"I can't talk to you right now, Max." She pushed at his chest and sighed when he refused to budge. "Let me go."

"No. Not 'til I'm certain you'll be all right." His sharp tone softened to a soft drawl as he slid his hand down her arm to twine his fingers with hers. "Come on, darlin', let's go for coffee. I know a good place."

The "good place" was the one they went to every time he had a home game—and the last place she wanted to be. The front of the café was filled with people winding down from hours of clubbing, but there were a few empty tables near the back where she and Max always sat in relative privacy and talked. Here, she felt smart, pretty, special. Here, the jolt came from more than caffeine. It came from just being around this man.

This man she apparently didn't know as well as she thought.

Max took her jacket to lay over the back of a chair before pulling it out for her. She perched on the seat, placed her purse on her lap, then clasped her hands together on the table. Max sat across from her and reached over to cover her hands with his.

He didn't speak at first, just looked at her, as though he sensed that, at the wrong word, the wrong move, she'd bolt. And she looked back and realized the last thing she wanted to do was leave. Being in Max's presence was like a vacation on a tropical beach. His blond hair always seemed windswept. His skin reminded her of smooth sand, glowing as though just kissed by the sun. She licked her lips, tempted to press them to the back of his hand to absorb some of his warmth. To inhale the fresh scent that clung to him, the scent of the ice, which on him smelled exactly like the surf catching the breeze.

"You came to the bar to see me." His tone was level, calm, but his hands shook with nervous energy. "Did something happen?"

Tell him!

But she couldn't. Not after what she'd seen.

Besides, vacations were temporary escapes. Not places to stay forever.

"No, nothing happened." She smiled at Max, then glanced at the door. What could she say to convince him she could walk out of there without blindly stepping into traffic again? "I just wanted to congratulate you—maybe have a couple of beers. I didn't realize you'd be . . . busy."

Brow furrowed, Max looked down at their hands and nodded slowly. "Yeah, well, I'm sorry you had to see that."

"Me, too." She flushed and ducked her head when he glanced up. "I was . . . shocked. To tell you the truth, I almost called the cops. I thought you and Callahan were . . . until she said she didn't want anyone to hear. Then I realized she wanted you both to do . . . well . . . whatever you were doing."

A familiar waitress stepped up to their table and flashed a brilliant smile, her gaze, as usual, lingering just a little longer on Max. "Max, Oriana, I'm surprised to see the two of you here so late. Do you want the usual or something decaf?"

"The usual," Max said.

Oriana nodded distractedly.

After the waitress left, Max leaned forward and squeezed Oriana's hands.

"Look, I reckon the whole thing seems pretty messed up, but—"

She pulled her hands free and shook her head. "You don't have to explain, Max. It's none of my business."

"Right, then." He rubbed his face with a hand and sat back. "I just don't want this to change things between us. It's not like I do stuff like that all the time."

You don't? Then why . . . ? She inhaled and decided she wanted him to explain. They were friends, and they'd always been able to talk. For some reason, he hadn't been comfortable telling her about this side of him. Maybe fate had decided to step in and show her who he really was before she made any rash decisions.

Like you did by jumping into a relationship with Paul?

No, that was different. Paul was . . .

Unreasonable, selfish, and sometimes even cruel. But still . . .

God, what had she been thinking hunting down Max in the middle of the night?

Not much beyond getting out of that house.

"I can't do this anymore," she'd said, stuffing all the clothes she could grab into a suitcase before slamming it shut. "It's over."

Paul had laughed. "Enough with the drama. We both know you've got nowhere else to go."

Upper lip stiff, head down, she'd hauled her suitcase to the door and grabbed her car keys. "Yes, I do."

"Right. Well, I'll leave the porch light on for you." Paul had followed her to the door, stood there, and watched her go. "And 'cause I'm such a nice guy, I won't say I told you so when you come back."

I'm not going back. She'd thought it then, and she thought it now. But the certainty was gone.

The waitress brought their drinks and retreated quietly, obviously having caught some of the tension between the two. Oriana sipped her mochaccino, savoring the espresso roast and rich dark chocolate topped with just a hint of cinnamon. Max made a throaty sound of pleasure and licked some frothed milk from his upper lip. Her pulse quickened. Damn the man for being so sexy. This would be much easier if he were ugly. Or gay.

Then again, probably not. Even if he were ugly, she'd still love the way he made her feel. And if he were gay, she'd wish he weren't.

Stop stalling. There's no easy way out. Get the facts and go from there.

She set her cup on the table and traced the glass handle with her pinky. "So you were waiting for Sloan to finish so you could—"

"Not this time. I was fine just watching." Max's cup clinked as he set it down. "I'm a voyeur. I get more out of watching than participating."

Her quickened pulse seemed to suddenly stop. She lifted her head and stared. The words left her mouth before her brain had time

9

to filter them. "A voyeur? No, I don't believe it. I can't see you sneaking around, getting off watching people having sex. You can have any woman you want." With those big shoulders, so muscular, yet relaxed like they could carry the weight of the world effortlessly. "Voyeurs are insecure freaks who use two-way mirrors and peepholes to invade people's privacy." And that smile, the one he was giving her now, the one that made her tingle down to her toes. "They—" She slapped her hand over her mouth to shut herself up.

Great friend she was. He'd confided in her, and in return, she'd insulted him.

But rather than take offense, he chuckled, then took another sip of coffee. "Don't hold back, Oriana; tell me how you *really* feel."

Her cheeks heated up. "I'm sorry. I—"

"Don't be. I'm used to it."

Like *that* made her feel any better. "Please. I want to understand."

He nodded and put his hands, palms up, on the table. When she gave him hers, he continued. "I was still in my teens the first time I ever did something that would classify as voyeurism. I walked in on a friend of mine having sex at a party. He shouted at me, told me to get out, but I just stood there—I couldn't move. Then I . . . well, let's say I did something embarrassing. The guy stopped being my friend after that. I talked to my dad about it—we've always been close, so I figured he should know I had a problem. His solution was to buy me a bunch of porn."

"Did that help?"

"For a bit, but I couldn't help fantasizing about being there in person. I never did anything about it 'cause my dad gave me a lecture about intruding on people's privacy, and his word is law. I buried my 'sick urges'—my words, not his—until I got old enough to go to strip clubs. Some of the girl-on-girl action helped a little."

"I'll bet." Oriana smiled, thinking—despite his strange urges—Max was a typical guy.

Max cleared his throat. "Yeah, well, I got exactly what I needed when Sloan and Dominik invited me to a club they go to. They were sharin' a girl and . . ."

The cafe seemed to heat up. Oriana inhaled sharply, leaning

forward. "And?"

"Sloan looked right at me and asked me to join in. I was already so turned on, I didn't even think twice. First time I realized being watched pushed all my buttons too. I could feel the eyes of all the people in the club on me—like they were all sharing the experience. Like it was one great big orgy." He shook his head and combed his fingers through his hair. "After that, me and Sloan went to the club together all the time. And . . . well, hell, I told him all my deep, dark secrets, and he acted like it was no big deal. Said so long as the people I watched consented, it was all good. And he consents a lot."

"I saw that." The coffee and the room and her blood cooled as she pictured them. Sloan surrounded by writhing bodies and Max drinking it in, savoring every moment of ecstasy before he joined them. Not something she could participate in. *Ever.* It was just too . . . out there. Paul's attitude, his offhand cruelty, even his lackluster lovemaking, suddenly didn't seem that bad. At least it was normal. She frowned at her coffee cup. "But you do know not everyone is into—"

"Things would be different with you, sugar." He ran his thumb over her knuckles, reaching out to tip her chin up with a finger. "I'd find a way to change. You'd be enough for me."

For a split second, she was tempted to say yes. But that wouldn't be fair. She held back a sigh and finished her coffee. "You shouldn't have to change for anyone, Max. There's nothing wrong with who you are."

"But I would. I'm not telling you this because I expect you to . . ." He studied her face for a moment, then withdrew his hands. "I just want you to understand what happened tonight."

The smile on her lips felt like it had been sewn in place. She stood and pulled on her coat. "I do."

"Good." He picked up the bill and shook his head when she opened her purse. "I've got it. Just give me a sec, and I'll walk you to your car."

"Thanks, but no. I need a few minutes alone to think." She focused on buttoning up her jacket so he wouldn't see the lie in her eyes. "Much as I understand, this is a lot to absorb. Besides, I'm parked right down the street."

"It's awfully late." He looked helplessly at the line in front of the cash register and the waitresses rushing to clean up after the crowd. "I'd be more comfortable if you'd—"

"This isn't Montreal. You're more dangerous than anyone I'll meet outside—*Hey!*" She giggled when he made a grab for her. For a second, things seemed lighter, brighter, their familiar playfulness a splash of yellow paint all over reality.

He caught her and wrapped her up in his great big arms, holding her close. Surrounded by his warmth, his strength, she felt her knees grow weak. She peeked up at him.

His eyes twinkled with mischief. He bent low and his lips brushed her earlobe as he spoke, letting his accent thicken his tone. "So you think I'm dangerous?"

Hell, yes. When he talked to her, in that smooth, rich voice— damn, the things he could have made her do. Thankfully, he didn't let the Southern playboy out often—with her anyway—but even without the vocal seductiveness and the face and the body, he played havoc with her concept of reality. He made her smile and laugh, made her believe in silly things like love at first sight.

But she was a Delgado. The responsible sister.

And he'd just proved he wasn't the man for her.

"You really shouldn't—" She squirmed out of his arms and the pain inside returned, even harder to swallow than before. "I have a boyfriend, Max."

His lips drew together in a thin, hard line. "After last time, I thought you were ready to end things with him. You kissed me."

Another blush flared up on her cheeks. She smacked his arm. "That's not fair. You gave me chocolate—and it was a kiss on the cheek. A friendly kiss."

"Ah, I see." He bent over and pressed a light kiss on her forehead. "Well, then, here's another." His cheek brushed hers. "And if things are going well between you and Paul, I'm happy for you, honestly. But I hope you've made it clear you won't tolerate him making you feel like shit about yourself whenever he's having a bad day."

She rested her head on his solid chest, breathing in his fresh scent, lightly tainted with beer. As she drew away, the overpowering aroma of freshly ground coffee beans took over, clearing her head.

"Of course." She hooked her purse over her arm and nodded at the waitress waiting nearby. "You sure you don't want me to pay for myself?"

"I'm sure." He patted her cheek. "Might make a dent in my savings, but you're worth it."

"All right, then I guess I'll see you around," she said, even though she knew she wouldn't. She swallowed when he let her go and started to turn away. "Thank you for . . . everything."

"Yeah, well, take care. And don't you worry." His jaw worked as he paused, head down, and shoved his hand into his pocket for his wallet. "I'll be here when . . . whenever."

The bells over the door tinkled as she hurried out, desperate to get to her car before his sweet acceptance of her choices ripped apart her resolve. Before she'd reached the end of the block, the bells sounded again. She glanced over her shoulder and saw him, standing there. The gentle weight of his eyes on her back remained until she'd reached the safety of her car.

Once inside, she eyed him through the rearview mirror. Her heart beat hard between her ears when he didn't move. Finally, he stuffed his hands in his pockets and took off in the other direction.

Make a U-turn! Go tell him the truth!

Shaking her head, she started the car, then pulled out. All the way home, her decision dragged her down. When she trampled up the front steps, she felt like all her bones were made of lead. The porch light blinded her as she fumbled in her pockets for her keys.

The door swung open. Paul sighed and gestured her inside. "Let's get this over with."

She closed the door softly behind her, then pulled off her jacket and went to hang it in the closet. "Get what over with?"

"You're sorry, you'll never do it again—"

Her shoulders stiffened as she turned to face him. "I'm not sorry."

His dark brown brows creased in confusion. "But you're back."

"Yeah. I'm back." She strode across the living room, kicked off her shoes, then plunked down on the stiff, white leather sofa. "And I'll be sleeping here tonight."

The grandfather clock in the hall ticked off the seconds in the silence. Paul's shadow wisped over her as he crossed the room.

"Hey, I'm giving the guys a break tomorrow." He scuffed his socks on the carpet and cleared his throat. "Maybe we can go visit your dad?"

Damn him, he always knows just what to say. Visits with her dad were . . . pleasant when Paul was around.

"I'd like that." Curling up on her side, she wrapped her arms around her chest. The dull ache wouldn't go away. Almost felt like something inside had been surgically removed. Maybe her heart.

"Okay." Paul bent down and kissed her cheek. "We'll talk more in the morning. I was a little rough on you . . . I like that you're so into the game, but this is my job. I see things differently than you do."

"I know." The wet spot where he'd pressed his lips felt cold. But for some reason, the spot on her forehead where Max had kissed her still burned. *So not right.* "But a win's a win. You've gotta give the guys more credit. The goaltender was off his game. If the first line hadn't pushed so hard—"

"That's what you don't get. If they'd focused on defense like I'd told them to—they deserved to lose after that performance."

"The first line worked their asses off."

Paul pushed away from the sofa. "You mean Max."

"Not *only* him." But *he* was probably the main reason for the fight. Maybe Paul sensed something between them. And if he did, this was all her fault. She reached out to touch the back of his hand. "I really hate when you call me stupid, Paul. Just because I can't understand why you'd get so upset about your team winning—"

"And you never will." He shook his head. "We'll talk more tomorrow, Oriana. Get some sleep."

Lying perfectly still, Oriana listened to the sound of Paul ascending the steps to their bedroom. She stared at the front door for a while, feeling trapped. If only she had the guts to get up and leave again. For good.

But this was her life. What she'd chosen. What she wanted. Normal. Stable. Things would get easier once she accepted all her dreams of some great romance were just that. Dreams.

But for now . . . she closed her eyes and drifted away into a place where reality didn't matter. Where Max waited with his teasing smile and warm embrace.

Chapter One

Rock on blades in the cold, shadowed spotlight,
The words "flag" and "freedom" stir you.
Do not be lulled by the song.
Hear the screams, knights of the ice, wield your stick swords.
Fly the wings, break away, never shy from the crush.
Play as though at war and hear the trumpet sound.

Standing in the shadow of the blocky beast of gray slate and glass, Oriana gazed up at the glaring light coming from the high window of her father's office. In her mind's eye, she could see the poem, written by her twelve-year-old self, etched on a bronze plaque. The plaque hung on the wall behind her father's desk among tarnished gold medals and faded blue ribbons. The original had been lost long ago, but she could still picture her father, holding the stationery with the pink carnation print, hands shaking as he read the meticulously handwritten words. His eyes glistening, he'd laughed and hugged her.

"Beautiful, sweetheart," he'd said. "You have no idea how much this means to me."

For a while, his words rang true, but, by now, that precious plaque had gathered years' worth of dust. The Delgado Forum, the largest building this close to the Narrows, was all her father cared about.

She inched closer to the wall.

Paranoid much? She rolled her eyes and laughed at herself. Even if she stood in the middle of the street, her father couldn't see her from way up there. And she was waiting for Paul, so it wouldn't matter if he did.

The muffled sound of Metric's "Stadium Love" came from her book bag. Heavy textbooks thunked on the sidewalk as she dropped the bag between her feet and crouched to unlatch the buckle. Reaching in to fetch her cell, her hand brushed the smallest book and heat skimmed her ears. She should have stopped at home and dropped it off. If anyone saw what she'd been reading . . .

Her fingers touched the cool, metallic edge of her cell. She snatched it out and closed her bag, making sure the strap was tight. The muscles in her thighs clenched as she rose, wobbling a little on her heels. Stilettos took some getting used to. Too bad the comfy sneakers in her bag wouldn't look half as sexy as the thigh-high leather boots she'd chosen to complete her costume for the evening. She wiggled her toes and winced at the sting of a broken blister on the inside of her left foot.

What was it Silver always said? Ah, yes. You wanna look hot? Suffer.

Then again, her little sister had started wearing G-strings in her mid-teens to avoid "gross" panty lines. In her late teens, she'd stopped wearing bras. Oriana didn't ask why—she really didn't want to know. Keeping up with Silver's warped fashion sense would take more free time, and, well, *guts*, than Oriana possessed. For school and special occasions, she wore nice, tailored suits. The rest of the time, she stuck with sweats. A little boring, maybe, but she hated having to constantly fiddle with her clothes and worry about how everything fit.

Looking around to make sure no one was watching, she ran a finger under the tight leather clinging to the flesh of her thigh. A cool breeze skimmed between her legs, reminding her of what else she was wearing. Better not to think too hard about the outfit beneath her white, mid-length wool coat.

She turned her attention to her phone, unwound the cord for her earbuds, then stuck them in her ears. When the highlight reel began, a smile whispered across her lips. The Friday night crowd bustling around her faded away. All she heard was the spectators' roar. All she saw was him.

Even on the small screen, she could make him out. Max Perron, number 40. A close-up of his face after a sweet slap shot sent tiny wings aflutter in her stomach. Sun-kissed ocean eyes glowed in a wickedly handsome face. Beautiful . . . even more so up close, filled with heat. She hadn't seen them in so long, not in person, not in any way that mattered, since the day he brought her flowers for her birthday and she'd told him their friendship was a bad idea. She'd ignored every call from him for what seemed like forever. Ignored them until they stopped coming.

A shriek pierced through the sounds blasting in her ears and brought her back to the present. She took out the earbuds.

"Tyler! Oh, I can't believe it's really you!"

The shrill cry came from a young woman dressed in a huge jersey who stepped out of the shadowed alcove halfway down the ramp on the side of the forum. The players came out of there after practices or games, and fans would lay in wait to get a glimpse of their heroes. But Oriana had a feeling this girl was more than a fan.

Tyler Vanek, one of the rookies brought up from the farm team the year before, stopped short and leaned an elbow on the brick wall beside the parking garage entrance, trying to look smooth.

"Hey. And you are . . . ?" His lips curved and his cheeks, soft and freshly shaven, glowed under the bare bulb that flashed on overhead. He raked his fingers through his tight, blond curls, and his eyes traveled over the girl as she hopped on her spiky, red heels.

The poise of a man, with the expression of a little boy eager to get his hand in the cookie jar. Maybe he didn't know *who* the girl was, but he'd clearly figured out enough to like his chances.

What did Max call them again? Oh, yeah, Puck Bunnies. Oriana smirked when the girl leapt forward with a little shriek. *Appropriate.*

Vanek braced and caught her before she could knock them both over. "Wow. You're feisty."

Ya think? Oriana stuffed her phone in her book bag and took out her sunglasses. The last dying sunrays had barely crested the city skyline, but she slipped the glasses on anyway. A side step up the sidewalk out of their line of sight put her in the perfect position to observe without seeming to. Not because she was into . . . *watching* or anything, but she was curious to see how far it would go.

Most of the players would offer a signature and gently detach themselves. The rookie obviously didn't know better. Bunny's lucky day.

Clinging to his shirt, the blond Jessica-Rabbit-lookalike rubbed one leg up his thigh. "Can we go somewhere?"

"I can't, I gotta get back." Vanek groaned as her hand

disappeared between their bodies. "But here's good."

With his back against the wall, he watched her get on her knees.

Oriana let out a huff of disgust and spun away from the pair. Then checked her watch. The spindly silver hands didn't move.

Stupid batteries.

Groans from below set her teeth on edge. Peeking at the lusty pair, she blushed. How could they do *that* out in the open? Loud slurps had passers-by glancing their way and doubling their pace. Vanek's baby face screwed up, and he clenched his hands in the girl's hair as she bobbed her head faster and faster. An old man slowed and took a good long look at the show before giving Oriana a toothless grin.

Cheeks blazing, she crossed her arms over her chest and faced the street. The image of another man getting sucked off by a girl on her knees played like porn on the big screen of her mind. She pressed her eyes shut and tried to force the images out of her head. Vanek's grunts brought them back.

What she'd witnessed in the alley had haunted her for nights after.

You made the right choice. Forget it.

But she couldn't. The way she felt about Max wouldn't go away. She might not want the kind of wild life Max lived, but her heart didn't care. Logic told her there was nothing wrong with the normal, stable life she intended to lead with Paul.

Then she recalled her plans for the evening. Okay, so desperation trumped normal.

Too late for her and Max, but with Paul, maybe, just maybe, she could salvage what they had. If only she wasn't the only one fighting for their relationship.

Where are you, Paul?

Tugging a curl loose from her bronze coiffure, she twirled it around her index finger and traced a big, silver hoop earring with her thumb. The scenario played over in her head like it had while she'd carefully picked out each piece of her outfit. Paul, all detached, sitting across from her in the secluded booth she'd paid extra to reserve at his favorite restaurant, looking at his cell every couple minutes. Then she'd take off her coat.

And he'd stare.

The snug, black corset dress she'd finally settled on, knee-length, slit up both sides to the hip, made her feel a little self-conscious, but what she wore underneath made her feel like a goddess. Maybe she should give Paul a preview in the car. He might not want to go out to dinner after all.

Page one of her new ... *relationship* handbook said a man like Paul needed direction. Needed to be caught off-guard.

Men in demanding jobs often feel like they have to be in control at all times. They can't find release in the bedroom because they're wound up so tight. Take their choices away and you'll find you've got a man ready and willing to please. Make him work for it. You'll both enjoy the results.

Could it possibly be that simple?

You're not even wet.

Oriana winced as another memory twinged like a splinter. The way things had gone the last time she and Paul were alone together, she was lucky he'd agreed to meet her at all. Whenever things got intimate, she screwed it up. Their sex life was seriously lacking, the very reason she'd taken the initiative to ask *him* out for once. And called her sister for some advice.

"Look for a book called *Lady in Charge*," Silver had told her. "If that don't work, ditch the loser."

She'd found the book online under "femdom" and decided her little sister was seriously unhinged. Dominate Paul? Really? But then she read the excerpt and decided to give it a shot. The bondage stuff looked ... interesting. Picturing silk scarves or lined cuffs securing her wrists—No, *Paul's* wrists to the headboard ...

Well, couldn't hurt to try. She couldn't very well make things worse.

Thinking of the graphic image on page 214 of a woman attaching a spiked ball stretcher to her lover's sack, she grinned and shook her head. Such extremes right off the bat would definitely make things worse. Better stick with the mild stuff. Like taking charge for the night.

For some reason, the very idea made her feel like she'd taken a big bite of something that smelled sweet and tasted awful. She mentally flipped the through the pages she pored over the night before, trying to find a single appealing scene. Maybe a simple role-play?

How would she broach the subject with Paul? "I want to try something…"

Her stomach did a little flip. Okay, no talking. Just a candlelit dinner, a little reveal of her sexy lingerie, and maybe some moves from the book. Tease him under the tablecloth and order him not to come. He'd be putty in her hands. The book said so.

Well, something's gotta work. Oriana made a face and checked her long, black, manicured nails. *According to that same book, the "honeymoon's" over.*

The streetlight overhead flickered to life and a shadow fell, her only warning before a massive form slammed into her. Teetering on her heels, her arms flailed. Her book bag swung out, hit the sidewalk, and skidded off the curb.

Without a word, the man plucked her bag off the street, ignoring the car that swerved to avoid him, horn blaring. He held it out to her.

She hesitated before taking it. The guy was huge, menacing with his face hidden in the shadows of his dark, gray hood. Without getting too close, she snatched the strap. Mouth too dry for a "thank you," she inclined her head and hoped it would be enough.

"Sorry about that." He lowered the hood, revealing a face just as familiar as the voice. His eyes ran over her, paused on her heels, then made their way up slowly. "Hey, don't I know you?"

Sloan Callahan. The man she'd seen with Max in the alley—had he seen her? The flap of her jacket hung open, and for a horrible moment, she felt completely exposed. Her mouth went dry, and she had a vision of that night. Only this time, the woman they planned to share wasn't Roxy. It was her.

Her eyes traced the scar from a slash that had almost taken his eye. The bound wooden blade of the stick had torn rather than cut, so the wound wasn't nice and smooth. White flesh streaked in two irregular lines through one brow, over one cheekbone, and up to his temple, creating a well-defined path.

Those who'd voted Callahan the most handsome man in the sport for three years straight—as if good looks made a damn bit of difference on the ice—considered the damage done to Callahan's face a tragedy. To her mind, the scars gave him a dangerous appeal. The kind of appeal that tempted good girls to do very bad things.

"Do I?"

Definitely. Oriana blinked. Did he know she was thinking about him and Max and . . . ? She shook her head. *Don't be a dumb ass. He asked if he knew you.*

Taking hold of the flaps of her jacket, she held it closed and craned her neck to study him over her sunglasses. "No. I don't think so." His dark eyes narrowed, and she swallowed. A moan from the ramp spurred her on. She pushed her sunglasses up with a finger and spoke loud so Vanek's captain wouldn't hear him. "Umm . . . I don't suppose you have the time?"

A crowd of teens approached, taking up most of the sidewalk. Rather than move across the sidewalk to let them pass, he stepped toward her. She retreated until her back hit a light post. His hand under her elbow kept her from toppling onto the street.

"It's eight-twenty, princess." He leaned his forearm on the post above her head and chuckled when she froze. "You waiting for someone?"

All she could do was nod as she peered up at him with wide eyes. Damn he was tall. And big. And hot.

More scary than anything. Should check him for weapons. Boy's dangerous.

Cold air skimmed over her breasts, causing goose bumps to rise on all the flesh not covered by the tightly-laced bodice. She wanted to do up her jacket, but he was too close. If she didn't move, he might not notice the slit of the dress had slipped to one side, exposing her thigh to hip.

You sure you don't want him to notice? said the naughty voice in her head, which usually indicated she had been spending too much time on the phone listening to her sister's raunchy tales.

She peeked up at Callahan, and heat flooded her cheeks when she caught his eyes on her breasts.

"Well, let's hope he's not too late. Someone might steal you away." Tiny creases cut through his scar, and something stirred deep inside. The way he looked at her almost made her feel desirable. He leaned a little closer. "I mean, dressed like that, standing on the corner . . ."

He pushed away from her.

"How dare—" She sputtered on the words she wanted to say and let her narrowed gaze spit all the venom her mouth couldn't. Might be better for him if he *did* have a knife on him. She was very tempted to see what kind of damage she could do with her nails.

But acting like a savage wasn't her style. She gave him the coldest look she could muster and glanced up the sidewalk to see if she could catch the eye of someone passing by. Just in case he went caveman on her. Not that he looked even close to doing so. His composure brought her to the edge of losing hers entirely.

A sparkle of amusement lit his black eyes, and he gave her legs another lingering look. "Hell, with those legs, I'm sure you'd get a decent offer. I'd make one myself, but I'm in too much of a hurry for you to make it worth my while." He winked and tugged his hood back over his head. "Maybe next time."

A little sting in the corner of her eye made her blink fast and shake her head. *Sticks and stones, Oriana. How would Silver handle this?*

Hands on her hips, she gave him a swift once over and sucked her teeth. "Callahan—"

"You can call me, 'Mr. Callahan.' We're not friends."

"Fine, Mr. Callahan." She clipped out each syllable, resisting the urge to kick him. "There won't be a next time."

Real smooth. Do you need Silver to script a decent comeback?

"So you say." Callahan cleared his throat. "Vanek, I'm heading in. You have two minutes."

The sharp sound of a zipper drew her attention to the ramp. Vanek gave her a sheepish grin, then nodded at his bunny while she scribbled something on a scrap of paper and stuffed it in his pocket. The bunny's heels clicked as she made her way up the ramp. Blonde waves bouncing, she disappeared around the corner.

"Nice try covering for the kid. I'm sure he'd thank you if he got her knocked up and she took him for all he's worth." Callahan took her sunglasses from her face and slipped them into her jacket pocket, effectively removing her only shield. "Did you enjoy the show?"

So much for hoping he'd forgotten. She glared at the gold embroidered team logo centered on his broad chest. A snake, just like him.

His finger brushed her cheek as he tucked a loose curl behind her ear. Her pulse sped up. Her gaze shot to his face. Those black eyes didn't belong to a snake. Or any animal she'd ever seen. They brought to mind the ocean at night when the surface was smooth and calm. And just cool enough to be soothing after a hot summer day. She could imagine immersing herself in the water, feeling soft waves lap up her thighs. Soon the moonlight would reflect off the glassy surface, like the streetlights reflected in Callahan's eyes.

The ocean always mesmerized her.

"Tell me, princess, did it get you off?"

But the ocean didn't have a big, stupid mouth.

Her chin jutted up. "I don't know what you're talking about."

"Sure you don't." He ran his thumb over her bottom lip. "So soft. I can imagine you in that position . . ." When she jerked away, he laughed. "But you don't know what I'm talking about."

Oh, god. She watched him turn away, unable to force her eyes off him until he disappeared inside the forum. Her mind locked on "the position" he'd implied. The bunny's position? Or the position of the woman he'd shared with Max? Neither option seemed as deplorable as it should have. Or likely to happen.

So not fair. The only man in history to reject Silver, hitting on *her.*

No, *mocking* her. He couldn't seriously think she'd ever . . .

Her nipples drew into hard little points and poked through the openwork details of her lace bra. Her body wasn't in accord with her mind. Then again, the intelligent arguments her brain came up with were weak.

Sex in public isn't my thing.

Not that she knew what her "thing" was.

Couldn't you consider trying something new? For Max?

She should have, but it was too late.

Is it?

Neither her brain nor her body had an answer. She hadn't spoken to Max in months. Maybe she should call him and apologize for the way she'd behaved. Maybe then they could discuss . . .

Get a grip. You have a man.

Who was an hour late. So much for their dinner reservations.

Heaving out a sigh, she smoothed her hands over her sides to make sure the dress hadn't inched up to reveal more of the *generous* thighs Sloan had admired. Then did up her jacket. The way things were going, he might be the only one who got to see them tonight.

Change direction of thoughts. Sloan isn't interested in my pudgy legs. I'm trying to impress Paul. Who'll be here . . .

The door of the forum slid open. Her father's secretary walked out.

"Hi, Anne." Oriana stepped into the pinched-nosed woman's path. "Is Paul—?"

Anne looked over the red rim of her spectacles and sniffed. "He'll be along shortly. Excuse me."

The secretary hurried to her bus stop. Her behavior might have seemed rude to some, but it didn't bother Oriana. Her father kept Anne busy. She had to get home to her kids.

Never mind that she would have found time to talk if Silver stood in her place. Because Silver wouldn't be standing here, waiting. No one kept Silver waiting for anything.

Then again, Silver wouldn't let them if they tried. Her little sister would have stormed into Daddy's office after ten minutes of sitting in the limo—not standing on the curb because the limo driver wouldn't dare tell *her* he had other places to be—and ranted until both the man of the hour and Daddy were tripping over each other making apologies.

Oriana couldn't do that.

A couple strolled by with steaming cups of coffee. The aroma lingered in the crisp, maritime breeze, fragrant tendrils of temptation, coming from the couple as much as the cups. A little café around the corner ground their coffee beans fresh for each pot right in front of the customers. The whole place smelled so earthy and rich, the caffeinated kick struck the second the door cracked open. Still her favorite haunt before and after exams, even though Max never . . .

Stop.

Coffee. Coffee would be lovely. A new plan formed and she smiled.

Maybe she couldn't do ranting. But she *could* do thoughtful.

Fifteen minutes later, cardboard tray in hand, Oriana strolled into the forum and made a beeline for the elevator. The echo of her heels on the glistening, black granite floors sounded like the tick of a giant clock. High rounded arches and marble columns gave the appearance of a cathedral; the huge black and white portraits of hockey greats like Gordie Howe, suspended from the pristine white ceiling looked like saints of old. Without crowds, it didn't seem like a place to enjoy rowdy sports. The last couple of times she'd met Paul here, she'd had to stop herself from looking for pews.

Eight months in Dartmouth and I still haven't been to a single game. Her steps slowed as she passed the big, red double doors that led to the stands. School work kept her busy, so she'd never questioned Paul and her father's refusal to let her watch the games from the press box.

Well, no one could stop her from buying a ticket. Then she could enjoy the full experience without Paul or her father spoiling her fun by telling her not to shout at the players. Imagining a treat of beer and nachos, she inhaled deeply, then wrinkled her nose at the sharp scent of lemon cleaner hanging in the air from a recently passed mop. Nope, fantasy just wouldn't cut it. Whether the men in her life liked it or not, she was going to the hockey game tomorrow night.

Movement to the far left quickened her pace.

The night guard pushed to his feet. "You can't be in here."

Her heels skidded on the wet floor, and her best imitation of Silver's haughty look froze on her face. The coffee tray went up.

She went down.

An arm hooked around her waist, and the coffee tray was swooped out of her hand. *"Careful."*

A flash of white teeth broke through the warm brown of the face above her. Bulging muscles flexed under her shoulders. Hard abs rippled under her hand. The feeling of falling intensified, and the room spun as blood rushed from her head to her core.

Oh, god! Whatever you want to do to me, the answer is yes!

Time to get her libido on a freaking leash. Maybe the granite cracking her skull would save her from embarrassing herself any further. She had the strangest urge to wrap her arms around his neck and press her body flush against his. Instead, she did her best to curve away from him.

Tray balanced on one big hand, the man set her on her feet. "That would have been a nasty spill."

The room leveled out. Black and gold filled her vision. Another freakin' Cobra's jersey. Her eyes traveled up and locked on big, pouty lips, a shade darker than his skin, outlined by a trim black goatee.

There was only one black player on the Cobra's roster. Dominik Mason. She'd watched a few of his interviews and knew he was the tough guy of the team, their enforcer. His smile usually meant someone would get hurt. A lot of people were scared of him.

But how could a man look scary with lips like that?

She blinked when the edges of his lips twitched and cleared her throat. "Um, thank you . . ."

He chuckled and handed her the tray. "Dominik Mason at your service, ma'am."

The way he said "service" made all the tiny hairs on her flesh rise. Deep as cavern wind, with a hint of hidden danger, his voice made her tremble, and she wouldn't pretend it was with fear. He wouldn't have to talk dirty to get a girl worked up. He could just say her name.

Did he know her name?

Enough! What the hell is wrong with you?

That book had messed with her head. Time to find Paul before she threw herself at the next guy who smiled at her.

Yeah, 'cause you're acting just like that bunny. Pathetic.

Oriana met his warm, brown eyes and pulled on the poise she used with the press. A mask that never fit quite right but tended to serve the purpose of redirecting questions to her father or Paul with a nod and a smile. "Thank you, Mason." She inhaled and gave him a stiff smile. "I really should get going . . ."

"As I said." The guard approached them, a scowl bunching the wrinkles on his face. "You can't be in here. We're closed to the public."

Mason crossed his arms and glanced at the little man. "You're new, aren't you?"

"Yes, but—"

"This is Oriana Delgado." Mason jerked his chin at her. "I don't think she qualifies as 'the public'."

He does know my name.

The guard's scowl melted away. He still didn't recognize her—no surprise there—but he wouldn't question Mason. "Sorry, ma'am." He tipped his hat and returned to his desk.

"Going up?" Mason pressed the button to the elevator at her nod.

Holding the tray with one hand, she used the other to adjust the strap of her book bag. "Are you?"

Please say no. Being alone with him in an elevator wouldn't be good. The hint of something spicy on his breath made her mouth water. Six floors up would be plenty of time for a taste.

You're projecting Silver again, Oriana. Stop before you do something stupid.

His lips curved like he'd caught the thought. "No. Unfortunately I've got a team meeting to get to. How about after . . . ?"

"I've got a date with my boyfriend."

"You're still with *him*?"

Could he sound any more disgusted? Of course, it wasn't exactly a secret that the players weren't fond of their coach. He was from Toronto, and a good half of the Cobras were from Montreal. There was bound to be some animosity.

That's what she told herself anyway. Wouldn't be loyal to admit her boyfriend was an asshole.

And the white picket fence you're dreaming of might start looking more like a cage.

"Yeah. It's been eight months." She shifted the tray so the hot parts weren't touching her skin. "It was really nice to meet you though."

"My pleasure, Oriana." He took her hand, gave it a little squeeze before retreating. "Don't let anyone give you grief about being here. Okay?"

The elevator door skidded open. She stepped inside. "Okay."

When the elevator doors clicked shut, she let out a breathy laugh. Keeping Delgado's daughter happy was part of the job. Just not *this* daughter. Good thing neither Mason nor the guard knew better. Or the guard wouldn't have let her in. And Mason would have ignored her, just like everyone did.

Self-pity now? You're on a roll.

The elevator dinged.

"Put him on injury reserve. I don't care if it means he can't play for the rest of the season, we need to bring up a new forward." Her father backed onto the elevator, the diamonds in his gold cufflinks flashing as he made a sharp motion with his hand in the assistant coach's face to cut him off and directed his next words at the general manager. "We're on a losing streak! We won't sell any seats if we don't get a win."

Oriana ducked to avoid getting smacked by the last excited gesture. Her father hadn't noticed her yet. And in this mood, she'd rather he not.

"We don't have the cap for another player of Callahan's caliber." Dean Richter, the GM, a man whose demeanor brought on the urge to salute, stopped the door with his shoulder and spared Oriana a dismissive glance. "However, we have a couple of draft picks—including the one we've been using—that might be suitable. I'll look into it."

When her father nodded, the GM stepped back and the door slid shut.

Case closed. But apparently Tim Rowe, the assistant coach, didn't see it that way.

"Sir, we have to consider the playoffs. And it was just an upper body injury." Rowe hooked his finger to the collar of his starched white shirt and loosened his tie. A muscle in his jaw ticked, belying the calm in his eyes. "We can't keep him on IR—the doctor cleared him to play. Give him a few games and he'll be—"

The olive shade of her father's faintly lined face turned blotchy red. "The playoffs mean shit out here when it comes to the bottom line, Tim. No one expects this team to make it that far! Fans come to the games expecting to see some action. Big hits, fights, and scoring!"

"Callahan is capable of giving you all that," Rowe said. "And he's a fan favorite."

"He *was* a fan favorite. Don't you fucking shake your head at me!" The veins in her father's temples darkened to a frightening shade of purple. "That's why Paul is the head coach! He gets that this is a business!"

She really, really didn't want to draw his attention, but she figured she'd better before he had a stroke. "Where *is* Paul, Dad?"

Her father spun toward her and scowled. "What are *you* doing here?"

Rowe opened his mouth. Before he could insert his foot by defending her, she answered. "I figured—since your meeting was taking so long—that I'd bring you guys some coffee. Me and Paul were supposed to go out for dinner, but—"

"The team was called in for extra practice," her father said. "You might as well go home."

"I just saw a couple of the guys taking a break—is Paul down at the rink already?"

"He's still in his office." Rowe met her father's glare with a shrug. "She deserves to know."

"Know what?" Oriana shifted the tray to one hand and touched Rowe's arm. "Is Paul okay?"

"He's fine." Her father cleared his throat. "He's heading down to the rink soon, but—"

The elevator dinged again. Her stop. "Well, I'll just drop this off with him and leave. I won't keep him, I promise."

"Oriana, he's busy!"

Not too busy to explain why he didn't have the decency to call and cancel their date. She strode across the hall, fingers denting the cardboard tray.

Rowe hastened to catch up with her. "Oriana, I should tell you . . . you don't want to—"

Third door on the left. She turned the handle.

Wet, rhythmic slapping came through the slit of the door. She swung it wide. Paul *was* busy. With Chantelle, the director of media relations. On top of his desk, working *real* hard.

The tray slipped from her hands as her grip went slack.

Chapter Two

The tops burst off the cups. Coffee splashed Oriana's legs. Pain sizzled up her thighs but didn't quite register. Her skin seemed to belong to someone else. Someone far away.

Slender thighs spread wide. Paul's face screwed up as he thrust hard, obviously experiencing more pleasure than he ever had with her . . .

A shout crossed the distance. "Hey!"

Tears blurred the bright lights of the hall. She blinked them away and swallowed against the bile in her throat. Her nails dug into her palms, and the sharp pain countered the numbness taking over.

Breathe. You don't care. Doesn't matter. You really don't care.

But she did. She'd cared enough to change everything for him. All for nothing.

The pages in that damn book she'd considered the salvation of her relationship flapped in her mind like a gust of wind had taken hold of them. The images mocked her—a powerful woman being worshiped by a man on his knees. Paul could never be that man. Never mind worship. Love and loyalty were too much to ask.

Someone touched her arm and she twisted away. "Don't!"

Paul swiped at the wet hair stuck to his brow and wrapped one hand around Oriana's wrist, trying to hold her in place while using the other to do up his pants. He let her go when his zipper stuck. "Stop it. I can explain."

"Can you?" She evaded his grab for her and stumbled out of his reach. "Let me guess. It's not what I think."

"It's exactly what you think. I have needs. You can't fulfill them." He folded his arms over his chest, lips drawn in a thin line. "We're good in every other way. I deal with all your flaws. Cut me some slack."

Did he really think so little of her? She bit the tip of her tongue and took a deep breath. "What flaws, Paul? What could I have possibly done to deserve this?"

"Look at you!" He gestured at her boots. "You're fucking clueless. Either it's baggy jogging pants to cover up the flab you're too lazy to work off or some ridiculous outfit that makes you look like you're playing dress up. What the hell are you wearing anyway?" He reached out to take hold of her jacket.

It was not the first time he'd implied she was fat, but it would be the last. She let her book bag slip off her shoulder and swung it at him. He sidestepped, caught the strap, and tore the bag from her hand. The buckle snapped, and her books flew out and skidded across the floor. *Lady in Charge* thumped into the wall beside Rowe, and Oriana's eyes went wide as he glanced down.

Rowe's brow twitched, but his expression was unreadable. He covered the book with his foot and smoothly slid it out of sight. Then he cleared his throat. "I think—"

Oriana's father held up his hand. "No one cares what you think. Paul, why don't you and Oriana go home and talk this over? Tim can manage the team for the night."

"No." Oriana forced her eyes away from the book under Rowe's shoe and turned to Paul. "It's over."

Paul arched a brow and looked past her to her father. "I won't have my partners invest another cent in the team if she won't be reasonable."

You think that's unreasonable? She opened her mouth, then snapped it shut when her father dropped a heavy hand on her shoulder.

"She will." Oriana stared at her father, and he shook his head. "She knows what she stands to lose."

With a curt nod, Paul disappeared into his office.

Her father eased the door shut. "Oriana, you have to understand—"

"I do not." She sucked air through her teeth, her whole body shaking as she tried to take in the utter betrayal of this man who called himself her father. He'd known about Paul and Chantelle, and, rather than tell her, he'd tried to cover for Paul. "How long has this been going on?"

"It doesn't matter. If you'd been keeping him satisfied, he wouldn't have looked elsewhere." Her father's cold, flint-colored eyes snapped. "You just got a hard dose of reality. It's about time. I've seen you mooning after the players. Is Paul just supposed to accept that?"

"I never cheated on him!"

"But you made it clear he wasn't enough." He straightened the lapels of his designer suit. "If I had the slightest inclination you were playing games, I would have discouraged Paul from pursuing you. It's too late. He's a savvy businessman, and he's used to getting what he wants. And, for *some* reason, he wants you."

"Tough." Something inside ached to scream at him, to demand to know when she'd stopped being his daughter and started being a commodity. But she didn't have the heart for it. "He can't have me anymore. We're through."

"Oh, really?" She jumped at her father's laugh. "Paul won't just let you go. You'll inherit a fortune if you don't screw this up." He leaned over her. "If you break up with him, I'll cut you off. Let's see you get your bachelor's without a dime to your name."

Her bottom lip quivered. She covered her mouth with her hand. "You wouldn't . . ."

His glare crushed the last of her pathetic delusions. They both knew he'd follow through with his threat. Losing the backing of Paul's business partners would cost her father more than she was worth. Reality lodged in her throat, hard enough to choke on. Her shoulders slumped and she gave a quick nod.

"Good, you *do* understand." He lips curled as he looked her over one last time. "Now go home and take off those ridiculous boots. I won't have my daughter walking around looking like a whore."

When her father disappeared into his office, Oriana stared down the empty hall, eyes burning with unshed tears. A rustle of fabric at her side reminded her she was not alone.

Muttering something under his breath, Rowe handed her the silver kerchief from his suit pocket.

Oriana took it and dabbed blindly at a stain on the hem of her jacket. Her skin stung where the wool grazed her thigh so she lifted the material to check the reddened flesh. Only a first-degree burn, nothing serious. Cold water, a bit of ointment, and she'd be fine.

Why did those words always sound so reassuring while volunteering at the clinic? Give the toddler a lollipop and the boo-boo's all better.

A sweet treat wouldn't do her any good. Pain was the least of her problems.

"I'm trapped." She felt for a wall to lean against, needing something solid behind her while her world crumbled. "I have to stay with him. Never mind my bachelor's. How the hell am I gonna pay for medical school?"

"I'm sure you'll figure something out." Rowe bent down and gathered her books, not looking up as he stuffed them in her ruined bag. "You're not the type to just lie down and accept defeat."

With a shaky, slightly incredulous smile on her lips, she shook her head. What a sweet guy. A little naive, but sweet. "What gives you that idea?"

Setting her bag on the floor between them, Rowe straightened. The bright pink cover of *Lady in Charge* glistened under the hall light as he held it up. He gave her a hard look. "This doesn't seem like the type of book a girl who lets her daddy run her life would read."

You're giving me way too much credit. Cheeks blazing, Oriana held out her hand. "Give me my book . . . please."

The stiff spine of the book cracked as Rowe opened it and turned away from her. "Hmm, nice graphics. Have you tried this one?" He held the book out to show her the image of a woman "pegging" a man. "If it got out that Paul let someone—"

Oriana grabbed the book, then her bag, and crammed it inside. "No, I've never tried any of it. I planned a special night with Paul, and I thought—anyway, it doesn't matter. If I try blackmailing either Paul or my father, they'll laugh in my face. I'm not Silver. Pissing *her* off means bad press."

"I'm sure you could stir up some bad press too."

He *really* didn't know her. The very idea of bringing that kind of attention to herself made her nauseous. But damn, having someone give a shit was nice.

You have someone—he's a phone call away.

True, yet, she didn't deserve help from *him*. Or Rowe for that matter, but she hadn't done anything to hurt Rowe. And she wasn't too proud to accept a bit of pity.

"Maybe I could, but they know I won't." Hugging her bag to her chest, she glanced up at him—man, why did everyone in this sport have to be so freakin' tall?—and ducked her head when he frowned at her. "Besides, if I do, my father will lose the team, and you'll be out of a job."

Rowe rubbed his shoulder and leaned forward, speaking low. "Your father will lose this team within the next couple of years whether Paul backs him or not, Oriana. I've been approached by several other teams for a head coach position. I'll be fine." He flicked a strand of hair off her shoulder and shook his head. "The question is, will you?"

Would she? No, not if she had to stay with Paul. And not if she had to give up the future she'd worked so hard for. She chewed on the inside of her cheek and shook her head.

"All right, then we need to focus on making sure your father doesn't cut you off before you can pay for school yourself."

Makes sense. She followed him toward the elevator, hands stuffed in her jacket pockets, and she weighed her few options. "I guess . . . I won't break up with Paul, at least until—"

He glanced over his shoulder and shook his head. "Forget Paul. He's not important."

"But—"

"Quiet." He grinned at Oriana's huff. "Let me think for a minute."

They passed her father's office. He hadn't closed the door, so she took a moment to watch him, standing in the middle of the room, staring at a portrait on the wall. Antoine's portrait, taken days after he'd been drafted for the minors. Weeks before he died. She did math in her head. Fifteen years, in two days. No wonder he seemed so cold. He always got that way while he mourned his only son.

Oriana gave up reminding him *she* was still alive when her father acquired the team and the forum. An abstract way to keep the dreams of his firstborn alive meant more to him than his living flesh and blood. Besides, Silver acted out enough for both of them.

But she couldn't let her father ruin her life in her dead brother's name. So how did she fix this?

Rowe waved her over, and she approached him, stepping carefully so her heels wouldn't click on the tiles.

"You know, with the right . . . evidence, you might not need to do anything public," he said. "The threat might be enough."

Oriana glanced at the open office door and kept her tone low. "What do you suggest?"

"Get creative, do something neither Paul nor your father would expect from you. Stop trying to be the perfect daughter." He pressed the call button for the elevator. "Your father was right about one thing. Paul clearly wasn't enough for you—'course, that's not your fault."

What's that supposed to mean? "I . . ."

"Have you seen Max lately?"

Little creases formed around his eyes when she bit her bottom lip and shook her head.

"You should. He talks about you a lot. To T.J. and Vanek." His brow lifted when her lips curved. "Dominik."

She swallowed.

He cocked his head slightly. "Sloan."

Ugh. She scraped her lip with her teeth and wrinkled her nose. She did not like the idea of Sloan and Max discussing her. What could they possibly have to say?

"Remember the time she caught us . . ."

Feeling Rowe's gaze on her face, she ripped her attention from the imagined conversation and focused on the present one.

"Have you ever experimented . . . sexually? With anyone?"

"*Rowe!*" She covered her mouth with her hand and glanced down the hall. Talking sex with Silver was weird enough, but with Rowe? She didn't want to go there. This all reminded her of Sex Ed in high school. *No, I'm not . . . doing it. Yes, I know about being safe.*

"Call me Tim." Suddenly he was very close, looming over her, and she couldn't look away. "Answer me, Oriana."

"No. Sex has always been . . ." She frowned. Why was she telling him? Why didn't she want to stop? "Boring."

"I've always liked your honesty." His broad smile of approval reminded her of her uncle Wayne. Her chest tightened as his face, weather-worn and full of laugh lines, filled her mind's eye. He'd become her surrogate father after her brother died, attended all her school functions, never missed a performance of her high school orchestra. He'd go on and on about her talent, told anyone who'd listen how well she played violin.

After he died, she stopped playing. She just didn't see the point anymore; she didn't impress anyone else. Not that anyone noticed *anything* she did.

"Hey, don't let them get to you, kid." Rowe—*no, Tim*— held out his hand. "Come on."

Oriana reached out but pulled back when her fingertips brushed his palm. "Where are we going?"

The elevator chimed and the door slid open.

"Down to the rink. I thought you wanted my help." Tim placed his hands behind his back, and his lips curved into a Cheshire cat smile.

That couldn't mean anything good. Oriana watched Tim turn away from her and step onto the elevator like he couldn't care less whether she followed or not. Which reminded her of Silver. She'd completely forgotten Tim and Silver had been close before he met his wife.

Kindred spirits. She took a deep breath and joined him on the elevator just in time to avoid the doors closing on her.

"What kind of help are we talking about?"

* * * *

The scrape of blades on ice echoed off the rink along with the odd shout from the trainers. Oriana followed Tim to the suicide box— the space between the benches for cameramen to take shots from ice level—and for a moment simply absorbed the sensation of actually being this close to the action. The air smelled like freshly fallen snow, moist with a nip of cold.

"You've never been here before, have you?" Tim put his hand on her shoulder, and she jumped. He laughed. "Hey, why so wound up? You're acting like I just snuck you into the teacher's lounge."

She gave him a sheepish grin and shrugged. That was exactly how she felt. Like she was out-of-bounds.

"Why are we here?"

"I thought you'd enjoy seeing the guys up close and personal." Tim jerked his chin in the direction of the rink.

One look and everything around her faded away. Her mouth went dry, and she swallowed spastically.

Max.

Completely oblivious to her presence, Max cut across the ice in a burst of speed, his blades a silver blur. Stopping short, he hip-checked one of his teammates, laughing his rich, skin-tingling laugh when the man shouted at him. Gliding backward, he made a come-get-me motion with his gloved hand.

Oriana rested her hands on the top of the boards, grip tight on the cold edge so she wouldn't hop over and run to him. Her heart beat hard against the cage of her ribs. She licked her lips as she imagined how he'd react if she gave in to the crazy urge. Would he be embarrassed?

No, not Max. He'd probably laugh and race over to save her from killing herself on her stupid boots. He would act like no time had passed because that was the kind of man he was. Everything would be forgiven. Forgotten. She envisioned him swooping her up into his arms. Then reason crept in. She didn't want to get him in trouble.

But she could see him after. And when she did, she would tell him how wrong she'd been. She smiled. *Maybe he'll let me make it up to him.*

"That's better." Tim gave her a little nudge, then leaned his forearms on top of the boards beside her. "Now, I have a very important question for you."

Tearing her eyes away from Max, Oriana looked up at Tim. "Yes?"

"How far are you willing to go to get the evidence you need?"

Good question. Oriana considered the lengths Silver had gone to when their father told her, in no uncertain terms, that she wouldn't be going to Hollywood to pursue an acting career. For months afterward, pictures of Silver filled the tabloids, pictures of her with different men, going into fetish clubs, coming out wearing half of what she'd gone in with. When big investors threatened to withdraw their support, her father not only agreed to let Silver go, he'd also paid all her expenses and gotten in touch with one of his contacts in the film industry to get Silver an audition.

A little too much for Oriana. She couldn't imagine doing something so extroverted.

She opened her mouth to tell Tim as much. Then the sound of a puck pinging off a goalpost, followed by a loud "Fuck!", brought her attention back to the rink.

"Try again, Callahan," one of the trainers called out.

Standing on the blue line, Callahan nodded and accepted a pass from the trainer. He glared at the empty net. Oriana held her breath as swung his stick, then slapped the puck with the stick blade. The puck zipped through the air in a black blur, too fast to follow. Another *ping*. The rink went quiet.

Callahan threw his stick toward the net and headed for the open Zamboni entrance. Oriana winced when he kicked the wall on his way out.

Someone cleared his throat behind her. "What are you doing here? You were told to go home."

Oriana's spine stiffened. She glanced over her shoulder at Paul. And Chantelle.

"I—"

"Came to see Max? I'm not surprised." Paul exchanged a look with Chantelle, and then they both looked at Oriana like she was a pathetic little girl with a crush. "Go ahead, throw yourself at him. He'll use you like he does all the other girls. Maybe then you'll appreciate what you have with me."

Wow. Oriana gaped after Paul as he drew Chantelle out of the box, whispering in her ear and kissing her neck. He obviously didn't feel like he needed to hide his affair anymore. That he'd gone so far as to tell her to go ahead and sleep with another man showed her just how confident he was that she wouldn't find a way to be free of him.

Tim rubbed her arm. "I'm sorry, sweetie. We'll figure out—"

Oriana grabbed his wrist. "You asked how far I'd go?" She ground her teeth and studied the men on the ice. Then she gave a curt nod and gulped at the sick feeling in her throat. "How's this? I'll do whatever it takes."

Chapter Three

The last of the men emptied out of the locker room, more subdued than Sloan had ever seen them. Friday night practice usually ended with the men converging to the closest bar for some down time. An excess of beer and women, then they'd all go home and crash.

But not tonight.

Fist pressed into the bench beneath him, Sloan took a deep, deep breath, fighting the urge to put a hole in the wall and risk breaking his hand again. One game without a goal and they were sending him to the freakin' farm team?

This had to be some kind of sick joke. With his stats, they couldn't seriously think they'd do better without him. Could they?

"You're not as ... resilient as you used to be, Callahan." The trainer made a face as though he could taste the bullshit smeared all over his words. "The center they brought up has the spunk the team needs."

In other words, the kid would rack up penalty minutes by getting in a fight every game and creaming the other team's players against the boards in the dirtiest, showiest way possible.

Sloan had tried to live up to the violent image the Cobras' owner wanted to portray, going so far as to throw down his gloves during a game midseason and call out the biggest guy on the ice. The crowd loved it. Coach Stanton loved it.

Too bad he'd broken his hand on the guy's helmet. He might have won the fight, but in the two months he'd been gone, the new kid had won several. The fans had a new hero.

"It's just for the last month of the season. We both know the team's not going any farther," the trainer said, as though he'd caught the gist of Sloan's thoughts.

And that was supposed to make him feel better? "I'm being sent down for reconditioning. It's humiliating. And they still expect me to play tomorrow?"

The trainer had the grace to look away. "I think they expect you to prove they're making the right decision. After tonight, I don't think you're ready to prove them wrong. Your stick handling is off."

Sloan slouched and rubbed his face with his hands. For fuck's sake, he'd been with the team for five years. Hadn't he earned more than two games to get back in the rhythm?

Before Delgado, definitely. But ever since the bastard took complete control of the team and the forum the year before, integrity meant fuck-all.

"Thanks for giving me a heads up, Randy," Sloan said, head down. "Stanton would have blindsided me."

Randy didn't comment. He shuffled out and left Sloan to change.

The door hit the wall. Two of his men stormed in.

"What the hell's going on?" one player pretty much roared. "Randy looks like he just downed a burger covered in maggots."

Brow arched, Sloan glanced at the team's top offensive-defenseman-slash-enforcer, Dominik Mason. White teeth bared, lips curled, the man reminded him of a big black bear with burrs in his fur. Took quite a bit to agitate Mason, so he must have some idea of what was going on.

Snapping up the towel he'd abandoned on the bench when he'd been sidetracked after his shower, Sloan rubbed his hair until the short onyx strands puffed up. He used his fingers to tame them. "I'm being sent down to the minors after the next game. Don't say nothing. It was decent of Randy to let me know."

"You've got to be kidding." T.J., the team's oldest and biggest defenseman, thirty-seven and a daunting six-foot-nine, folded his arms and leaned on the lockers, making them creak. "You're the best player we've got."

"I'm not productive enough for Delgado."

The door opened again. Sloan tossed the towel in the general direction of the biggest pile on the floor, then propped his hands behind him on the bench to watch the team's finest gather, all bristling at the injustice while Mason shared the news.

"You should have gotten an assist on my goal Wednesday."

"This is bullshit."

Vanek, the left winger, and his best friend, Perron, another defenseman. Sloan grinned. They were a loyal bunch.

"Nothing we can do about it, guys." Sloan slapped his thighs and stood. "Let's just enjoy our last game together."

Perron eyed the sleek, black cell phone in his hand and gave a curt nod before stuffing it in the pocket of his baggy, gray jogging pants. "Or we can figure out a way to keep you on the roster."

Pulse quickening, Sloan sat back down and schooled his features. He didn't want to look too excited, but they didn't call Perron "The Catalyst" for nothing. "Tell me what you've got."

* * * *

Max left the men in the player's lounge and approached the bathroom across the hall. He knew his vague "Trust me" hadn't satisfied Sloan, but that was the best he could offer until he made sure his plan worked for everyone involved. He reached out to push the door open and noticed his hand shaking like he had pregame jitters.

He clenched his fist and knocked. "You in there, sugar?"

No answer. Well, hell, he shouldn't be surprised. Even if Tim was right and she needed his help, that didn't mean she'd accept it. Her reasons for rejecting his friendship—for rejecting *him*—hadn't changed. He still saw the flowers she'd left to die on the passenger seat of his pickup that night, on her birthday, when he'd told her he loved her.

You went too far. You had no right.

But things had changed.

"Look, Tim called me and . . ." He rested his forehead on the back of his fist. "I'm . . . I'm here if you need me, Oriana."

The door opened a crack. Oriana peeked out at him, eyes rimmed with tears. "That's what you said when I stopped being your friend."

Shit. She likely thinks I'm going to rub it in. He pinched the tense flesh between his eyes and eased the door open. "I was pissed off when I said it, but I meant every word—" *Every word? Including "have a nice life" and all the crap after?* "I mean—"

"I know what you mean."

Her arms crossed under breasts, which seemed dangerously

close to spilling right over the top of her corset-style bodice. For a second, he wondered how she could breathe with the laces done up so tight, but then he forced his gaze to where her nails dug into her bare arms. Then up to her face.

Fresh tears spilled down her cheeks. Her lips trembled.

"Come here," he said, holding out his hand. Deep inside, part of him braced for rejection the way he'd brace for a solid check into the boards. But he knew on the outside he looked calm. In control.

She sobbed, put her hand in his, then threw herself into his arms. "I'm sorry. You were right. You were right and I was so stupid—"

"None of that, love." Face buried in her hair, he closed his eyes and absorbed her scent, her warmth, grateful for the chance to be close to her again. Maybe not for long, but he'd take what he could get. "We both know why you were with Paul. The important thing now is gettin' him out of your life."

"Yes." She sniffed and looked up. "Then we can—"

"One thing at a time." He tapped her nose and smiled so she wouldn't take him cutting her off too hard. Much as he wanted to, he couldn't let her finish that sentence. She'd end up offering something she'd regret. "Tim said you were willing to do *anything* to make your dad and Paul back off. Did you mean that?"

Her tiny nose wrinkled and her nostrils flared. "Definitely. Why, do you have an idea?"

"I might." But she wouldn't like it. Fuck, he wished he could come up with something else—*anything* else. Instead, he had to use the one thing that would remind her of why she'd ditched him in the first place. "What would you think of involving the other guys?"

The look on her face was priceless. Lips parted, cheeks cherry red, she stared at him like he'd just asked her to strip and strut around the forum naked. His lips quirked. The next part of his plan was almost as bad.

"The other guys?" Her voice squeaked and she turned even redder. "How many of them?"

Hell, she thinks I mean the whole team! "Just four. My line and two defenseman."

"Ah." She rubbed her bare arms, then covered her cleavage with her hand. "And what exactly do I do with them all?"

"You don't have to do anything." He reached out and curved his hand under her jaw, angling her face up so she could see the camera in the hall right between the locker-room and the bathroom. "We'll just make it look like you did."

Her hand slid up to her throat. "Oh."

Oh? Frowning, he studied her face. She blinked at him and pulled away.

Very strange. She seemed nervous, but Mason always said dilated pupils combined with rapid blinking and—he watched her tongue dart over her bottom lip—*that,* were signs of arousal. His blood surged downward and his palms got damp. He'd been worried about scaring her, but his suggestion seemed to have had a very different effect.

The metallic heels of her boots clicked as she walked across the room, watching him through the mirror. "So you think evidence that I'm . . . fooling around with the team . . . you think that will be enough?"

"I don't know—Paul's got some pride; I don't see him wanting to be associated with something like that, but this is more about your father." He paused, meeting her eyes in the reflection. "I have a reputation, Oriana. There are a lot of rumors about me sharing women. If I bring the guys in here, and then walk out with you half naked—"

All the color left her face. "Half naked? You want me to walk out of here—"

He quickly stepped up behind her to hug her before she got all upset for nothing. "In a jersey or somethin', I know you're not into exhibitionism."

"Max." She squirmed in his arms until she was facing him. Her fingers hooked over the collar of his white undershirt. "I might—"

Please don't say it. Not unless you . . . Breath held, eyes shut, he waited. And waited.

"Um." She gave his shirt a little tug. He looked at her, and she looked away. "Let's get this over with."

"Sure." He ground his teeth, then glanced at her hand. "You'll have to let me go."

"I know, I just . . ." Her fingers slid up the length of his throat. She licked her lips again, deliberately, as though savoring the last drop of something sweet. Or slightly salty. "Will you—"

"God, woman! You're going to drive me insane!" He took her face between his hands and kissed her, groaning when her lips and body fitted against his. Slick, peach-flavored lip gloss smeared everywhere. The depths of her mouth held pure, hot sin. But the tentative touch of her tongue was almost innocent. Letting out a gruff sound, he deepened the kiss, loving how she clung to his shoulders and took everything he gave. In this moment, she accepted him. Because her head wasn't telling her not to.

This woman—this unhindered, passionate woman—usually hid from the world. But he'd gotten glimpses in the past of all her many facets. The sweet, eager-to-please girl. The clever imp. The hot-blooded tease—who didn't often come out to play.

I won't let you stash them and be all proper, darlin'. Not this time.

He caressed her tongue with his, then grazed the sensitive spot on the roof of her mouth. She bunched up the collar of his shirt in her hands like she was afraid he'd get away. And he wanted to stay with her more than she'd ever understand.

If only his needs were different. Or hers.

But his body's needs seemed normal enough now. His pulse raced and his dick got hard. Like any guy who wanted a woman.

"I'm willing to try, Oriana." He sucked on her bottom lip, then moved down to kiss the slender length of her throat. "Not here, but when this is done, we'll go out to dinner and act like a regular couple. If you can forget what you saw and what I said—"

"No. I won't forget and I won't pretend." Oriana retreated a step and put a finger on his lips. "I already told you I wouldn't do that to you."

He felt like she'd just thrown ice water in his face. She wouldn't even give him a chance. Not that he blamed her. What she'd seen him and Sloan do would traumatize most women.

Her fingers stroked along his cheek, then delved into his hair. She rose up on her tiptoes and gave him a quick kiss. "You said we should take this one step at a time. How about we do that?"

"Yeah." Drawing her into a firm embrace, he pressed his lips to her brow before backing. "Let's do that."

* * * *

Black leather boots, a book bag, and a white jacket were strewn across the bathroom floor. Sloan followed Perron, confused as hell when he saw who was inside. He hadn't expected to see *her* again. Wasn't sure he wanted to.

Oriana Delgado sat on the wide, gray laminate counter, bare feet on the edge of the white sink, forehead resting on the mirror. The reflection showed him her face was blotchy, like she'd been crying. Sloan didn't feel an ounce of pity for her. What could this stuck-up brat possibly have to cry about?

"Oriana," Perron said. "They're here."

Her eyes pressed shut, she gave a jerky nod, then hopped off the counter. Looking unsteady on her feet, she turned to face them. "I—"

Perron stopped her mid-turn and ran his hands down her back. His fingers brushed the exposed flesh of her ass where the bottom of her dress had twisted to one side. Sloan's mouth went dry. That heart-shaped butt was just made to fit in his palms, made for him to squeeze while he . . . *fuck!* Even outside, all covered up, she'd tempted him. Now, with her all rumpled and temptingly vulnerable, it was impossible to feign disinterest.

She squirmed as Perron's hand covered her ass. "Max—"

One firm arm around her shoulders held her still as Perron tugged down the hem of her dress. "There you go, love. Not tryin' to take advantage—you were giving the boys a show."

Yeah, she was. Thanks for ruining it, buddy.

"Oh, god." Oriana hid her face under Perron's arm, whispering. "This isn't embarrassing enough?"

"It's all right, darlin'." The southern drawl Perron usually hid in order to fit in crept into his tone as it deepened with concern. He kissed the top of her head and murmured into her hair. "Would you like for me to ask them?"

Whiskey-colored eyes flicked from one man to the next, paused on Sloan, and closed before she pressed her face to Perron's chest and mumbled. "No, I will. I'm just . . ."

Sloan grinned. *Surrounded?*

Mason moved into the room, and the door drifted shut behind him. "Is this about Stanton? Are you ready to leave him?"

"I can't leave him." Her lips parted in a wide O before she snapped them shut.

"Oh, please—" Sloan scowled when Perron gave him a dirty look. Did the man seriously think he'd waste his time listening to her drama?

Before Sloan could tell them all to enjoy the evening and take off, Mason crossed the room to stand over the girl in full white-knight mode.

"What does that bastard have on you?"

"N-nothing—" Oriana seemed to be trying to burrow under Perron's jersey. Her words were muffled against his chest. "Forget it. Max, please bring me h . . ." She shook her head. "Somewhere."

"Are you sure?" Perron frowned, massaging her shoulders when she didn't answer. "You can trust them; I wouldn't have suggested this otherwise. Just spit it out."

She gave him a you-can't-be-serious look, angled away from him, and crossed her arms over her chest, causing her breasts to strain against the tight black laces of her corset. Sloan struggled with the overwhelming urge to wrench her out of Perron's arms and bury his face in her cleavage.

Which would likely get him slapped. Unless he showed her what a decent guy he could be. His pulse thrummed low in his gut, then descended a little more. *Yeah, time to play nice.*

"Relax, Perron." He shoved his hands in his pockets and took a step back. "She'll talk when she's ready."

Her grateful smile told him he was headed in the right direction.

"I can do this." She bent to pick up her jacket and sucked in a shallow breath. Her words sounded strangled, like she couldn't breathe right. "Just give me a minute."

She straightened and her face went white. One hand hovered over her chest.

"Fine." Perron took the jacket from her and laid it on the counter by the sink. "But in the meantime, how 'bout you get out of that dress."

Fuck! Much as he'd love to see her strip, he couldn't see the girl doing that with them all watching. Probably wouldn't take much for *Perron* to get her naked, but if he planned to seduce her, why drag the rest of them along? What the hell was the man up to?

"Out of this . . ." She gulped in air like she was standing on the edge of a pool, about to take a plunge into the deep end. Then she gave each of Sloan's men a long look—while avoiding looking at him at all—and let out a noisy breath. "Yeah, I guess that's a good place to start." She put her fingernails between her lips and backed toward the stalls. "I'll explain when I . . ." She smacked the stall door and stumbled inside. "Please don't leave."

The door clicked shut.

"What's going on, Perron?" T.J.'s pale eyes flashed with rage. He tried to step between Sloan and Perron. "You better start talking or—"

Sloan sidestepped and did his best to keep the big man out of arm's reach of Perron's throat. "Calm down. He'll tell us."

"Not for me to tell." Perron leaned his elbows on the counter behind him. At a loud *thump* from the stalls, he cleared his throat. "Need some help, darlin'?"

"Umm . . ." The girl sounded like someone was choking the life out of her. She groaned and there was another thump. "Maybe someone could give me something to change into—"

Vanek skirted around them. "Come to the locker room with me. I'm sure I've got something. You'd float in the other guys' clothes, but I'm not that much bigger than you."

Sloan grabbed Vanek by the back of his shirt when he reached for the door. "Go get the clothes. She'll change in here." Sloan's eyes narrowed when the boy opened his mouth to interrupt. "Alone."

"No!"

Every man in the room went still at Oriana's shout. Something crashed into the wall hard enough to make the stalls shake. A sob got Sloan moving. Perron reached the stall a step ahead of him.

"Oriana?" The muscles in Perron's forearm flexed as he took hold of the top of the door, looking ready to tear it right off the hinges.

"I'm okay . . . I'm just . . ." Oriana sniffed, then sighed. "I'm stuck."

"Do you want me to come in there and help you?"

"Would you?"

A devilish smile slanted Perron's lips. "Gladly."

Sloan mentally counted all the reasons he shouldn't knock his friend's perfect teeth down his throat. He got stuck on *one* . . . when Mason spoke up.

"I've got a better idea." Mason folded his arms over his chest and gave Perron the look he usually saved for when playtime was about to get real serious. Whips and chains serious.

Now you're in for it. Sloan leaned on the wall by the stall and smirked when Perron nervously glanced his way.

When Mason cleared his throat, Perron jumped. "What?"

"You obviously know something. We've all been asked to stay, and neither of you are telling us anything." Mason waited for Perron's nod, then continued. "If you want to keep this between you, fine. But if we're being included, for whatever reason, I want to know why. Now."

The locked clicked. The door opened a crack. Oriana peeked out at them and spoke so quietly Sloan had to hold his breath to hear her. "Don't blame Max; he's doing this for me. I need something I can use against my father. He threatened to cut me off if I break up with Paul. Changing his mind shouldn't take much—he won't risk me going as far as my sister did—"

"What does Silver have to do with this?" Sloan's sharp tone had all the men staring at him, but he didn't give a damn. He'd known Silver for all of a month—couple of years after Delgado acquired the team. She had to be the most self-centered, high-maintenance woman he'd ever met. Not his type at all, and she hadn't taken it well when he'd say so.

Tough. He didn't perform on demand.

Oriana gave Perron a helpless look. Perron held up a hand and shook his head, probably having guessed where Sloan's thoughts had gone. "No one has to do anything. She's just gonna walk out of here with all of us; make it look like something was going on by getting out of her clothes—"

"I'm liking this idea so far." Vanek sidled between Sloan and Mason and pulled off his jersey. He bunched it up to toss it to Oriana. "Even if this don't work, imagine what the guys will say—"

"You're not gonna look like some big stud if that's what you're thinking, Vanek." Sloan snatched the jersey, feeling Oriana's eyes on him as he paced to the sink. He fisted the jersey in his hand and rested his knuckles on the edge of the sink. "As a matter of fact, she's just going to use us to get what she wants—should be something in this for us, but there won't be."

The stall door opened all the way. He watched Oriana's reflection as she slipped out and moved to stand next to Perron.

"What do you think should be in it for you, Mr. Callahan?"

Sloan shrugged. "At least a little show . . ." Her bottom lip quivered, and he groaned. "Shit. I'm kidding. Don't start blubbering." He tossed the jersey to Perron. "Help her get changed; I wanna get this over with."

Expecting Perron to take her into the stall, Sloan hefted himself up on the counter to sit and wait. Oriana crossed the room and bent down to pick up one of her boots.

He had a second to wonder why before she flung it at his head. The sharp heel nicked the arm he shielded himself with, then clattered on the floor.

"What the hell!"

She came at him so fast he thought she'd claw at him like an angry cat. She stopped a foot away and dug those very sharp-looking nails into her palms. Fists pressed to her sides, she stared at him, opening her mouth twice before she finally spoke.

"I don't use people and I don't 'blubber.' I would really appreciate your help—I know I'm not much to look at, but still . . ." She blinked fast and held her hand up when he pushed off the counter and stepped forward. "Please don't make fun of me anymore. I don't like it."

Make fun of her? What the . . . "I wasn't—"

"Shut up." Perron glared at Sloan like he'd just called the girl some nasty name and rubbed Oriana's arms. "You are beautiful. But you don't have to—"

"Please get it off me." Oriana turned her head away from the men. Perron slung the jersey over his shoulder and went to work on the knotted ribbon of her corset.

Sloan studied her stiff posture and frowned. "Perron—"

"Not now, Callahan." Perron murmured something to Oriana, and she nodded.

The corset opened wide, revealing soft round breasts covered by sheer black lace, quivering with the rapid rise and fall of her chest. Lovely—but the girl looked ready to hyperventilate.

Taking hold of the bottom of her dress, Perron gave Oriana a bracing smile. "Arms up."

Oriana put her arms up. Her face was sickly white.

Sloan couldn't take it any longer. "Perron, stop. She can't—"

"Yes, I can." Oriana took a deep breath. "Do it, Max."

Perron started lifting the dress but paused when she winced. He knelt and looked at something on her thigh. "Ouch. Why didn't you tell me you got hurt?"

"It's just a little burn."

"It's pretty red." Perron didn't sound so sure of himself anymore. He stood and took her hand. "Come on, we'll go to my place. I'll take care of this, and then—"

"I want it off!" She twisted her hand free when Perron shook his head and grabbed the hem of the dress like she wanted to tear it from her body. "I wore this for him and I hate it! Like my father said, like Callahan implied . . ." She hissed in air through her teeth. "I look cheap."

Jesus, her father and Paul had done a number on her. Never mind the dress, the girl didn't look comfortable in her own skin. And he hadn't helped matters with his crude comments. The reddened flesh made him think of the marks he'd leave if he got his hands on her, but concern overrode his baser impulses.

He held out his hand. "Oriana—"

"I'm fine, Mr. Callahan." A few deep inhales, and she actually managed a smile. "Just stand back and enjoy the show."

"We certainly will." Mason used the husky tone all the ladies seemed to like, yet his eyes trailed over Oriana in a way most women found offensive. Strange contradiction, 'specially since this woman didn't seem the least bit offended.

She flushed and ducked her head. "Maybe you can help me, since Max won't."

Perron grabbed her by the hips before she could go to Mason. "I didn't say I wouldn't."

"Stop stalling and do it then."

Aren't we bossy? Sloan shook his head when Perron simply grinned and obediently stepped up to her. Peeling the dress up over her head, he gave them all an unobstructed view of her beautiful body. Her black lace bra and panties were so sheer he could see her puckered nipples and waxed pussy. His gaze trailed over the exposed flesh, butter smooth, naturally tanned—he wondered whether she'd mark easily. The head of his dick scraped against the inside of his zipper. Lousy time to go commando. He shoved his hands in his pockets and did his best to unobtrusively shift his dick away from the metal teeth. *Damn, damn, damn.*

Perron lowered the jersey over her head, then pulled her hair free of the collar. "There you go. What does my *lady* require now?"

At the emphasis on "lady," Oriana's lips parted. "Tim told you about *that?*"

"Yes, ma'am." Perron gave her a mock bow. "Command me, Mistress. I am eager to serve."

Sloan groaned. "Tell me you're not going to make us watch this."

"We've got some time to kill." Perron shifted his gaze to Sloan in the barely perceptible way he did when he was about to make a blind pass. "If nothin' else, watching me make an ass of myself ought to be entertaining."

"Not really," Mason said under his breath.

Shaking her head, Oriana put her hands on her hips. "Be serious, Max."

"Try it," Perron said.

Oriana smoothed her hands down her sides and bunched the bottom of the jersey in her hands, tugging as though she wanted to make it longer. She licked her bottom lip and pointed at the floor in front of her. "Come here. I liked the position you were in before. Get on your knees; I'm going to kiss you."

At Sloan's side, Mason coughed back a laugh. Perron glanced

over and winked. Then he got on his knees and waited.

Cupping Perron's face in her hands, Oriana leaned down and pressed a chaste kiss on his lips. When Perron made no effort to return the kiss, she let out a frustrated sound and raked her fingers into his hair. Sloan winced when she jammed her mouth over Perron's and their teeth clinked.

"Shoot." She touched Perron's bottom lip with her thumb. "I'm sorry—"

"Don't worry about it. You 'bout done?" Perron rose at her nod. "I've a mind to ask you something."

"Okay." Oriana clasped her hands in front of her and rocked on her bare feet. As the silence lengthened, she wrung her hands and glanced across the room. Perron cleared his throat and she jumped. "What?"

"One step at a time, right?"

"Right." She gave the hem of the jersey a sharp tug.

Perron gave her a level look. "Good. Go sit on the counter."

At the command in Perron's tone, Sloan stood a little straighter and noticed Mason doing the same. T.J. stood near the door, arms crossed, brow furrowed. Vanek had gone almost as white as Oriana.

Oriana approached the sink, stopped, and shook her head. "I'd rather not."

Perron closed the distance between them. "Why? Are you afraid of what might happen? I might could tell *you* to get on your knees instead, but that'd be going a bit too far."

"You're missing the whole *Lady* in charge, Max."

My cue. Sloan sidestepped to the sink, then slid along the counter until he stood right behind Oriana. Her spine stiffened, but she kept her eyes on Perron.

"You don't really want to be in charge, Oriana." Sloan let his breath out slowly so she'd feel the heat of it on the back of her neck. She shivered, and he grinned at Perron over her shoulder. The man had read her perfectly. "Think how it would feel to be at another's mercy. To surrender."

"You're making fun of me again." She shifted, as though to get away from him.

He put his hands on her hips and turned her to face the mirror.

"When you look in the mirror, I don't think you see what I see—what any of us sees." He pressed a soft kiss on the sensitive hollow behind her ear and whispered. "I'm not making fun of you. But I need to know what you want."

Her hair brushed his lips as she turned her head to look at him. Eyes wide, lips parted, she looked ready to do anything he asked. To surrender to *him*.

Chapter Four

iss me. Lost in Callahan's dark eyes, Oriana willed herself to say the words. Another second and she'd beg him to devour her as his hungry gaze promised he would.

Max touched her cheek and whispered. "Is this what you want?"

What I want is . . . She ground her teeth and fisted her hands at her sides. *What I want is wrong.* "Let's get this over with. You want me to sit on the counter? Fine."

She spun away from Max and almost fell when she slammed into Callahan. He caught her arm.

"Without the attitude, Oriana." Callahan's tone snapped like a whip.

The bones in her legs liquefied. Only Callahan's hand under her elbow kept her on her feet. The smooth material of her jersey skimmed her nipples, and the sensation was like a spark of static electricity. She bit back a moan and hissed through her teeth.

Why did he affect her like this? He was a jerk. Mean and arrogant and . . .

Damn fine. She could practically hear Silver going on and on about all the things she would do with Callahan once she got him alone. *Sloan's got a body you just want to run your tongue all over. I'll tell you what he tastes like.*

Silver had basked in the players' attention, flirting and using first names like they were all good friends. She'd been uncharacteristically grumpy after *Sloan* turned her down.

Maybe I'll be able to tell her what he tastes like. Oriana's mouth watered at the thought. She pressed her thighs together as lower things throbbed and moistened.

Only one other man ever made her feel this way. She glanced at Max, standing a foot away, watching her. If she went through with this, he'd be doing that a lot. In all honesty, she could deal with indulging his kink—once in a while. Having all the attention of two men on her at once would be nice. But here? *Now?*

He's not the only one watching.

She shifted away from Sloan and hugged herself. "I'm not on your team, *Captain.*" She mumbled to the floor. "Max got on his knees for me. I'll follow his orders. Not yours."

"We'll see." Sloan's gruff tone told her he wasn't happy, but he got out of her way.

For some strange reason, she was disappointed.

Max didn't give her time to dwell. He hooked an arm around her waist, then tipped her chin up with a finger. "I'm still waitin' for you to 'follow my orders,' sugar."

Uck, should have kept my mouth shut. "Sorry." Licking her bottom lip, she glanced at the counter. "I'll do it."

"One minute." Max slid his hand to the nape of her neck and squeezed when she tried to slip away. "Dominik."

Leaning against the tiled wall beside the sink, looking rather bored, Dominik arched a brow. "Yes?"

Max gestured to her. "Help her up."

The muscles in Dominik's jaw tensed. "Getting a bit full of yourself? I don't take orders." His expression gentled when his eyes met hers. "You sure you want to do this?"

Her insides went all gooey. She might have nodded, or just gawked at him like she'd gone brain-dead. Was he talking to her or Max? She couldn't tell. Dominik's hands circled her waist, and oxygen went elsewhere. Probably sucked up by all the insanely big men.

The sharing, the . . . *arrangement,* went on between just Max and Sloan, didn't it? Dominik's involvement threw her completely off-balance. To be blunt, she could probably fuck Sloan once then tell him to get lost. He was too mean to get attached to. But Dominik— things could easily get complicated with him.

Her gaze flicked from Dominik to Max, then past them to the three other men. T.J. looked pissed, Tyler eager, Sloan . . .

Sloan's lips moved, and she could almost feel them on her flesh again, soft despite how hard he always seemed.

"Go for it," he mouthed.

"I'm sure," Max said. He dropped his hand and backed up a bit. "You're a master, Mason. I've seen what you can do without layin' a hand on a sub."

A sub? Oh hell. She'd seen the term in her book. He didn't mean . . . "Max—"

"No, Oriana." Dominik took one hand from her waist, then slid the very tips of his fingers along her jaw. "Look at me."

She couldn't imagine looking anywhere else. The gold flecks in his dark brown eyes entranced her, reminded her of a gold mine she'd visited and the gold veins running through the rocks beyond signs that read "Danger."

Too appropriate. The man really should have "Caution" stamped on him somewhere. Maybe smack dab in the middle of his forehead where a girl couldn't miss the warning.

Dominik chuckled and picked her up by the hips to sit her on the edge of the sink. "So pensive. What's on your mind?"

With him standing close enough for her to bask in his body heat?

She shifted back as far as she could without falling into the sink. "Caves. Your eyes . . ." *Damn, damn, damn.* "I mean—"

"Caves?" He rubbed his chin with his thumb and forefinger and tilted his head to one side. "Now I'm curious. Why do my eyes make you think of caves?"

She folded her hands on her lap and focused on keeping the edge of the jersey from slipping up any farther. Bad enough the undersides of her thighs were directly on the cold counter. A little more and the men would get another eyeful of her see-through panties. Were any of them looking? She snuck a glance at Max and Sloan. Both were studying her with disturbing intensity. What about T.J. and Tyler? She leaned over a little farther to see around the muscular black shoulders cutting her off from the rest of the room.

"Oriana." Dominik gently pried her hands apart and lowered them to her sides where he held them in a loose grip. "I asked you a question."

A question? She blinked at him, confused. Then she remembered. *The caves.* "I visited a gold mine in Timmins, Ontario. Your eyes made me think of it . . ." *Lame much?* She shrugged. "They're pretty."

Someone snickered—probably Tyler. A yelp cut the snicker short.

"I hadn't taken you for a girl who'd explore the darkness." The resonance of his tone echoed in her bones. Little tremors ran up her spine. He moved closer but still touched nothing but her hands. "I find tours rather tame, though. Would you consider something a little more . . . thrilling?"

Yikes. She had a pretty good idea where he was going with this. She moved to slip off the counter. "Dominik—"

"Do. Not. Move."

She froze.

He smiled and stroked her inner wrists with his thumbs. "Now, as I was saying—maybe I could take you with me cave diving this summer. Nova Scotia has some beautiful underwater caves." He pressed his hips between her knees and brushed the hair off her shoulder with his chin. "Some consider it dangerous, but I know what I'm doing. I could teach you."

"Umm . . ." She worried her bottom lip between her teeth. "I don't know."

"You don't have to decide right away. Just consider the adventure, the chance to try something new." His breath teased the flesh over her quickening pulse. "Which is what you're doing now. Right?"

Before she considered the question, the answer came. "Yes."

"Good girl." He backed away and straightened. "I want you to close your eyes."

Her eyes drifted shut.

"Sloan was right. You don't want to be in charge; you don't want control. Imagine giving it up. Imagine me holding you right where you are." She felt him shift and something grazed the jersey between her breasts. His heat swept through the fabric like a gentle caress. "And doing whatever I please."

Oh, yes. His words made her imagination run wild. Carnal images of things she'd never thought of trying flashed behind her closed lids like erotic stills. Everything inside her cried out for her to make the fantasy a reality. Pure hot lust spilled over, dampening the swatch of lace between her thighs. She hadn't been this wet in, well, *ever.* This man's voice alone made her feel like her pussy was being stroked and teased by a very skilled tongue. She imagined Max drinking her in with his eyes, enjoying the way she responded to the man he'd given her to, and her core throbbed. She gasped and let her thighs part. Dominik could do whatever he pleased. So long as he did *something.* She opened her eyes, ready to beg.

Dominik was on his knees. "So you spilled that coffee after all." He pressed a light kiss over the burnt flesh on her thigh. "I shouldn't have left you."

And who said kisses didn't make the pain go away? The scent of citrusy soap wafted up as her deep inhales made her feel a little dizzy. She put her hand on his shoulder to steady herself. "I was the one who left."

"Yes, well, you won't be given that option again."

Good. Her toes curled as he pressed another kiss farther up her thigh. *Mmm, very good.*

* * * *

Sloan watched Dominik graze his lips up to the crease between Oriana's thigh and hip and shook his head. Dominik was so damn good—hell, just watching turned *him* on. And he wasn't a voyeur.

"Thanks, Dominik. I'll be takin' it from here." Perron took Dominik's place in front of Oriana and eyed the red blotch on her thigh. "I think you'll be okay. I've got some aloe to put on it back at my place."

"Your place?" Her swallow was audible. "But . . ."

"You don't want to go home?" Perron waited for her to shake her head, then rubbed her knees. "Then come with me."

The defiance in her eyes brought out the dominant in Sloan. He couldn't just watch anymore. Perron was being too soft. Dominik had backed off. She needed more.

He held out his hand. "Enough. Come here."

Before she had time to consider obeying, she'd hopped off the counter and put her hand in his.

He curled his fingers into her palm and smiled. "Very nice."

A hesitant smile graced her lips, but then she glanced at Max through the corner of her eyes. Her lips parted, and her already flushed cheeks grew even redder. One look told Sloan all he needed to know. Max had his thumbs hooked into his belt and his fingers laced over his very erect cock.

"There's a lot you need to learn about your lover boy, sweetheart." Sloan splayed his hand on the small of her back and pressed her butt against the counter. "But you already have an idea of what he needs, don't you?"

She swallowed, once, twice, then nodded.

"I think he's waited long enough." With that final statement, he claimed her lips. His hips ground into hers as she curved into him. Blood pumped into his dick, and his balls throbbed. All he had to do was sit her on the counter and flip those see-through panties off her pussy, then stuff her full of his cock and make her scream . . .

"Fuck. Callahan, stop." Perron took a firm hold of Sloan's shoulder. "This is why I asked Dominik. You always take things too far, too fast."

"She's ready." Sloan felt a growl rip out of his chest. "Tell me you don't see it."

"Maybe, but she'll regret doing this here, now."

"Fine, but later—"

"Not if you don't get a grip." Perron glared at him and reached for Oriana. "Come on, love."

Confusion flickered through the glaze in her eyes. She snatched her hand from Sloan's and reached for Perron. Then hugged herself and retreated a few steps.

"Wonderful." Perron muttered. "Let's go."

Asshole. Sloan watched Oriana gather her things and follow Perron out, submission buried under uncertainty. Dominik watched her and Perron, displeasure darkening his already black features. But experience prevented him from contradicting the command she'd chosen to follow.

They were taking Perron's lead. So not good.

Sloan headed for the door.

T.J. blocked him. "She doesn't seem the type to be into the kinky stuff."

Sloan took hold of the big man's arm and pried his hand from the doorframe. "You don't know her."

"Neither do you."

"I will." Sloan barred his teeth and glared at Vanek when he moved to intercede. "Intimately."

Vanek moved to stand by T.J. "We'll see about that."

"Coming, boys?" Dominik cracked his knuckles and gave them each a pointed look. "This isn't going to be a problem, is it?"

"Not at all." Sloan skirted by Dominik and T.J. and made his way to the elevator. Perron and Oriana were long gone. The three other men joined him before the elevator doors could close. Tension filled the small space like thick black smoke. Each man had his own idea about what Oriana needed. Not one was willing to discuss it.

Damn, he hated competing with his boys for women. They always had plenty to choose from when they went out together. They couldn't *all* share her—could they?

Guess it's up to Perron. Sloan grinned at the thought. This might work in his favor after all.

Chapter Five

The rolling thrum of drums and wailing guitars filled the car, followed by vocals with a growling undertone, loud enough to make the seats vibrate. Avenged Sevenfold. Max tapped his foot in time to the beat. The restless energy the music gave him was perfect just before games—but not so much for dates. Well, not for dates with most women anyway. He glanced over at Oriana, sitting stiffly at his side, gazing out the window. Her loose hair hid her face like a silky, bronze shield, but the white-knuckled grip on her purse told him all he needed to know.

Mason's gentle commands and careful seduction had gotten her guard down, but Max and Callahan had screwed that up by acting like a pair of toddlers fighting over a hockey stick they had to share. *Me first! No me!* Freakin' pathetic.

And his genius plan . . . he'd rushed her out of there so fast, that probably wouldn't pan out, either. But everything in the locker room had gone beyond something staged for her father's benefit. The possibilities almost overwhelmed him. He was willing to bet they'd overwhelmed her.

Max rubbed his thumbs over the ridges of the steering wheel. *How do I get her to relax now?*

The music should have helped. Back before she'd stopped talking to him, she'd gone through all the CDs he kept in the car and pulled out this one. Face all red, she'd confessed that she'd bought the album on her phone. When he'd told her that was cool, she'd seemed so relieved, as if she'd been afraid he'd think less of her for liking such hard-core music.

Nothing could, but saying so wouldn't be enough. Paul and her father made her doubt herself so much that her confidence was a fragile thing. She needed a break from it all. Maybe a vacation somewhere with some good memories to erase all the bad.

That's it! Spinning the steering wheel, he swerved off the road home.

Oriana gasped and grabbed his knee. "Where are you going?" She sat forward and her hand moved farther up his thigh. "Max?"

"Just a sec, sugar." He put his hand over hers and squeezed. "Trust me."

Fifteen minutes later, he pulled up in front of the Halifax Public Gardens and parked the car.

He gestured vaguely at the passenger side door. "Get out."

She opened the door, and her heels clicked on the pavement. Then she perched on the edge of the seat and glanced back at him. "You never used to be so bossy."

"I didn't know you needed it." He pulled out his cell phone and dialed Dominik's number. "Go. I'll be there in a minute."

One eye on Oriana, Max let Dominik know they'd taken a detour and settled in to listen to the *Master's* instructions. *Aw hell, should I be taking notes?*

"Max, you do know she's submissive, right?" Dominik sounded more concerned than he ever had with the subs he'd let Callahan and Max practice with. "She's new to this. You have to take it slow."

"I know that." Max watched as she paced in front of the wrought iron gate, back and forth with leisurely steps, like she could wait all night. The odd dirty look tossed his way undermined her patient act. He took a bit longer than necessary just to see what she'd do. "But I should have done this months ago. She needs to know I'm not letting her go."

Mason was silent for a while. Then he answered in a cool, detached tone. "Yes. She does."

"Not sure how long we'll be, but you might want to wait up."

"I plan to," Dominik said, before hanging up.

Perfect. His lips curved up as Oriana flounced up to the gate. She stopped and clasped her hands behind her, rocking on her heels as she studied the garden's crest. Her brief show of temper might not seem like much to some, but it showed him she'd gotten comfortable enough not to hide how she really felt.

"Wealth from the sea." He heard her whisper as he joined her.

He moved up to her side, sounding each step so he wouldn't startle her, then took her hand. "You remembered."

"I remember everything about the day you brought me here. I still can't believe you knew more about this place than I did—I've lived in Nova Scotia most of my life!" Her eyes shone as she looked up at him. "You made me feel like a tourist, but it was wonderful."

"Believe me, it was my pleasure. My dad used to spend days teaching me the history of the places we visited when I was a kid. Instead of bedtime stories, he'd read me travel books." He glanced down at her hand in his. For the first time since they'd met, touching her didn't feel like trespassing. It felt right. He stroked the soft flesh of her inner wrist and smiled when she shivered. "Most of the women I've dated get bored real quick when I go on about 'points of interest,' but you seemed genuinely interested—"

"I was." She turned to face him and touched his cheek with her free hand. "I am."

I know, darlin'. That's why we're here. He drew her closer to the gates. "How 'bout another tour?"

"The gates are locked."

"They're easy enough to climb." He paused and glanced down at her boots. *Shoot. Should have thought this through a little better.* "Ah, well maybe not in those."

She giggled, shook her head, then sat on the walkway to unzip her boots. "Problem solved."

"That's my girl." Not even a question about getting caught. Of course, she was probably feeling a little reckless tonight, but if so, he might as well enjoy it while it lasted. "Up you—"

Scrambling up the fence, she hooked an arm around a rung and held out her hand. "Do you need help?"

He tongued his bottom lip and let his eyes trail from her bare feet, up to her bare thighs. "God, yes." He climbed the fence, cursing when his running shoes slipped. His whole body vibrated with a heightened awareness of her, so close, so . . . available. "But not with this."

On the other side of the fence, he hopped down, then caught her in his arms. Lowering her slowly to her feet, he trapped her with his hooded gaze and brushed a soft kiss over her lips.

Her fingers dug into his forearms as she aligned her body with his. "Max . . ."

"Not yet, love." He frowned as she started to protest. "We need to have us a little chat first."

Tiny teeth dented her bottom lip. "You don't want me?"

Aw, Christ. That's the last thing I want her to think. "'Course I do."

Her eyes went down to his crotch. "Doesn't seem like it."

His arms fell to his sides. *Shit,* he'd really hoped she wouldn't notice *that.* Truthfully, the thought of having sex with her here hadn't even occurred to him. But, considering the lengths she'd been willing to go to with Paul—including getting a kinky book which seemed way out there for her, no wonder any type of rejection hurt.

Every inch of his heart and soul wanted to taste her lips, to hold her—and yet his body . . .

I'm not the only one with needs.

His frown deepened. "Do you really think I brought you here just to fuck you against the fence?"

Her eyes widened, and she put her hand on the center of his chest. "No! I—"

"Good, then come with me." He took hold of her wrist and arched a brow when she tried to tug away. "We should talk about what happened tonight. But if you're more interested in getting off, that's fine." He pointed at a patch of dry grass alongside the path. "Take off your panties and lie down. I'll use my mouth and tongue and teeth on that sweet little pussy—make you come so hard, you'll scream. Then I'll bring you back to my place."

She stared at the grass and pressed her thighs together. Considering his offer probably aroused her even more than before. But he'd intentionally made sure his tone didn't compel obedience. Giving her the option to refuse.

"What do you want to talk about?"

Curious little minx. Another thing he loved about her and the very thing he'd counted on. He shrugged and skimmed his fingers up her outer thighs. "Guess it's not that important."

Little goose bumps rose up on the bare flesh under his hands. Her thighs quivered. His mouth watered. Tasting her, all hot and wet for him—hell, they could talk later.

She grabbed his wrists and shook her head. "No. Let's talk. We can . . . you can . . ." She blushed. "Later."

He swooped her up in his arms and laughed at her squeal. "And I will. But first . . ."

Letting his words trail off, he carried her across the park until they reached the bandstand. Then he climbed the steps and set her on her feet, facing away from him. She placed her hands on the green railing. He wrapped his arms around her waist and rested his chin on her shoulder.

The gardens, which were a riot of colorful blooms throughout late spring and summer, showed only the first signs of stirring from their winter's rest. The merest hint of the coming beauty, but Oriana would recall the way it had looked in September when they'd been here last.

"I thought you could use a break before we head to my place."

"All the guys live with you, right?" At his nod, she inhaled and gave a little shudder. "And they're waiting."

"Let them wait. A few hours is nothing compared to months." He pressed his cheek against her silken hair and closed his eyes. His tone lowered to a whisper. "Promise me you'll never do that again."

"I shouldn't have done it in the first place."

"Shh." He brushed her hair aside with one hand and laid a gentle kiss on her cheek. "No regrets. Just your promise."

* * * *

Oriana's throat felt tight. But she managed to say the words, "I promise."

The promise seemed to satisfy him, for he simply held her close and took in the scenery, but she didn't understand how he could forgive her so easily. Before this night, the last call she'd taken from him had been on her birthday, which she'd spent alone because Paul had "business" to tend to.

As soon as she'd told him she had no plans, he came and picked her up, bearing an armful of yellow tulips. Her favorite flower—Paul usually bought her roses, which should have given her a clue. But, right then, all she could think was her feelings for Max were becoming stronger and that was unacceptable.

Even worse, she could see everything she felt reflected in his eyes. Which just wasn't fair.

After a long drive out to the piers, after he blurted out *those three words*, she decided it was time to tell him their friendship was a bad idea. She'd hoped to spare him some pain, but the way he stilled, having just said "Happy birthday" and leaning in to kiss her cheek, she might as well have stabbed him in the gut.

On the mildest of winter nights, his passion had cooled fast as hot syrup drizzled on snow. White-knuckled fist pressed to the hood of his refurbished black pickup truck, he nodded slowly.

"Why?"

Oriana's gaze had fallen on the flowers, abandoned on the passenger seat, the yellow petals, wilted from exposure to the cold, stark against the black leather. What could she say?

Because when you flash those dimples, reality shifts. I forget that I'm in a good, solid, relationship and you . . . need things . . . things I can never give you. If only I hadn't seen . . . if you hadn't told me . . . This has to end before I do something crazy. Like fall for you.

All good reasons, as far as she was concerned. He would have understood; Max was good that way. But she hadn't bothered explaining because he'd have found a way to change her mind.

Feeling like she'd put her heart in a vise, like each breath tightened the clamps, she'd taken out her sunglasses. Her hands had shaken as she slipped them on. Brow arched, she'd given him the icy Delgado smile. "Think about it, Max."

"I see." The dimples disappeared. The muscles in his jaw ticked. "Reckon I should tell you to have a nice life. But you won't, 'cause he'll make you miserable." He ran his knuckles down her cheek. "I'll be here when you figure that out."

Max made a gruff sound in his throat, dragging her from the past into the present. "Stay here with me, sugar."

"I'm here." She bit her lip, then turned in his embrace to face him. "And I'm not going anywhere."

"All right then." He lowered his forehead to hers. "So, tell me—are you good with what happened tonight?"

"In the bathroom?" Her nose wrinkled when he nodded. "I guess so. It's just . . . I'm not sure why I reacted the way I did. To Mason and . . . and Callahan. He's one mean son-of-a-bitch."

"That he is," Max said, his lips curving into a fond smile. "But he's loyal. And you couldn't ask for a better friend."

"I don't think he wants to be friends with me," she said dryly.

"No, but he's attracted to you." His gaze burrowed deep into hers, as though he could see into her very soul. "Which surprises you."

"Naturally." She twisted her lips and looked down at her bare feet. Why hadn't she grabbed her boots? Her toes were getting cold. "What would a man like him want with a woman like me?"

"Don't do that, love." Max sighed and shook his head. "You are everything a man could want. Passionate, full of life, always giving more than you take—we'll have to work on that, you hear?"

"Yes, sir." She giggled at his stern look. "Are you really into all that dominant stuff?"

"I am."

"Well . . . what if I'm not into being dominated?"

He chuckled. "Let's be honest, shall we?"

Umm, no? She pressed her tongue between her teeth. "How about I'll think about it?"

"That will do." He lips slanted into a lazy smile. "For now."

* * * *

Max grinned when she spun away from him and stared out at the park. There were things she wasn't ready to accept about herself. Which was fine. He was a very patient man.

"So why did you bring me here?" she asked.

"You seemed to find peace here last time." He shrugged. "I thought you'd enjoy a chunk of nature—"

Her soft laughter resonated through him as he pressed his lips to her throat. "A chunk of nature?"

"Yeah. Why, would you prefer a 'taste'?" His voice turned husky, and she shifted closer. *Good, very good.* He knew this tone turned her on—not as much as when Mason used it, but . . .

The image of her with Mason played out in his mind and got him as hard as he'd been then. He moved his hips away from hers and cleared his throat.

"Reckon I should tell you I plan to steal you away very soon."

"You already did."

"Yes, to a place you've already been." He held her still when she tried to wiggle closer. "But you've never seen the view from the St. Joseph's oratory or walked through the sanctuary garden. You haven't savored some of the best smoked meat in the world or heard the tam-tams near the Cartier monument."

This time, he let her go so she could turn to face him. "Montréal?"

He brushed her hair away from her eyes so he could enjoy the glow of excitement, sparkling like golden liquor in a crystal glass. "You haven't been to Montréal in about eight months, right?"

She shook her head. "I don't feel like I was ever really there. Much as I loved the atmosphere and culture, I didn't experience half the stuff I would with you."

He clenched and unclenched his jaw a few times to keep from grinning like an ass, but another tinkle of laughter told him she wasn't fooled. "So we should go?"

Her shoulders lifted in an offhand shrug. "I'll think about it."

Lips pressed together, he tried for an uncompromising expression and failed miserably. Then he chuckled and backed her into the railing. "Brat. How about we leave the first week of May?"

"But—"

"You're done with school for the semester."

"Yes, but—"

"So what's the problem?"

"Arg!" She stomped her foot and grabbed a fistful of his shirt. "Will you let me speak?"

The shade of red that rose high on her cheeks as she got more and more flustered was absolutely adorable. He should tell her off for interrupting and being grabby with him, but he was having too much fun. Mason could teach her to be a proper sub if that's what she wanted. When they were alone, like this, he didn't see any reason to get all serious.

"Go ahead," he said.

"What if you make the playoffs?" Her hands smoothed out his shirt, lingering near the spots on his chest that made him twitch. She lightly played her fingertips over his hard nipples while her tongue slid across her lips. Her thoughts seemed to have strayed. "Or even the . . . um . . . the finals?"

"We won't." He bent down to nibble up the length of her throat. Her pulse fluttered against his lips fast as dragonfly wings. "Which means we can spend a few weeks in Montréal before we head to the Alamo." He grazed the shallow behind her ear with his teeth.

"Oh—*Mmm*." The bright red shade of her cheeks had faded to a light blush of pleasure. Then she went still and the color faded. "The Alamo? In Texas? You want me to go to Texas with you?"

Well, hell. This wasn't the reaction he'd expected. "Yeah, I do. You used to talk about going all the time."

"I'd love to, but—" Her brow furrowed. "Don't you stay with your dad while you're there?"

"So?"

"So, you've told me so many wonderful things about him, like how *protective* he is of his kids." Misery painted shadows around her eyes. She hugged herself and made a halfhearted attempt to twist away from him. "He'll hate me for how I treated you."

"How you . . ." He groaned and pulled her in for a hug. "Silly, he won't hate you. Even if he knew what happened—which he doesn't—he'd understand. He's made his share of mistakes. Namely stayin' with my mother for years after their relationship fell apart."

"After she *cheated* on him." She mumbled between the hands she had covering her face. "What if he finds out—"

"Stop worrying." He curved his hand under her jaw, tipping her head up. "And kiss me."

The way her lips parted for him, the way she groaned when he moved his hands under the jersey to hook them around her waist, was . . . very nice. But his body lagged way behind where the rest of him wanted to go. Possessing her mouth with the deep thrusts of his tongue, he let his mind slip to when he'd last been hard. Two recent memories played over in his head. Oriana with Mason. Oriana with Sloan.

Blood rushed to his groin. He looked down at the woman in his arms, a woman he'd willingly have waited a lifetime for, and imagined sharing her with one of his closest friends. Or both. Or *several*.

He groaned as Oriana's hand glided over his stomach, then down to cover his stiff erection. Without his jeans to muffle the sensation, he would have come right then. *Rein it in a little, Perron.*

Ice, helmets, smelly gloves, ugly guys with no teeth—there, he'd regained control of his body. He traced a finger along Oriana's hip bone, dipped under the elastic of her panties, touched her silken folds.

Which weren't as moist as he'd expected.

"You not into this, babe?" He kept his tone neutral so she wouldn't think he was upset. Not that she'd been explicit, but he'd known she and Paul had problems with sex. 'Course, he'd blamed Paul—and still did—but maybe there was more to it.

"I'm into it. I just—" Her hips wiggled, and she tried to clamp her legs shut as he lightly tapped his fingertip on her clit. "I keep wondering what you're thinking about. Just me? Or me with the men?"

A half-truth, but he'd go along with it. "Honestly?"

She nodded.

"I was thinking about you and Mason, about how beautifully submissive you were." At that, her breath hitched, and she grew nice and slick around his fingertips. He dipped two fingers inside her and smiled as her eyes glazed with pleasure. "And then with Callahan—" Her hot, tight pussy squeezed his fingers. "You seemed a little scared, but there was a dark passion in your eyes."

Her lips formed silent words before she whispered, "Max . . ."

In this perfect setting, the two of them under the moonlight, with only sleepy plants watching, they could give each other some satisfaction. But how shallow would it be? He withdrew his fingers and caught her elbow with a hand when she swayed.

"No!" She held on to him, her eyes wide. "I want you!"

"Do you now?" He cupped her breasts and grazed his thumbs in slow circles around her nipples. His gentle ministrations had her bucking her hips and moaning out loud. "Tell me who you're thinking of, love. Just me, or more?"

* * * *

"More!" Oriana gasped as he rolled the jersey up to her throat and bent down to kiss the swell of her breasts. "Oh!"

Without a moment's pause, he bared her breasts and began suckling the taut flesh of one, then the other. The sensation coiled around her clit, and her insides clamped down on nothingness, aching to be filled.

"Please." She pressed against him, her hips seeking his with aimless forward thrusts. "Max, please!"

"This will be enough, darlin'." His tongue traced the edges of her areola, coming closer and closer to her nipple. He let the moisture left behind cool while he brought his lips to hers and stole her breath with a fierce kiss. His palms covered her breasts, molding them gently, leaving her nipples untouched. "I never would have asked you to be with the men. I would have done everything in my power to be the man you needed, but you want them, don't you?"

"Mmm." She threw her head back as he lightly brushed his fingertips over her nipples, and every nerve in the tiny nubs greedily absorbed the sensation. Being neglected had made them hypersensitive. She almost wanted to pull away; it was almost too much, but his words had her ready to come apart. Visions of hot hands and mouths all over her made her knees lock and her core clench convulsively.

"Tell me. Tell me exactly what you want us to do to you." He caught her nipples between his fingers and thumbs, rolling them, tugging lightly before lowering his mouth to flick each with his tongue. "Don't come until you answer me, Oriana."

"Ah!" Her eyes teared as she fought the urge to surrender to the building climax. "Everything! Anything! Just . . . just . . ."

His tongue fluttered over the tip of her nipple, faster and faster. He sucked the nipple, playing it carefully between his teeth, then resumed the fluttering. "Very good. You may come now, sugar."

At another flick, pleasure burst from her breasts and flared out from her cunt. She cried out as the sensations came together and ignited from everywhere at once. Her knees gave out, and Max held her tight as she rode the violent orgasm until she was deliciously spent.

Supporting her with an arm around her waist, Max straightened her bra, then her jersey. Her skin tingled as the material touched her, and she whimpered, suddenly, desperately needy. She wanted to strip and beg him to take her again and again.

"Don't give me that look." He palmed her cheek and kissed her. "It's getting cold. We'll head back to my place and get you warmed up. See where your head's at."

"Where my head's at?" She blinked at him as he draped his jacket over her shoulder. "But you said—"

"A bit of mental stimulation, Oriana." He glanced down at her bare feet and shook his head, cursing under his breath. "Mason would kick my ass if he knew I had you out here like this."

"But—"

He shook his head again and she groaned. No more talking. He obviously wanted her to make her decisions with a clear head.

But exactly what would clearheaded Oriana decide?

To tell the truth, she had no idea.

Chapter Six

Oriana decided she'd lost her mind. The men in her life had pushed her over the edge. Not just Paul and her father, no; Max could take some of the blame, too. Or most of the blame. Only he could make coming to his house, alone, to . . . umm . . . with *five* men sound . . .

Sound crazy. *Slutty.* A little hot considering she had her pick of some damn fine studs—*Ugh.* No. She'd regained her senses on the drive over. Once they reached the house, she'd made a mad dash for the first-floor bathroom—almost settling on a closet when she'd opened the wrong door.

She'd said she needed to go. She'd really just needed to hide.

Phone tucked between her shoulder and her ear, she leaned on the beige marble counter and prayed her sister would answer. Silver would know how to handle a situation like this.

"Hello?" Silver said groggily.

Oriana felt bad—for about a second. Then she recalled all the times she'd bailed her sister out of worse messes. *You owe me, sis.* "I need your help."

The reaction she got after explaining her situation was odd.

"Blackmail? Oh, you naughty girl!" Silver sounded so proud. "And you made sure the security cameras caught you leaving the bathroom with the boys in nothing but a jersey?"

"Yeah. Do you think it will work?"

"It might. *If* you've got the nerve to tell Daddy you'll have the recording sent to the media if he doesn't back off."

Exactly what she'd hoped.

"The only problem is Daddy might call your bluff. Or the men might tell the truth, and you don't want it to be their word against yours. You'll look stupid."

"Oh." *Well, that sucks.* "So what do you suggest?"

Silver groaned loudly into the phone. In response to what she'd said? Or was something else was going on in her sister's room? "Daddy doesn't give me my own way because of idle threats. He knows I'll follow through; he's had to cover up me doing so a few times. He's all about image."

"Silver there are five men outside this door. You can't seriously think I could—"

"Why the hell not?" Her sister giggled, then gasped. Definitely multitasking. "Think about it. You stay with Paul and let him walk all over you, or have a fuckfest and ditch him all at once. You might have to follow through with your threats. Shouldn't you enjoy yourself if everyone's gonna think you're a hussy anyway?"

"I guess . . ."

Wimp. You seriously need your little sister to make this okay for you?

Silver sighed. "Don't do anything you don't want to, but I think every girl should have at least one gang bang."

A gang bang? No, nothing with Max would be as crude as that. But where would things go from here?

One step at a time.

This was a pretty big step.

A loud moan in the phone made Oriana blush. The sound of a man's murmur, followed by another's laugh, almost made her drop it. Her mind drew up an image of herself in bed between Max and Dominik. Or Sloan. She tried to hold the phone steady as her hand shook. Static filled her ear.

A deep voice replaced her sister's. "Silver's busy now. Can she call you back?"

The line went dead before she could answer.

Tapping at the door made her heart skip a beat.

"You all right in there, Oriana?" Max called.

"Couldn't be better." She gathered her wits, straightened the borrowed jersey, then threw the door open.

Max stood off to one side, arms crossed, and a smile on his lips that didn't reach his eyes. At her other side, Sloan hooked his hand to the doorframe over her head.

He scratched his chin and looked her over. "You know, if you're uncomfortable *being* with all of us, you and Max can use my room. I don't share."

Uck, how much had he heard? She folded her arms over her head and racked her brain for a way to put him in his place. Maybe she should tell him what she'd decided.

Which is what exactly?

Dominik made a gruff sound of disgust and pushed off the black cube coffee table where he'd been munching on what looked like frozen fruit. "Don't be a dick. She never said she wanted to be with any of us."

"Right." Sloan arched a brow at the other man, then shrugged. "Just want to make sure she understands she's got options."

How generous. She opened her mouth.

"Smooth, Sloan." Max took Oriana's arm and led her a bit away from the others. "Don't listen to him. He's just sore 'bout being shipped to the minors."

"Oh." She traced the embroidered details of the Cobra emblem on her chest and mentally shelved a rude comeback. She'd almost forgotten her father and Paul were planning to destroy more than just her future. "I'm sorry—I didn't know until—"

"Right." Sloan met Max's glare and returned it. "Forgive me if I'm skeptical about the innocent act, but princess here lives the sweet life because her father's a cold, calculating son of a bitch. He probably brags about who he'll screw over next while their cook serves supper."

"Unless I'm with Paul, my father doesn't waste time having supper with me." Oriana shook off Max's comforting touch and strode across the room to face Sloan. She jabbed a finger into his big chest, poking the cobra on his T-shirt in the eye. "And you're one of the highest paid players in the league, so don't you dare look down on me because my family has money. That doesn't change who I am." *Or what I can do for you.* She smiled grimly. "All I want to do is finish school and be a doctor. All you want to do is play hockey with the team you love. We'll both get what we want if—"

"If?" The bitterness faded from Sloan's face. He grabbed her wrist to stop her poking and jerked her against him. "Are you really gonna go through with this?"

Oriana arched her neck so she could meet his eyes. "*This?* I'm not sure what you mean. I've got all the evidence I need."

"And suddenly everything Max wanted is okay."

"Is that why you hate me?"

The silence of the room was so thick, every inhale like air sucked in through a stopped-up straw. One of the men cleared his throat. The springs of the sofa creaked.

"I don't hate you. I just don't buy the complete 180." Sloan's grip loosened, and his thumb stroked her knuckles. He tilted her chin up with a finger so he could look in her eyes. "And are we playing this game again? You know exactly what I mean."

Dark green. His eyes weren't black like she'd first thought; they were a deep, dark green. Oriana's mouth went dry. She had to swallow a few times before she could get a word out. "I will tell my father that if he cuts me off or sends you to the minors, the security footage goes straight to the press."

"I appreciate that." His hand slid up to her cheek, and his thumb caressed her bottom lip. "And coming here with us will certainly help." He gave her a soft smile. "But that doesn't explain why you haven't left yet."

Oh, God. Do I have to spell it out? "I don't want to go home. Paul will be there."

"The offer of another room stands."

Cool air skittered down her spine as someone moved up behind her, lifting her hair and smoothing it over one shoulder. The familiar ice and ocean scent soothed her as Max whispered, "Let me handle him." His tongue stroked the curve of her ear, leaving moisture which warmed with his breath, but chilled as he moved away. She shivered and he rubbed her arms briefly before he put his hand on the small of her back and guided her to the armchair beside the sofa. "Make yourself comfortable."

"You're cutting us out of decisions that include us all again, Perron," Dominik said from behind her as she sat. She glanced up at him when he braced his hands on the back of the chair. "We assumed you took some private time to satisfy the woman, but you haven't, have you?"

The woman? When had she become "the woman?"

"Well, we . . ." Max ran his tongue over his teeth, head cocked as though seriously considering his next words. "Oriana had some things to think over."

"Did she now?" Dominik caught her chin in his hand and leaned over her. "How's that working out for you, little one?"

She had to close her eyes to block out the intensity of his regard. But she couldn't stop the truth from passing her lips. "It's not."

"Shall I take a guess as to why?"

Mouth dry, she nodded.

"Your man has figured out what you need, but he's letting you take the next step because he doesn't want to scare you off." He combed his fingers into her hair and tugged. "I don't think you scare that easy, Oriana."

The way he said her name, like he knew exactly what his voice did to her—maybe "the woman" would be better. "The woman" didn't make her skin recall the way his hot breath had caressed her. And he didn't think she scared that easy? Well, she was pretty damn afraid of what she'd let him do if he asked in *that* tone.

The edges of Dominik's lips drew up slowly. "Well now—"

"Assuming you're right, Mason—" Max walked around the chair until he was in her line of sight and stopped right behind Dominik "—what do you suggest?"

"Why don't you start with giving her some space?" T.J. asked.

"Perhaps . . ." Dominik straightened and folded his arms over his chest. "Do you want some space, pet?"

Pet? She rubbed her arms as goose bumps rose. What normal woman would be okay with being called "Pet?" Or be turned on by all the implications of that word. *Maybe I'm not normal.* All right, then, she should tell them what she wanted. But how? She couldn't very well just strip and say, "Take me, boys."

Or could she?

"So what's it going to be, Oriana?" Sloan asked.

Her palm itched to find something to throw at him. Why couldn't the man give her a minute to think?

"We can start by . . ." *Damn.* She had no clue. And no matter how deeply she inhaled, she couldn't seem to get *enough* air. Not a good sign. She wouldn't have much fun if she passed out.

"Why don't we watch a movie?" Tyler popped his head out from the first bedroom off the sitting room. "I've got some good ones—"

"No one's in the mood for Disney, little man." Max grinned at Tyler's scowl. "I don't suppose you have any grown-up movies?"

"Hey, I've got fucking porn if that's what you want."

"Are you even old enough to watch porn?"

Uck, men! She rolled her eyes, but the light exchange seemed to make the air a little more breathable. Smacking the arms of the chair, she stood. "A movie would be great. Let's see what you've got."

Max caught her wrist. "Anything you want, love. Don't be shy."

He's so not talking about the movie.

"Anything?" *What would you think of a game of Yahtzee?* "What exactly do you mean by *anything?*"

"Anything, anybody. There are five men here, Oriana." He paused as though to let her absorb his words. "Take your pick."

Shouldn't you pick?

The fact that he wasn't making the choice for her thrilled and scared her all at once. The possibilities were overwhelming.

Keep it simple. Don't pick a man. Pick a movie.

"No chick flicks!" Sloan called out as she joined Tyler in the bedroom.

No kidding. She giggled when Tyler stuck his middle finger up in Sloan's general direction.

"Ignore those jerks. We'll watch whatever you want." Tyler pushedup the gray bed skirt and pulled out a suitcase. He flipped open the lid and sat back on his heels.

The entire suitcase was crammed with DVDs. She knelt beside him and scanned the titles, all in alphabetical order.

"Wow, this is quite a collection. Do you cart this with you to all the games?"

"Yeah, I'd go nuts if I didn't. On the road, I watch them on my PVP while the guys are watching sports." He pulled a slim black video player out of the top flap of the suitcase. "My mom bought me this and my own TV/DVD combo when she heard that I'd be staying with Max and sharing a room." He ducked his head and blushed. "She fusses over me a lot, but she's a good woman."

Oriana smiled. He might be all man, but he was adorable. And embarrassed. She looked at the movies and selected one.

"*Slap Shot?* I haven't seen this in so long." She paused. "But if you don't like watching sports—"

"It's not that. I just don't watch anything but hockey. *Slap Shot* is one of my favorites." He cocked his head. "You like it?"

"Like it? Seriously?" She cleared her throat and did her best Denis Lemieux impersonation. "'You do that, you go to the box, you know. Two minutes, by yourself, you know, and you feel shame, you know. And then you get free.'"

Tyler burst out laughing. "Hey, that was pretty good!"

Cheeks blazing, Oriana wrinkled her nose and shrugged. "I practiced a lot when I was little. My uncle loved my impersonations."

"You're a really cool chick, you know that?" He reached out and smoothed a few strands of hair off her cheek. "I meant to thank you for trying to distract Sloan."

Distract Sloan? Oh! The bouncy bunny at the forum! "It didn't work."

"Doesn't matter." He inched closer. She didn't move. "Thank you anyway."

"You're welcome." She whispered as his lips touched hers.

His kiss was tender, sweet, like her first kiss in the tree house with the boy next door—she couldn't have been more than seven. But then Tyler pulled her against him, and the kiss changed. Silken, wet, hot, and not the least bit childish. He urged her lips apart, tasting her with teasing little dips of his tongue. Her heartbeat quickened as every spark of lust triggered that night ignited like gunpowder in her veins. His fingers grazed her belly, and her muscles twitched.

"Oriana."

Please don't stop. She whimpered when Tyler's lips left hers.

Then she realized Tyler hadn't spoken. Her gaze shot to the door.

Sloan clucked his tongue. "Naughty girl, taking advantage of the kid like that."

"Fuck off, Sloan." Tyler flattened his hand on her stomach and nuzzled her neck. "Perron said she could have anything she wanted."

Anything. Yes. Her eyes drifted shut, and she tried to forget Sloan, standing there, watching. Impossible. Her thoughts drifted to him joining her and Tyler on the floor, and her head spun.

"You guys coming?" Max called from the other room.

Suddenly, her blood ran cold. She scrambled away from Tyler and hauled in a lungful of air, praying it would clear her head. What if Max had come instead of Sloan?

He wants to watch.

But he couldn't see anything from the other room.

"Come on, Oriana." Sloan held out his hand. "Don't overthink things. No one's gonna be mad."

"Are you sure?" She let him help her to her feet, hoping he was right.

"Yes, but if you're worried, we'll keep this between the three of us." He touched her bottom lip and grinned when she shivered. "Your lips are a little red, but it's dark in the other room. No one will notice."

She peeked past him. The only light in the sitting room spilled out from the open bathroom door and the faint flash from the TV. She could hear the men talking quietly amongst themselves. Max's rich laugh rang out, and she felt every taut muscle in her body relax.

Maybe they wouldn't notice. They seemed pretty distracted.

Sloan circled her palm with the rough pad of his thumb. "There's a lock on the door if you want to stay in here with me and Tyler."

"Good idea." Tyler hopped to his feet and darted to the door.

A big, black hand smacked the door before Tyler could pull it shut.

"Not really," Dominik said, pushing the door open. "I'd hate to have to kick the door in."

"A little excessive, Mason." Sloan's low tone held a hint of danger.

Dominik didn't appear intimidated. "You think so? Why don't we ask the only man here who really knows her?"

As though he'd been called, Max came up behind Dominik. His narrowed eyes went from Oriana to Tyler, then fixed on Sloan. "What the hell's going on in here?"

"Nothing. Mason's just paranoid." Sloan's shoulder hit Dominik's as he stormed out of the room.

With a gruff sound in his throat, Dominik lunged for Sloan. Oriana leapt forward and grabbed his arm.

"Please don't. This is my fault. I didn't think—"

Halfway across the sitting room, Sloan stopped and turned slowly. "Do you honestly believe either me or Vanek would have done anything to hurt you?"

"Of course not!" She didn't, she really didn't. But she should have considered how easily things could have gotten out of hand.

Sloan stared at her, swallowed, then nodded. "Right. Look, the rest of you have fun. I'm out."

"Chill, Callahan." Max shook his head and raked his fingers through his wavy blond hair. "This is getting a lot more complicated than it needs to be." He stepped forward and took Oriana's hands between his. "I thought taking things slow would be a good idea, but I was wrong."

"You were?" She closed her eyes as he slid his hands up her arms, bunching the sleeves of the jersey to stroke sensitive flesh. "But this is so . . ."

"Oriana." Max tapped her nose and smiled when she looked at him. "I meant what I said. You will take what you want. Do you understand?"

No. "Yes."

"Good." He laced his fingers behind her neck and rested his forehead on hers. "So how do you want to do this?"

How? Umm . . . Faintly, she heard her Bon Jovi ringtone coming from the sitting room.

"I should get that." She scrambled around the men and grabbed her book bag from where she'd dumped it beside the sofa. After fishing out her phone, she held it to her ear.

"Hello?"

"You sound out of breath. Am I interrupting anything?" Tim sounded amused.

"No," Oriana said, keeping her back to the men, perfectly happy pretending they weren't there waiting. "What's up?"

"Silver called me. She thought you might have forgotten the evidence you worked so hard to obtain." He sighed. "I'm in the bar down the street from Max's place. I had a feeling you'd still be with them, but—"

"I'll meet you in the bar." She pressed "end" and dropped her phone on the sofa. Sitting on the floor, she pulled on her boots and glanced at Max who'd come up beside her. "I'll be right back."

Max frowned. "I'll come with you."

"No!" She stood and held on to the arm of the sofa while her legs adjusted to the height of her boot heels. "I need to . . . I won't be long."

Chapter Seven

The door whispered shut, and Oriana was gone. Sloan shook his head and cursed. They couldn't have handled that worse.

Perron moved to follow her.

"Max."

Every man in the room turned to Mason, who sat on the arm of the sofa, his steady gaze speaking volumes above his tone.

"She's had a fucking hell of a day, and I screwed up." Perron crossed the room and set one hand on the sofa by Mason's hip, leaning close. "I'm not leaving her alone."

"Go with Callahan, but for god's sake, don't let him take charge. Give her a taste of what she needs. A small taste." Mason's brow lifted when Sloan scowled. "If you can refrain from reminding her she's a 'poor little rich girl.'"

The perception of the man in training mode really freaked Sloan out. He caught himself rubbing the long scar on his face and stopped. No doubt Mason would read something into it. "I don't think she's a 'poor little rich girl' anymore."

"Then what's the problem?"

Where should he start? "Do you really think she knows what she wants? I'm used to dealing with girls who have more . . . experience. I would've gone along with whatever she was ready for, but she took off."

"And if you can't figure out why, maybe I *should* go with Perron." Mason rose from the sofa and rolled his arms behind his back in a fluid stretch. "I'm fairly confident I won't push her too far."

And I will? Sloan's scowl deepened. Just because he hadn't been voted a club master like Mason didn't mean he couldn't handle a sub. Of course, Mason wouldn't have suggested him going with Perron if he doubted that.

One thing confused him though. Why would Mason goad him into going at all? He obviously wanted the girl too.

"Perron is right. She shouldn't be alone right now." T.J. shifted toward the door, obviously ready to take the job of comforting the girl if the rest of them couldn't get their act together. "I'll bring her to my room and let her chill there."

The very idea of T.J. taking Oriana anywhere alone twisted Sloan's gut. Not that he would be anything but utterly respectful, but whatever Oriana's needs were, she would inadvertently push to get them fulfilled. And Sloan would damn well be there when it happened.

"I'm going." He frowned at T.J. who blocked the door. It was becoming a bad habit. "I'll bring her here unless she'd rather be alone. Then she can crash in my room. I offered first."

What a grown-up statement. Still, T.J. moved, so Sloan walked out and didn't bother looking back. Dominik could handle the boys for a while. Sloan's only concern was one emotional female.

"This is my fault," Max said when they hit the street. "I gave her too many choices right off."

"Ya think?" Sloan cracked his knuckles against a metal fence. "Five men . . . four, if you figure she's already sure of you. She freaked just seeing you watching me with a woman. Never mind the knife. Did you really think she'd go along with you watching her with all of us?"

"I know she will." Max stuffed his hands in his pockets, and Sloan could tell he was making some mental adjustments. "I won't go into details, but we talked. She won't come right out and say it, but, well, she's attracted to you. And Dominik. She kissed Vanek."

"Jesus, Perron." Sloan shook his head as the man he considered his best friend stepped off the curb and paused to let a car pass. "I know how you feel about the girl. How does this not bother you? If she was mine, I wouldn't want to share."

"I can't help what gets me off any more than you can. And she . . ." Perron stopped short and groaned, rubbing his thighs as though the muscles were cramped. "She's been irrelevant to the one man that matters most to her. She stayed with Paul to make her father happy; did you know that? All of us, wanting her—she needs this. Which works out, you know? This isn't just me being generous."

Sloan nodded. "You two mesh well. But jealousy could make things messy."

"I won't get jealous. Never have. When I watch a woman I like with another man, it's liberating. Seeing the woman getting fucked is hot, but it's like she doesn't have to be with just me. That she's got the dick of a man she's into ramming into her pussy, that she knows I'm still there, or, if I'm not, that she's thinking about me . . ." Perron shook his head. "I can't explain it better."

"You don't have to. I get it." More than he wanted to admit. Sloan had a possessive streak, but he understood the appeal of sitting back and enjoying the show, knowing a woman had him on her mind, would be his when the fun was over. Then again, if the woman belonged to him, he'd set some limits. A lot of limits.

But Oriana didn't belong to him. If she belonged to anyone, it was Perron.

"I want to give her tonight. I can't say what will happen tomorrow," Perron said.

Sloan nodded and squeezed his friend's shoulder. "Then let's handle tonight."

"Right." Perron squared his shoulders. "Our girl needs us. That's all that matters."

Our girl. Sloan trailed after Perron. *I really wish you hadn't said that.*

They headed into the bar. Sloan spotted Oriana the second he breached the dark threshold. Impossible to miss that big, black-and-gold jersey skimming those curvy thighs. The silver glint of snakes wound around her boot heels caught his eyes for a second. His gaze moved up slowly, taking in the bare olive lengths, entranced with the idea of having them wrapped around his waist.

Then she reached out and picked up a bottle of beer. Her lips parted slightly at the rim of the bottle flooded his mind with an entirely different set of images.

A man took the bottle from her and set it on the bar. He leaned close, and red filled Sloan's vision. The three men waiting back home—and Perron—were all the competition he was willing to put up with.

As he crossed the bar, their exchange stopped him short.

"I'm glad Silver called." The man, Tim, pulled a DVD from his pocket and handed it to Oriana. "She said if it doesn't have a pulse, you're not big on details."

"Thank you, Tim." Oriana took the DVD and looked at the jersey she wore. "Uck. I can't believe I came here like this. I looked just like those puck bunnies I'm always making fun of."

The assistant coach laughed. "You make a cute bunny. But at least you wouldn't have been down here for long. Figured one—or more—of the boys would come looking for you."

Oriana's gaze followed Tim's, and her eyes widened as she caught sight of Sloan and Perron. She hadn't expected them.

Good. Keeping her off balance would work in their favor.

Trapping her with his hard gaze, Sloan gestured to the bartender. "Molson Canadian."

The bartender recognized him, so the bottle was slid across the bar without a tedious exchange of pleasantries. When Sloan drank, he usually didn't chat. Max ordered vodka and cranberry juice. Sloan spared him a quizzical glance before focusing on Oriana.

"So Silver knows everything?" He brought the beer to his mouth. "Shoulda figured you didn't come up with that crazy plan on your own."

Brow furrowed, Oriana leaned her elbows on the bar and took her beer in both hands. "I called my sister because I thought *my* plan was crazy." She picked up the disc she'd dropped on the bar. "I got the support I needed from her. The only problem—according to Silver—is making sure when I say we all screwed like rabbits, you guys won't say otherwise." She tilted her head to one side. "You won't, will you?"

"We won't." Sloan took the disc from her and slipped it into the pouch of his sweater. "But be honest, Oriana, you want more."

The indecision in her eyes threw him off. Had he read her wrong?

"What brought you down here, honey?" Tim put his hand over her wrist and lightly squeezed to get her attention. "I'd planned to drop the disc off at Max's place, thought you'd all be there. Was a bit worried about interrupting, but . . ."

"You wouldn't have interrupted anything." Oriana looked down when Sloan arched a brow at her. "I couldn't . . ."

"Really." Tim's steady gaze tore Sloan's from Oriana. He gave Sloan the look he usually saved for players who showed up to practice hungover. The one that clearly said "You dumb fuck." His tone remained soft when he addressed Oriana. "You know, *real* Doms are a rare breed. Yet the Cobras ended up with three—four, if you include me. Would you like to know how that happened?"

She nodded and shifted closer to Tim."Yes, please."

"I found them. Dominik first. Then Sloan." He smiled. "I got lucky with Max."

Sloan recalled the odd conversation his agent had reiterated, asking how into *"the lifestyle"* he wanted to be. Asking if Sloan wanted discretion. If he'd ever belonged to a private club. And would he like to?

The Cobras made him a decent offer—not what other teams were willing to pay, but who cared? He was fucking sick to death of hiding who he was. Not that he advertised it now, but he didn't have to sneak around like he had in Colorado.

Tim finished explaining how he'd tempted a few kinky guys to join the team.

Oriana's lips twisted. "I can't see my father allowing you to pick players—"

"The GM picks the players," Tim said.

She nodded. "Yes, but—"

"He's my halfbrother."

"Dean Richter is your brother?" She shook her head as though the concept of shared genetics escaped her. "But his parents have been happily married for fifty years!"

"And mine have been just as happily married for about that long. Let's just say we were raised in a household where alternative lifestyles were the norm. The details aren't important. The important thing is Dean figured out that one of the biggest problems the team had in Tampa—besides crappy attendance—was a lack of actual team play. We hoped getting a few guys who shared more than a love of the game might create some unity. It worked. You'll notice—soon, I think—that Sloan, Max, and Dominik play very well together." At the implication in Tim's tone, Oriana blushed and ducked her head. He whispered something Sloan couldn't hear, then tapped under her chin with a finger. "Now look at Sloan."

Her eyes snapped up, and Sloan could almost feel the heat

flushing her cheeks spill into him. He put his hands on the stool by her hips and spun it so she faced him.

Tim inclined his head at Sloan in approval. "Tell him what you want."

* * * *

"You're a lucky girl," Tim had whispered. *"Don't be too afraid to appreciate what you've got."*

"Sloan." Oriana chewed at her bottom lip and caught Max's eyes on her. His gaze blazed into her. She placed her hands on her knees and focused on Sloan's mouth. *I can do this.* "Sloan, I want you to . . ."

One arm hooked around her waist, Sloan curved his hand around the side of her neck. His thumb aligned with her jaw, he tipped her face up and kissed her, gently, as though he found her lips delicate and delicious. She needed him closer, deeper. She pressed against him, and he growled. His fingers dug into her flesh, hard enough to keep her from moving, but not enough to hurt. Words weren't necessary. She understood.

He'd taken over. More would come on his terms—or not at all.

Lust, hot and sweet as mulled wine, poured down her throat, pooling in her belly before drizzling down further. Her lips softened under his, and her will folded. Resistance evaporated as though it couldn't take the heat. But she wasn't worried. Sloan would take care of her.

Air seized in her throat as though Sloan had both hands wrapped around her neck. Max had said Sloan moved too fast. How far would he take things?

Max won't let him. Max will . . . Her pulse raced. She opened her eyes to make sure Max hadn't gone anywhere.

There. Just out of arm's reach. She needed him closer, holding her hand, giving her an anchor to safety and sanity. Her hand slid across the counter toward him.

Max pushed off his chair and gently took her hand in his. His palm was sweaty, his skin hot. A peek downward showed her just the kiss had gotten him hard. But the simple gesture proved that her comfort was more important than his pleasure.

She relaxed and curved her neck as Sloan grazed his teeth down the length of her throat. He bit down lightly on a tense muscle. Chills washed over her, and she whimpered. Sloan tightened his grip on her hips and slid her to the edge of the stool. He pressed his hard length snug between her thighs, and she almost forgot where they were, almost begged him to continue.

Tim nuzzled the other side of her neck, then drew away as her spine stiffened. "What's wrong?"

Frowning, blinking away the erotic haze, Oriana shook her head to clear it. *What's wrong?* "I'm not . . ." She inhaled deeply and let the air out slowly. "You're married, Tim."

"Ah." Tim chuckled and stepped back. "I'd tell you my wife doesn't mind me helping with a scene—to some extent—but that would only confuse you." He sighed and checked his watch. "Speaking of my wife, I better head home before she takes out the whip." His eyes took on a hint of mischief. "Although . . ."

Oriana's eyes went wide. *Tim lets his wife use a whip on him?*

Well, why not? He obviously had some experience. She'd figured him for a Dom, but maybe he was a switch? Were any of her men switches? Would they want her to . . .

"Jesus, Tim," Sloan said, rubbing her arms. "Scare the hell out of her, why don't you?"

"About that." The humor faded from Tim's eyes. "You might want to watch that recording before you try to use it. When you left the bathroom, you looked pretty freaked out. And the men looked pissed. Don't know if that's the impression you want to give."

"Not really." Oriana tried to slip away from Sloan. He slid his hands up her thighs, stopping at the edge of the jersey. She bit her lip and looked at Max. When he shrugged, she picked up her beer and took a sip. "But I'm sure we can come up with something else."

Grinning, Sloan bent down to lick a drop of beer from her bottom lip. "Does that mean you're coming back?"

Rather than answer, she set the beer on the bar and gave him a little nudge. Before he could get out of her way, she eased off the stool and let her body glide down his. He groaned when she wiggled her hips.

"I'll think about it."

He flipped up the bottom of the jersey and dug his fingers into her ass. "You keep that up and I won't wait."

"You can't do anything here." She hiked her chin up, shoveling defiance over rampant desire. This guy was way too cocky. Time to bring him down a notch. "Save your threats, Mr. Callahan. I'm not scared of you."

Tim cleared his throat. "Just a suggestion, Oriana, and then I'm out of here." He laughed when she tried to twist away from Sloan. "Taunting your Dom is a bad idea. Especially when he's a sadist."

Oriana gulped when Tim walked away. She suddenly realized Max had released her hand and stepped away from her to finish his drink.

Leaving her alone to deal with Sloan.

"I was joking." She pressed her hands against Sloan's chest and gave him the most innocent look she could muster. *I'll be good. I promise.* "You're not going to hurt me, are you?"

His answering smile didn't bode well. "Oh, I'll hurt you," he said. "But not here. And not tonight." He picked her up and dropped her on the stool. "Finish your beer."

"But—" She shut her mouth when his eyes narrowed. Okay, maybe she *was* a little scared of him. The rush of adrenaline in her veins made her skin cold. With a shaky hand, she brought her beer to her lips.

Sloan placed his hands on her upper thigh and framed his thumbs along the rim of her panties. She choked on a mouthful of beer as her clit throbbed.

Max's presence behind her made her insides clench with need. He patted her back. "Breathe, darlin'."

She gasped and tried to close her thighs. Solid hips worked between her knees. Hands clamped just above them.

A little whine escaped her as she realized whose hands held her open. "Max . . ."

Sloan's thumbs stroked her pussy.

"Oh!" She covered her mouth with her hand and shook her head. "You can't—"

"But I am." Sloan nibbled along the side of her throat as his fingers slipped into her panties. "And you want me to. You're so wet, babe. Be honest, you'd let me fuck you now if I wanted to."

Yes! Oh god, yes! She shifted her hips forward and pressed her face against his chest to stifle her moans as one thick finger penetrated her. Part of her mind objected to letting him do this, here, where anyone could see. Reason made her say the words out loud. "We'll get caught."

"That's part of the thrill." Sloan strained to fill her with another finger even as he picked up his beer. If anyone was looking, they'd assume he was having an intimate conversation; his face betrayed nothing more. "Would you like another drink?"

His calloused fingers, all slicked with the spill of moisture, thrust in and out slowly, gentle and erotic. Not quite enough to make her scream—unless it was for more. Her whole body quivered, chanting "Deeper, faster, harder!", drowning out her whispers of reservation.

Lips sucked at her neck, then a tongue trailed a hot path up to her ear. Max whispered. "He asked you a question, love. Would you like another beer?"

"Mmm." Her eyes rolled back as Sloan teased her clit with his thumb. The rim of the beer she held bumped her bottom lip. She drained the bitter dregs and blindly attempted to set the bottle down on the bar. A searing wave of arousal made the bottle slip from her hand. Max caught it just in time.

"I think she's had enough," Max said.

Enough? What? No! She whimpered, sure Sloan would leave her a quivering mess—unfulfilled and longing.

"I agree." Sloan pressed his thumb down on her clit and resumed dipping his fingers into her, again and again, fast and hard, until she was sure everyone in the bar could hear the rhythmic wet slap of his palm on her pussy. "Just give me a minute."

Another finger joined the others. Stretching, twisting. She fell back onto Max. Sloan flicked her clit, once, twice, then drove his fingers in deep. Her spine bowed, and her hips bucked. A violent orgasm tore through her, and only Max's lips on hers kept her from screaming.

Sloan dragged a few more spasms from her and casually withdrew his fingers. He covered her with her lace panties and patted her pussy, making her jerk and moan. Not enough. Need *everything.* *Please!*

"How about we take this back to my place?" Max helped her off the stool, holding her when her legs refused to solidify. "I think she's had her taste. Time for a full course."

Had my taste? This was planned?

Reason slammed into her skull. She glared at Max, then Sloan. "I can't believe you just—"

"Oh, stop it." Sloan brought his glistening fingers to his lips and sucked them, one at a time. "You wanted me to."

I did. But that doesn't matter. "Not here!"

"Liar."

Her shocked senses made her tense up. She wanted to spit in his face. "Fuck you."

"Fuck me?" Sloan clamped his hand around her wrist like a shackle and towed her out of the bar. "As you wish."

All the way down the street, Sloan tightened his grip every time she tried to wrench free. She cursed him in her head and out loud until her lame-ass objections sounded silly, even to her. There was no denying it. She could have asked him to stop at any time. And, if he hadn't listened, Max would have made him. Still, he didn't have to be such a jerk now.

In front of the house, Sloan finally let her go.

She rubbed her sore wrist and muttered under her breath, "Asshole."

"What did you just call me?" Sloan took a step toward her.

Max blocked him. "Take it down a notch, Callahan."

Sloan's stance went from barely contained violence to the calm of a predator stretched out on a rock in the sun. Harmless. Unless you dared make a sound.

Oriana's whole body went rigid, but, as they made their way up to the porch, she realized he wouldn't attack her. Yet.

She grazed her bottom lip with her teeth. After everything that had just happened, one thing still bothered her. Maybe talking would ease the tension. "Sloan, can I ask you something?"

"Shoot."

A deep breath, and she blurted out her question. "You're not really a sadist, are you?"

Chapter Eight

Sloan's roaring laughter echoed out onto the street, and Oriana scowled. Tim's warning fresh in her mind, she wondered if smacking her Dom would be as bad, or worse, than taunting him.

"Aww, babe. Don't be mad." Max hugged her from behind and whispered in her ear. "You have to admit, the question's kinda ridiculous. He's all turned on, and he promised to hurt you."

Bad time to play 'one of the boys,' Max. She jabbed her elbow into his gut hard enough to make him grunt, then skirted out of reach. "I'm going to pretend you did not just say that."

Her heels thudded on the steps as she turned her back on him and stomped up to the house. The men spoke quietly, then one caught up with her.

"Oriana, wait." She could still hear the laughter in Sloan's tone as he took her hand and spun her away from the door before she could open it. "I didn't mean to laugh, just . . . well, considering your recent research, I didn't think you'd be so clueless."

Screw bad ideas. She put her hands on his chest and shoved. "You've got to be the biggest jerk I've ever met."

Shadows swept away the amusement lightening his features. "I find that hard to believe considering your taste in—"

A mutter and a cough, and Oriana turned to see the front door hanging open.

Dominik stepped away from T.J. and Tyler and held out his hand. "Everything okay?"

Oh, that voice. Little tremors raced over her flesh as though she'd ventured naked into a cool spring shower. His concern barely masked his displeasure. He didn't seem to like Sloan and Max upsetting her.

They were lucky she didn't relish being fought over. Silver considered scuffling part of foreplay. May the best man win.

But I'm not Silver. And, for the first time, that didn't seem so bad.

She put her hand in Dominik's, and her whole being went calm and still. Somehow, his strength seemed to fill her. She smiled up at him. "Everything's fine."

The men drifted away from the doorway, but not far. As Dominik led her inside, her shoulder brushed T.J.'s chest. She peeked at him, and he gave her a grim smile. He seemed . . . disappointed.

A wave of uncertainty crashed into her. Before Dominik could bring her any farther into the house, she dug in her heels. "Are you sure everyone's comfortable with this? Maybe I *should* take one of the other rooms."

Not necessarily alone. She squeezed Dominik's hand, hoping he'd catch on.

"Maybe you should make up your mind." Sloan stopped short when Dominik put a hand on his shoulder and said something too low for her to hear. Sloan sighed and rubbed between his black eyebrows. "Hell, do whatever you're comfortable with. I'm not up for playing games."

"Then you don't get to play." Dominik's tone was gentle, but firm. He turned to Oriana. "What about you?"

She pressed her lips together to hide a smile, then cocked her head. "Why? Will you play without me if I say no?"

Dominik went still, then roared out a laugh. The tension in the room shattered like sugar glass. Even Sloan chuckled.

God, that felt good. All the deep masculine laughter, rumbling like thunder before a storm breaks. She couldn't remember ever making someone laugh like that before. Maybe in high school, but that seemed like so long ago.

"No, brat, we won't play without you." Dominik tapped her chin with a knuckle. "So, what's it gonna be?"

Near the bar, beside the large TV stand, Vanek uncapped a bottle of water and watched her as he gulped the whole thing down. T.J. slouched on one of the wing chairs that angled away from the sofa, as though whatever she decided wouldn't affect him at all. But the way his fist, resting on the arm of the chair, repeatedly tensed and relaxed told her otherwise.

Max, Dominik, and Sloan were the hardest to read. For all Sloan's frustration and Dominik's amusement, both wore blank expressions. The captain was taking the Master's lead, and both looked like they could stand there all night and wait for her to make up her mind. Max's expression almost matched those of the other two men, except for the slight quirk of his lips.

Her blood retreated from her fingers and sizzled all the way down to her core. The fear of making the wrong choice created an urge to run for her life. Only her life wasn't in danger.

She rubbed her hands together, startled when she felt a hand on her arm. Max. His touch assured her she wasn't making this decision alone.

"How far are you planning to take this . . . game?" she asked Dominik.

"As far as I think you can manage," he said.

Sloan's lips curled. "Which will be further than you think you can, little girl."

Nodding slowly, she felt her pulse steady and took a deep breath. "I guess I better say yes." She gave Sloan her sweetest smile. "I might be clueless, but I know better than to piss off this sadist."

"Do you really?" Sloan stepped up to her. "And why's that?"

"Well, he might beat me with his hockey stick." She traced a big C on his chest. "You find roughing sexy, Captain?"

Max spat out a laugh. "I would say mocking a sadist isn't brilliant either, doll."

Sloan shook his head, lips moving as though in silent prayer. "If you keep pushing, Oriana, I'll teach you Submission 101 right now."

T.J. slammed his fist on the arm of the chair and stood.

That didn't look promising. She skipped across the room, putting herself in front of T.J. and just out of Sloan's reach. With a fake little shudder, she glanced over at Sloan and gave him Bambi eyes.

"Should I be afraid?"

Hands settled on her shoulders. "Yes." Dominik's tone dropped an octave, and its deep resonance made her shudder for real. "When we decide to introduce you to that aspect of our lives, *pet,* you'll have to follow our rules."

"*When?*" She swallowed so her voice wouldn't squeak again and looked over her shoulder at Dominik. "I thought we were limiting the . . . *fun* to tonight."

"Tonight won't be enough for me." He rubbed the muscles running along her neck. "But it's a start."

A start? The little adventure turning into something long-term hadn't occurred to her. Max enjoyed watching—she might be able to deal with that—but what Sloan enjoyed . . .

"Nothing serious yet." Dominik leaned over her shoulder and kissed her cheek. "This isn't something you jump into. Perhaps a few commands to add some spice, but I really don't think you'll need it."

"What if I decide I do?" Silly thing to butt heads about, but this all felt too fast, too slow, too confusing. "Speaking of which, how does giving me commands I won't obey spice things up?"

Dominik's fingers tightened around the nape of her neck. "When I give commands, you'll obey."

"*Try me.*"

His eyes narrowed, and his generous lips drew into a hard line. She dropped her gaze to the pointy tips of her boots. Cool air brushed over her butt as he lifted the bottom of her jersey. She inhaled and closed her eyes, prepared for the warmth of his big hands molding into her flesh.

He pinched both cheeks. Hard.

"Ow!" She squirmed when he hooked an arm around her waist, and she drove her heel down toward his foot. He hauled her up and sat on the sofa with her straddling his thighs.

"You're not ready, little bunny—"

She glared at him. "Don't call me that!"

When he grinned, she swung her hand toward his face. He shifted away just in time to avoid getting slapped. Then he latched onto both her wrists and held them against her knees.

He didn't look all that surprised that she'd tried to hit him, but she was shocked by her own actions. She didn't do violence. *Ever.*

"Eyes on me."

The soft command jolted her from her thoughts, enough power behind it to send a tingling charge along her flesh. She bit her lip and looked at him.

"Stop pushing. Sloan doesn't deal well with switches, and I haven't decided whether you are one. And Max doesn't have the experience to ease you into this. You have plenty of choices—but rushing things isn't one of them."

Choices. Damn, she was tired of hearing that. Arousal buzzed in her veins with painful insistency. She felt like a junkie desperate for a fix. But how the hell could she make them understand?

The answer came to her. She let her body go slack and leaned into Dominik, whispering, "I don't want any more choices."

Shackling both her wrists with one hand, Dominik used the other to nudge her chin up. Creases formed around his eyes, and he studied her for a moment. "No, I guess you don't." He released her wrists. "Stand up."

She scrambled to her feet awkwardly, wishing she'd taken off her boots when she'd come back from the bar. Someone grabbed her elbow when she swayed, and she glanced over and gave Tyler a grateful smile. He smiled back, but his eyes were wide and his skin had gone white. He looked as nervous as she felt.

"Take off the jersey," Dominik said.

The sleeves of the jersey fell over her hands as she fumbled with the shirt. Her fingers weren't working right. She wanted to obey, more than she'd ever wanted anything, but . . .

Tyler pushed her hands away and put his hands on her hips.

His lips formed a silent "You ready?"

When she nodded, he took hold of the shirt and eased it up. His knuckles skimmed her sides, and she heard him hiss in a breath as she lifted her arms and he pulled off the shirt.

"You're so . . . wow." Tyler shook his head and blushed. "I'm sorry; I'm not used to wanting a girl more than she wants me."

"But I do want you." She touched his cheek, sensing that he needed comforting more than she did. His awkwardness lessened her own. She wasn't the only one new to this.

He ducked his head. "Yeah, maybe, but you didn't throw yourself at me because of who I am. It's a nice change."

Poor kid. He'd been in the sport his whole life, destined for greatness from the day he'd put on a pair of skates. She'd thought he didn't know any better when he'd let the blonde bunny go down on him, but it was more than that. He didn't know anything else.

"You're a little young for me." She grinned when his blush darkened. "But I have a feeling you'll make me forget our age difference. You're the kind of man I wish I'd met in university, before I came here."

"You probably had plenty of men chasing after you."

She shrugged. "Yeah. Hoping to get with my sister."

"Silver?" Tyler wrinkled his nose. "Sloan told me about her—"

"Family is strictly off-limits." Dominik pushed off the sofa, and his powerful essence slammed into her. She backed into Tyler. The muscles in Tyler's chest rippled against her back. His erection pressed against her butt. Her knees shook, and she clung to Dominik when he took her hands. He gave her a tender smile. "Lie down on the coffee table."

She felt around for the first solid thing she could find and sat hard. The square block felt nice and sturdy beneath her. She latched on to Tyler's forearms as he eased her down onto the table. The coolness of the smooth surface seeped into the flesh of her bare back, and she was suddenly aware of the fact that she wore nothing but her bra and panties. Her practically transparent bra and panties.

"Clasp your hands above your head, pet." Dominik circled the table, observing her the same way she'd seen doctors observe patients during an exam. "Tyler, hold her wrists so she doesn't move."

She positioned her hands. Tyler grabbed her wrists.

Trapped, I'm trapped! She tugged at her wrists and shook her head. "But—"

"If you want to stop, say so now." Dominik latched onto her ankles and leaned over her. "Otherwise, I gave you an order."

Pressing her eyes shut, she nodded. Fingers hooked under the elastic waist of her panties. Desire spilled hot and wet from her core, and she knew the men could see it as her panties were peeled down her thighs and over her calves. Gone. Her last shield was gone.

"Sloan, Max, hold her ankles."

Hands clamped onto her ankles, held them apart. She refused to open her eyes to see who was where. She didn't care. Things were finally happening. Which was good. Had to be.

"What about me?" T.J. asked, sounding ready to be excused.

"Her bra has a front clasp. Undo it, and see if you can get her to relax," Dominik said. His voice came from somewhere near the end of the table. Big, warm hands pushed her thighs open wide.

"Oh, God. Am I really doing this?" She didn't realize she'd spoken out loud until she heard T.J. chuckle, seconds before he kissed her.

Firm, yet gentle as she relaxed, T.J.'s kiss told her she was in the presence of a man who knew his strength, who kept it carefully in check because if he didn't, he'd hurt her. And he didn't want to hurt her. He only wanted this moment to show her all he could give. She moaned into his mouth. The scent of sweat and faint cologne came off him in waves. Every plunge of his tongue into her gasping mouth made her feel like a small sun had nestled deep inside.

"You're doing this." He gasped against her lips as he undid her bra, then covered her breasts with his hands. "I don't know why, but I'm happy to be included."

Her nipples puckered up beneath his palms, and the sweet sensation joined the feeling of Dominik massaging her thighs.

"Why?" She had to ask. She couldn't understand why these men were so interested in her. Was it because she'd made herself available?

"You always seemed so unattainable." T.J. cupped her face in his hands, and she opened her eyes. He smiled at her. "I'm sure the others will have all kinds of proclamations to make, but honestly, I just want you because I never thought I could have you."

Good enough. Not for tomorrow, but for right now.

"You have me." She watched him lower his head to take one of her nipples in his mouth. He sucked, and an electric wire strung out from her nipple to her clit. Her hips shot up. The feeling of his lips on her, of the other men's hands holding her, stroking her calves and her sides, was glorious.

"So soft."

"Smooth."

"Beautiful."

Their reverent whispers made her feel like she was glowing from the inside out. Didn't matter who said what. They wanted *her*.

"This is going faster than I wanted, Oriana," Dominik said before kissing the crease between her pussy and her thigh. "But you're so wet, I can tell the slow pace is becoming torture. Keep your eyes closed, and just feel what we're doing. Because we're going to . . ." He pressed his lips to the top of her mound with enough pressure to tease her clit. Sparks zipped along her nerves, and her head tossed from side to side. "Worship." He tongue snaked between her lips, and she could already feel the tidal wave of an orgasm rising with violent insistence. "Every inch of you."

She clung to the sensations tearing through her, wanting to make them last a little longer. The whole thing seemed surreal, five men all focused on her like her reactions were something precious to behold. Dominik's tongue slid along her folds, teasing her cleft with shallow dips. She expected him to add his fingers—but, no, he used nothing but his tongue to penetrate her while he shoved her thighs even farther apart. His teeth grazed her clit as he lapped at her. Her pussy became a gourd of hot syrup, spilling into Dominik's mouth.

Climax came closer, closer. The muscles in her thighs shuddered as she grasped at the edge. Her body cried for relief, but not yet, not yet . . .

The urge to give in ripped at her, almost painfully. She tried to close her thighs, stop Dominik before he sent her plummeting into the hot depths. She twisted her ankles—the men's grips tightened in response, solid as shackles. The leather of her boots chafed her ankles.

"If you don't stop tugging, Oriana, I'm going to hurt you," Sloan said from the end of the table.

The threat threw her off her precarious perch. She bucked up against Dominik's mouth. A hard suck on her nipple, and she lost the will to fight. All the pressure building up inside rippled out, boiling past tolerance, dragging her under the crashing waves of heat. A hot, shaky mouth swallowed her screams. Not T.J.'s; his mouth was on her breast. Tyler's.

"Shh." He breathed against her lips, and a choked sob blasted air over her face. "You're okay. Please tell me you're okay."

His worry dampened all the vicious sensations, and she dropped from the high of pleasure so fast she was sure she'd fall into oblivion. But she regained her senses enough to press the hand he'd released to his sweaty cheek.

"I'm okay." She gasped in air like she'd been forced underwater for far too long. "Are you?"

"No," Tyler said, then laughed. "Another minute and I'd have proved I'm not much of a man."

"You're not the only one." Max unzipped one of her boots and tugged it off. After he tossed it aside, he kissed the top of her foot. "Oriana, I want you so bad I'm about to give the guys a show."

Oriana sat up and watched Sloan take off her other boot. His black hair was slicked back from his face, and he was breathing hard. Turned on or pissed? With him it was hard to tell.

Dominik knelt at the end of the table and rested his chin on his folded arms. "What now, bunny?" He lips curved when she frowned at the endearment. "Was that enough, or do you want more?"

Drawing her knees to her chest, she hugged them and looked at the men. All but Tyler had fixed their features into closed-off expressions, as though to tell her they expected nothing. Tyler shifted from foot to foot and stared at his sneakers. He wouldn't ask for anything, but he couldn't pretend like the others.

"I thought Doms made the decisions." She clenched her thighs as her insides throbbed. More sounded good. Talking didn't.

"That's a cop out, Oriana, and you know it," Dominik said. "None of us has earned that distinction. But all you have to do is say the word and—"

"Say *the* word?" She threw her legs over the side of the table and stood. The carpet felt rough under her bare feet; her head felt light and airy. But going after what she wanted made her feel solid. She cocked her head and took slow backward steps toward the bedroom. "Which one? 'More'?"

Dominik frowned. "*Oriana . . .*"

"Or 'harder'?"

"Sounds good to me." Tyler started across the room and grunted when T.J. elbowed him in the gut. "Hey!"

Oriana couldn't help but smile. This was more like it. She ducked into the bedroom, then poked her head out. "How about 'Now'?"

Silence followed as she made her way through the dark room. A sliver of light sliced across the bed from the slight part in the curtains, forming a white, translucent spear point that ended in the middle of the comforter. The shadows made the blue fabric look black, made the whole room a little gloomy, but the gloom couldn't touch her now.

I'm doing this. I'm doing this because I want to. Nothing else matters.

She climbed onto the bed and reclined on her side. The evening had begun with plans for pleasure with a man who gave her none. For the longest time, she'd blamed herself. But not anymore. Paul never tried to find out what she enjoyed, and she'd made that effort for him. She didn't feel guilty at all.

How the evening would end—the possibilities excited her. Five men who cared very much how she felt. Maybe just tonight, but that was enough.

Padded footsteps brought her attention to the doorway.

"Max." She tongued her bottom lip as he pulled off his shirt and threw it on top of a pile of luggage in the corner. The shadows brought out every defined curve of muscle, the hard slope of his chest, the tight ripple of his abdomen.

The way his biceps glided when he crawled onto the bed reminded her of how a really big, strong animal looked prowling after prey that might bolt at any second. Made her want to bolt for a second just to see if he'd catch her.

Bad girl. Don't push him.

"Do you have any idea how long I've wanted this?" His gaze skimmed over her, and she expected it to be hot when it stopped at her face. But it was tender and warm. "Even after you told me to get lost, I couldn't help thinking, every time I saw you, that I would have you one day."

"Have me?" She rolled her eyes and refused to let it bother her. Had she really expected proclamations from him? After the day she'd had, no way. They were living out his fantasies and hers. No need to make a big thing of it. "You could have spared me all the lines. I've got to say, they were good. You almost convinced me—"

He kept talking as though she hadn't said a word. "And once I had you, I planned to keep you so fucking satisfied that you'd never want to leave. So that I could keep you."

"Keep me?" She hissed in a breath when he bent to kiss the hollow of her throat. Her unstable detachment faltered. "What about now?"

"Nothing's changed." He nibbled along her collarbone, then up her throat, pausing by her ear. "Do you want me to lock the door before the others come in?"

Chapter Nine

"Only if *you* want to." Oriana's emphasis on "you" told Max all he needed to know. She would forget about the other men in a heartbeat—okay, maybe not that fast, but fast enough to make it clear that the two of them were what mattered most.

"How did I get so lucky?" He pushed up on his hands and looked down at her, amazed at the beauty spread out beneath him. All his, if he chose not to share. But she wanted him to. She'd given herself to him like a precious gift, one he could . . . lend to those he trusted.

She was the embodiment of everything he would have asked for if he had one wish. A woman who knew him and all his odd quirks. Who accepted him.

"You must have been a saint in a past life." Her tone was dead serious, but her eyes sparkled with laughter. She finally let out a throaty chuckle and cupped his face in her hands. "Face it, Max. You're a good man."

"Says you."

"Yeah, says me. I might be stupid relationship-wise, but I'm not blind." She held up her hand when he opened his mouth to protest. "I cut you out of my life, and you didn't hold it against me. You let me come to terms with things in my own time."

"I didn't expect you to come to terms with anything." He rolled off her and rested on his side with his head propped up on his hand. "But whether or not you did, I was gonna be there for you when you needed me."

"I know." She wrinkled her nose and trailed a fingernail up his chest, then down. "Which makes me the lucky one, doesn't it?"

He shuddered as blood pumped into his dick, so hard and fast he felt a little light-headed. But he shook his head to clear it and took hold of her chin. "You're crazy if you think that."

The door creaked open, then slammed shut. Both he and Oriana peered through the darkness, listening to the raised voices from the other room.

"Give them a few minutes," Mason said.

"She'll change her mind," said Vanek, sounding like a kid who'd just been told he wasn't going to Disneyland after all.

"Then she changes her mind," Sloan practically snarled. "Deal with it."

"We all know how Max feels about her. He can't seriously want this," T.J. cut in.

Max held his breath, not sure how the rest of the men would respond to T.J. voicing what they all believed. The darkness pressed in on him, along with the self-doubt he could never escape. What kind of man would be okay with sharing a woman like Oriana? Fine, she was okay with it, but were they? And, if not, how would he find someone he trusted enough to give them both what they needed?

Oriana grabbed his hand. Her nails dug into his palm. "If you boys don't hurry up, we're starting without you!"

The door swung open. Tyler poked his head into the room.

"You sure?"

"Yes." Oriana pulled Max's hand to her chest and shivered. He reached down to pull the sheets over her, and she gave him a grateful smile. "But only if you are."

She spoke loud enough for all the men to hear, but Max knew the question was directed at him. He nodded and sat up, still holding her hand.

"I've never been more sure of anything in my life." He kissed her fingertips. "And I'm gonna make sure you don't ever forget tonight. This is just the beginning. I promise you'll never regret giving yourself to me." His breath caught in his throat. "Or to them."

* * * *

Tyler dropped onto the bed and used the sheets to pin Oriana down as he crawled over her. She arched a brow at his stern expression. With his golden curls glistening like a halo in the light from the main room and his bright, blue eyes slightly hooded, he was more a seductively sexy angel than a tough alpha male.

I've got more than my quota of dominant males. She blew a strand of hair off her face and tried to sit up. "Tyler, you don't need to—"

"Quiet. I'm going to kiss you." He settled his weight on her. "Then I'm going to—"

"Just kiss me." She laced her fingers around the back of his neck and pulled him to her, tasting his lips with the tip of her tongue. He groaned when she sucked on his bottom lip, then tilted his head to one side and deepened the kiss. His tongue slipped into her mouth as his hand slipped under the sheets, over one breast.

"Thank you." He whispered as he slid his lips along her jaw and down her throat. He shoved at the blankets and pushed her breasts together. Burying his face between them, he let out a lusty sigh. "Mmm."

Being at the mercy of all the men had been wonderful, but even with just Tyler, she felt sexy and wanton and . . . *Oh!* Sharp pain-pleasure shot through her chest when Tyler bit down on one of her nipples. She gasped into Max's mouth as he bent down to kiss her. She caught sight of Sloan, standing behind Max, not moving until he had her full attention. Then he reached over and flipped the sheets off her.

"Keep your legs wide open, Oriana," Sloan said before she could close them. He leaned over her as Max nipped her bottom lip. "Don't let Tyler give you the illusion of control. As you can see, he's not the only one here."

As though the captain had set up the play, Tyler moved down, and T.J. climbed onto the bed. T.J. held her thighs apart while Tyler spread her pussy lips and dipped his tongue between them. Wave after wave of pure, sweet pleasure flowed inside her, rising up and rippling back down as Max set his teeth in her throat and Sloan molded her breasts in his hands. Sloan rested his chest on the bed and rolled one painfully hard nipple between his finger and thumb.

"How long do you think you can hold back this time, sweetheart?" Sloan pinched her nipple and flicked the tip with his tongue. She whimpered as the sweet sensations became hot, sizzling through her veins and along every nerve.

Someone's hand curved under her ass and a thick finger, or maybe a thumb, pressed hard against her cleft before slipping inside.

She whimpered as the heat reached a boiling point. Her hips

shot off the bed, and she ground her pussy against Tyler's mouth. Her whole body trembled as she did her best not to twist away from the four men whose only goal seemed to drive her mad with pleasure.

"I—Oh, please, please . . ." She groaned as another finger stretched her, slowly, so slowly she could feel every callous drag against her inner folds, every knuckle straining past tight undulating rings of muscle. "I need . . ."

"You need to let go, Oriana." Dominik's rich voice came from somewhere to her right, across from Sloan and Max. "After you do, there will be more. So much more."

She tossed her head, wanting to do as he said, but instinctively taking a stranglehold on the climax, unable to release it just yet. She just couldn't believe she would feel this wild, unadulterated ecstasy ever again.

"Harder, T.J.," Max rasped out, breathing hard like he was in the middle of a rough workout. "But be careful. I've seen Paul in the locker room. He's not a big guy."

No! Not yet! The wet sound of fingers thrusting into her was almost loud enough to drown out the low keening sound coming from her throat. She clenched every muscle in her body and tried to distract herself from the men working so hard to pitch her over the edge. The edge was wonderful. She didn't want to let this slip away.

"She's so fucking wet, Perron." T.J. paused and growled. "You lick me again, Vanek, and I'm gonna throw you."

Oriana let out a breathless laugh and felt the threatening orgasm recede. She could hang on a little longer, just a little longer . . .

"Stubborn." Dominik clucked his tongue, then gave her a deep, searing kiss. "One of these days, I'm going to punish you for being so willful. Come, Oriana." His hand curved under his jaw, and his fingers dug into the tense muscles. "Now!"

"Ah!" She was tumbling, tumbling over the edge, clawing at the ledge of control. "Dominik . . . I'm gonna—" She twisted and groaned. "Max!"

"Do it, baby." Max smoothed her hair away from her face, kissing her forehead, her cheeks. "I wanna watch you come while Vanek eats that sweet pussy."

Oriana screamed, and all five men held her down as she jerked and writhed under them. A burst of pleasure, then another, exploded inside her. Little white specks of light filled her vision, and she pressed her eyes shut as she drifted down from the aftermath of the orgasm. She was sure that would be it, that her body couldn't take anymore, but then something hot and wet prodded her clit and flung her right back to the precipice of another climax. She moaned and looked down her body at Tyler. His fingers filled her, glistening when he drew them out. He sucked them clean, and her whole body started shaking as he did it again and again.

"I can't . . . I can't!"

Max hushed her as she came down from another violent orgasm. "You can, my love. You'll be surprised by how often you can."

* * * *

Sloan could tell her resistance had crumbled with the last orgasm. Finally, she was ready to let them give her all the pleasure they could. Enough for now, but he couldn't wait for the day he'd take the option of denying herself, and him, away from her.

But one thing at a time. He watched Mason slide his hand over her ribs, over her stomach, his eyes fixed on her face as he explored every inch of soft, supple flesh—probably taking note of all her sweet spots for future use. Before long the man would know her body better than she did. A bit of training, and he'd stimulate her with a command. If Mason wasn't such a loyal friend—well, Perron might want to keep his guard up anyway.

Mason bowed his head and flicked his tongue over Oriana's puffy little clit. Her muffled cry was followed by a low groan. Perron. Sloan shook his head. His friend was way too into this to worry about losing his girl.

Most of the men seemed too involved to worry about much.

T.J. draped her thighs over his shoulders and his face disappeared between them. Considering T.J.'s complaints about Vanek licking his fingers, he was oddly quiet about Dominik's tongue so close to his own. At one point Sloan heard Mason quietly instructing the other man. Then T.J. did something that made

Oriana's whole body arch off the bed.

Watching Oriana being devoured by the two men, Sloan hadn't noticed Perron covering both her breasts with his hands. He and Vanek were running out of body parts to play with. And he'd be damned if he'd let Mason take over.

Time to get creative.

Sliding to the foot of the bed, Sloan reached between T.J.'s chest and Oriana's arched hips and squeezed one lush ass cheek.

"You know, Oriana, if we're going to share you, I've got one very important question." He slipped his fingers into the crease of her ass and prodded at the puckered little hole, nice and wet from her juices and the men's saliva. "Have you ever had anal sex?"

Oriana gasped when he pushed the tip of his finger inside. Her hips bucked, but the press of T.J.'s and Mason's mouths kept her from going too far.

"Damn it, Sloan." The tight little ring of muscle clenched around his finger. "No. I've never had anal sex."

Sloan pulled his finger out, then shoved it in a little deeper. "Would you like to?"

Perron whispered something to Oriana, gave her a quick kiss, then leaned forward to get a better look at what Sloan was doing. Sloan smirked at him. There was no way he could see anything past T.J.'s and Mason's big heads.

Vanek left the bed, went to his suitcase, and returned seconds later to sit across from Sloan. The end of the bed was getting crowded.

"Here, let me try something," Vanek said.

Sloan moved his hand and let Vanek take his place. When Oriana squirmed, he put his hand back between her ass cheeks and felt Vanek's lubed-up finger thrusting in and out.

"How's that, Oriana?" Vanek was moving faster, watching Oriana's lips part. Her thigh muscles tensed, and she bowed her back. "A little more tempting, no?"

"Yes." Oriana raked her fingers into Max's hair and tugged him down to kiss him, looking like she couldn't breathe and she wanted him to do it for her. "That's . . ."

"Slow up, Vanek. I want to try something." Sloan waited until

Vanek stopped moving and gathered some of the lube to slick up his own finger. Then he carefully worked the digit beside the one already inside. "That's what, babe? You've got two guys with their tongues all over your pussy, two with their fingers in your tight little asshole, and one fondling your tits. Five men at once. How bad do you want to be fucked?"

Chapter Ten

Oriana froze at Sloan's crude words and studied his shadowed features. Maybe just his idea of talking dirty. No big deal.

"Bad enough that I don't want to have a conversation about it." She glanced down when Dominik shifted over her. Sloan and Tyler withdrew their fingers, and Dominik braced his hands on either side of her hips, his posture tense—almost protective. Only, the way he licked her juices from his lips made her think that he'd rather devour her than keep her safe.

She shivered as he lowered his dark head to press his lips to the center of her chest. He worked his way down with little kisses. She closed her eyes and rested her head on the pillow. His soft, hot lips, felt so nice on her flesh. Soothing even.

A hand clamped around her breast. She gasped as Tyler sucked a nipple into his mouth. He nipped her just as Dominik lapped up between her pussy lips. Her hips jutted up as a shock of pleasure flashed through her. Dominik's thick tongue slipped inside her, and she twisted away from the overwhelming sensations, almost dislodging him.

"Oh, no, you don't." Max sat on the bed and leaned across her stomach. His elbow braced at her side, kept his weight off her, but the press of his body trapped her. An evil smile played at his lips. "You're gonna lie there and take it. I want to watch your face while you come in his mouth, and then I'm gonna hold you while he stuffs his big, black cock into your tight little pussy."

She could almost feel Dominik stretching her already. Her pussy moistened as though ready to ease his passage, and he sucked hard on her slick folds. Wonderful, but she needed more.

"Sounds fun." Sloan strolled around the bed, shoved his hands in his pockets, and arched a brow. "So what's the lineup, boss?"

His words were cold, so cold, but they couldn't pierce the wildfire spreading through her as Dominik fucked her with his tongue. Tyler moved from one breast to the other to toy with her nipples with his teeth, and she clawed at the sheets.

T.J. moved into her line of sight, standing just behind Max. "You sure about this, Perron?"

The tight lines around the big man's bright blue eyes gave her the impression that he was the one having second thoughts. She couldn't have that. One look at the outline of his dick pressed against his zipper gave her an idea.

She tried to sit up.

Max laughed and pushed her flat on the bed. "We distracting you, dollface?"

"A little." She yelped when Vanek stretched her nipple with a hard suck. "I—I need a different kind of distraction. T.J. . . ."

"Yes." T.J. moved a little closer. He gulped when she grabbed him by the belt and tugged.

"You're wearing too many clothes." Her hands shook as she tried to undo the buckle. A fierce heat was building between her thighs. She wouldn't be talking much longer. "I can't suck your dick with your jeans in the way."

T.J. blinked, then shook his head. "Don't need to tell me twice."

He stripped, and Oriana closed her thighs against Dominik's face, hoping he'd understand and give her a minute to enjoy the unveiling. After one last lick, he rested his chin on the top of her mound.

T.J. knelt on the bed and curved his hand under her neck to prop her up. The slit of his dick glistened with pre-cum. Oriana flicked her tongue out to taste it. Salty sweetness. She couldn't remember the last time she'd given a man a blow job. Paul hadn't liked her doing it. Maybe she wasn't that good?

"That thought didn't look pleasant." Max caught her jaw in his hand and guided her mouth over the head of T.J.'s dick. "If they're not doing it for you, sweetheart, I can take over."

Dominik thrust his tongue into her pussy. T.J. pushed deeper into her mouth. She moaned around him as Tyler gently bit her nipple.

No more thinking. Only feeling. The climax caught her unaware, and she rode it out, moving her head up and down, saliva slick on her lips as she gulped around T.J.'s dick, desperate to share some of her pleasure with him. Fingers raked into her hair, gripped tight, helped her move. Lips pressed over the rapid pulse on her neck.

"You won't be happy until he comes, will you?" Sloan whispered against her throat. "Look at him. He's close."

Oriana gazed up at T.J. Every muscle in his body strained against his flesh. Jaw clenched, eyes closed, he grunted and jerked his hips. She swallowed as she took him deep.

The crinkle of a wrapper made her pause. Sloan wouldn't let her turn her head. Dominik's mouth left her. Tyler shifted away.

T.J. grunted, and she focused on him. Steady motions. She could feel him swell in her mouth. A little faster.

The mattress shifted. Hands around her waist lifted her, careful not to pull her away from T.J. She grabbed T.J.'s hips as he slid to the edge of her lips. Sucked hard as more hands spread her thighs. Her knees settled on the mattress on either side of someone's hips, and her legs shook as she straddled the man. A thick, hard cock prodded her slit, stretching her slowly before it filled her.

"Mmm." She moaned around T.J.'s dick as her core wrapped around the throbbing invasion of someone she couldn't even see. She tried to rise up when it started to feel like too much. Whoever it was, he was huge. Her body couldn't take it.

"Shh." Fingers brushed her cheek. "Relax. Dominik's a big boy. But you're so wet, if you don't tense up, he'll slip right in."

It was Max who spoke. His tone was strained, but not like it disturbed him that another man was inside her. He sounded turned on.

"Fuck, she's tight." Dominik panted beneath her, and she splayed her hands over the slick, sweat-coated flesh of his massive chest. "Maybe it was a bad idea for me to go first."

"I'm longer, and both T.J. and Sloan are thicker," Max said, sounding so matter-of-fact she wanted to hit him. Did they actually measure each other's dicks?

But T.J. throbbed in her mouth, so close she could taste it. One more hard suck . . .

Dominik thrust up. She cried out, and T.J. came. Cum hit her tongue, her cheek. T.J.'s knees hit the floor with a thump.

She heard another wrapper rip.

"Now, Vanek." Max cleaned her lips and cheek with a tissue,

then kissed her.

A slippery finger pressed against her asshole, circling the puckered rosette before pushing inside. Before she fully adjusted to the slight burning sensation, another finger strained to enter alongside the first. She tensed around Dominik's dick and sat up.

"I missed these." Sloan grinned and curved his hands under her breasts, molding them together before closing his lips over her nipples.

Tyler shoved his fingers inside her, drew them out, then shoved them in again even more slicked up. He spread his fingers, and she did her best not to fight him as he stretched her. Her legs quivered, and her thighs tensed against Dominik's hips as she gulped in air. It only hurt a little, but the sensation of him fingering her there felt so very wrong. Like something she shouldn't be doing.

"Oriana." Dominik's dark eyes locked with hers, and the intensity within them stole her breath. He nudged Sloan aside, then smoothed a hand over her hair, pulling her closer. His lips brushed softly over hers. "You will tell me if it's too much."

"Yes."

Tyler's fingers twisted, and she choked on a sob as a new set of nerves blazed to life inside her. For a moment, agony and rapture were one. Then her body adjusted, and all she felt was pulsing need. She pressed down on Dominik, on Tyler, suddenly desperate to take them in deeper.

Tyler withdrew his fingers, then fit his naked body against her back. The latex covered head of him strained for entrance. "Just breathe in and relax as much as you can."

The lube eased him past the tight ring of muscle, but then a fiery pain made her whole lower half clench. She hissed in through her teeth, tempted to tell him to stop. This *was* too much. She couldn't do this. She was full, so full. How could she possibly take more?

"You're not breathing, pet." Dominik circled his hips, and his dick swirled inside her. Her mouth opened wide, and she gasped. He smiled at her. "That's a little better."

"I want some of what T.J. got." Max stood and his lips quirked as she turned her full attention to his hands undoing his belt. He dropped his jeans and his boxers, then bent to take off his socks.

"Would you mind?"

"No." She whimpered at the sting as Vanek took advantage of the distraction and worked in another inch. "Three men at once . . ." She shifted her hips and willed her body to adjust to the two now lodged inside. "How could I refuse?"

Sloan traced a circle around her nipple and kissed it once before glancing down at Dominik and Tyler. Deep lines formed around his pursed lips. "That's so fucking hot. Big black man, a boy who's barely legal, a sexy Latino woman taking them both. Get in her mouth, Texan. You're the perfect cast for an awesome porn."

Oriana froze. Dominik went still. Vanek cursed.

"You ruin this for her, and I swear to God, Sloan . . ." Max's dick brushed her lips, but she could tell he didn't want her to take him in her mouth yet. His rigid posture promised violence.

I won't let Sloan ruin this. "He can leave if he's not enjoying himself." She kissed the tip of Max's dick. "But he can't ruin anything. I want this. I want Dominik and Vanek to fuck my body while you fuck my mouth. If T.J.'s up to it, maybe he can suck my breasts—"

T.J. got up on his knees and leaned over her. "I'm up to it."

"Good." She hissed in a breath when his lips closed over the nipple Sloan had abandoned. "Oh, yes. That's good."

She arched her neck and swept her tongue up Max's hard length. Tyler and Dominik took her cue and drove into her, slow at first, then faster as she eased into the motions, meeting each thrust. She could feel Sloan's eyes on her as she took Max in her mouth and writhed between the men, but she didn't care. Let him watch. The ecstasy was building into something pure and wild, bringing her up to heights beyond the reaches of the pettiness of jealousy. She was being fucked to enlightenment.

Tyler's hands on her hips slammed her down onto his cock, onto Dominik's. Hot and wet, she slid on them, faster and faster. The muscles in her thighs worked as she rode them both. Her head bobbed as she matched each rise and fall with her mouth on Max. T.J. gasped around her nipple as she pressed her breast to his face. Every sensation hit her at once, and she couldn't go on. Her muscles tensed. She couldn't move anymore. But she had to . . . she had to . . .

The men took over. Tyler and Dominik found a steady rhythm, one in while the other drew out. Max's hands on her head kept her still while he thrust into her mouth. T.J.'s arms wrapped around her, his tongue laving each nipple until the oversensitive tips throbbed in time with the beat of her heart.

Hanging on the edge of yet another orgasm, she whimpered when it slipped away again and again. She felt like she was climbing to a peak, but every time she got close, the ground crumbled. The sensations began to overwhelm, the need for satisfaction almost painful.

"Slow down a little, boys." The mattress creaked as Sloan sat hard. He put his hand on her thigh and massaged the tense muscles. "She's overstimulated, her nerves will go numb, and she won't feel anything if you keep it up."

Dominik immediately changed his pace, rotating his hips beneath her, stirring the heat until her core simmered. T.J. gave Tyler a shot in the arm when he kept pumping into her.

"Slow down."

"I can't!" Tyler grunted and slammed in hard. His fingers dug into her hips, and she could feel his hot cum filling his latex sheath. "Sorry, I . . . sorry . . ."

"Shh." Oriana let Max slip out of her mouth and looked at Tyler over her shoulder as he withdrew. "I've already come a few times. It's only natural that I'd last longer."

Dominik twisted under her, breathing hard through his teeth. He reached up and touched her cheek. "Just give me a minute and I'll—"

Oriana gently nudged T.J. away from her breast and bent to kiss Dominik. Teasing his lips with little flicks of her tongue, she dropped her hips, then lifted until she was almost off him. She rode just the tip of him until his back bowed and then ground on to him, undulating her body over his.

"Stop! Fuck!" Dominik wrapped his arms around her. He drove up, and a shudder passed through him as he came. His whole body went slack, and the rapid pulse beating in the thick veins of his dick slowed. He pressed his eyes shut and shook his head. "Jesus! I'm getting too old for this."

"You're only a couple of years older than me, you ass." Max helped Oriana climb off of Dominik. Even without an orgasm, her legs were shaky and weak. And he'd noticed. "Wait until you're T.J.'s age. Then you can complain. Might have to start using Viagra. Looks like I'm the only one in my prime."

"That's not nice." Oriana clucked her tongue and turned in his lap, closing her hand around his erection. When she squeezed, he jumped. "T.J., Dominik, and Vanek made me feel like *I'm* in my prime. Like maybe I'm not so bad at this after all." She stroked him with a loose fist. "But you lasted so long . . ."

Eyes hooded, Max leaned back against the bed frame. "Self-control, darlin', it's nothing against you. Though if it helps, it's never been tested quite so much." He ground his teeth and stared up at the ceiling. "But I don't want to come in your mouth . . ." He caught her wrist when she stroked faster. "Or your hand."

She rose up on her knees and moved to take him inside her. "Then why don't we—" An arm barred across her belly, and she scowled at Sloan as he picked her up. "What do you think you're—?"

"Give your body some time to come down from the edge, Oriana. Me and Max will bring you back up the right way."

"*We* will?" Max draped the sheet over himself and held out his hand for Oriana. "After what you pulled?"

"Momentary insanity. I'm sorry." Sloan's brow creased, and he took Oriana's face in his hands. "Forgive me?"

As if she could resist that "I've-been-a-bad-boy" look. After playing with her at the bar, he'd probably expected to feel a little more included, but there was only so much of her to go around. Either way, she liked this vulnerable side of him.

Smiling, she curled herself into his arms. "I forgive you. Tonight is me being greedy. You're all mine." His abdominal muscles clenched and released, she smoothed her hand over it. "Even you."

Chapter Eleven

The soft body in Sloan's arms grew slack with sleep. His boys had worn his girl out.

No, not *his* girl. He glanced at Max who'd bumped his arm while stroking Oriana's hair.

"You're a lucky man, Perron." The edge of his lip curved in a tense half-smile. "I've never met a woman like her. I mean—we've shared before, and it was fun, but this was . . ."

"Intense." Max nodded slowly and wound a slick, bronze strand around his finger. He let it slip away and sighed. "Oriana gives without restraint. She's been that way as long as I've known her—which is why Paul was no good for her. He never made her feel good about herself. He never loved her."

Like you do.

She felt so right in his arms—he had to put her down. It would be really bad if he started getting all confused about his own feelings just because he liked holding her. *Not mine, not mine, not mine.* The words pounded in his head, echoing the heavy beat of his heart.

He carefully slid Oriana onto the bed and watched Max pull the rumpled blankets up to her chin. He heard the door shut. The others had slipped out.

"I think the men are all half in love with her. I've never seen them take such good care of a woman." Sloan laughed and shook his head. "They were ready to take whatever they could get."

Max cocked his head. "But not you. You wanted it all. You still do."

"Tonight, Max. I'll be happy with tonight."

He stretched out behind Oriana's sleeping form, resting his arm just below the one Max wrapped around her waist. A cocoon of warmth enveloped him, filling the humid air with the musky scent of woman, wrapped up with the scent of man, tipped with the fragrance of floral perfume. Lilacs, Sloan thought, nuzzling Oriana's neck. How fitting that she smelled like the flower that shared the bouquet of its tiny buds more openly than any other. The sharing he could manage. Losing her in the end . . . not so much.

Enough with the sentimental bullshit. Take what you can get, Callahan.

"You don't have to settle for one night," Perron said quietly. "You know that, right?"

Yeah, he knew that. But he still didn't get it. He studied his best friend's peaceful features, cheek on the same pillow as Oriana's, cuddled close and perfectly comfortable. Just like a normal couple. With a spare.

I'm no fucking spare. He let out a gruff sound of frustration. "Aren't you scared she'll choose me over you?"

"Why should I be? I'm not forcing her to choose." Perron's eyes stayed shut, but creases formed on his forehead. "Will you?"

"No way, man." Sloan's pillow billowed as he plunked his head down. Glaring at the ceiling, he forced his tone to sound light. "I wouldn't do that to you."

"Don't that to her, Sloan. Or yourself." Perron using his first name made him sit up and stare. The last time the man had done that, Sloan had been going into surgery to get his face put back together. Thankfully, he didn't sound like he was gonna cry this time. "She might be good for you."

"Go to sleep, Perron, you're starting to sound like Doctor-fucking-Phil."

Perron grunted, and Sloan grinned.

She might be good for me, eh? Well, maybe I'll be good for her, too.

* * * *

Dominik rested the rim of the wine glass against his bottom lip as the balcony door opened. Oriana stepped into the moonlight, and the faded white T-shirt she'd borrowed from either Sloan or Max billowed around her. She leaned against the sturdy white railing, gazing out at the black expanse of the ocean, oblivious to him.

He decided to wait awhile before making himself known. Give her the illusion of privacy, see what he could learn about her. Within moments, one thing was clear. The girl found peace in the sound of waves crashing in the distance, in the cool night air saturated with the scents of the sea. Perfectly still, she closed her eyes, seeming to absorb it all. This gave her peace.

Something they had in common.

Max's house had two balconies, one on the east side, one on the south side. The south side one was connected to Sloan's room—he'd gotten to pick first since he'd moved in before the rest of them. This balcony belonged to Dominik, and over the years he'd added little personal touches to mark his territory. An antique bistro set in the corner, close to where Oriana stood. A small rock garden against the wall by the door with a small, inlaid fountain. Hanging plants curtaining off the area where he sat on one of two wooden lounge chairs with thick red padding. Several succulents in his room which would join the decor when the weather got warmer.

His private sanctuary. The men only came here when they needed to talk—more often than not, Max or Sloan, wanting his guidance. Both believed becoming "true masters" would save them from their twisted desires.

Lately, Sloan's faith in even that seemed to be slipping. Their last conversation had gotten pretty intense.

"I made the bitch bleed, Mason." Sloan had fisted his hands against the wall so hard the bricks grated his knuckles. He'd bowed his head between his arms. "You still gonna tell me I'm not sick?"

Not likely. I'm getting pretty fucking tired of repeating myself, *Dominik had thought. Out loud he'd said. "Did she want you to?"*

Sloan's shoulders curved inward. "Yes."

"Did you lose control?"

"Of course not."

"Did you leave any lasting damage besides the shallow cuts, which I assume you took good care of?"

"Fuck, Mason, I said I must be sick. Never said I didn't know what I was doing. 'Course I took care of her." Sloan lifted his head and sighed. "I guess this means I'm not getting your vote at the club."

"You're not ready, Captain. Give it another year and we'll talk." Dominik grinned to lighten the mood. "Am I getting an A on my jersey this season?"

"Over three hundred penalty minutes last year, Mason. Sorry, not happening." Sloan laughed. "Get it under two this year and we'll talk."

If he could deal with two insecure baby Doms, a natural submissive testing the waters would be easy. She wouldn't be the first sub he'd helped train. Granted, he rarely had sex with trainees, but he'd shared with both Max and Sloan before. His combined experience would benefit them all until the men came up with a lasting arrangement.

Max and Sloan can't take care of her. A voice snarled from the deepest, darkest caverns of his mind where he'd stashed his own insecurities—and his possessiveness—long ago. *She needs you. She'll always need you.*

The sappy country music he'd been listening to before Oriana came out was giving him crazy ideas. He powered off his MP3 player and slid the earphones off his head, letting them hang over the back of his neck.

Across the balcony, Oriana buried her face in her hands and moaned. "What am I doing?"

A question he could answer. "You're regaining control of your life, pet. Your methods may seem a little . . . unorthodox to some, but you did something unexpected, saw what you wanted, and took it."

She jumped, stared at him, and then let out a sharp laugh. "Unorthodox? Yeah, I guess you could call letting five guys fuck me and boss me around unorthodox."

Dominik stood and Oriana took a quick step back. "Fuck you? When did any of us fuck you?" He strode across the long balcony, and his lips curved up as the wall blocked her retreat. His hand on the railing prevented her from slipping past him. "As I recall, you continued fucking me when I told you to stop. I fully intend to punish you for that."

Her eyes went as big and round as the full moon overhead. "You do?"

"Yes." He held out his hand, then waited. She placed her fingers on his palm. He shook his head and took hold of her wrist. "Even if a punishment isn't immediate, it's always inevitable. Understand?"

The pulse under his palm quickened. Nervous little bunny. "I think so."

"Good." He towed her with him to the lounge chair, then released her. She fidgeted while he reclined on the chair, and her eyes flicked uneasily in the direction of the door. He counted down from ten. By the time he reached one, she'd stopped fidgeting. *A quick study in patience.* He smiled. *Next lesson.* "Now strip."

"I don't—" She clamped her lips shut and ground her teeth. Without another word, she peeled off the oversized shirt. She was naked underneath.

If she's a switch, I'm a fucking Bruin. No switch that he'd ever met obeyed commands this readily outside of play. He trailed his gaze over her, admiring the body he'd touched and tasted and possessed, from her curvy thighs and her delicious pussy, all the way up to her equally delicious lips.

"Brave girl," he said. "I didn't think you'd be comfortable being so exposed outside, but, aside from a negligible protest, you did as you were told. I'm impressed."

Her teeth worried her plump bottom lip, but her eyes glowed with pleasure. She'd likely forgotten they were outside, yet, even with the reminder, her need to please overrode her shyness.

"Come here, Oriana." He sat up and patted his knee. "Sit."

She perched on his knee and folded her arms over her breasts. "Is my punishment over?"

"Punishment?" He pried her arms apart, then arched a brow when she tried to put them back. Her eyes narrowed. She licked her lips. Then lowered her arms to her sides. "Fingers laced behind your neck." When she complied, he wrapped an arm around her waist and scooted her up his thigh. Her small, soft body fit nicely against his big, hard chest. "That wasn't a punishment. I just wanted to look at you."

"Oh." She bowed her head. "So I guess now you'll—"

"Now, we'll have a chat." He watched her chest rise and fall with each rapid inhale, causing her breasts to jiggle. Interesting. The idea of a "chat" increased her anxiety more than the prospect of being punished. That would have to change. "Are you okay with what happened earlier?"

"Sort of." She ducked her head. "As long as I don't think about it too much."

Should I be insulted? After wetting the tip of his finger with his tongue, he traced the pale, brown areola of one breast. Her little wiggles forced him to shift her away from his swelling cock before she crushed it. "And why's that?"

She curved her spine, and her eyes fluttered shut. "Because I *liked* being fondled by all of you. Once we started, I couldn't care how slutty I might look. But I'm afraid of what will happen tomorrow. We can't keep doing this."

Probably not. *But...* "There will be plenty of tomorrows. There's only one tonight."

"I know." She hissed in a breath as he circled his fingertip closer and closer to her very hard nipple. Her eyes shot open when he pinched it. "Ouch!"

"Straddle my thighs, Oriana." His jaw clenched as the thick head of his dick rubbed the rough insides of his jeans. "Keep your hands behind your neck, then stay perfectly still. Your punishment should fit the crime. Once you've come a few times, I may show mercy."

The swift way she complied gave him primal satisfaction. Her arousal sweetened the salty sea air. He had all the time in the world, and he planned to use it.

A *whoosh* and the balcony door swung open.

"You fucking whore."

Rage lashed at Dominik, cushioned by discipline. He flipped Oriana onto the lounge chair, then stood.

Looks like Sloan forgot to lock the damn door again.

"Get dressed, you little skank," Paul said, knocking over a pile of smooth stones as he tried to bypass Dominik. "We need to talk."

"I have nothing to say to you," Oriana whispered, sounding vulnerable and a little afraid.

The dominant in Dominik tamped down his baser needs for violence. She should feel safe here. Beating the other man bloody wouldn't accomplish that.

"I don't care if you're my coach." His tone sounded gruff but dead calm. "Leave or I'll fucking make you."

* * * *

Oriana retrieved her shirt. *I can't believe this is happening. This can't be happening!*

A grunt cut off Paul's shouting. "You're gonna regret that."

Shit. She pulled the shirt on, then grabbed Dominik's arm before he could shove Paul again.

"What do you want, Paul?" She put her hand on Dominik's chest and let out a sigh of relief when he didn't try to step around her. "I'm sorry if I wasn't clear. It's over."

The door burst open, and Max emerged, followed by Sloan, who preempted his lunge for Paul, and T.J., who hovered in the doorway. "You've got some nerve coming here! She chose you! She chose you, and all you did was hurt her!"

She chose you. The words dropped on her like a great big stone landing in the center of her chest. Max hadn't forgotten or forgiven anything. He'd just shifted the blame to Paul.

"Please, Max! Let it go!" She moved toward Max, then scowled at Dominik when he pulled her back.

He shook his head and nodded toward Max who elbowed Sloan in the gut and tried to wrench free of his choke hold.

Sloan grunted and tightened his grip.

"Callahan, let me go," Max snarled. "I'm gonna kill him."

"I believe you." Sloan shoved Max into a wall and held him there. "That's why you're staying put."

She'd never seen Max lose it like this. She had to get Paul out of there before things got out of hand. "Paul—"

"How dare you be all bitchy about me and Chantelle when you're doing half my goddamn team!" Paul's nostrils flared, and his lips curled as he looked her over. "You're just like your sister. Only she doesn't hide the fact that she's a dirty little slut."

Oriana spun, and her hand whipped out. A loud *crack* silenced every single man on the balcony. Pain flared up from her palm. A blood-red hand print bloomed on Paul's cheek.

"Don't you ever talk about my sister like that. At least she had the sense to see you were scum from the very beginning." Her eyes burned as she thought of Silver, and of Max, trying to convince her she could do better than Paul. She never listened. Why didn't she listen? Blinking fast, she shook her head and laughed. "Explains why you never liked her, though. She saw right through you."

"I'm sorry. This isn't about your sister. It's about you." Paul rubbed his cheek and leaned forward. "What the hell are you doing?"

"Whatever the hell I want. That's what single women do."

"You have no idea what I've done to get investors interested in this team. If I tell them to pull their money, your father will lose everything. He dumped it all into keeping this dream alive. He'll be left with nothing. Are you ready to do that to him?"

Am I? She closed her eyes and pressed her cheek to Dominik's chest. "Why me, Paul? Why do you want me?"

"My partners felt good about me being with the owner's daughter. Made me look nice and stable. And then you go and do this." Paul shook his head. "I was ready to propose."

"You've got to be kidding." T.J. fisted his hands at his sides, and Oriana wondered if she should worry about the big guy. Despite his size—or maybe because of it—he never fought on the ice. If he took a swing at Paul, he'd probably kill him. But he looked too calm to commit murder. "Oriana's a smart girl, Coach. And too good for the likes of you. Give it up already."

Paul ignored him. "Come home, Oriana. I'll forgive you for whatever you've done. We'll make it work."

"No." Oriana bowed her head. She'd tried again and again to make it work, but never again. Dominik's strong arms around her seemed to steel her resolve. *I'm done. For real this time.* "My father will have to find another way to keep the team."

"He won't find another way, and you know that. Please, Oriana." Paul took a step forward and held his hand out. "You know he wants this for your brother. Antoine would have been better than all of *them* put together. Your dad showed me the tapes of him playing. Your mother took that future from him. Can you really take what your father has left?"

Guilt and regret spilled through her, like alcohol poured over a torn scab. She winced. "That's low, Paul. And you know what? I didn't know my brother very well, but I doubt he would have wanted me with someone like you. Not if he loved me." *Unlike my father.* She cleared her throat of the clogged-up feeling. "Seriously, what's your problem? Chantelle's perfect for you. Why don't you stay with her?"

"She's nobody! You get everything if your father doesn't let this pathetic team go under! I've put eight months into this. I'm not giving it up!" He took a step toward her. T.J. blocked him. "I'll ruin you. I swear to God, if you don't come with me now, I'll fucking ruin you and your new fucking harem."

"Give it your best shot." Dominik petted Oriana's hair as she wrapped her arms around his waist. "Figure you woulda learned by now, *Coach*. You can't call every game."

"I'll *win* this one, asshole!" Paul swiveled on his heels and grabbed a bottle of wine off the floor by the lounge chair. Straightened and hurled it. Dominik brought up his arm. The bottle shattered.

Glass and wine and blood rained down. Dominik tucked Oriana's face under his arm, but she could still see the red sparkles, dancing like mad fireflies, zipping in and out of the white haze of her mind. A childish voice cried out Dominik's name. The voice belonged to her.

* * * *

Dominik held Oriana against his chest, gritting his teeth as agony ripped up his nerves and his grip went slack.

"Dominik! He's hurt!" Oriana groped for his arm and smeared her hand in his blood. The color drained from her face. "Help him!"

"Shh." Dominik let his bloody arm fall to his side. "It's not a big deal. You need to sit down and breathe, pet."

"No, sir." After a deep inhale, she wrapped the wound up in the bottom of her shirt and put some pressure on it. "I won't follow orders while you're bleeding to death."

Bleeding to death? He shook his head and smiled. *Whatever you say, bunny.*

He watched T.J. hustle Paul into the house, his sheer size making Paul's struggles pointless.

"Get your fucking hands off me!" Paul shouted. "I'll destroy you, bitch! I'll fucking destroy you!"

Still holding on to Max, Sloan called out, "Punch him for me, T.J.!"

"Mason won't be able to press charges."

"Do you want to press charges?" Sloan asked Dominik.

Did he? He pressed his lips to Oriana's brow. Ice cold. He shook his head. "Just get him out of here, T.J.!" His head spun and he swallowed. "Take her, Callahan, she's about to pass out."

"Or you are. Go sit." Sloan released Max and swooped Oriana up in his arms. He carried her to the lounge chair, keeping one eye on his friend. "Think you can pull yourself together long enough to help Mason?"

Max nodded, then disappeared inside, coming back seconds later with a dish towel to compress the deep cuts in Dominik's arm. "You all right?"

"Yeah." He looked at the glass shards in his fountain, the blood and wine forming a nasty red puddle. His sanctuary was trashed. He let out a long sigh, then turned his back on the damage. That could wait. "Let's check on Oriana."

"Oriana Delgado is a whore!" Paul shouted from the street. "Hear that? The rich bitch is a whore! She's fucking all the Dartmouth Cobras!"

"Shut your mouth before the neighbors call the cops, Coach," they heard T.J. say from below. The front door slammed shut.

Dominik stepped inside and closed the balcony door behind him. Oriana didn't need to hear any more of that shit. He decided to change the subject. "Don't know if you wanna be a doctor if you can't take the sight of blood." He covered his bloody arm with the dish towel and took a knee beside Sloan. "Get her some water, Sloan."

"Yes, Master Mason." Sloan stood and shot Oriana a wink. He frowned when she didn't respond and hurried to the mini-fridge. "She's not going into shock, is she?"

"I don't know." Dominik took his phone out of his pocket. "Should we give Doc Henry a call?"

"No need." Giving him the fakest smile in history, Oriana pushed up to a sitting position. "I'm fine. I don't know what came over me." Her eyes looked very shiny. "Don't worry about me. Let's take care of you."

"It's not the blood." T.J. locked the door, grabbed the bottle of water from Sloan as he passed, and went to the bar. Ice clinked in a glass, and he spoke with his back to them. "It's Mason."

Max had just gotten a fresh towel, which he was wrapping around Dominik's arm. His grip suddenly tightened. "What about

Mason?"

Pain erupted in Dominik's arm. He growled and jerked away. "Fuck, man."

T.J. brought Oriana the glass. "When Sloan's face was opened up by that slash—" he arched a brow when she winced "—I held the skin together with my hand. I didn't like that my friend was hurt, but the blood didn't bother me." He sat on the arm of the sofa and put his hands on his knees. "Last winter, my daughter had an accident when we went on a ski trip. I almost passed out when I saw her blood on the snow."

Dominik's head shot up. His eyes locked with Oriana's. She flushed and looked away.

"I'm taking a walk." Dominik was out the door before anyone could argue with him. He couldn't show her how much it pleased him that she cared. She shouldn't care . . . not *that* much.

But she did. So what the fuck was he going to do about that now?

* * * *

The door opened again before it had fully shut. Sloan paused, torn between the urge to go after Mason and the instinct to hover over Oriana.

Vanek balanced three pizza boxes on one hand while he motioned over his shoulder with his thumb. "What's *his* problem?"

"Don't ask." Max disappeared into the bathroom. He came out with a fresh towel in his hands and headed straight for the door. "I'm gonna make sure he gets that taken care of." He looked pointedly at Sloan. "Take care of my girl. See that she gets what she needs."

The stickiness of wine and blood covering the trembling girl soaked through his jeans and smeared his bare chest. Sloan knew exactly what she needed.

He eyed T.J. who was rubbing his face with his hands.

And he had an idea of how to take care of another problem while he was at it.

Chapter Twelve

Wine and blood streaked through the water, stark against the white porcelain tub. Beneath the scalding spray of the shower, she bowed her head and tried to stop the constant replay of the scene in her mind. But every time she closed her eyes . . .

She put a hand on the tiled wall and sucked in air. The sweet scent of metal wafted up with the steam. The bathroom tilted.

"Whoa, careful, honey." T.J. caught her around the waist and lifted her out of the bath. He sat her on the big marble counter between the twin sinks and draped a towel over her shoulders. "I think you've rinsed off enough. Can you draw her a bath please, Callahan?"

The shower sputtered, and she stole a glance at Sloan who bent over to rinse out the tub. From the stiff set of his shoulders, she could tell he was pissed. And no wonder. Look at all the trouble she'd caused.

"Hey, look at me." T.J. stroked her legs with the ends of the big towel. His hands curved around the top of her thighs, so high that his thumbs skimmed along the crease of her mound. He smiled when she lifted her head and blinked at him. "You did absolutely nothing wrong. This isn't your fault. Paul's an asshole, and that's all there is to it."

"He wouldn't have come if I hadn't . . ." She groaned and pressed her legs together. His thumbs pressed right over her swollen clit, and her groan became a moan. "I should have just told my father what I told Paul in the first place. I shouldn't have dragged you all into it. Now Dominik's hurt and . . ."

Sloan straightened and folded his arms over his chest, leaning against the wall across from them. "Dominik's cut himself worse shaving. Believe me, none of us would trade what happened tonight to avoid whatever Paul's planning."

T.J.'s thumbs massaged her, and she clenched her thighs to stop him. "But now me and Max—"

Christ. She bit her lip as T.J. settled one arm on her shoulders

139

and leaned her back. His hand covered her pussy, and her pulse quickened. "Let me help you relax. Max won't mind."

"But he's not . . ."

"But I am." Sloan crossed the bathroom and rested his folded arms on the counter by her hip. "He told me to take care of you."

All the heat and the moisture building inside seemed to boil and spill in response to his words. She didn't understand why. Then T.J. filled her with one big finger, and it didn't matter at all.

"What did Paul mean when he mentioned your brother?" T.J. slid his finger up and circled her clit gently with the wet tip. "What did your mother do to him?"

A question? Did he just ask her a question? *Now?*

He stopped moving when she didn't answer.

"She killed him." Cold settled deep in her chest, the cold sense of loss for a brother she'd never really known. "She was an alcoholic. She got drunk one night, and he got in the car to try and stop her. I was nine—they left me alone with Silver—they never came back."

A deep thrust and the cold dissipated. She wiggled her hips and let her thighs open wider.

"Do you miss him?" T.J. asked, hooking his fingers inside her.

"Can't. Never spent any time with him. He was gone all the time for sports stuff and I—" She hissed in a breath when T.J. rolled her clit with his thumb. "But Daddy took it hard. Antoine was his favorite."

"Bath's ready." Sloan patted her knee and lifted her off the counter when T.J. backed away. "A good soak and you'll feel all better."

Her lips parted. *That's it?*

"I'll be right back." T.J. grinned and walked out.

Oriana gritted her teeth and nudged Sloan aside to step in the bath. *Mmm, very nice.* She closed her eyes and got comfortable. Well, if T.J. wouldn't . . . She dipped a hand under the bubbles.

And glared at Sloan when he grabbed her wrist.

"Patience. He's coming." He chuckled when she huffed. "Paul really didn't do it for you, did he, baby?"

"You have to ask?" She laid back and let her eyes drift shut. "So are you and T.J. going to . . ."

"Just T.J. I'm waiting for Max." His finger traced random shapes on her palm, and she sighed. "It's nice to know you're looking forward to it."

"Can I ask you something?" She opened her eyes to watch him nod. "Why all the questions?"

"T.J. didn't want to take advantage of you if you were too vulnerable. He's noble like that." The respect in his tone reflected in the soft glow of his eyes. "If you were really upset, he would have brought you to the bedroom to cuddle. But you're more worried about Mason than anything else."

No point in denying it. Her brow furrowed. "You must think I'm a cold-hearted bitch."

He squeezed her hand and frowned. "Why? Your brother died fifteen years ago, and, like you said, you hardly knew him. My mother died when I was born. My stepmother abandoned me and my dad for a rich guy when I was twelve, then committed suicide a year later. I don't pretend to care just because people might think I should."

The rawness of his tone made his every word a lie. Not what he said about her brother, but what he said about his stepmother.

She laced her fingers with his. "How's your father?"

Little creases formed around his eyes, and his whole bearing loosened up. "He's really proud of me. Tells everyone about his son 'The Pro.'" His lips twisted. "He won't be too happy about me being dumped in the minors."

"You won't be."

"You can't stop it, Oriana. I think we both know your plan won't work now."

Plastic tearing brought their attention to T.J., standing in the doorway.

"I thought you'd keep her simmering for me, Callahan." He dropped something in the trash and approached the bath, one hand behind his back. "Now I've got to start over."

"Sorry, she distracted me." Sloan patted her hand and got out of the way. "Never thought a woman could do that just talking. Amazing what she can do with that mouth of hers."

T.J. laughed. "Don't I know it." He pointed at Oriana. "Mouth and eyes shut. I've got something special for you."

She pressed her eyes shut, but couldn't help but ask. "What?"

"Shh." The water lapped at the sides of the bath, and he pried her legs apart. "Don't move."

Buzzing, the sound, then the feel as something slipped inside her. She gasped as the vibration spread, then swirled around and around. It withdrew, glided in, then left her again. Her eyes shot open and she stared at the vibrator in T.J.'s hand. The end of the dark blue, rubber rod curved inward, and she watched it slide in and out of her. She'd never owned a vibrator, but the way it made her feel—*damn*, time to buy herself some toys!

"I'm afraid I don't have the stamina of the rest, doll face." Water dripped from T.J.'s hand before he covered one breast. "But I'll be damned if I let this opportunity pass without having you come under my hands at least once."

He spread her pussy lips with his fingers and manipulated her clit, rubbing at either side of the hard nub while drawing the thick rod in and out. The slickness of her joined the water already filling her. Water slapped the edges of the bath, and her butt slipped against the smooth porcelain beneath her as her hips rose to meet each thrust. She reached out to cling to the sides of the bath. Little spasms in her core told her she was close. Climax hovered, just out of reach.

What the hell was wrong with her?

A hand pressed against her cheek. "I want to hear you scream, Oriana." Sloan's lips covered hers, and his tongue slid into her mouth. He bit her lip when she tried to kiss him back. "Watching you being fucked with that vibrator's got me so hard. I almost can't wait for my turn."

"Then don't." She whimpered as the edge of an orgasm came and went. "Take me now."

"No." His hand tightened around her jaw and he kissed her, the press of his lips as firm as his words. "Come. Come while I watch another man open you up and get you ready for me. My dick's bigger than what he's got stuffed inside you."

She was empty. Then suddenly full. The vibrations sped up.

"Ah!" She screamed into his mouth as her core tensed and released. An undercurrent of lava seemed to flow up into her womb and spill out until it coursed through every vein. Water sloshed onto the floor as she rode the vibrator, drawing the sensation out. Then it became too much. She whimpered.

The vibrator went away. Someone picked her up. A towel covered her. Strong arms carried her from the bathroom. She felt boneless, and it was wonderful. Her cheek rested against a hard chest, and she let the sound of a steady heartbeat lull her.

"Having fun, boys?"

Max. She looked at him. At Dominik. Both standing in the main room, expressions unreadable. A gruff sound brought her attention up to Sloan.

"What do you think?" he asked, the muscles of his arms tightening around her.

She chewed at her lip and hid her face against his chest. The throb from the aftermath of her pleasure stilled. For all Max's talk of giving her this one night, he couldn't have expected her to carry on without him.

She'd gone too far.

Chapter Thirteen

"You should have heard them," Vanek said around a mouthful of pizza. "They had her screaming and— Ow!" He rubbed his head where T.J. had cuffed him. "What was that for?"

"You've got a big mouth." T.J. put his hand on Oriana's shoulder. "They're not mad, sweetheart. Look at them."

Sloan tensed as Oriana pushed out of his arms. T.J. better be right.

Dominik approached her first. "Just a few stitches. No big deal." He titled her chin up with a hand and kissed her. "Would have been a bigger deal if you'd have gotten hurt."

"There was so much blood." She leaned on Dominik and let out a heavy sigh. "I had to get it off me. Everything else just . . . happened."

Max stepped up behind her and touched her shoulder. "What *happened,* exactly?"

Oriana shifted. Dominik put his arm around her shoulders and tucked her against his side. Sloan's tongue ran across his teeth as he stifled the urge to snatch her away from the other men.

"You wanna get off on the details, Max?" T.J.'s lips curled, and his nostrils flared. "Whatever's going on between you two, you gave her carte blanche for the night."

"Yes, I did," Max said, more to himself than anyone else. He mumbled something under his breath Sloan couldn't make out and shook his head. "Just askin'."

"So, how many stitches did you get, Mason?" Cardboard scraped the coffee table as Vanek took another piece of pizza. From his tone, he'd missed the entire exchange. Or was choosing to ignore it. "Oriana's right; there was an awful lot of blood. Cleaned it up best I could, but I think all the fish in your pond-thingy are dead."

Nice way to change the subject. Sloan rolled his eyes and scrambled to come up with something else.

But Dominik took the offered "out". "There were no fish in— and it's a fountain, but thanks for taking care of that for me."

"You're welcome." Vanek pointed at Dominik's arm. "I'm guessing thirty."

"Fifteen. I'm gonna have a few sweet scars." Dominik pulled off his jacket and hiked up the sleeve of his black sweatshirt. "Almost looks like lightning."

Very true. Dominik's peeled-off bandage revealed sewn skin in three long lines angled from one another. Once the swelling went down, it would look pretty cool.

But if her pallor was anything to go by, Oriana didn't agree. Sloan caught Dominik's eyes and nodded at Oriana. Much as he didn't like how close Dominik and Oriana were getting, she needed him now.

Dominik bent to pick her up as she swayed. "Whoa there, sweetie. Completely forgot how much seeing me hurt affects you." The regret in his eyes couldn't hide the pleasure in his tone. "Come on, I'll bring you—"

"No!" Oriana smacked the center of Dominik's chest and scowled at him. "Don't be a dumb ass. If you pick me up, you'll tear open your stitches."

Now that was a funny sight. Sloan knew Dominik well as a Master and as a hockey player. For a moment, he'd relaxed into an easy going one-of-the-guys. Concern shifted him to Dom. Now the two were at war as Oriana herded him toward the bedroom.

"I want you in bed. Now."

"Oriana—" Dominik's eyes narrowed. He didn't like taking orders from subs.

Girl was gonna get it.

Suddenly, Dominik's features lightened and he laughed. "All right. But only if you come with me."

Lips pursed, Oriana folded her arms over her chest. "To sleep."

"Deal." Dominik took her hand and laced their fingers together. "I enjoyed taking you, Oriana, but I can't imagine anything better than holding you all night long."

"Have fun!" Vanek dropped a pizza crust in the empty box and rubbed his hands on his thighs. "I'll crash on the couch."

"Why don't you head up to bed?" Dominik combed his fingers through Oriana's wet hair and brought her fingers to his lips. "You need your rest, rookie."

"'Cause I'm not stupid. If she wakes up during the night all antsy, I wanna be nearby. Bad enough I couldn't join the fun in the bathroom. Too crowded."

"Well, I'm gonna get some sleep while you guys figure this out." T.J. went to Oriana and kissed her brow. "Had fun and all, but I'm done for the night."

"Goodnight, T.J." Oriana groaned as Dominik worked one hand between the folds of her towel. "Stop that! We're going to sleep, remember?"

"Mmm." Dominik tugged at the towel until it opened and fell to her feet. "You still won't need this."

"There gonna be room in that bed for one more?" Max took a hesitant step toward Oriana, then smiled when she reached out to him. "I wanna 'hold' you, too."

The trio headed for the bedroom, and Sloan frowned when Oriana gasped. So much for sleeping. Maybe he and Vanek should join them.

The door was shut firmly behind them. The lock clicked.

"Guess they won't be needing us tonight." Vanek propped his feet up on the table and nudged the pizza box toward Sloan. "Hungry?"

"Go fuck yourself, Vanek." Scowling at Vanek's laugh, Sloan stormed out of the room. Closed inside his own, he paced, hands raked into his hair. How had he managed to miss out on everything? Oriana wanted him as much—if not more—than the others. So what had gone wrong?

Besides you running your mouth? Pretty much everything.

After stripping off his shirt and jeans, Sloan went to his bed and lay on top of the forest green comforter, arms folded under his head. Calm. Control. *There's no fucking rush. This isn't over for you. Not by a long shot.*

Tomorrow, he'd take his place with her. Maybe start her on some training. Then, after the game, they'd play.

Chapter Fourteen

Limbs wrapped around her, heavy and warm. The sun streaked through the part in the curtains, blazing through her closed lids and causing her head to throb in time with the dull ache between her thighs.

A wonderful feeling, until she woke enough to face what she'd done.

Images flashed behind eyelids she pressed shut. Five men, having their way with her. Vanek and Dominik. T.J. and Sloan. Then Max and Dominik again.

She didn't regret it, but she was afraid to see how the men would treat her. Like a plaything to be used for their amusement? Or would they be disgusted by how wanton she'd been?

Only one way to find out.

Untangling herself from Max and Dominik, she crawled off the bed and looked around. She certainly couldn't face them naked.

A suitcase caught her eye. Inside, she found a pair of jogging pants and a T-shirt. After combing her hair with her fingers, she checked her appearance in the mirror above the dresser.

Her lips were swollen, her cheeks flushed, but, other than that, she didn't look too bad. Her eyes held a sparkle that made them almost pretty.

Hell, I enjoyed myself last night. Whatever happens now won't take that away from me.

Squaring her shoulders, she walked up to the door and unlocked it. Then she eased it open.

"Good morning, gorgeous." Tyler tossed the remote on the coffee table and stood. "Damn, you're a sight in the morning."

So far, so good. She went to the sofa when he waved her over and accepted his kiss.

"I made you some breakfast." A tray slammed on the table in the little kitchenette. Sloan set a knife and fork by a plate and held out his hand. "Come eat."

Fruit salad and homemade waffles. Her mouth watered as she took a seat, and she whispered thanks as he poured her a glass of orange juice. She cut herself a piece of waffle, eyes on Sloan as he took the seat across from her.

"We've got a game tonight," he said, picking up the newspaper from the tray and flicking it open.

"I know." She put the piece of waffle in her mouth, watching him cruise the headline. "I was thinking of going—"

"You're coming." Sloan laid the paper on the table and smiled at her. "The Cobras are gonna crush the Blue Jackets. You wouldn't want to miss that, would you?"

"No." The syrup felt thick on her tongue. Too sweet. She took a gulp of orange juice. It didn't help. "Should I put money on it?"

Sloan's hand settled on her knee. Her fork fell out of her hand and clinked on her plate. At little early for . . . She swallowed and peered up at him. At least he didn't look like he thought any less of her.

"You're the owner's daughter. Might be frowned on." His hand stroked up her leg, sending a spike of awareness between her thighs. Then he stood and held up a finger. "Dominik! Perron! Get up, you lazy bastards!"

Grumbling came from the bedroom. Sloan rounded the table and took her hand to pull her to her feet.

When Sloan sat in her chair, she cocked her head, confused.

"Sit down and finish your breakfast."

Oh, hell, no.

"But—" She glanced across the room to watch Max and Dominik emerge, both deliciously rumpled and wearing nothing but boxers.

Sloan lifted her up and sat her on his knee. "Wasn't I clear enough?" He wrapped his hands around her waist and slid his fingers under the waistband of her jogging pants. "Eat up. We've got a big day planned."

Max took Sloan's abandoned seat. "So we get to chill before the game?"

Since Max didn't appear bothered by the fact that she was in Sloan's lap, she peeked at Dominik and relaxed. He simply smiled at her before taking her glass and gulping down half her orange juice.

"The last time I let you laze around before a game, you ended up minus six. We're heading to the gym for a light workout, then to the rink to warm up." Sloan's fingers slid inside her pants, brushing the top of her mound. "Food, Oriana."

She tried to get up and whimpered when he pulled her back. The hard muscles of his thigh ground against her, and she could feel the crotch of the jogging pants dampen with her lust. The tip of his finger grazed her clit.

Picking up her fork, she speared a big piece of waffle and crammed it in her mouth.

"There you go," he whispered, withdrawing his hand to set it on the table. "How's your knee, Vanek?"

Tyler snapped his gaping mouth shut and shook his head. "What?" His cheeks flushed. He rose from the sofa and brought first one knee, then the other, to his chest. "Little sore, but nothing I can't handle."

While Sloan questioned each of the men, Oriana cleaned her plate of the tasteless food. Not that the waffles weren't good, but her focus had turned from her taste buds to something . . . lower.

Sounded like the boys' schedules were full. They wouldn't have time for her, but maybe if she could have a few minutes alone?

"Where do you think you're going?" Sloan put his hand on her hip when she slipped off his lap.

"Shower." She dodged his hand and headed to the bathroom.

"You had a bath last night."

"Well—" She gave Dominik a helpless look when he blocked her path. They just weren't playing fair this morning.

Dominik cupped her cheek. "Go ahead, babe. Wash all me and Max's sweat off. I'll bring you by your place later to pick up a change of clothes. But I want you to wear my jersey to the game." He grinned when she nodded and let her pass.

"Oh, and Oriana," Sloan said, lifting his arms over his head to stretch.

She sighed and glanced over her shoulder, one foot in the bathroom. "What?"

"Don't get yourself off."

Snorting, she entered the bathroom and slammed the door behind her. As if.

But under the hot spray of the shower, she found herself obeying despite her best efforts to do otherwise. Her body refused to respond to her touch—she let out an aggravated scream between her teeth, then another when she heard a chuckle from right outside the door.

Bastard! Grinding her teeth, she reached down and turned the cold water on full.

Chapter Fifteen

Portland Estates Boulevard was sprinkled with nice family-sized homes and bungalows. And trees, so many Dominik double-checked the GPS on the dashboard of the rental to make sure he hadn't left the city. When Oriana referred to her place as an apartment, he'd expected a blocky complex in the shopping district. But this was a typical, suburban neighborhood. A good place to raise kids.

Oriana lived here with Paul. The very thought made him feel like he'd swallowed lumpy, sour milk. If he had his way, either Paul or Oriana would vacate the apartment very soon. He'd force the issue if he had to.

Right, she'll love that. Oriana might be sexually submissive, but she gave no impression of needing someone to run her life for her. Which didn't mean he couldn't broach the subject. But as a friend, not a Dom.

Then again, they hadn't been friends long enough for him to offer that kind of advice. Even calling them "friends" seemed preemptive. Friends talked, and not once in their time alone had Oriana showed any desire to chat. Despite what had passed between them, he felt like one of the chauffeurs on her daddy's payroll.

"Where to, ma'am?"

The sound of Oriana unsticking her bare thighs from the leather seat disturbed the silence. From the corner of his eye, he observed the way she rubbed her knees and pursed her lips. Her eyes flung fiery daggers at him as though blaming him for her discomfort.

"I'll have to do something to earn those dirty looks, bunny." He chuckled when she gave him another. "If you recall, Sloan's the one who ordered you not to pleasure yourself in the shower."

Her lips moved like those of a goldfish suddenly plucked from a safe little glass bowl. Fingers denting the flesh of her thighs, she jutted her chin up. "You're assuming I did what he said."

"Either that, or your panties are on fire." He chuckled when she let out a kitten-like growl. "You're a lusty woman, Oriana. Nothing to be ashamed of."

"Uck, as if I can't go a few hours without sex. Just because I—"
Her cheeks turned hot pink. "I'm not a damn nympho."

"Never said you were." He pulled up in front of a building that
looked more like a large townhouse than an apartment and
confirmed the address. Throwing the rented Lincoln in park, he
opened the door, but paused when she didn't move. "What is it? Are
you worried that Paul's here? Didn't the concierge say he left
yesterday with a few bags?"

Fiddling with the hem of the jersey he'd loaned her, she nodded
slowly. "Yes, it's not that."

"Then . . . ?" He scanned her face, her posture, for any kind of
clue. His well-honed patience waned when he came up with nothing.
"Tell me what's on your mind."

With an aggravated *huff*, she sat up straight and put her hands on
her hips. "Why didn't you let me change your bandages? I'm good
for more than gyrating my hips and giving head you know." She
reached out and gently traced the crooked medical tape on his arm.
"Tyler did a lousy job."

Ah, I see. His insides warmed, and he smiled. As a Dom, he spent
more time than not taking care of others. As far as he was
concerned, it was his duty. But someone wanting to take care of him
was a nice change.

*She's training to be a doctor. The need to heal is instinctive. You're just
another patient.*

But then he considered why he hadn't let her dress his wounds.
T.J.'s observations about her behavior when he'd gotten hurt rang
true. Maybe her feelings for him made this something more.

He touched her cheek and waited until her eyes met his. "Baby,
I'd love nothing more than to let you nurse me, your touch—" *Don't
go there. You'll just make this harder for her. She's Max's girl.* He forced
himself to keep talking before the painful acknowledgement could
show on his face. "Honestly, I didn't want to look like less of a man
in front of you. With Tyler, I can act all tough, but seeing the
concern in you beautiful eyes—"

"You could never look like less of a man to me, Dominik." She
touched his bottom lip. "Why would you even think that? Everyone
knows how strong you are."

"Everyone?" Her body heat flowed over him like the gentle rays of the sun on a summer morning. He could stay right there, just basking in her, forever. "Including you?"

"Especially me." She sighed when he moved in for a kiss and flattened her hand against his chest. "But you're still human, and, sometimes, you've got to drop the macho act."

"Done." He laughed as she wrinkled her little nose. "Kiss me, and I'll let you patch me up."

"Let me?" Her dainty brows disappeared under the sweep of her bangs. She rose up on her knees and shoved him back into his seat. "You're assuming I'll give you a choice? I'll have you know I've been scheming to get you inside, knock you down, and strap you up. Maybe add a gag so you wouldn't snarl while I tended to your boo-boo."

"You could try." He drew her into his lap, fit her snugly against him, and brushed his lips over hers. "But I can't see you trying that hard. You're the one who wears the straps in this relationship."

Biting the tip of her tongue, she blinked at him. "Relationship? Dominik, I—"

"Don't worry, I've no intention of pulling out a coll—ring." His words sounded smooth despite the tightness of his throat. And the way her whole body loosened up, she didn't suspect a thing. "Relationship just sounds better than arrangement."

She winced and shifted back a little. "Yeah, I guess it does."

Her shapely ass molded over his thighs. The way she straddled him gave him the urge to unzip his pants, rip away the cotton barrier of her jogging pants, and bury himself inside her. If she considered this nothing more than an arrangement, why not indulge himself while he had the chance?

He set his palms on her sides and framed her ribs with his fingers and thumbs. *Because she might change her mind.*

"Can I ask you something, Dominik?"

"Mmmhmm?" He kept his eyes on his thumbs as he counted up her ribs. Her pulse, her breath, sped up under his hands. Her nipples jutted out, but not all the way; he'd seen them bigger, harder, and nice and red from being sucked on. His mouth watered as he pictured sucking them to full size through her shirt.

"You don't feel used, do you?"

His gaze traveled up from her breasts to her face. His lips turned down when he saw the way her eyes seemed to beg for understanding. "Excuse me?"

She brought her shaky fingers up to her lips. "Well, you know . . . what we did . . . it's only because Max needs—"

Acidic rage coursed through him as though a needle full had been injected into his veins. The way she'd touched him, held him, the way she'd reacted when he'd gotten hurt—she was going to pretend all that was for Max?

Of all the unwritten rules Oriana could have broken, she had to choose that one.

He managed not to shout, but his tone was gruff. "Get off me."

"What?" She scrambled off his lap and out of the car. "I don't understand—are you mad?" When he didn't answer, she stomped her foot on the sidewalk. "Say something!"

Rubbing his hand over his face, he reminded himself that most people thought nothing of lying to one another. Friends, family, lover—the truth was never a given. For all he knew, she was lying to herself as well. But he had to make her understand.

"Yes. I'm mad." He unfolded his large frame from the car, purposely moving toward her before she could clear the door. Then he put his hand on her shoulder, taking away any illusions she might have about slipping away. "We can talk about anything . . . *everything*. You can tell me as much or as little as you want, so long as it's the truth."

"When did I lie?" Her gaze flicked from his arm to his face. "If Max wasn't a voyeur, I wouldn't have gone through with it."

This time, he wished she was lying. But she'd looked him straight in the eye while telling him she wouldn't have slept with him without Max's stamp of approval. Not that she hadn't wanted to, but her own desires wouldn't have been enough.

"I appreciate your honesty." He held his arm out toward her front door. "Go get your stuff. I'll wait here."

"You're upset."

He shook his head, careful to give no outward sign of his own lie. "I like knowing where I stand."

* * * *

The picture window at the end of the hall looked like the perfect postcard image enlarged. Once the home of a wealthy shipyard owner, the house had been converted into several large loft-style apartments by her father only months before she'd returned to Dartmouth. Oriana had always thought that he'd hoped to lure both her and Silver back with the lavish accommodations, knowing without being told that neither would ever move back in with him. He'd had to settle for her alone. Silver wouldn't give up her glamorous lifestyle for anything he had to offer.

And why should she? She didn't need anything from him. Unlike Oriana, Silver had made it on her own.

I will, too. Oriana fished her keys from her pocket, then unlocked her door. The scent of stale Chinese food came out with the cold draft from the air conditioner. She stepped in and closed the door behind her.

The natural light spilling in from the tall windows lining the white walls seemed to emphasize the mess Paul had left for her. His dirty clothes were strewn across the floor as though tossed there from their open bedroom on the second floor. The modern glass table at the far end of the open room was covered with open containers of take out, a bottle of wine, and two long-stemmed glasses. Coral lipstick marred the crystal rim of one glass.

Paul had brought Chantelle here. To their home.

Stumbling over to the cubic, white leather sofa that split the sitting area from the dining area, she sat hard. A plain, white envelope lay on the ottoman in front of the sofa. She picked it up and used her nails to pick at the sealed part of the letter. Her hands shook, and she finally just let the letter flutter to the floor. All the white around her blurred as tears gathered. Dark brown broke through her washed-out, colorless vision. Warmth caressed her cheek.

"Come here, sweetie." The sofa creaked a little as Dominik sat beside her. She buried her face under his arm and sobbed. "Shh, it's okay. About time actually."

"Huh?" She hiccupped on another sob, then almost choked on a laugh. "You mean about time for me to fall apart? Over Paul?"

"Yes." Dominik settled back on the sofa, drawing her close. "I hate the guy, and right now, you probably do too. But you didn't always."

"I should have. If I'd known who he really was—"

"What did you see in him?" he asked, the low timbre of his voice for once soothing, rather than arousing. "Maybe if I understood, I could help you get through this."

What did she see in him? God, how to explain?

"From the first day, he saw how uncomfortable I was with all the attention from the press. He took me aside and told me that my father needed all the media attention for the team. He admitted that the team probably wouldn't last long, but said my father would appreciate us both doing our best while it did. Stability at the top would encourage the investors to hang on. And a family man looks more stable than a power hungry tycoon, which is how most see my father . . ." She laughed and closed her eyes. "Because that's what he is. But I improved his image. Paul said people were curious about me."

"That must have scared the hell out of you." Dominik curved his hands around the back of her neck, massaging with the tips of his fingers.

His touch grounded her. She nodded and bent her head forward as his fingers moved up to her nape with a bit more pressure. "But Paul prepped me for each appearance. He told me to keep my answers short and simple. I came off as shy and sweet to the press, which was perfect. My father was thrilled with my performance, but it didn't take long before he took it for granted. The only time he paid me any attention was when the three of us went out for supper. Then he'd ask me how things were going at school. Paul warned me in advance not to tell him about the courses I'm struggling with."

"So basically, Paul was like a bridge between you and your father." Dominik squeezed her shoulder, then smiled when she looked up at him. "He gave you the relationship you'd never had before."

She'd never seen it that way, but he was right. And Paul must have known how much she wanted that bond with her father. He'd used it, used *her.*

"God, how could I have been so stupid?"

"You weren't stupid. You were naïve," Dominik said firmly, as though stating a fact. "What I don't understand is how Paul had you going for so long. You lived together. You've admitted the sex wasn't good—"

"We didn't spend much time together. Between road games and school . . ." She rolled her eyes at her own ignorance. "Sometimes he left days early, saying he wanted the extra time to get you guys prepped for a 'big game.' It happened more and more often over the last few months. During my last school break, I got hooked on romance novels." Dominik's raised brows made her blush. "Okay, erotic novels. I started wondering what I was doing wrong. I bought sexy lingerie and planned romantic evenings. That's when things changed. When we first got together, Paul was sweet and considerate in the bedroom. Nothing earth-shattering, but it was . . . pleasant. But weeks, sometimes months, would go by without us doing more than falling asleep with our backs to one another. We hardly even kissed unless there was a camera in the vicinity. When I came on to Paul, he acted like he was doing me a favor. And he would say . . ."

Dominik's muscles tensed, and she felt like she'd laid her head on stone. His breathing became hard and fast. He let out a low growl when she didn't continue.

"What did he say?" He sat up and pressed her head against his chest, right over his heart. "No. Don't answer that. I want you to forget everything that bastard said to you. From this point on, you are to see yourself as I see you." He nudged her chin up and claimed her lips in a fierce kiss, like he'd force her to swallow his words if he must. "As a beautiful, *generous*—"she giggled when he gave her a second to breathe. Then he sucked on her bottom lips and she groaned"—woman who's strong and smart and too good for the likes of Paul. Got it?"

"Yes, Sir." She grinned when his chest puffed up. Her book had given a brief rundown of the honorific titles granted a Domme and how hard one had to work to earn them. Obviously, the same was true for a Dom. And even though she couldn't claim Dominik as hers, she had no problem giving him the respect he deserved.

"Good girl."

His approval made her feel all glowy inside. She smiled at him and fingered the button of his black pants. Why not take advantage of their time alone?

Covering her hand with his own, Dominik clucked his tongue and shook his head. "I thought you were going to take care of me."

"I'm trying to." She frowned when he stood. "You don't want—"

He shook his head. "I always want with you, sweetie." He kicked a pair of Paul's boxers and scowled up at the bedroom. "But this place reeks of Paul and his whore. Let me help you clean up and—"

"You've got a game in a few hours." She plucked the envelope she'd dropped off the floor and stuffed it between the cushions. "Come to think of it, I don't have the stomach to clean up Paul and Chantelle's mess. I'll take care of your arm at the hotel. Just let me pack some stuff and—"

"I saw the letter, Oriana." He strode up to one of the windows and stuffed his hands in his pockets. "No use hiding it. You don't have to tell me what it says if you don't want to."

"It's not that." She went to the small closet under the stairs leading up to the bedroom and took out a small suitcase. Keeping herself busy would snuff the nagging curiosity. Why would Paul leave her a note? What more could he have to say? "You can read it if you want. I'm not interested."

"What did I tell you about lying to me, Oriana?"

She tensed, prepared for him to cross the room and grab her, but he hadn't moved. The built-up adrenaline died a bittersweet death. Odd, but she'd kind of wished he had come after her for breaking his number one rule. The idea excited her. His inaction concerned her. Would he wait until they got back to the hotel?

Clearing her throat, she hugged the suitcase to her chest. "Are you going to punish me?"

He gave her an amused look over his shoulder. "Yes. But not now. I'll let you stew for a while."

"Hmph." She rolled her eyes and stomped up the stairs. Tossing everything she might need for the next few days in the suitcase, she considered her punishment. *Lady in Charge* had a whole chapter on disciplining wayward submissives. Dominik obviously couldn't use a cock cage on her, but he could use something equally unpleasant. She tried to think of the worst things imaginable and came up with everything from whippings that left her back a bloody mess—which didn't seem Dominik's style—to being denied orgasm for eternity. A little excessive, but even being forced not to come once would be pure torture.

Punishments aren't supposed to be pleasant. You only get punished if you do something wrong.

And she had done something wrong. He hadn't asked for much. He didn't expect her to bare her soul. He'd asked for nothing but truth between them.

Finished packing, she returned downstairs and dropped her suitcase by the door. Then she walked up to Dominik and wrapped her arms around his waist.

Pressing her forehead against his back, she whispered. "I'm sorry. I really am interested in the letter, sadly enough. Can you just read it and tell me what it says? Please?"

He turned and kissed the top of her brow. "Sure." He tipped her face up with a finger and kissed her lips. "And consider your punishment served."

She stared at him as he went to the sofa and plucked the letter from between the cushions. "That's it?"

"This time," he said, tearing the letter open. "You learned your lesson, right?"

She nodded.

"Well, that's the point of a punishment. But I'm warning you . . ." His expression turned stern. "Next time, I won't be so lenient."

"Okay." She bit her lip and decided there wouldn't be a next time. She liked it much better when he was happy with her. "So . . . ?"

He unfolded the letter, scanned it, then crumpled it in his fist. "He's staying with Chantelle. He's giving you a few days to 'smarten up,' then he'll call you."

"Really." She rubbed her eyes with her fingers, feeling the threatening sting of tears. Not again. She would not waste another tear on that pathetic excuse for a man. "Well, I hope he's in for one hell of a shock."

She took her phone from where she'd stuffed it in the deep pocket of Tyler's shorts and dialed the number for the concierge. After instructing him to have someone come and pack up Paul's things and have them shipped to Chantelle's, she hung up and gave Dominik a stiff smile.

"Well, that's done. Now all I have to do is change the locks, and I won't ever have to deal with Paul again." She picked up her suitcase and opened the door, wishing she didn't have to come back here, but accepting the fact that she had nowhere else to go. "Shall we?"

Dominik took the suitcase from her, pausing at her side to tuck a strand of hair behind her ear. "You don't really believe that, do you?"

"For today, I do." She let out a sigh of relief when he nodded, as though satisfied with her answer. Then she moved past him as he held the door open for her. "I don't want to think about tomorrow, not yet."

Tomorrow, she'd have to face her future. Without Paul, which was good.

But her relationship with Max only really needed one other man. She assumed he'd choose Sloan.

Out on the street, steps away from the rental, she stopped Dominik with a hand on his arm.

"When a submissive chooses a Dom, they'll do anything to please him or her—"

"Essentially. Why do you ask?" Deep creases formed between Dominik's eyes, and he seemed to be trying to read something in her expression. "Do you think Max will want more than you're prepared to give?"

"You told me not to lie to you, Dominik." She dropped her gaze when he scowled. "Please don't ask me that."

"Fine." He drew away from her and went to put her suitcase in the trunk. Then he stopped by the driver's side door and looked over the car at her. "But you better come to me if his demands become unreasonable."

She nodded, hoping not making the promise out loud wouldn't

be considered a lie.

Max asking me to commit to one other man wouldn't be unreasonable.

But the commitment might just be more than she was prepared to give. Her heart felt like it had been split, but not in half. She couldn't even see how the pieces fit together anymore. But she knew she needed them all to be whole.

Chapter Sixteen

Music erupted from the speakers of the stadium. The crowd rose from their seats for the singing of the national anthems. Sloan held his helmet under his arm and took his place dead center on the blue line. His tongue touched his bottom lip, still slick with Oriana's peach-flavored lip gloss. *That kiss topped them all.*

As usual, there were plenty of empty seats in the forum. Being the owner's daughter, Oriana claimed a seat right by the rink where the Cobras came on the ice. When Sloan came out, she'd hopped out of her seat and leaned over. He'd climbed up, and the crowd went wild as they kissed. Suddenly, weird sixties-style guitar strumming cut off the AC/DC riff. The Monkees' "When Love Comes Knockin'" played out, making him feel like a putz. A very lucky putz.

The fans laughed. They cheered. Then the kiss replayed on the scoreboard. Oriana's cheeks got redder than the maple leaf on the flag, and she hid her face inside her jersey.

Adorably shy, but he had to give the girl one thing, putting herself out there had taken some guts. Maybe her original plan hadn't gotten Paul to back off, but their public display should do it. He'd look like a fool if he tried staking a claim now. And her father would probably do anything in his power to stop her from showcasing her relationships with him and the other men again. Fine, she hadn't kissed all the men, but she'd kissed him while wearing Mason's jersey. That would get people talking.

Our girl's a winner. Sloan grinned. He was proud of her. And he was even more determined than ever to make her just as proud of him. Of all of them.

The crowd roared as the teams met at center ice. The ref dropped the puck; Sloan won the face-off. He passed the puck to T.J. who whipped it to Vanek. Vanek evaded a check and streamed to the other end of the rink. Sloan rushed the opponents' net with Perron. Fanned the puck. Kicked it to the other side of the net. The puck hit a Blue Jacket defenseman, and Mason stopped it with his stick and redirected it to Vanek who tucked it in the net just as the goaltender skidded to block Mason.

Red lights blared, and Sloan crashed into Vanek, hooking his arm around the boy's neck to congratulate him. Mason, T.J., and Perron slammed into them, whooping like madmen. You'd have thought they'd never scored before.

Play continued. Sloan and his line played more minutes than they ever had before—either Coach Stanton's idea of revenge, or he'd finally smartened up and decided he wanted to win. In any case, by the end of the game, Sloan had two goals and three assists. They beat the Blue Jackets seven to three. Let Delgado send him down after that. The fans would throw a fit.

But the victory couldn't compete with the lust that built as he showered, thinking of the woman who would finally be in his arms. Of the body he would possess before the night was over.

Oriana's love for the game glowed in her eyes as she twirled into the sitting room. She went from one man to the next, hugging them, kissing them, recapping the game with a fervor that made him so hot he was tempted to haul her over his shoulder and carry her to his bedroom. But she made them watch the highlights of the game and fell asleep on the sofa, her head on Max's lap, her feet on T.J.'s.

All the lust eroding him was replaced by something tender as he watched Max carry her to his room. Dominik bowed out with a tight smile and went to his own room, as did T.J. and Vanek. They were giving him his turn.

He took his place on the bed.

"Don't wake her up," Max said as Sloan snuggled up behind Oriana.

"I don't plan to." He laid his head on the pillow and smoothed out her hair. "She's something else."

Max lay on his back, careful not to move the arm Oriana rested on. "That she is."

* * * *

A little wiggle and Sloan was instantly awake. His dick stirred and thickened when a hand passed over it. He groaned, then grinned when Oriana giggled. Eager little minx.

Her gaze led his down. Both her hands were on his bare chest.

Sloan sat up and shoved Max's big hand off his thigh. "What the hell, man!"

Grumbling something incoherent, Max rolled over and resumed snoring.

Oriana laughed. "I didn't know you two were so close. Maybe I should give you some privacy?"

Sloan chuckled. "Get over here."

He clamped his hands around the nape of her neck, pulled her up, and brought his lips down hard. Her tongue flicked out, and she gasped when he caught it with his teeth. He gently tugged and sucked until breathy little whimpers filled his mouth with her hot breath.

"I think I need to remind you what team I play for."

The way she clung to his hair, like she wanted to control how far and fast things would go, made him smile. He twisted out of her grip and pressed a kiss between her breasts.

"If you want me to stop, just say so." He kissed the underside of one breast, just above where it sat atop her ribs. "Otherwise, hold on to the top of the mattress and don't move."

He could feel the pulse thrumming beneath his lips speed up.

"What happens if I move?"

"I'll assume you don't want me to take control. So I won't. And I refuse to take you any other way." He grazed her other breast with the day-old scruff on his chin. "You didn't get off last time because you focused on the pleasure of the others and took none for yourself. I don't play that way, babe."

Her arms stretched over her head, then slid down to her sides.

One brow raised, he took a push-up position over her, his knees by her hips, and looked pointedly at her hands.

She looked pointedly at his cock. "You want me, Sloan."

"That I do." He sat up and put his hands on his thighs. "I want you to come in my mouth, I want you to come while Max and I fill you up—nice and slow—then I want you to come again when we both come deep inside you."

"That sounds . . ." She shuddered, which was answer enough.

Then Max spoke up. "That sounds perfect." He braced his

elbow on the bed and his head on his hand. Then he patted the top of the mattress. "Come on, sugar. Do what the man says."

Oriana's eyes narrowed as she studied Max's face, like she was looking for a sign of some sort. Waiting for *him* to take charge.

The heavy-lidded look Max gave her made Sloan laugh. "If you're waiting for Perron to take the lead, you'll be waiting all night, sweetheart."

"Don't push it, Callahan," Max said.

"Or what?"

"Or I'll make you leave."

A hand smacked over Sloan's mouth before he could respond. Another covered Max's. Oriana glared at them. "I'm ready."

Her hands moved from their mouths and hooked to the top of the mattress. Her knuckles were white. Her whole body quivered like a plucked bowstring beneath him.

Sloan dropped his mouth to one plump breast. He kept his eyes on Max as he used his tongue to roll a hard little nipple against the roof of his mouth.

"Jesus." Max inhaled and licked his lips. His hand hovered over his crotch, then gripped it as he pretended to adjust himself.

Sucking as much of Oriana's breast into his mouth as he could, Sloan released it with a plop and circled the extended nipple with his tongue. "Your girlfriend's tits taste salty from having all the men pressed against her after the game. Kinda nasty and erotic all at once."

Max's hand closed over his dick under the cotton of his boxers.

"I wonder how they would taste with cum all over them." Sloan tilted his head in thought and licked around the jutted nub. "I've never tasted another man's cum, but you have. You kissed her after T.J. came in her mouth."

With a gruff sound in the back of his throat, Max freed his cock and started stroking it.

Oriana moaned. "Sloan, stop."

Lifting his head, Sloan arched a brow. "If you're sure . . ."

"That's not what I meant." She glanced at Max, and her cheeks turned a bright pink. "Oh."

"Yeah." Sloan slid his hand down her back and took a firm hold of her ass to press her soft belly against his hard dick. "Do you feel that?"

Her stomach muscles jumped. "Yes."

He moved his hand down her thigh and hooked it under her knee to draw it over his hip. "All yours."

Another whimper. Her nails scraped the mattress, and he felt her shift. She was going to move. And he'd have to follow through with his threat.

Which really sucked.

Clamping a hand over her wrists, Max fixed that little dilemma. "Don't. I need to see his mouth on you. He wasn't kidding when he said he'd stop."

Oriana hissed through her teeth. "Hold me, Max. Don't let me go."

That precious vulnerability again. God, Sloan loved it. He glanced at Max and caught the tenderness he felt reflected in the azure depths of his eyes.

"I'll hold you, love." He inclined his head at Sloan. "And I won't let go unless you ask."

"I won't."

Sloan cupped her breasts in his hands and squeezed as he moved down, grazing her ribs with his teeth, nibbling her side when he found a sensitive spot that made her arch up and gasp. Lower still, he found another spot under the soft slope of her belly. A shudder passed right through her. She was already close.

Time to pull back a little.

"Has Max ever told you about the women we've shared?" He positioned himself on his side between her legs. Her thigh muscles tensed against his back, and he knew she didn't like picturing them with other women. He stroked one hand down her side and pressed it to her belly. "Have you ever heard of DP?"

Her muscles flexed. "No."

"Double penetration. Some consider it two men in a woman at once, one in her pussy." He bowed his head so his breath teased her slick flesh. "The other in her ass." He reached around and slid a finger along the tightened crevice of her butt. "But one woman taught us otherwise."

"Sloan." Max sat up but kept a firm hold on Oriana's wrists. "She doesn't need to hear this."

"She might enjoy it. I won't get graphic." Sloan smirked at Max's scowl and zig-zagged his fingers along her hip to the top of her mound. "Let's just say we both fit snug inside her—" He slicked two fingers over her clit and dipped them into her slit. "Here."

Oriana twisted her hips and shook her head. "No. I can't. I couldn't."

Sloan dragged his fingers out, then drew a moist finger eight around her clit. "We didn't enjoy it. Our balls squished together wasn't as fun as it sounds."

"Mmm." Oriana sighed as he skimmed around her clit again. "I can't imagine it would be." She tongued her bottom lip. "But it must have been interesting to have your cocks rubbing together."

Max sputtered. Sloan stared. Her impish grin made him laugh. He shook his head and pushed his fingers in until she squirmed against the press of his big knuckles.

"Never thought about it like that." He rolled his eyes at Max when Oriana's eyes fluttered shut. Hell, if it got her off, let her think what she wanted. "Then again, I never thought I'd see Max get so hard giving me something that could be his alone."

The muscles of her pussy gripped his fingers, and her juices spilled around them. He brought his fingers to his mouth and sucked, conscious of Max watching.

"You know you belong to him now." He gave her soft mound an open-mouthed kiss. "Which means he can give this pussy—" his slick fingers slipped between her ass cheeks and teased the little hole "—and this ass—" he flicked her clit with his tongue "—to anyone."

"Oh." Oriana opened her thighs a little and lifted up to him as he sucked her clit between his lips and dipped his fingers into her pussy. "Sloan. Max . . ."

Close. So close. Her pulse beat hard and fast around the thrust of his fingers. Sloan turned his hand so he could prod her rosette with his thumb. A bit of pressure and he filled her.

But she was holding back. Not intentionally, but she needed something more. Something he couldn't give her.

"He's right, my love." Max pumped his cock slow, jaw clenched, holding out on his own pleasure. "I gave you to Vanek and Dominik and T.J. And now I'm giving you to Sloan."

Oriana tensed and relaxed. "Why?"

"Honesty, right?"

They'd had a talk he hadn't been privy to. He went still and waited on the outcome.

"Always." Oriana bit her lip. "We agreed to one night, but this isn't over, is it?"

"No." Max released his dick and ran a finger down her cheek. "Honey, Sloan reads me better than anyone—that's why we're so good together on the ice. How do I explain this so it makes sense?" He looked at Sloan. Sloan shrugged. Damned if he knew. "When I'm on the ice, and I've got the puck, I like knowing I can take the shot—or that I can pass it off and let someone else put it in the net."

"But not just anyone." Oriana turned her head to lay her cheek on Max's bare thigh. "'Cause they might not get a goal."

"Exactly." Max bent down and kissed her, soft and sweet. Didn't seem to fit the carnal act a threesome should be, but for some reason, it seemed right. "I love a girl who knows the game."

"I know it." Oriana hooked her ankles around the back of Sloan's neck. "And I still want to play."

Chapter Seventeen

The air left the room like a giant vacuum had been turned on. Max took it from her mouth. Sloan took it from . . . below. But she really didn't need to worry. Her men would take good care of her.

Her men. She smiled at the thought. Maybe she couldn't tell Max now, but he'd given her much more than he could understand. More than she could ever have asked for. As much as she belonged to him, *they* belonged to her.

And what would she do with them all?

She brought one hand up to trace the rough curve of Max's jaw as he kissed her.

Whatever she wanted.

No. She corrected herself with a slanted curve to her lips. *Whatever Max wants.*

"Did you just move your hand?"

Shit.

She put her hand back where Sloan had told her to keep it. "No."

"Liar." Sloan laughed and arched up, leaving her core empty and cold. "I've decided to amend my demands. They were a little unreasonable."

"Ya think?" Oriana smirked. She'd felt his erection against her thigh too often to buy his "I'm-in-control" act. "So what's the penalty, Captain?"

Sloan's dark green eyes sparkled like dewy grass under moonlight. "Five swats and we'll carry on."

Oriana rolled her eyes. He was going to spank her?

Big deal. She'd been spanked as a child. Her father's displeasure always stung more than the little taps on the ass. And Sloan didn't sound pissed.

He smiled. "Each. I think Max deserves his share for trusting you to keep your word."

Now she frowned. Put that way brought guilt. Max had let her go to kiss her. To give her the truth she'd demanded. He *had* trusted her.

She looked at Max. His brow furrowed.

"You respect me that little, love?"

Oh, that just wasn't fair. They'd distracted her.

"I forgot."

Lame much?

"Then you agree. Sloan's being fair."

What?

"Come here, Oriana." Sloan drew away from her and sat on the edge of the bed. He patted his lap. "Unless you wanted to stop?"

Are you insane? She glared at him. She could still feel the pressure, deep inside, slicking her wetness where it didn't belong. But it felt so good.

Sloan's eyes narrowed. "I'm not a patient man. Either you take your punishment, or I'll go take care of myself in the bathroom and let Max handle you however he chooses."

She looked at Max.

"Gotta have rules." His lips curved, and he kept stroking himself like he didn't have a care in the world. "I'm thinking if Sloan leaves, I'll get Dominik. He's got bigger hands."

Her bottom lip stuck out as she glanced from him to Sloan and back. Then she crossed her arms over her breasts. Her nipples throbbed against her wrists, and the sensation skipped down to her core.

"What if I won't let anyone spank me?"

The elastic of Max's boxers snapped on his waist. He rose until he loomed over her. With a firm hold of her chin, he looked deep into her wide eyes. "I say you will."

A quiver of fear, strangely erotic, rode over her flesh. *Well, since he put it that way . . .*

She bowed her head and crawled to Sloan. The moisture between her thighs made all her protests seem shallow. As though the thought of being punished turned her on.

Without another word, she positioned herself over Sloan's thighs, praying he wouldn't notice how wet she was. "Be gentle."

He caressed her butt with one calloused hand. "Be quiet and I'll do my best. If the boys hear you cry, they'll come in to see what's wrong. And I'll make them each take a turn."

Her hips wiggled and she moaned. Each of the men taking a turn didn't seem like much of a threat. She almost said "Go ahead," but she bit her lip instead. She had a feeling Sloan would find a way to take the fun out of it.

"Like that idea, do you?" Sloan barred one arm across her thighs and held her in place with his hand on the small of her back. "Then go ahead. Be as loud as you want."

She pressed her lips together and shook her head.

A hand came down hard on one cheek. Pain flared over her butt. She yelped and turned to glare at Max.

His grin was positively wicked. "We never specified who'd go first." He rubbed the sting from her flesh. "We like taking turns."

Sloan's hand left her back. Went up high. Came down.

Oriana pressed her eyes shut. He gave her a little tap. Then a harder one on the other cheek when Max moved.

Two fingers dove into her, and she cried out. Thrust. Smack. Thrust. Smack. She lost count as she teetered over the edge between pleasure and pain and barely stopped herself from screaming "More!" If Sloan knew how much she was enjoying this, he might take things further than she was ready to go.

Maybe not. Maybe he can tell . . .

Before she could finish the thought, they picked her up and dumped her on the bed. Her legs were spread. A tongue plunged into her pussy while fingers held it open. Teeth tugged at a nipple. The sheets rubbed against her butt as she squirmed, and the burning flesh of her bottom seemed to ignite. The fiery sensation billowed into her core, setting off countless bursts of pure ecstasy. Her body wrenched and twisted and bucked, completely out of control. Wave after blazing wave crashed within, and she screamed.

Her body was going to burn up, sizzle out. "Oh, God!"

A hand covered her mouth while the tongue inside her prodded her folds, causing the last spasms to linger.

"Shh." Max kissed her cheeks, moved his hand, and kissed her lips, his own damp with the tears she hadn't felt spill. "That was beautiful, baby. Do you have any idea how happy it makes me to know we can do that to you?"

Slowly, so slowly she knew one touch would set her off again, she came down from the mind-numbing high. She gave Max a tremulous smile. The intensity had almost been more than she could handle, but his words made her feel solid. Whole.

The sound of a wrapper ripping tossed her off balance. They weren't done with her. They might never be done with her. Which was perfect. She didn't want this to end.

"Are you sore, sweetie?" Sloan knelt on the bed beside her and pulled her up on her knees, facing him. His hands petted her bottom, and the slight sting turned sharp. He chuckled when she hissed. "And I don't mean here."

"Well that's the only place I'm sore, you jerk." A pinch on one butt cheek made her glare at Max who'd gotten up on his knees behind her. "Hey!"

"Answer him, doll. He's trying to be nice."

"*Nice?*" Her lips parted as Sloan slipped between her thighs, grazing her clit before he went still. His dick felt hot and swollen between her quivering thighs. She reached for him, needing to be filled.

"Nice." Little creases formed around Sloan's eyes as he smirked. "Next time, I'll use my belt."

Her breath hitched. *No! Or maybe yes?*

At that moment, she knew she'd enjoy anything he chose to do to her. Which was a little scary. What he chose to do could hurt.

"Keep your hands at your sides, lover. I won't have you rushing me." Sloan's brow lifted when she wrapped a hand around his dick. "Max?"

Her wrists were pulled behind her. She tried to twist free. But she couldn't. She was at their mercy. Her whole body shook violently.

"Say the word and we'll leave you alone." Max nipped her ear, then used his knees to spread her thighs wide as Sloan swirled just the tip of himself over and around the part of her that desperately wanted him inside. "Or say nothing and . . ."

Sloan filled her with one smooth thrust.

"We'll give you what you need."

Held up on her knees, with her thighs spread, trapped against

Max's solid chest, Oriana could do nothing but let Sloan take her at his own pace. And that pace was so slow she felt like she would melt. With each glide in, he would grind deep and then slide out. She tried to twist her hips, and he grabbed them. Her core clamped around him, and she used the rhythmic tighten-and-release within to match his steady motions. She had to make sure he enjoyed it too.

And judging by the tense lines around his mouth, his restraint caused him pain. Fast and hard would be better. If only she could make him let go.

"Dominik was right; you're a stubborn little thing." Sloan grunted and slammed in hard. Then stopped. "Max."

The grip around her wrists loosened a little, then something slid around them. She looked over her shoulder, and her lips parted as she watched Max cinch a belt around her wrists.

"Sorry, my fur cuffs are locked in the toy box." Max kissed her shoulder, then pushed her head down so her brow was pressed against Sloan's chest. "Don't twist around too much; the leather will cut into your skin."

"Or do." Sloan raked his fingers into her hair and tilted her head back. "You should get used to having our mark on you."

His mouth covered hers, and he swallowed her shallow cry. She could already feel the belt chafing her flesh, and she imagined where—and *how*—they might mark her next time. Strangely enough, she liked the idea of having a reminder of their time together with her even when they were apart. A little twisted, but she wouldn't lie to herself. She wanted it. Wanted whatever they would give her.

Something cool and wet squirted into her from behind. It drizzled down her thighs, and Max spread it between her cheeks. She heard the distinct sound of him donning a condom.

A finger, then two, entered her and withdrew. Something bigger took their place.

"She's ready."

"Yes!" She tugged at the restraints, whimpering when Sloan slipped out of her. "Please, I'm—Ah!"

Both men drove into her at once.

"Mmm." Oriana let her weight fall on Sloan as they buried themselves inside her. Now, she thought, they would pound and release until they all collapsed.

Instead, they pressed against her, hardly moving at all.

Max curved his hand under her chin and forced her to face the other side of the room. "Look at that, love."

The image in the mirror above the dresser showed her a scene far beyond anything she could have ever imagined. Bodies aligned in a tight embrace, flesh glowing in the dim light, limbs tangled. Erotic and beautiful.

"There will be times when we just fuck you, Oriana." Sloan tugged her hair and gave her a wolfish grin. Then he loosened his grip and smoothed the strands over her shoulders. "But this time, we want to give you more. Give you something I don't think you've ever had."

He took her face between his hands and kissed her. Max ran his hands up her sides and worked them between her and Sloan. Molding her breasts in his palms, he slipped from her, then entered her again with shallow thrusts. Sloan circled his hips so his dick stirred. His balls bumped her thighs, slick with moisture.

Flames lapped over her like oil lit on a calm pool of water, an intense spill of blue and white, spreading fast and smooth.

"Come, babe." Max drove in deep and stayed there as Sloan dragged out and stroked in. "Now."

Sloan groaned and arched, hitting something in her core that made her fall into that fiery pool, drowning in heat. Max grunted and dropped his forehead on her shoulder. In the throes of ecstasy, sight and sound faded, but she didn't miss the words.

"I love you."

The words came strong and clear from Max. And in his passionate daze, she could have sworn she saw Sloan's lips form them, too.

Chapter Eighteen

D ominik had planned to call it an early night, but the lingering excitement from the game and—something else—had him feeling restless. Lying in his room listening to moans and groans muffled by walls that seemed to have become paper-thin—yeah, his firm resolve to leave the cozy threesome had taken a serious beating. So he donned his leathers and headed to the club. The fifteen-minute drive gave him some perspective. A detached scene with a sub who knew exactly what she wanted—and didn't want—from him would help him get a grip.

The club was walking distance from the forum in an area where loud music and people coming and going in fetish wear wouldn't disturb the neighbors. At the door, Wayne, one of the club's beefy bouncers, tipped his leather cap in acknowledgement and stepped aside to let Dominik pass.

Avenged Sevenfold's "Nightmare" kicked off with a trilling drum beat, adding to the already hard-core atmosphere. People who wanted a little slap and tickle went elsewhere to indulge their kinks. The Blades & Ice club catered to a fair number of sadists, which meant edge play was pretty much the norm. Dominik didn't get off on serious pain or making a sub bleed, but it didn't bother him as long as it was consensual.

As if Dean would put up with anything less. As he passed, a dungeon monitor stopped by a scene where a Domme was piercing her sub's dick. After making sure she was taking all the necessary precautions, he moved on, walking a bit stiffly, as though feeling sympathy pain.

Snap! A shudder ran through Dominik as the slick cut of a cane sang above the music and a crescendo of screams. He took a seat at the bar, ordering a double CC on the rocks and swiveled on the stool to watch Dean decorate the already flush red asses of three bound subs with a thin, looped length of birch.

One of the subs turned her head and whined something to Dean.

Dean threw his head back and roared out a laugh. "You want more, precious? Well isn't that a shame. Tim!"

Tim stepped from the shadow of the open doorway of a playroom where he'd likely been watching a scene. "Yeah?"

"Unstrap your wife." Dean gestured to the side of the roped-off area. "She can switch with you all she wants, but if she wants me to top her, she either fully submits, or we don't play. I want her kneeling over there. She can watch the good girls have fun."

Making a face, Tim undid his wife's restraints and helped her off the sawhorse. "Thanks, bro. I'm looking forward to the rest of the night."

Tim's wife, Madeline, patted his cheek before moving gracefully to take her place as instructed. "I won't take it out on you, love. This is all on me—I should know better."

"Yes, you should." Dean rested his cane on his shoulder and gave her a dark look. "Now, if you don't mind, you're interrupting my scene. You know what that means, don't you?"

"Yes, sir." Madeline settled on her knees and ducked her head to hide a smile. "Discipline. Will it be a spanking or a big butt plug?"

"Neither, smart ass." Head cocked to one side, Dean seemed to consider for a moment. Then his lips curved into a positively evil smile. "I have a new fucking machine I'd like you to try out, my pretty little guinea pig."

Madeline paled and peered up at Dean with wide eyes. "Here?"

"Where else? Club discipline takes place at the club," Dean said, sounding completely unaffected by her reaction. But when she didn't protest, he added in a significantly warmer tone. "Being put on display isn't your thing, but if you do well, I'll reward you. How does a private session between you, me, and my bullwhip sound?"

Soft pink spread over Madeline's cheeks. "Wonderful, sir."

Dominik shook his head and smiled. Both Tim and Madeline were masochists and switches. He marveled at the way they managed to indulge their kinks. Tim trusted his brother to give Madeline what she needed without going too far. Under Dean's hands, she could reach the ecstasy of pain without penetration. It was a strangely amicable arrangement.

"Don't think I don't see you there, Mason," Dean called out as he unzipped his leathers and donned a condom. "As you may have noticed, I've got my hands full. Care to join me?"

Why not? Dominik drained his glass and pushed off the stool. Crossing the room in three long strides, he let out a gruff laugh. "I don't know, Dean. You've got her warmed up." He stroked the bowed back of the quivering sub. "But she doesn't know me. Maybe we should acquaint ourselves first?"

"Maybe." Dean drove two fingers into the pussy of the sub in front of him, languorously thrusting in and out as he eyed the sub Dominik petted. "What do you think, Tara?"

"Whatever Master Dean wishes." Tara pressed her face into the leather padding and moaned as Dominik grazed his fingers over the welts on her ass.

"Good answer." Dean chuckled. "Go for it, Mason. Her thighs are still awfully white."

Inclining his head, Dominik strolled over to the wall and chose a studded leather paddle. He returned and held it out in front of Tara. "Will this do?"

"Oh!" She shivered and almost nodded. Her lips dented her bottom lip. "Yes, sir!"

Without warning, Dominik hauled off and smacked her midthigh, just below her glistening wet pussy. She let out a straggled cry, and he hit her again and again until her sobs drowned out the music. Another and she'd come. Or he could deny her and toy with her a little longer. Sink his dick into her and take everything she was more than willing to give.

Only one problem. He wasn't even hard. Any thought of pleasure brought him back to another woman, a woman who would never belong to him alone. A woman who needed him.

Why? He asked himself as he gave Tara one last hard smack with the paddle and watched her buck and scream. As he curved his body over hers and helped her ride out the last waves of her orgasm, his mind took him from the club to Oriana, who was in the care of two other men. Men who he'd trust with his life. But who he couldn't quite trust with her pleasure.

What if they pushed her too far?

Max won't. Max will take care of her.

No doubt about that. Max knew Sloan better than anyone. And he knew Oriana.

But he's not me.

How fucking arrogant was that?

Shortly after having freed and tended to Tara, Dominik sat with Dean at the bar, nursing a beer and making small talk. The unwritten rule of leaving the game at the door limited them to discussing the weather and family.

"Is your mom doing better?" Dean asked, holding his bottle between both hands and leaning forward. "Last I heard, she has diabetes? Is it bad?"

"Not as bad as it could have been. She doesn't take care of herself, and she still bakes like she's feeding a house full of teenage boys." Closing his eyes, he recalled the aroma of his mother's house from when he'd visited her during the holidays. The gingerbread cookie and pumpkin pie scents lingered for days, and he was sure he gained a couple of pounds just thinking of all he'd eaten. "My sister moved closer so she could keep an eye on her. Mom doesn't consider licking the spoon cheating on her diet."

Dean chuckled. "She's a nice lady. You've got to get her to come down for a game soon as she's feeling up to it."

"Will do," Dominik said. "So how's Jami?"

For a second, it looked like Dean might slug him. His grip tightened around the neck of his bottle, and his knuckles went white. Strange reaction, considering his daughter was his pride and joy and usually his favorite subject.

"Wonderful," Dean said dryly as he released his bottle and sat back. "She dyed her hair purple and got a tattoo."

Damn. "Isn't she seventeen?"

"Nope. Eighteen. For all of a week." Using his fingers to massage the center of his brow, Dean let out a gruff, aggravated sound. "Daughters will kill a man. Never have any." He went still and looked up. "Speaking of daughters, what have you been doing with Delgado's?"

"No shop talk, Dean."

"How is you and half the team fucking the boss's daughter shop talk?"

"Since I consider you a friend, I won't knock your teeth down your throat for talking about her like that." Dominik drained his beer and slammed the bottle on the bar as he stood. "This time."

"Don't go there, Mason." Eyes narrowed, Dean studied Dominik's face. "How much do you think you guys can get away with?"

Despite the rage boiling up within, Dominik walked out without another word. All the way home, all he could think about was what Oriana's plan was doing to her reputation. Maybe she didn't care, but—damn it, the idea of anyone thinking badly of her made him sick.

The scent of maple syrup and vanilla hit him when he stepped into the house. He glanced at the clock on the wall as he made his way down the hall. It was 4:00 a.m. Who the hell was baking at this hour?

"Ouch!"

Dominik hurried into the kitchen and frowned at Oriana's back as she pulled a cookie tray from the oven with a dish cloth, not letting it go even though the cloth obviously wasn't protecting her.

"What the hell do you think you're doing?" he demanded as he snatched the tray and slammed it on the stove. "We have oven mitts."

"Shh!" She glanced toward the hall and bunched the bottom of her kitten-patterned nightgown in her fists. "Everyone's sleeping and I couldn't find them."

"I don't care—" He dragged her to the sink and ran the cold water over her red fingertips. "Why are you up?"

"Couldn't sleep after . . ." She blushed. "I don't cook much, but I enjoy baking cookies. I figured the guys would enjoy them in the morning."

"Hmm." Dominik tried to keep looking pissed, but the cookies smelled delicious. "Mind if I sneak one?"

"Are you still mad at me?"

"I was never mad." He shut off the water and then drew her wet fingers to his lips. "I just don't like seeing you get hurt."

She smiled. "I know the feeling. How's your arm?"

"Not bad. Maybe you can take a look since you're up?"

Her smile broadened, lighting up her whole face. "Now you definitely get a cookie." She touched his cheek. "Thank you for letting me take care of you."

He kissed her palm. "Thank me by letting me take care of you."

"Gladly." Nibbling at her bottom lip, she eased away from him and turned to the stove to check the cookies. She picked one up, passed it from hand to hand, then giggled at his arched brow. "They've cooled down a bit. Tell me what you think."

He stuffed the cookie in his mouth, chewed, and groaned as the maple walnut flavor filled his mouth. "What is this?"

"Maple walnut shortbread. My grandmother's recipe." Oriana's eyes became distant. "She taught me how to cook and bake—I inherited all her recipes."

"Wow." He reached around her to snitch another cookie. "My mom would love you. Maybe you two can exchange recipes one day."

"Maybe." She scuffed her slippers on the tiles. "So . . . how about you go get comfortable in the living room? I'll bring some cookies and then fetch the first aid kit."

"Sounds like a plan." He watched her divide the cookies onto two plates, six on one, sixteen on the other. Then he wandered into the living room, shedding his shirt before lounging on the sofa. He picked at his bandage, trying not to think about how much he enjoyed having Oriana around. It was temporary. She'd eventually want to go home. She had a nice-sized place, so Max and Sloan might even move in with her if things went well.

Stop moping, Mason. She's not gone yet.

Key word. *Yet.*

"Troubling thoughts?" Oriana knelt beside him and laughed at his surprised look. "Doms aren't the only ones who can be observant. Want to talk about it?"

"No need." He relaxed as she peeled the bandage from his arm and meticulously cleaned the wound. "We promised to take care of each other. I'm good with that."

"So am I." She wrinkled her nose. "Actually, I'm thinking I may need you more than I thought. I may actually be a nympho!"

His heart stuttered. *I need you.* He laughed as he gave her a one-armed hug. "You're not a nympho. You just finally enjoy sex. Nothing wrong with that."

"Yes, but—"

"But I will make sure neither you nor the boys overdo it." He brushed her hair away from her face and kissed her forehead. "Deal?"

She stayed in that position, breathlessly whispering. "Deal."

And she let him. For the next week, aside from games, she spent most of her time with Max and Sloan, but all it took was a look from Dominik for her to tell them she'd had enough.

They hadn't made love since the first time, but something told him he shouldn't count himself out just yet. The wonderful words she'd spoken reflected in her eyes every time she looked at him.

I need you.

Chapter Nineteen

"**R**oom service!"

Sloan tossed the blanket aside and stood, ready to throttle Vanek. "Can't you knock!"

The curtains were thrown open. Oriana hid under the covers. Max threw an arm over his face and curled into her.

"It's his room." Dominik strolled up to the bed and plopped down, peeling the sheets away from Oriana's face. "How you doing? You gave us quite a scare last night."

Anger flew as Sloan watched Oriana blink and rub her eyes. When she'd passed out during their lovemaking, he and Max had panicked. Max had shouted her name until Dominik burst into the room with Vanek on his heel. Vanek had been as useless as the rest of them, but Dominik woke Oriana, asked her a few questions while she was conscious and told them she was all right. Just overwhelmed and exhausted, nothing serious.

Whatever Dominik said, Sloan couldn't forget the disgust in his expression. Lately, he'd been acting like Sloan and Max were too stupid to take care of Oriana without him. 'Course it didn't help that she blacked out the one night Dominik had stayed out late, but, still, even he couldn't have expected multiple forced orgasms would be too much.

You keep telling yourself that, Callahan.

"I brought you the works." Vanek picked up the tray he'd left on the dresser and set it on Oriana's lap when Dominik helped her sit up. "Mason said you'd need protein and plenty of fluids—"

"Wait." Oriana stared at the food and shook her head. She looked at Sloan. "What happened?"

"You fainted on us." Sloan stole a piece of bacon from her plate and fought to keep his tone light. "Sensory overload. No big deal."

Oriana gaped at him like he'd grown two heads. "No big deal?"

"Oriana, you were physically and emotionally drained. It caught up with you." Dominik rubbed the back of her neck and grinned when she shivered. "You're not used to all this attention. I don't think you've ever got off so hard in your life. We'll have to work on that."

Max propped himself up on his elbow and put his hand on Oriana's knee, stroking down to her ankle and back up. "We've decided to ease off a bit. You scared the hell out of most of us."

"Most?" Oriana nibbled on a piece of toast, eyes drifting shut as Dominik massaged her shoulders.

"I've had a couple of subs pass out on me—before I gained enough experience to prevent it." Dominik used his thumbs to work the corded muscles along her neck. "Why do you think me and Max didn't have sex with you last Friday after everything?"

Sloan blinked. "You didn't?"

"Nope." Max grinned and blew a strand of wavy, blond hair out of his face. "We did a bit of oral, but that doesn't count."

Vanek plopped down on the end of the sofa, sitting in a way that made it obvious all the talk had gotten him hard. "So what we doing today?"

"I thought you were heading home to see your mom." The way Vanek's ears reddened at Sloan's words made all the men laugh. The ribbing about his ritual of calling his mom before every game had lost its effect the season before, months after Vanek blurted it out during his first interview.

Apparently, Oriana's presence changed things. Kid didn't want her to think he was a momma's boy.

"That's next week." Vanek made a face and snatched a piece of bacon out from under Sloan's hand to feed it to Oriana. "I've got other plans for today."

Oriana licked the bacon grease from her lips and took hold of Vanek's wrist to suck the rest from his fingers. "Like what?"

"Enough of that." Dominik chuckled when Oriana frowned at him. "Do you know there's often a penalty for frowning at your Dom?"

"Well, you're not my Dom." Her voice hitched, and her spine went stiff as she handed the tray to Vanek. "So enough with the idle threats."

Max laughed. "She's pushed for so many spankings this week that I'm seriously starting to think she enjoys them. Not a fitting punishment, if you ask me."

"Hmm." Dominik threw his legs over the side of the bed and put his foot down on the sheet Oriana was trying to pry free to cover herself. "Well, I guess I'll have to pick something else out of my arsenal. You seem eager for another taste of submission, bunny—"

"I told you not to call me that." Oriana folded her arms over her chest and scowled at him. "And you said I wasn't ready."

"And, by the way you keep testing me, you're determined to prove that you are."

Sloan sat on the bed beside Max and mirrored his relaxed, cross-legged pose. Dominik was right, she had been pushing. Just the day before, she'd *accidentally* dumped a bowl of cereal into Dominik's lap when he mentioned having swung by Blades & Ice and taking a paddle to a sub. Being a smart girl, she'd no doubt figured out that Dominik was the most dominant of them all, so pushing his buttons would eventually get a reaction.

Just not the one she wanted.

"I need to get my clothes." The whine in Oriana's tone made it clear she knew she wasn't going to like what Dominik had planned. "Give me the sheet so I can—"

"No." Dominik stood and took a step toward her, then another until she skirted back. The wall blocked her retreat. The door was too far.

Her chest rose and fell under her arms in time with her jerky breaths.

"Sit down. I'll get you something to wear."

Dominik walked out without waiting to see if she'd obey. She gave Sloan and Max a sweet, helpless look.

Max patted the bed. "Better do what the man says, honey. Don't think you'll like him taking you over his knee when there's no pleasure involved."

The way her eyes widened and her cheeks turned nice and pink, she liked the idea of Dominik's hands on her ass. But the creases in her brow told Sloan she didn't understand why she liked it.

I'll show you, babe. He licked his bottom lip and watched her perch on the edge of the bed. *Very soon.*

She grabbed a pillow and hugged it to her chest.

When Dominik returned with a dress and some tights, she took them from him and laid them on the bed. Sloan grinned when she shook her head.

"I need a bra. And panties."

"No you don't." Dominik rested his hip on the dresser and crossed his arms. "Consider yourself lucky that I don't want you to get cold. If it was summer, you'd wear just the dress."

"Jerk," Oriana said under her breath. She yelped when Dominik crossed the room and shoved her onto her back. "Hey!"

Dominik folded her legs over her head and gave her a solid smack on the fleshy part of her already red ass.

"You son of a bitch! Let me go or I'm going to—" Another smack and she screamed something incoherent.

"Stop it, Mason!" Vanek shot to his feet and tackled Mason. White-faced, speaking through gritted teeth, he put his hand on Mason's throat and raised his fist. "You hurt her, you bastard."

Sloan grabbed Vanek before the boy could punch his long-time protector. His reaction sobered them all.

How could they have forgotten that he'd been raised by a single woman who'd gotten roughed up by several boyfriends? Sloan and Max might have known Dominik wasn't giving Oriana anything she didn't want, but Vanek saw it as abuse.

And Oriana's reaction didn't help. She dropped to her knees at Dominik's side. "I'm sorry. I didn't mean for this—"

"Don't apologize to him!" Vanek struggled against the arm Sloan barred across his chest. "A woman should never be treated like that!"

Lips parted, Oriana looked up at Vanek. "He wasn't really hurting me." She ran her hand down Dominik's chest, stood, then padded up to Vanek. Still naked, but the vulnerability was gone. "It stung a little, but Dominik was right. I was testing him. I wanted . . ." She shook her head and held out her hand. "Give me your hand, Tyler."

Vanek's shoulders hunched, and he reached out. Oriana guided his hand between her thighs.

"Fuck." Vanek groaned and cupped her pussy, then wrapped an arm around her neck and pulled her against him. "You're so wet."

"Yes." Oriana pulled Vanek's shirt out of his jogging pants and lifted it up. When Vanek let her remove it, she pressed her breasts to his bare chest. "Do you think I'm a freak for enjoying that?"

"No." Vanek stroked her, then lowered her to the bed and bent over her. "But I don't understand."

Heels on the edge of the mattress, Oriana spread her legs and let Vanek pump his fingers into her. She clawed at the sheets until Max grabbed her wrists and held them in one hand.

"Neither do I." Oriana tossed her head from side to side, her hips rising to meet each plunge of Vanek's fingers. "But I won't deny what I need anymore. And I won't let anyone else deny me either."

The light scent of her arousal rose up to Sloan as he watched Vanek fuck her with his fingers. He was hard as hell, but, for the first time, he felt like he understood Max. The way Oriana unleashed her passions turned him on. She hadn't surrendered to Vanek, but she had surrendered to her own desires. No one had forced her to give in to her nature; she'd done that all on her own.

Had to be the hottest thing he'd ever seen.

Chapter Twenty

"Wouldn't think of it." Tyler tugged his pants over his hips with one hand and took the condom Max handed him.

Oriana watched him roll the latex sheath over his dick, wishing he'd hurry. She couldn't understand how she could want this *again*, but it didn't matter. She did, and Tyler would give it to her. Nice and simple.

"So how should I . . . ?" Tyler positioned himself between her thighs, then wrapped his hands around her waist to slide her to the very edge of the bed. "Is Max holding you down enough? I can't beat you like Mason did."

"I don't think I need—" She bit her lip, arching up as Tyler filled her. "This is . . . mmm, Tyler."

"I love hearing you say my name." Tyler hammered into her, his jaw clenched in a smile. "Say it again."

"Very good, Vanek." Dominik knelt behind Tyler, and she felt him take hold of her ankles, spreading her legs apart. "A bit of pain helps, but she needs to give up control more than anything." She watched him push his shoulder against Tyler's thighs, causing him to slam into her harder. "Take it from her."

Suddenly nothing was between her and Dominik. In her mind it was him, deep inside her, taking everything she had to give. She tore her mind away from the image and focused on the man above her. Tyler was safe.

Why?

She gasped as her thighs were pushed farther apart. The answer wouldn't come. Pleasure trapped her in the moment.

Tyler threw back his head and groaned. "I fucking love this, Oriana. Max and Mason holding you down for me. This pussy all mine."

"Ugh!" Oriana rocked in time with each violent thrust. "D— Tyler!"

"Again!" Tyler clamped his hands around her waist and stopped moving when she simply moaned. "Say my name again!"

When she lifted her hips, he drew out.

"No, Tyler!"

"Hold her, Callahan." Tyler swirled the slick tip of his dick through her folds while Sloan put one arm under her hips and the other over her stomach.

When Tyler thrust into her again, she clenched every muscle within, determined to hold him deep inside and milk him until he came.

"No, Oriana." Tyler stopped moving and dropped his hands on either side of her head, sucking in air through his teeth. "I will not come before you do. Stop clenching down on me, or I'll pull out and get you off with my mouth."

"I'll stop!" She whimpered when he slid out. "Please!"

He eased back into her, and her whole body tensed up. The way he dragged in and out of her made the already swollen tissues within sore. The men had been right, her body needed a break. But she would make sure Tyler enjoyed himself first.

"Don't overdo it." Dominik rammed his shoulder into Tyler's ass when he stilled. "We were supposed to leave her alone today. Since you decided to go for it anyway, don't push her too far."

Tyler seized up and bowed his back. She was close, but not close enough to come before he did.

It's okay; I like knowing I can . . .

Sloan reached between her and Vanek and V'd his fingers on either side of her clit. She tugged at her hands but couldn't get them free. The friction of Sloan's fingers rubbing that sensitive little nub jolted like the strike of a thousand tiny lightning bolts. She panted and her movements became as erratic as Tyler's. And Sloan rubbed her a little harder, making quick little circles around her clit, speeding up when Tyler did, almost as though it was a race to see who would come first.

His words confirmed it. "If he comes before you do, Oriana, I'll tie you to the bed and use T.J.'s vibrator on you until I'm absolutely certain you're sated." He kissed her shoulder, then chuckled. "Can't guarantee you'll be able to walk afterward, though, bunny."

"Don't call—" The pulse deep within beat harder, harder. Not hers. The mushroomed head of Tyler's dick seemed to swell even more with each plunge into her smoldering depths. "Tyler, slow down!"

Tyler grunted and buried his sweaty brow in the curve of her neck. "I can't . . . Dominik won't—"

Dominik's laughter filled the air, strong and rich, tingling up her spine and drizzling over her soul. "I bet my Ken Dryden rookie card he comes first."

Cheater! She tried to scowl at Dominik as he continued to ram his shoulder into the back of Tyler's thighs, forcing him to continue his jarring pace. A pace Tyler couldn't continue for long.

"You're on." Sloan pulled his hand out from between her and Tyler and licked the tips of his fingers. "Don't disappoint me, honey."

He dipped his hand back down and slicked his fingers over her clit.

* * * *

A buzzing from the floor distracted Sloan. He glanced over at his jeans on the floor and reached out with his free hand.

"Wanna pass me my cell, Perron?"

Max grinned and reached down without releasing Oriana. He flicked open the phone and held it to Sloan's ear.

"Hello?"

Oriana and Vanek tensed against his hand.

"Is this a bad time?" His father sounded amused. "I can call back."

"Naw, I'm just hanging out with the boys." Thank god it was his father. This wasn't the first time he'd called while Sloan played, and he was good at going along with the game. "What's up?"

"I'm docked for the day. I was hoping you'd come down since your next game's Tuesday."

Groins and thighs clenched around his hand. Vanek cried out. Oriana muffled her screams in the heavy blue comforter rumpled up beside her.

"Love to." Sloan withdrew his hand as it grew slick. He scrubbed it on the sheets. "I want you to meet someone anyway."

"Sounds good. I'll see you then."

The dial tone sounded. Sloan smirked. Poor dad. He had an adventurous streak, but chose to act out on it by sailing the high seas. Investing in the lobster venture his father had spent years saving for kept him a little closer to Digby, but the urge to leave shores far behind overcame the man now and then. Sloan knew his father paid women for the rare pleasure he allowed himself. But it didn't stop Sloan from tempting him. There were a couple of Dommes he'd met who would be perfect for his father.

If he could ever lure his father from his boat long enough.

"Guess we've got a draw," Dominik said to Sloan as he straightened and thumped Vanek on the back.

Sloan gave Oriana a long look. Her eyes widened, and her throat worked as she gulped. He had a feeling she was recalling his threat.

"I guess so." He let out a heavy sigh, then smiled as though he'd just had a fabulous thought.

Max picked up the white sheet folded at the bottom of the bed and wrapped it around Oriana, cuddling her against his side as she shivered. Vanek stumbled away from the bed and almost fell twice while trying to pull up his pants.

"Max, Coach just called. He wants you to . . ." T.J. paused in the doorway and shook his head. "What happened to giving the poor girl the day off?"

"She apparently didn't need it." Sloan pushed off the bed and leaned over Oriana. "I'll go pour you a bath so you can clean up. Then you can come meet my dad."

She grabbed the front of his boxers when he backed away. "Ask me, Sloan."

Needed another lesson, did she? "Oriana, you don't want me to—"

"Stop right there. I'm fine being submissive in bed, but I won't let you boss me around all the time. Not for stuff like this." She released his boxers with a snap and sat back on her heels. The blanket covered her enough that he could focus on her face. On her warm smile.

God, she was gorgeous. He realized he'd rather her come because she chose to anyway. "Will you come with me to Digby to meet my father? You can see his boat, and I'll bring you to the lighthouse and—"

She pressed her fingers to his lips. "Yes. I'd love to."

The tail end of T.J. and Max's conversation wiped the goofy grin off his face.

"He wants to talk to me?" Max bared his teeth in a smile. "Good, 'cause I've got a thing or two to say to him."

"Max, don't." Oriana reached out, but Max rolled out of reach and off the bed, then grabbed his clothes.

In that state of mind, there'd be no talking to him. He didn't even look at her before walking out.

"Shit, I didn't realize he'd act like that." T.J. glanced at Oriana. "I'd go with him, but I promised my daughter—"

"Your daughter . . . how old is she?"

"Just a few years younger than you." T.J.'s lips slanted. "Which I hadn't really thought about until she called."

"Too weird for you?" Oriana gave him a sympathetic smile.

T.J. shrugged, then looked at Dominik. "Wanna make sure he doesn't do anything stupid?"

"Sure." Dominik took a step toward the door, then paused. "You know that little coffee shop around the corner from the forum?"

Oriana nodded.

"When you get back, I wanna take you there . . . if that's okay?"

Master Mason, nicely asking a sub to go out with him. Would wonders never cease?

"I'd love to." By the way she fought not to smile, she'd caught the effort Dominik put into asking and not telling. "But only if I get to choose my own clothes."

"To the coffee shop? Done." Dominik pointed at the clothes he'd given her earlier. "Today you wear these."

When Dominik left to catch up with Max, Oriana stuck out her tongue, giggling when Sloan made a grab for her.

"I'm going to take a quick shower." She evaded him at the last second. "Getting a bit tired of being manhandled."

He crawled across the bed, slowly so she'd think he'd given up. "You're a horrible liar. If you were tired of it, you'd stop tempting us." He lurched forward, hauled her onto the bed, and pulled her under him. "Tell me when you've had enough."

"I've had enough!" She gasped when his fingers grazed her ribs. "Really, Sloan, I need a break."

"You sure?" He nibbled along her jaw, then kissed down her throat. "'Cause I can keep you in this bed all day."

"No, you . . ." Oriana let her words trail off. "I want to meet your father. He sounds great."

Sloan's brow furrowed. He pushed to his feet, then helped her up.

"He is," Sloan said. "But he's nothing like the snobs you're used to."

"The snobs I'm . . ." Oriana threw up her hands and stomped across the room. "I'll have you know, most of the people I hang out with are students, and none of them are snobs." Her chin jutted out. "And neither am I."

When she slammed the door, Sloan winced. Now why the hell had he said that?

So much for having a pleasant day getting better acquainted. He thought of the three-hour drive ahead of them.

It was going to be a long trip.

Chapter Twenty One

"So he said, 'Look, you little punk, if you don't want your brains splattered all over the ice, you'll stay the hell away from my goaltender.'"

Leaning forward, Oriana gave a sharp inhale. "Thornton? From Minnesota? He's what, almost a foot taller than you? Weren't you worried that you'd get creamed?"

Vanek draped his arm across the backseat and toyed with Oriana's hair. "Naw, I knew I could take him."

"So what did you do?"

Sloan couldn't help but grin as Vanek embellished the tale. The tension between him and Oriana had grown slack at some point between Vanek's excited minor league chatter and his colorful retelling of his first days as a pro. The boy made it very hard to stay in a bad mood.

". . . well, then Thornton picked my pocket and shot toward the net. Giroux had him covered, and he didn't have any backup. I could tell he was gonna plow our goaltender—like a revenge thing. So I sped up, overtook him, and rammed into him with a good, solid hip check. Never seen such a big man fly so high. He landed in a heap, and Giroux gloved the puck."

"Nice." Oriana rubbed her hands together, then motioned for him to go on.

"Well, the ref blew the whistle, and Thornton came at me. He dropped his gloves and tore off my helmet. I didn't have time to react before his ham-sized fist was in my face." He paused for effect. "But he didn't get one hit. Mason spun him around and clocked him right between the eyes. One punch. KO. Callahan and Perron had to drag Mason back before he kept hitting the guy. He completely lost it."

"I wish I could have seen that." Oriana ducked her head when Sloan arched a brow at her through the rearview mirror. "I don't mean Dominik losing it. I mean the game. Sounds like good, old-school hockey."

Hell, could a man fall in love with a girl just for sharing his greatest passion? He could almost laugh at the notion, if only he didn't feel something building between them.

Whatever it was, it would go nowhere if he kept acting bipolar around her.

"What Vanek fails to mention is what a cocky rookie he was. And still is." Sloan drummed his fingers in time to the music, which was turned low so as not to drown out conversation. "I don't usually have patience with new kids being that arrogant, but he plays good enough to back up all the bragging."

"It's too bad the Cobras don't have more than one good scoring line. You might be cup contenders." Oriana sighed and fiddled with the buttons on her jacket. "If Nova Scotia had the population, the team would thrive."

"Aw, none of us is really worried about it. If the team goes belly up, we've got the stats to get picked up by a bigger team." Vanek took her hands and kissed her knuckles. "I'd give my left nut to get a contract with the Habs."

"But you'll be separated."

The look on Vanek's face would have been comical, if the fact that the kid had been deluding himself wasn't so freakin' sad. Much as a game might be old-school, the league had taken on the mentality of any big corporation. Players were moved across the board like chess pieces. Playing for the team in the city where you were born was a brief treat rather than a lifetime commitment.

By next season, Sloan would be playing with strangers. And his linemates would become rivals.

Turning off the dirt road onto a gravel one, Sloan gazed up at the quaint log cabin in the center of a semicircle of recently pruned white cedar trees. Movement between the branches caught his eye, and he slowed the car and cut the engine.

"Hey, Oriana." He waved her over. "Come here."

Oriana wiggled between the seats and leaned against the dashboard. "What is it?"

Setting his hand on the small of her back, Sloan pointed. "See that?"

She squinted and moved forward so her face was practically pressed against the windshield. "A deer?" She looked down at him and smiled. "Do you think it will run off if we get out real quietly? I've never been this close to one before."

"You can try." He slid his hand over her butt, loving the snug fit of the tights Dominik had chosen for her, and loving even more that she didn't object to his casual touch.

Actually, she didn't seem to notice as she eased the car door open and moved away from him. He heard the gravel crunch under her shoes and watched the startled buck dash out of sight.

He got out of the car and walked around it to stand at her side. "Maybe next time. They eat the foliage from the cedar trees—my dad had to put gates around these ones when they were saplings to keep the deer from killing them. Actually, if you want to try some deer steak, my dad's probably got some in his freezer."

"Deer steak?" Oriana stared at him like he'd just told her they were going to have puppy tartare. "You eat that?"

How to answer without her thinking he was a monster? He decided he better not tell her he preferred the meat of a deer he'd shot himself. She probably wouldn't take it well.

Thankfully, the door to the cabin opened, distracting her. His father came out, looking like a lumberjack in his red plaid shirt and ragged jeans. Sloan watched Oriana fiddle with the hem of her dress and wondered what the rich girl would think of the most important man in his life. Vanek came out to join them, and Sloan decided to intercept the pair as they approached his father.

"Dad, this is Vanek, the rookie I told you about." He let Vanek shake his father's hand, then pointed to Oriana. "This is Oriana Delgado."

Oriana winced at the emphasis he put on her last name. Then she squared her shoulders and skirted around him. "It's a pleasure to meet you, Mr. Callahan." She took his father's hand and leaned close. "You seem like a nice guy. How did you manage to raise such an uptight kid?"

Sloan's jaw dropped.

His father laughed. "My son's got issues with your father—which I'm sure you know. I hope he hasn't given you too much grief about it."

"Oh, he makes sure I pay for the sins of my father." Oriana's lips quirked. "But I'm dealing."

"Good for you." His father's ruddy cheeks crinkled as he looked Oriana over. "Well now, that outfit's got to go. Me and my buddies planned a game for Sloan's visit. Do you play?"

"Not since I was a kid." Oriana shoved her hands in the pockets of her jacket. "But I'd love to, sir. Are there going to be other girls?"

"Of course." His father hooked Oriana's arm with his own. "And I have a feeling you'll fit right in. But don't call me sir. My name's Jim."

They disappeared into the cabin. Sloan leaned on the hood of the car and pulled a pack of cigarettes from the inner pocket of his open sports jacket. He didn't smoke often because he needed his lungs clean for speed on the ice, but he needed to steady his nerves.

Vanek held out his hand, and Sloan passed him a cigarette. Not the time for a lecture, and he didn't have it in him to play hypocrite.

"If you were worried about how she'd act around your dad—" Vanek took the Bic lighter Sloan handed him and flicked it. The slight breeze forced him to cup his hand around the flame "—why'd you bring her?"

"Last time my dad docked, he asked me why I don't introduce him to the 'special' ladies in my life." Sloan sucked at his cigarette and shrugged. "Figured it was about time I did."

Vanek pushed up onto the hood of the car and hunched over. "I think my mom would like her. Do you think I should introduce them?"

Oh, boy, this could get awkward. After a few hot nights, Oriana was being passed around for the dreaded "meet the parents" thing. Only Max really had the right, but it was easy to forget. Oriana was just as affectionate with him and Vanek as she was with Max. And then there was Dominik.

T.J. was the only one who could really be considered a one-night stand. And he hadn't even fucked the girl.

But had any of them really? Sloan had a hard time pinning the crude word on what had passed between them. He had made love to her. The inevitable aftereffects were creeping up on him.

When Oriana came back out with his father, the "aftereffects" cracked him upside the head.

Dressed in clothes his packrat dad had kept since Sloan was a teen, Oriana was transformed. Snug black Levis, the jersey from his days playing for the Hamilton Bulldogs, her hair up in a simple jaunty ponytail, Oriana looked young and vibrant. A pair of his old hockey skates slung over her shoulder, she hopped in place and giggled when his father poked her in the ribs, motioning for her to go on while he locked the door.

She tripped on the last step, and the skates fell off her shoulder. Sloan lunged to catch her. Vanek was a step ahead of him. He watched the boy twirl her around. They fell onto the grass, and Vanek bent to kiss her.

"Well, now." His father joined him and arched a brow at the cigarette. He smiled when Sloan dropped it and ground the cherry into the gravel with the heel of his shoe. "I expected to meet your sweetheart, not your boy's."

"It's . . ." Sloan shook his head and combed his fingers through his hair. "Complicated."

"I can see that." Dark green eyes fixed on his face, as all-knowing as they'd always been. "But you don't like things simple. You planning to make a bid for her?"

Seeing her like that with Vanek, all playful, after seeing her bond with Max and her intensity with Mason, despite the fact that they'd been platonic all week, he almost put himself out of the running. But the inclination felt wrong.

He had a place with her. He just had to figure out what it was.

"You two coming, or do you need some privacy?" He went to his open driver's side door and planted a neutral smile on his lips. "'Cause I'm itching to hit the ice."

Oriana scrambled to her feet. "We're coming. I've got some moves to show you, Captain."

"I take it you're not planning to play on my team?" Sloan rested his forearms on the hood of the car as she circled to the other side.

"No way." She blew at the bangs that had come loose during her roll in the grass and grinned. "I fully intend to knock you on your ass. Only fair that I'm not the only one sore."

A blush spread over her cheeks when his father chuckled.

"Quite the handful, aren't you, cutie?" He patted her hand and winked. "If I was ten years younger, I'd give these boys a run for their money."

Face red as fall leaves, Oriana ducked into the car.

His dad was right, a handful. But a good one.

And she'd made his father smile. And laugh. Had to admit, it made him love her a little.

Chapter Twenty Two

Skate laces tied tight, Oriana stood and let the other woman dress her in all the necessary protective gear. The pads felt weird, heavy, like wearing armor. She rolled her shoulders to make sure she could move despite the weight.

"Good?" asked the girl, who'd been introduced as Chicklet. She popped the gum she chewed nonstop. "Not too tight?"

Oriana nodded absently, then glanced at the other three women in the locker room. They had their backs to her and were whispering.

"They don't seem happy that I'm playing."

Chicklet snorted. "They're thrilled. They just won't show it because you're the opponent. Once your name was picked for the red team, the head games started. Don't let it get to you."

Ah. One of the girls looked over, and Oriana gave her the snobby look she usually reserved for pushy reporters.

"That's the spirit!" Chicklet said. After handing Oriana a plain red jersey, she combed the bangs of her short brown hair away from her face, then put on her huge goalie mask. "Ready?"

"Yep." Jersey on, stick in one hand, helmet hanging from the other, Oriana wobbled toward the door. "I might be a little rusty, but I promise, nothing gets to the net unless I'm glued to the boards."

"Good enough." Chicklet swung out her stick, smacking Oriana's padded butt with the blade. Oriana let out a muffled shriek and Chicklet laughed. "Guess I can figure out why Sloan likes you so much. You're into that 'chain 'em and beat 'em stuff.'"

"Well . . ." Oriana already felt like she was boiling inside all the equipment; flushing didn't help. "I don't—"

Chicklet held up one gloved hand. "Just an observation, kid. I'm bisexual, so I don't presume to judge."

Looking to be in her late thirties, Chicklet displayed a confidence Oriana wished she could emulate. The bold proclamation should have shocked her, but, considering what had passed between her and the men over the past week, she found herself taking it in stride.

The only thing that surprised her was what Chicklet knew about Sloan. She'd gotten the impression that he kept that part of his life private.

"So, you and Sloan, have you been friends long?" She stopped halfway down the long hallway and braced her hands against the gray stucco wall, rolling her ankles in the skates to relieve some of the strain.

"Ever since he moved his dad here five years ago. His dad served in the Navy for twenty years, making Sloan your typical military brat. He's lived all over the place. The only constant was hockey—his dad made sure he was on a team, no matter where he was deployed. That's how we met. Even though Sloan had been playing in the minors since he was seventeen, his father was so used to asking around for local teams that he did it automatically before he'd even settled in. People in town thought he was nuts—why the hell would Sloan Callahan want to play with us? But Jim's such a nice guy, I told him to come watch us play a few times, see if his son would be interested. Found out the old guy was a pretty decent player himself." Chicklet stuck her stick between her wide, black leg pads, and rested her chin on top of the handle. "We get together every weekend. Took a few months before Sloan had the time to visit. By then, everyone was excited. We'd all heard so much about Sloan, it was like we knew him. A bunch of guys organized a barbeque as a kind of 'welcome to the neighborhood.'"

Oriana pushed away from the wall and rocked on her skates. "What happened?"

"Sloan didn't show up." Chicklet grinned, her puckish face small behind the white cage of her mask. She chomped harder on her gum. "People were pissed. They decided he was a jerk, but they acted all sweet around him whenever they saw him after 'cause they didn't want to upset Jim. I didn't feel the same—I knew the man could take it. They came into my bar one night, and I flat out ignored Sloan."

"What did he do?" Oriana asked, leaning so far forward she almost fell over. Sloan wasn't the kind of guy who would react well to any kind of disrespect. And Chicklet didn't seem like the type of woman who would let him spank her for it. "He must have been mad."

Chicklet laughed. "He sure was. He cornered me at the bar and asked me what my problem was. So I told him. 'You ain't better than us,' I said." Her chewing slowed. "He nodded, then said, real quiet like, 'I know.' So I asked him why he didn't show up. Apparently, he doesn't like crowds. Can you believe that? Famous hockey player like him."

Didn't seem to make sense. Sloan obviously wasn't shy—he dealt with the press just fine. Something about Chicklet's tone told her there was more to it.

But what?

"He deals with crowds almost every day during the season," Oriana said, thinking out loud. "Never seems to bother him."

"Nope." Chicklet's teeth flashed, then disappeared as she blew a big pink bubble. "I don't think it does."

"Then . . ." Oriana looked down the hall, listening to the faint sound of music coming from the arena, thinking back on the log cabin with boxes full of Sloan's things stacked up in the attic. Of the room Jim showed her, Sloan's room. "This is the first real home Sloan's ever had."

"Cute and smart." Chicklet popped her gum. "Sloan wanted normal here. He knew he couldn't have it, but the big fuss his first day threw him off. He felt like he had no control."

Oriana traced her upper lip with her tongue. "I can see that being a problem."

"You don't know the half of it. Sloan's got violent tendencies he works very hard to restrain. He uses fighting on the ice, and rough stuff in the clubs, as an outlet," Chicklet said. "He won't put himself in situations where he might lose his cool. He wasn't feeling right about things, so he stayed away."

The door at the end of the hall opened, and the ruckus from the arena blasted into the hall like big speakers turned full blast. The fresh scent of new ice drifted in, followed by the overpowering aroma of popcorn and cheap beer. A man in a red jersey propped the door open with his stick.

"Coming?" he asked.

Not yet! Oriana hooked her gloved hand around Chicklet's arm before she could step away. Chicklet frowned the same way Dominik did when she got grabby. She let her hand fall. "Sloan . . . told you all this?"

Chicklet blew at her own face as though to cool herself off, then nodded. "Yes, but it's not like you think. Sloan's not my type—I like pretty boys that let me dress them up. But I knew how to get Sloan what he needed."

Sweaty fist clenched in her gloves, Oriana turned her head to dry her upper lip on the sleeve of her jersey. "Someone who likes pain?"

"Loves it."

"Is she here?"

"Number seven, Lindsey Moore." Chicklet arched a brow. "Why?"

"No reason." With a slight shake of her head, she started down the hall. Between the layers of pads, the wool socks, the humongous gloves with the strange stink of stale pickles—no wonder she was feeling off. A bit dizzy, nothing more. A drink and she'd be fine.

The glaring arena lights reflected off the ice, temporarily blinding her. Then her vision cleared, and all she could see was the stands. Packed with people.

Cameras, she could do. Sitting in a crowded stadium, hell, even kissing Sloan in front of all those people hadn't been so bad. Actually, it had been kind of nice.

But these people were going to watch her struggle to keep up with two pros and people who played once a week. She hadn't even skated since she was thirteen! She was going to make an ass of herself, and they'd all be there to witness her humiliation.

"Skate a few laps to warm up," Chicklet said, propelling her toward the rink. She leaned close, then whispered. "Sloan and Lindsey are already out there—looks like they're getting reacquainted."

True enough. One look and she spotted Sloan, the biggest person on the ice, skating backward while a clunky woman wearing a black jersey with the number 7 plastered on her back, followed. Oriana could tell the only reason the woman looked clunky was because of all the equipment. The graceful way she glided across the ice reminded Oriana of Silver. Every movement was meant to entice. But even Silver wouldn't have looked that good with that bulk.

Sloan's laughter echoed across the cold expanse of the rink like the toll of a massive bell. Oriana bit the tip of her tongue and surged forward, sweeping the pile of pucks off the boards by the red team's benches. They clunked onto the glassy surface like a dozen rubber stones. She grabbed a stick and stepped onto the ice. Her left skate slipped. She toppled to the right. Her arms flailed, and her stick went flying.

The world spun. Her chin struck something solid. Something warm. "Oomf!" Her teeth gouged her tongue and blood filled her mouth. But she hadn't hit the ice. She was still standing.

Firm arms wrapped around her waist and led her closer to the boards. She glanced up and smiled tremulously at the boyish angel face above her.

"You said you could play." Tyler skidded a little ways from her but kept one hand under her elbow. "I thought that meant you could skate too."

"I can, it's just been . . ." At another boom of laughter, she ground her teeth. "A long time."

"Hmm." Tyler slid backward on his skates, then forward, never moving his supportive hand. "Were you any good? If you were, your body will remember."

She blushed and ducked her head. Her helmet felt like a furnace. "I could do some pretty cool spins, and I was fast." Fast enough that she'd made it through the tryouts for the Queens County minor hockey league bantam team. They told her she had skill. She dropped out when her father absently told her women had no business playing the sport. And he didn't respect those who tried.

One of many stupid moves she'd made on a long list while trying to please her father. A list she planned to mentally crumple and burn. Her wild week would mark a fresh start.

If only she could manage it on her own two feet.

"Your body doesn't forget much, sweetheart." Tyler backed her into the boards and pressed against her. "You'll probably be able to recall the feeling of me being deep inside you years from now." His gaze shifted from side to side, then he pressed a quick kiss on her lips. "Not that I won't be giving you constant reminders."

Tyler's words made her feel very old. Only the young leapt into relationships head first and believed things would last. She couldn't see the future as bright and shiny; too much was bound to go wrong.

But she had today—maybe tomorrow. Plenty of time to make some memories.

"Keep that up and I'm gonna think you only want me for one thing." She folded her arms over her chest, slipped, then grabbed the boards with both hands.

"Right now, I do." He put his gloved hand on the small of her back and eased her about a foot away from the boards. "I need you watching my back. We've got about five minutes to get you used to the ice again."

Right then, she didn't think five years would be enough, but after a couple of laps around the rink, she felt secure enough to speed up. The cold air stirred by sheer velocity made her feel more awake and alive than she'd felt in a long time. Tyler kept up without much effort, but she didn't care. She giggled when he reached for her and spun away. Then flew backward, crossed her skates, and spun again.

She'd never make pro, but she was more than competent. An asset to her team. Which was good enough.

"All right, speedy." Tyler caught her arm and swung her around. "Let's see how you stick handle."

He handed her the stick she'd dropped, then plunked down a puck between her skates.

She grinned and stroked the shaft of the stick with her gloved fist. "Seems like you thought my 'stick' handling was just fine."

His jaw nearly hit the ice. Then he grinned and shook his head. "I'm starting to understand why the guys like spanking you so much." He positioned the blade of his stick near hers. "Come on; let's see if you can get away from me."

I don't want to get away from you, she thought, but she tapped the puck, sidestepped, then rammed her shoulder into Tyler's stomach when he lunged for her. He grunted and almost fell over. She took advantage of his fumbling and jetted across the ice, careful to keep the puck centered on the white tape wrapped around her stick blade. She couldn't move as fast as before, but she didn't lose the puck once as she circled the net.

"You go, girl!" Chicklet clanged her stick against the goalpost. "Damn, I'm glad you're wearing red."

Me too. Slowing at center ice, Oriana panted and glanced over at the bench when Tyler called to her. They were about to get started.

Snow sprayed up from the ice and coated her legs. She tripped on her skates, righted herself, then glared up at Sloan.

"Not bad," he said, reaching out to smooth a sweaty strand of hair off her cheek with his thick, gloved finger. "But we're still going to cream you."

"You sure about that, Captain?" She smirked and jutted her chin toward Tyler. "Tyler scored twenty-five goals his rookie year. You haven't managed that in two seasons."

She left Sloan to chew on that little fact and joined her teammates at the bench. Tyler handed her a bottle of purple Gatorade. She took a swig and made a face as the flavor of watered-down Jell-O coated her mouth.

Tyler leaned over the boards as she took a seat. "What did you say to him? He hasn't budged since you skated away."

"I reminded him your stats are better than his." Sucking her tongue, she looked around for a bottle of water to get rid of the lingering gag-worthy taste. A man next to her spit a mouthful of red fluid in the general direction of the ice. She hid her mouth with her hand and discretely did the same.

"Ouch." Tyler straightened and smoothed his red jersey. "You've got a mean streak, Oriana. I hope I never get you riled up."

"I'm not . . ." She let her words trail off when the referee blew the whistle. Tyler skated to center ice.

To face Sloan.

The referee dropped the puck. Sloan swiped it out from under Tyler's stick, passed it to his defenseman. And drove into Tyler, knocking the smaller man right off his feet.

Oriana cringed, but Tyler sprang up without missing a beat. He chased Sloan, intercepting a pass just inside the defensive zone. Then he snapped the puck across the ice to the red team's left winger. The man fumbled the pass, but Tyler was already close enough to retrieve the puck. Sloan barreled after him, looking like a bull being taunted by a matador.

Near the boards, Tyler looked up just in time to avoid getting crushed. He scrambled forward, reached back for the puck. Sloan held him at arm's length and kicked the puck loose with his skate. Then he took a shot. The puck completely missed the net.

"Between the pipes, Sloan!" Chicklet called out with a laugh. "Need glasses, old man?"

A defenseman from the red team cruised across the ice to touch the puck. The referee blew the whistle.

"You're up," the deli owner slash coach said from behind Oriana. She glanced over her shoulder, nodded, then climbed over the boards.

The black team had iced the puck, which meant they couldn't make a line change. Oriana took her position and eyed Sloan. Lindsey stood beside him, speaking low. He shook his head and motioned for her to take the face-off. Then he slid into position across from Oriana.

"Ready, babe?" he asked.

Oriana blinked. His question tore her right out of her game mindset. She felt like her skates were glued to the ice. She heard the rap of sticks, the slash of blades, but for a moment, they meant nothing. All she could see was him, coming toward her.

Way too fast. If she didn't do something, he'd skate right around her. The goaltender would be vulnerable. She ground her teeth and pushed off, jabbing her stick awkwardly between his feet. Shoving her elbow into his ribs, she forced him around the back of the net.

He chuckled when her stick finally connected with the puck. "Watch out."

Something hit her side and all the air left her with a loud *Oomph!* Kneeling on the ice, she gulped in air and shook away the buzzing in her head. She looked up just in time to catch number seven skating away.

"Bitch." She hissed before scrambling upright and jetting after the girl. Her blades slashed the ice as she raced across the rink. The girl didn't have the puck, but Oriana didn't care. She hit her with every ounce of strength in her body.

The rink twirled around her. She fell with Lindsey in a tangled heap.

"Interference!" The referee shouted, blasting his whistle before pointing at the penalty box. "Two minutes for the red team."

"That was petty," Sloan said, hauling her to her feet. His frown looked very dark under the shadow of his helmet. "Did you forget that this is just a game?"

Twisting away from him, Oriana retreated toward the penalty box. "I guess I did."

Stuck in the penalty box, Oriana thought about her behavior and couldn't help but be a little disgusted with herself. If any other player from the black team had checked her, she would have considered it part of the game.

"Just a game." Sloan's words played over and over inside her head. She watched him score and hung her head. How stupid to have forgotten that was all this was. Not just on the ice. The entire week had been one big game, a bit of lusty, grownup fun. And if she started acting all jealous, the game would end that much sooner.

She wasn't ready for that. Not yet. So she'd better smarten up.

The part of *Slap Shot* that she'd quoted to Tyler came back to her. Go to the box and feel shame. Yep, she could definitely relate.

When she got free, she returned to her defensive role and tried to make up for costing her team a goal. She managed to block a shot and make a few decent passes, but things still didn't feel right.

She approached Sloan during the fifteen-minute break. Shuffling her feet, she did her best to keep her eyes on his face as he turned from Lindsey and arched a brow at her.

"Yes?" he asked after a long silence.

"I'm sorry." She glanced at Lindsey and the words lumped up in her throat. "Really, going after you like that was uncalled for."

Lindsey shrugged and smoothed her stringy blond hair into a fresh ponytail. "It's all right. Emotions get real ramped up during a game." She gave Sloan a sly smile. "Right, Sir?"

Sloan's pressed his lips together, his eyes trailing over Lindsey. "Sometimes." He shook his head slowly, then tipped the water bottle in his hand to his lips. Capping the bottle, he looked at Oriana again as though surprised that she hadn't left yet. "Was that all?"

"Yeah." Oriana tripped backward, feeling like he'd just given her a good, hard shove. "See you on the ice."

Her eyes burned as she made her way to the locker room. Chicklet met her at the door. The tight, irritated look on her face vanished the second she stepped up to Oriana.

"What's wrong?"

"Nothing." Oriana tried to step around her, then sighed when Chicklet barred her arm across the doorway. She rolled her eyes and crossed her arms over her chest. "I took things too seriously. I know better now. It's not a big deal."

"Why do I have a feeling you're not talking about the game?" Chicklet sighed when she shrugged and took her arm. She shoved the locker room door open. "Everyone out. Us girls need to talk."

The men filed out of the room. Tyler paused beside Oriana and shucked her helmet off her forehead.

"You okay?" He frowned at her nod. "Doesn't look like you are. If you're not enjoying yourself, we can leave."

She forced a thin smile to her lips. "I'm enjoying myself. Honestly."

Not at the moment, but she would—as soon as she put a lock on her irrational emotions.

"Fine, but you better tell me if something's up," Tyler said.

"I will."

He hesitated, then cuffed her chin gently with the gritty knuckles of his stinky glove. "And don't worry about that goal. I've got this."

"I know you do." She bit her lip and decided to let him believe the score bothered her. "I just wish I hadn't taken such a stupid penalty."

His relief was obvious. He grinned and leaned in for a kiss. "I take them all the time—not as much as I used to, but still, I get wanting to retaliate." He slid his lips across her cheek and whispered in her ear. "Felt good though, right?"

That made her smile. "Actually, it did."

"Good." He pressed a soft kiss on her cheek and stepped back. "I'll let you girls talk."

The second the door to the locker room closed, Chicklet dragged her to the benches between the lockers and forced her to sit.

"Now talk." She put her hands on her hips, looking lopsided with her huge goalie gloves and lumpy pads. She continued before Oriana could say a word. "Please tell me this isn't because of what I said about Sloan and Lindsey. I just wanted to get you emotionally invested in the game."

Oh, that's just nasty. Oriana stared at Chicklet, then burst out laughing. "Well it worked—a little too well actually."

Chicklet dropped her hands to her sides and slumped onto the bench. "Shit, kid, I didn't mean—you gotta know he's not really into that twit. She was a good time."

"So was I."

And there it was. She'd finally said it. She'd been a good time for Sloan and all the other men.

They were a good time for me, too. She kept her lips fixed in a smile that felt plastered to her face. "Actually, the whole thing with Sloan and Tyler and . . ." The smile twisted when Chicklet's eyes widened. Maybe she shouldn't tell her *everything.* "Well, it was kind of a rebound. I'd just found out my boyfriend cheated on me."

Sounded so reasonable. If she didn't know better, she might have believed her own lies.

Thankfully, Chicklet did. "I see. I'm a little surprised Sloan would bring a girl he wasn't serious about to meet his dad, but what do I know?"

The locker room door swung open. The referee grinned at them. "Break's over!"

Oriana stood and took a deep breath. The talk hadn't changed much, but she did feel a little better. Even if she'd portrayed herself as a slut, at least she didn't seem quite so pathetic.

Really, getting hung up over a guy after a gang bang. She chewed hard on her bottom lip to hold back the hysterical laughter that bubbled up inside. *Silver would find that pretty damn funny.*

Chicklet followed her to the door. "So—if you don't mind me asking—what exactly are you and Sloan to one another?"

She didn't mind the question at all. Saying it out loud would reaffirm what she already knew. "Friends."

Fuck friends. She added to herself. *Because that's what Max needs us to be.*

A tight ache settled in her chest, and she inhaled deep to loosen it. Once she got back to the benches, she grabbed a bottle of water and gulped the whole thing down, but that didn't help either. She just missed Max. The feeling would go away as soon as she saw him again.

But every time Sloan passed her on the ice, the ache got a little worse. Like she'd swallowed something big and hard whole. And was trying to swallow more.

Chapter Twenty Three

hird period. The teams were tied. Tyler scored on a soft shot. Sixteen seconds later, one of the high school players deked Sloan and beat the goaltender stick side.

Sloan usually hated playing here. He refused to ruin the rare games he played in his father's adopted home town by complaining, but he considered performing for the locals about as fun as having his jaw wired shut. The people on the ice didn't play; they watched him in awe while circling the rink at a pathetically slow pace. He didn't see the point.

Today was different. Oriana's presence helped them relax, and Tyler's enthusiasm spurred the red team to attack with no holds barred. Which forced the black team to strike back. Sloan almost felt like he was playing a real game.

A quick change put Oriana on the ice just as he crossed the red line. He grinned as she swept her stick from side to side to cover the passing lanes. The hard line of her delicate jaw told him she'd do everything in her power to keep him from breaching her defense of the red's zone. Swishing his stick through the water still coating the ice after hasty repairs, easily keeping the puck on the blade, he slowed and looked her over.

"You really think you can stop me, Oriana?" He let her get close enough to touch the puck, then spun smoothly away when she jabbed at the rubber disk with her stick. "You might as well give up; you can't win."

"Enough with the head games, Sloan. I'm not impressed or intimidated." Oriana widened her stance, retreating in pace with his advance. "Just make your move."

"All right." He glanced to the left and careened a pass to the plumber playing forward. "How's that?"

Oriana scowled, then turned to chase the man with the puck. Sloan watched her dive to block the shot and winced. The girl was going to be sore after the game.

The plumber saucered the puck over her. Chicklet snapped it out of the air and poke-checked the plumber when he charged the net.

The plumber spiraled out of control and hit the post. Sloan paused for a second to make sure the man wasn't seriously hurt, then turned to Oriana.

"Look at you." He slid up to her side, laughing when she swiped a glove hand down her soaked side. "You're all wet, babe. Doesn't take much, does it?"

Her cheeks reddened and she fisted her hands at her sides. Breathing hard, she blinked fast, probably trying to come up with a clever come-back. "Fuck you, Sloan."

Oh, you can do better than that. He chuckled. "Not here. We'd shock the locals."

"Oh, you . . . !" She let out a muffled screech, her narrowed eyes tearing. "Right now, you are the last person in the world I'd even consider sleeping with. And I've got four other guys perfectly willing to give me anything I want. Consider that before you say anything else."

Better. Much better. He nodded and watched her skate to the reds' bench. She didn't like what he had to say? Fine. He'd give her exactly what she'd asked for. Might not be what she really wanted, but she'd learn.

Back on his own bench, Sloan took off his helmet and emptied a bottle of water over his head. The arena felt like a sauna, which explained why the ice was still wet. The weather in the spring often made for unstable conditions. During a game that actually mattered, he didn't let that affect his play, but here, he'd taken care not to give his all and risk an injury. He eyed Tyler, zipping across the ice at breakneck speed and decided he should take the boy aside and remind him a win here wasn't worth his career.

Lindsey leaned over and nudged him with her elbow. "I don't know why you brought her here."

Sloan shrugged and reached for another bottle of water, not in the mood to talk, hoping Lindsey would catch on.

But she didn't.

"I mean, really, look at her!" Lindsey's nostrils flared. "She's been all over that kid since she got here! They're not dating, are they?" When Sloan didn't answer, she made a gagging sound. "That's just gross."

"Why?" He glanced over at the red team's bench. Shift over, Tyler shuffled past the other players and took a seat at Oriana's side. He pressed against her, his cheap, borrowed helmet pushing hers almost off her head as their brows touched. Sounded sappy as hell, but they looked kind of cute together. He shook his head when Tyler slipped his hand under Oriana's jersey and she giggled. Didn't the boy know there was no tickling in hockey?

"He's what, eighteen? She's way too old for him."

What the hell was Lindsey going on about? "He's twenty-one. There's only three years between them. It's not like she's cradle-robbing."

"It's a fact that women mature faster than men," Lindsey said, as though his statement was based on ignorance. "So those three years are more like ten."

"That's the stupidest thing I've ever heard." Sloan chuckled and shook his head. "You don't seriously believe that, do you?"

"Not really." She gave him a sheepish grin, then ducked her head. "That's not what's bugging me, to tell you the truth." She lowered her voice, glancing at the rest of the bench to make sure no one was listening. "When she's not groping the kid, she's staring at you. All the girls were whispering about it in the locker room. Is she one of those trashy puck bunnies who chases pro-hockey dick?"

Sloan crushed the bottle in his fist. "No, she's not."

"Well, she certainly acts like one."

Without saying a word, Sloan stood, then vaulted over the boards. He tried to immerse himself in the game, but no matter how fast he skated, he couldn't escape Lindsey's words. That anyone had such a low opinion of Oriana had him seeing red.

How could they keep this up without everyone thinking the same? Should it matter? Fine, she'd started all this with the intention of blackmailing her father, but things were different now. What would happen in the long run, he didn't know, but one thing was certain. He'd make sure Oriana never regretted what had passed between them.

As he calmed, his rage dropped from almost-boiling-over to a manageable simmer. His control was still a little off, but, so long as he wasn't pushed too far, he'd be fine. No one would get hurt.

"No smart-assed remarks now, Sloan?" Oriana's smoldering, whiskey eyes seemed to glow behind her visor. "Figure out that they won't get you anywhere?"

Say nothing. He feigned to the left and passed her on the right. His skates slipped, and he slowed until he could feel the steady slice of his blades on ice. He heard Oriana panting as she struggled to keep up with him.

"Come on, tell me how you're going to beat me here, then beat me again when we're alone." She smacked his shin pads with the blade of her stick. "Tell me how much you want to hurt me."

Oh, God, I want to hurt you. But he fixed his sights on the goal. He'd get nowhere with her if he gave in. If she riled him up now, she'd get more than she was ready for.

As he closed in on the net, Chicklet came out to meet him. Amateur mistake. He let the puck skid about a foot away from him, kicked it to the left, then twisted his wrist for a backhand shot.

Pain exploded through his cheek and jaw. White sparks burst in his vision. His control snapped. He closed his eyes, inhaling, exhaling, praying for a few precious seconds to pull himself together.

Oriana's stick clattered to the ice, and she grabbed his arm. "I'm so sorry!"

He jerked away and snarled, "Don't touch me."

"Sloan, please . . ." Her soft, feminine voice filtered through the buzzing in his ears. "You're bleeding; let me see—"

She can't see me like this. She won't understand.

"Back off." When his eyes met hers, she went white. He must look like a monster. He didn't want her scared of him, not here, not like this. But he had no idea how to avoid it. His eyes narrowed when she didn't move. "*Now,* Oriana."

"No." She glared at him as she took hold of his jaw and reached up to compress his bloody lip with her sleeve. "I'm training to be a doctor; you don't really think I'll just leave you like this."

He let himself slide backward out of reach and gave her a cold smile. "Funny, because you weren't so calm when Dominik got hurt. Guess you're right. There are others to cater to your needs. And, like any spoiled brat, you'll lash out at those who don't kowtow to your every whim."

"Sloan . . ." Her tone warned him he was going too far.

But he couldn't stop. His discipline on the ice didn't allow for emotions. His discipline was all that kept him from surrendering to violence like a mindless animal.

Something inside him shut down. He couldn't do this if he cared how she'd react, so he did his best not to. "I said back off. Now!"

"Fine." She licked her lips, nodded jerkily, then swallowed. "That's fine."

Blood spilled over his chin and splattered on the ice. His vision was still a little fuzzy, but the buzzing in his ears was gone. He skated over to the black team's bench and grabbed a towel. The men and women in black jerseys watched him like he had a bomb strapped to his chest and a trigger in his hand.

It took him a few seconds to notice that no one was playing anymore. Everyone either sat or stood perfectly still, on or around the rink. Staring at him.

Blood roared and crashed inside his skull. He clenched his jaw, released.

Relax, relax, relax.

The mantra usually worked, but he couldn't recall ever losing it this bad before. Not since he was very, very young. He'd learned to suppress the anger, the urge to lash out, until an appropriate—and pleasurable—time. But now he couldn't seem to . . .

Fingers snapped in his face. "Sloan, pull yourself together."

He blinked at his father. Cold washed over all the hot rage, leaving him numb.

His father towed him away from the benches, snatched the towel, then slapped it over Sloan's lip. The swollen flesh throbbed. His father kept his voice very low and calm. "What set you off?"

What? His brain didn't seem to be functioning properly. He did his best to answer anyway. "Oriana—"

"Because she cross-checked you?" His father put more pressure on his lip, his usual calm gone. "You don't usually lose your temper with women. I don't like this."

Blinking, Sloan shifted away from his father. "I didn't lose my temper with her. I just needed some space."

"That still doesn't explain why you lost it in the first place. You get sticks in the face all the time."

"It wasn't just the damn cross-check." Sloan felt the eyes of all the people in the arena like hundreds of cold fingers crawling all over his flesh. He had to get out of there. "I was already pissed because—well, Lindsey said something nasty about Oriana. And I didn't like it."

Lame, so fucking lame. He'd gotten all unhinged because of stupidity. He prayed another team didn't find out about this kink in his *impenetrable* armor. They'd expose his weakness, and he'd end up killing someone on the ice.

For some reason, his father smiled. "That's good to hear, Sloan. You'll have to find a better way to deal, but I like where this is going."

Sloan's brow shot up. "You do?"

His father patted his shoulder. "Yes. You've only ever reacted this extreme to people insulting *me*. And not since you were a boy. I never thought you'd let yourself care about anyone, let anyone past all those boundaries you put up, but you have."

"I haven't known the girl that long, Dad."

"So you *don't* care?"

"I didn't say that."

With a smug smile, his father nodded, then gestured toward the benches. "Good, because Oriana's gone."

"What?" Spinning on his blades, Sloan's gaze swept over the benches, then the bleachers. He ground his teeth when he saw, true to his father's words, that Oriana had taken off. Tyler's absence reassured him a little; at least she wouldn't get lost out there alone. But it irked him that she'd had the gall to leave without telling him. "This time, I'm using my fucking belt."

"Don't overdo it, son," his father called after him as he made his way off the ice, doing his damnedest to remain composed. "This is your fault."

Is it? Sloan slammed the red metal arena door against the wall, leaving the sound of the game resuming behind him. She'd cross-checked him in the face, and, somehow, this was his fault? He let out a bitter laugh. *Either way, she's still gonna pay.*

Making quick work of ditching his skates in the locker room and donning his sneakers, Sloan hurried out into the hall. Then huffed out a sigh of relief when he spotted Tyler.

Only Tyler was alone.

Chapter Twenty Four

Under the awning of the Mom-and-Pop-style restaurant, Oriana pressed her watch into the bent old man's hand.

"This watch is sterling silver—an antique." She pointed at the dent-laden, silver pickup. "The For Sale sign says 'Five hundred, negotiable.' You'll get more than that if you pawn the watch."

"I don't doubt you." The old man squinted at the silver band, shaking his head slowly. "But I don't feel right about this. You look upset, honey. Why don't you come in and let me buy you a coffee? Then I'll drive you wherever you want to go."

The soft ocean breeze wafted over her and cooled the sweat-coated flesh under her T-shirt. She'd stopped in the locker room just long enough to shed all the protective gear and ditch Sloan's old skates. She had no doubt Sloan and Tyler would come after her, so she'd stolen out through a side door and kept out of sight when Tyler called for her. She hated worrying him, but she knew he'd bring her back to Sloan. The man was his captain; Tyler wouldn't stand against him.

Or maybe he would, but she didn't want that either. All she wanted was to go home. And the sign in the window of the beaten-up truck gave her the perfect opportunity. She didn't have any money on hand, but she'd entered the restaurant that the truck was parked in front of, figuring her watch would make decent currency. She'd asked around and found the owner. Her luck ended there. The old man was perfectly willing to help her, but not on her terms. Every time she broached the subject of the truck, he hedged as though not sure he wanted to sell it at all.

"Do you have a map?" Oriana asked, doing her best to keep her irritation out of her tone. "I'm pretty good with directions. If you tell me how to get onto the highway, I can manage the rest myself."

The old man's wrinkles crumpled around his eyes and mouth like thin paper. He shivered and glanced at the restaurant. "I do, but—"

"Oh, good. Then it's all settled." She gave him her sweetest smile. "Actually, you're right. I might change my mind about the watch. How about you hold onto it for now, and I'll come back with the money next weekend."

"I suppose—"

"And since I'm so very grateful for your help, I'll pay you double what you're asking." Breath held and fingers crossed, she willed him to say yes. The Dartmouth Cobra cap attached to his belt loop gave her an idea. "And I'll throw in a pair of tickets to a Cobras' game—"

His patchy white eyebrows hopped up to his receding hairline. "Playoff tickets?"

She opened her mouth to tell him the Cobras wouldn't make the playoffs, but she didn't see killing his dreams helping her cause. So she just nodded.

"Can't turn down an offer like that." He gave her a gummy grin, dug into the pocket of his corduroy pants, then handed her a key. "Promise me you'll take care of yourself?"

"I will!" She leaned forward and pressed a soft kiss on his cheek. "Thank you!"

Shortly after, sitting on the cracked plastic seat of the old Chevy pickup, Oriana rested her head on the steering wheel and let relief fill her. Soon, she would be with Max again, safe from Sloan's violent mood swings and his cocky attitude.

Screw Sloan, she thought as she shifted the truck out of park. *Dominik can take his place easy. And Tyler. I'll have to make this up to him . . .*

Her insides felt strange, kind of like a bowl of hot porridge topped with ice cubes. Cozy and warm at the thought of the men who wanted her, cold at the idea of Sloan's absence. She'd hated him ignoring her even more than she hated him laughing at her. But mostly she'd hated how he'd pushed her to lash out.

How he pushed you? The little voice in her head that sounded like her sister laughed at her. *So suddenly you're not responsible for your own actions?*

She tuned out the voice like she tuned out Silver rambling about her latest sexathon. Shifting gears, she eased her foot off the gas and let the truck roll. The scent of stale cigars rose in a draft from the floor of the passenger's side. The cruddy red carpet was covered with ash and big orange burn marks. She made a face and sighed, rolling her window down to air out the humid, stinky cab.

Maybe it's not a town car, but it's my way to get away from Sloan.

"Oriana?"

Slap, slap, slap. She glanced over her shoulder and saw Tyler, running almost alongside the truck's cab. Fast, but not fast enough to catch up if she accelerated.

"Get a lift with Sloan, Tyler!" she called out, putting a bit more weight on the gas pedal. "I'm going home!"

Tyler shook his head and ran faster. She poked her head out the open window. The cool wind slapped her face and stole her breath. Big, fat trees and tiny houses rolled by at a crawl, and Tyler seemed to be running in place. His face blurred as her eyes watered, but she could see that he'd finally stopped running.

Waving his hands frantically over his head, he shouted, "Oriana, hit the brake!"

Oriana faced forward. A large form strode into the middle of the street. She slammed her foot down. On the wrong pedal.

The truck lurched, then jerked to stop when she hit the brakes. She shifted to park and sat still just long enough for all her organs to settle back where they belonged.

Leaning against the hood of the truck, Sloan watched her, his lips in a tight, amused slant.

He's so dead.

"You stupid son of a bitch!" Oriana threw the driver's side door open and stepped up to Sloan, smacking his chest with wild slaps. "I could have killed you! Are you insane?"

"No." Sloan caught her hands and used her own momentum to twist her away from him, facing the truck. He latched onto both of her wrists and held her against the cab as though placing her under arrest. His tone was cold, sharp, like a freshly edged blade on ice. "Are you?"

Violent tremors took over her body as she strained her neck to look into his eyes. They didn't look feral like they had after she'd hit him—they were steady, impassive. Which was somehow much more frightening.

"N-no." She rested her head against the top of the gritty fender.

Her head felt light with fear, both from almost running Sloan over and from being utterly at his mercy. Much more and she'd pass out. "Please—I—I can't breathe. Let me go."

"You sure?" He leaned close and cocked his head as though to better hear her answer.

Am I sure? She inhaled and wrinkled her nose. Gasoline and fish saturated the air. She smelled like an ashtray, and her muscles burned. Part of her wanted to go home, take a long, hot bath, then curl up in bed with a man or two. Another part wanted to stay put and see what Sloan would do.

Too bad she was pissed at him, a little detail she'd almost forgotten. She let her mind go over all the reasons why and worked herself back up to indignant fury.

"I'm very sure," she said. He loosened his grip and she wrenched away from him. Tyler stood by the Chevy's bumper. Close enough to stop Sloan if he snapped. Not that she was scared or anything. "After what you pulled today, I'd much prefer if you keep your hands to yourself."

"Really." His hands fell to his sides, palms out. A classic I-mean-you-no-harm gesture. But the way the muscle in his jaw ticked meant something else entirely. "Would you mind telling me what I did?"

She blinked at him. He had to be kidding. Didn't look like he was, but . . .

His eyes narrowed, and his hands curved, as they would if wrapped around someone's neck.

Shivering, she hiked up her chin and ticked off his transgressions on her fingers. "You were ignorant to me in front of that girl Lindsey; you mocked me, laughed at me, then ignored me. Then you told me to go away. So I did."

"I see." He looked at her hand, then held out his own. "You've snarked at me, been rude, attacked one of my players in a fit of rage, then attacked me in another—"

"I wasn't trying to hit your face."

"But you'll admit you weren't just defending your goalie."

Lips parted, mouth dry, she stared up at him, feeling the platform of her anger crumble around her. She'd blamed him for everything, but she was as much at fault, if not more. Technically,

Sloan talking smack was well within the rules of the game. What she'd done wasn't.

"I hit you because I was frustrated." The smudge of blood at the edge of his lip was glaring evidence of her transgression. She dropped her gaze to his shoes and mumbled, "I hate being ignored."

"Ah." He tipped her chin up with a finger. "I think I understand. Your father ignored you a lot, didn't he?"

She shrugged. "He was busy most of the time—which I could deal with. But when I disappointed him . . ." She tried to turn her head, but his fingers held firm to her jaw. So she let the words spill out while staring at the stark, white scar on his cheek. "He would ignore me for days. He did the same to Silver, and she would throw a fit. She'd break things and swear at him, but nothing worked. He'd have the maid clean everything up and act like she was invisible until she broke down. Then he'd summon her to his office and let her apologize and pick her own punishment."

"And what did you do when he ignored you?" Sloan cupped her jaw and leaned in until she couldn't help but look into his dark eyes. "I can't picture you hitting him."

"I don't hit—well, I didn't until you and Dominik . . ." She paused, her own actions confusing her. Both Sloan and Dominik were capable of pushing her past any sense of self-control. "I would go to his office three times a day. Bring him breakfast, lunch, and supper. Then I'd wait until he finished eating. I'd tell him how sorry I was and watch his face, hoping for a sign that he'd heard me. But . . . nothing in his expression showed that he did. He wouldn't acknowledge me until I gave up."

The admission hurt. Suddenly, it was very clear what her father had been doing. By cutting his daughters off from himself even more than he usually did, he'd assured ultimate surrender. His affection became a coveted prize, and, if they displeased him, they lost it.

"Thank you for telling me, Oriana." Sloan's tender tone pulled her out of the dark, lonely pit she'd fallen into. He kissed her while pulling her into a firm embrace. "Now I know whenever you need to be punished, you also need to be reminded that I still care. I'm sorry I did something to trigger your messed-up childhood."

She let out a shallow laugh. "I didn't have a messed-up

childhood."

"Anyway, that's irrelevant now." He set his hands on the door behind her and nodded at Tyler. "You do need to be punished."

All her morose feelings fled like they wanted no part of his plans. She trembled and put her hands on his forearms, hard as steel bars, trapping her. The crotch of her borrowed jeans dampened, and heat flooded her cheeks.

"I do?" She surveyed the empty street, noting the empty driveways, the houses with dark windows. Dusk, and no one was home. But still . . . "Not *here?*"

"Everyone's still at the arena. We've got a bit of time before the game ends and they all head home." The edge of his lips quirked. "But not much."

In other words, she'd better hurry and accept the punishment, or he'd do it with an audience.

She didn't want to stall, but maybe she could talk him out of punishing her at all? "Why do I need to be punished?"

"You know why." He reached between them and unzipped her jeans. "Now tell me, you don't like to be embarrassed, do you?"

Stupid question. She clenched her thighs when he started pushing her jeans down. "No, I don't."

"Oriana, if you make this difficult, I'm going to strip you and bend you over the hood of the truck. Then I'll go with my original idea of using my belt on your pretty ass. I doubt you'll be able to get dressed before someone shows up."

"I want you to stop." She did. She didn't. She couldn't make up her mind. But she held his wrists to prevent him from going further.

For what seemed like forever, he studied her face. Then he pried her hands from his wrists. "And if I believed you, I would. You're not crazy about doing this outside, but the last thing you want is for me to stop. You'd be very disappointed if I took you at your word."

"No." She groaned and her knees locked, but the muscles in her thighs went slack. He peeled her jeans down. The moisture smeared between her legs cooled as the breeze kicked up.

"Yes." He shoved his hand in his pocket. "I want the truth, Oriana. You know I'm disappointed in you, and you'll do anything to make it up to me, won't you?"

Anything? She watched him pull something out of his pocket. The last time she'd seen him reach into his pocket with a woman at his mercy, he'd taken out a small blade and held it against her throat. Maybe she *was* willing to do anything to make amends.

Anything but that.

She swallowed. "You're not going to use your knife on me, are you?"

He shook his head. "No. Don't take this the wrong way, but I don't trust you enough yet."

Shouldn't the trust be on her end? His hands covered her pussy, and her hips jerked.

"I'll just assume the feeling is mutual."

Mutual? She squirmed as his fingers tapped her clit, creating little spikes of pleasure to zip up in time with the steady tattoo. Then she nodded and let her head fall back. *Oh, yes. Mutual feeling sounds right.*

"You still haven't answered me."

What? She waited for an explanation, but none came. Then she remembered. The truth. He wanted the truth.

"I'll do anything but bleed for you . . ." His fingers stilled, and she whimpered. "Unless . . ."

She'd made him bleed. Shouldn't she let him . . .

"No blood. Not tonight." His fingers slipped in her folds as moisture spilled, and he made a gruff sound in his throat. "Jesus, you tempt me—the way you respond . . ." She peeked at him and the flesh around his eyes crinkled. "Soon. Very, very soon."

"Um, you two are freaking me out." Tyler folded his arms over his chest, his gaze flicking from Sloan's hand on Oriana's crotch to somewhere in the golden horizon. "Is there a reason you wanted me here?"

Sloan nodded. "Do you know what this is?"

Tyler shuffled closer, took one look at whatever Sloan had in his hand, and grinned. "Uh-huh. Those things are fun. My ex-girlfriend use to put one in her pussy before we went out to fancy restaurants. By the time we got home, she'd be so wet—"

"Good, well, I want you to use this on Oriana while we have a little chat." He dropped a shiny, black object into Tyler's palm, and scooted over while Tyler knelt in front of her. "Every time it seems

Game Misconduct

like she's getting close, stop."

"Stop?" Oriana stared at Tyler's hand. She couldn't figure out the purpose of the tiny thing, but since Tyler didn't get off on pain, she wasn't too worried. But why stop?

Both men smiled at her, then carried on their conversation.

"Okay," Tyler said.

"I mean it."

"Gotcha, Captain."

Sloan slid his hand from between her thighs, and Tyler took his place, spreading her pussy lips apart with his fingers. Oriana tried to see what he was doing, but Sloan clamped his hand around her jaw and forced her to look at him.

"Hook your fingers to my belt, honey." He waited until she'd complied before continuing. "If this gets to be too much, tug twice, and everything stops. Understand?"

If what gets to be too much? She licked her lips, not sure whether she should agree or go along with whatever he would do to her. Her brain turned to mush as all her attention fixed on Tyler's prodding fingers. Her thighs quivered as he exposed her clit and pressed something hard against the tip of the exposed nub. Then her entire world started vibrating.

"Ah!" Electric pulses zinged up every nerve. Pleasure assaulted her, and her nipples pebbled in response. "Oh, *yes!*"

"What will you do if it gets to be too much?" Sloan whispered against her lips.

"Tug." She gasped as all the muscles inside her contracted, and Tyler slid one finger in. She dropped her hips to take him deeper but his finger circled, teasing her. "Tug twice."

"Good girl." Sloan traced her lips with his tongue. His hands slid down to her throat. "Now, I need you to understand something."

I understand! Don't stop, don't stop!

Sloan made a motion with his hand at the edge of her vision, and the vibrations ceased.

Uh, I hate you! She glared at Sloan and spread her thighs as far as she could, hoping Tyler would take the hint.

But he didn't.

"What?" She felt like screaming, but someone might hear.

232

Sudden panic had her looking over Sloan's shoulder, over her own. The street was still empty, but the distant sounds of cars told her it wouldn't be for long. "Please! What?"

"What, who?" Sloan's thumb stoked her throat, up and down, up and down. "Who am I?"

Mindless with need, she tossed her head back and groaned. "Master, Captain . . . Oh, God!"

"'Sir' will do." Sloan motioned again, and the vibrating thing touched her clit. "I don't expect us to see eye to eye on everything, but I do expect you to talk to me when something is bothering you."

"Okay." Sounded good. Anything that kept things going sounded good. She whimpered as Tyler filled her with one finger, pumping deeper and deeper until her pulse matched his thrusts. She teetered on the brink of climax and pressed her eyes shut.

Tyler withdrew his finger.

"No!" She tried to push down again, but Sloan pressed his thumb against her larynx.

"Don't move." His tone warned her of the danger of disobeying, told her she'd regret it if she did.

For some reason, she couldn't resist pushing a little, just to see how far he'd go. She wasn't afraid—yet. But she wanted to be.

"Tyler, please—"

A bit more pressure on her windpipe and she cut herself off. Mouth opened wide, she gulped in air, but not enough. She couldn't get enough

"Keep going, Tyler," Sloan said.

Danger, pleasure, all wrapped into a fiery ball of ecstasy. The flames spiraled up, out of control. Two fingers filled her, then three, moving faster, harder. She felt like the sensations were smothering her. One lungful of air and they would disappear. She pressed against Sloan's hand, held her breath when the press of his thumb wasn't enough.

"Don't do that." Sloan stroked up and down her throat, hard enough for her to feel, light enough for her to breathe if she chose to. "I wanted to see how you'd take to a little breath play, and obviously you enjoy it, but we'll have to work up to me actually controlling how much air you can take in. Trust, sweetheart. It takes time."

"I trust you, I trust you!" She spoke without drawing in air, almost there, almost . . .

"You're smarter than that." Sloan took his hand from her throat and patted her cheek. "I'll earn your trust, not take it while you're desperate to get off." He glanced down. "Okay, enough, Tyler."

Tyler removed his fingers and the tiny vibrating thing. Then he stood.

"I'm not sure I get what you're doing, Sloan." He put his fingers to his lips and sucked, rolling his eyes as though savoring some delicacy. "But I'm enjoying this so far."

"Tyler." With one hand, she blocked Sloan's attempt to pull up her jeans. With the other, she reached for Tyler. Her fingers brushed the telling lump angling up to his belt. "Please, I need—"

"No. You want." Sloan stepped between her and Tyler, then opened the driver's side door of the truck. "I'll decide what you need."

A second longer and she'd have Tyler doing whatever she asked; the uncertainty in his eyes made it obvious. But Sloan wouldn't let that happen.

And she felt pretty silly standing there with her jeans around her knees. Lips pursed, she jerked them up and elbowed past Sloan. "I don't get you."

His arm whipped out and barred across her belly. Her back hit his solid chest. He ground his erection into her butt.

"Well, get this." He licked up the length of her throat, then bit her earlobe. Hard. She yelped, and he covered her mouth with his hand. "I'd love to fuck you right here, but you wouldn't enjoy being watched by the very same people who saw you throw a fit on the ice. Making you desperate enough to beg was punishment enough. I don't imagine you get off on humiliation."

As if on cue, a bright red Volvo rumbled up the street, slowing as it passed. The couple in front glanced over, then away. The two little boys in the backseat pressed their faces against the window and waved.

Bitter shame poured down her throat and puddled in her gut. Her hand fluttered over her throat.

"I feel sick." Her stomach lurched, and she bent over. Hands on her knees, she inhaled deeply. "Oh, God. What's wrong with me?"

Sloan rubbed between her shoulder blades and held her hair away from her face as she gagged. "You're like a kid in an amusement park, sweetheart. You're jumping on the biggest, fastest rides before you're ready to handle the small ones. Paul cheating on you made you reckless. Which is fine. You explored a part of yourself you never would have otherwise. But it's time to slow down a little. I'll help you, and if you trust me at all, trust me to know how far you can go."

The back of her throat burned, but the urge to vomit passed. Sloan's words, along with their implication, soothed her. He'd told her from the start he could read her. Her every movement, every breath, told him what she needed. Even when she wasn't sure, he knew.

She felt exposed yet safe with him. Not completely; he still frightened her with his intensity and his promises of pain, but she had a feeling that was intentional. The ever-present uncertainty added a thrill, a delicious sense of danger. No matter how many times she said he didn't scare her, they both knew he did.

Trust took time, granted, but fear—there was no reason not to enjoy that now.

Straightening, she leaned against him, enjoying the comforting way he rubbed her arms, almost wishing they could stay like that for a while. But her body craved what she'd been denied. The dampness between her thighs, the lust blazing in her veins, demanded more than his gentle touch.

"So, if I'm not ready for extreme exhibitionism—what am I ready for?" She turned in his arms, stroked his rippled abs, then let her hands drift lower. When Sloan cursed, she peered up at him with an innocent smile on her lips and massaged his cock through his jeans. "Or will my punishment last all night?"

"One of these days, you'll push me so far, and I'll whip you until you feel like I've peeled the flesh from your ass and your back." His smile got bigger as the blood left her face. When she started shaking, he sniffed her hair as though he could smell her fear. "But it could take months—even years—before we can share that kind of pain, before you'll understand the rapture of agony."

Months, years. Yep, I agree. We'll go there later. Much, much later. Her fingers shook as she played with his unadorned silver belt buckle. "And until then?"

"Lucky for you, torturing myself doesn't appeal to me. And poor Tyler." He nodded toward the sidewalk where Tyler kicked a rock between his sneakers, letting out a heavy sigh before glancing their way. "He doesn't deserve this. He's been a good sport."

Sloan's games were driving her nuts. She wished he'd get to the point. "So where are we going?"

"The lighthouse." He motioned for her to get in the car, then shrugged and climbed in when she didn't move. "I told you I'd take you. The plumber owns the one out near Bay View. He's got a camper there he said we can use for the night. In exchange for rink side seats the next time he's in Dartmouth."

Seats for a pickup and a private visit to a lighthouse, complete with accommodations. Would luxury suites at the Dartmouth forum be worth a few souls? Did she really want to know?

The passenger side door opened with a tired screech. Tyler climbed into the cab. "Can we do something? I'm hard enough to hammer nails."

"Charming, Vanek." Sloan braced an elbow on the steering wheel, shook his head at Tyler, then gave Oriana an expectant look. "You coming?"

With one last lungful of clean air, Oriana stepped onto the ledge of the door. She'd come to terms with giving in to Sloan. Once they reached the cove.

"Go sit on the toolbox in the back." Oriana pointed to the wooden box bolted to the floor in the small space behind the seats. "This is my truck. I'm driving."

Sloan frowned. "Listen, pet—"

"I'm dressed, and we're not having sex, Sloan." She folded her hands over her knee and leaned forward, lashes fluttering. "Don't call me 'pet.' My truck, my rules. Go sit."

"You're gonna pay for this," Sloan muttered before he hunched over and folded himself onto the box. "I hope you know what you're doing, *sweetheart*."

"Why, Sloan, I thought you could read me so well." Tossing her hair over one shoulder, she climbed into the driver's seat and buckled herself in. "Can't you tell?"

His narrowed eyes met hers through the rearview mirror, then widened slightly. Whatever he saw seemed to please him, because he relaxed—as much as possible given the cramped space.

She might not be ready for the behemoth ride, but she could handle more than a merry-go-round. Sloan was like the ticket-master, measuring stick in hand, sizing her up. And from the looks of it, she'd passed.

Chapter Twenty Five

The truck's headlights illuminated an overgrown path almost completely obscured by the dense woods. Oriana squinted at her map, sure Sloan's directions were off. Not that she'd ever been to a lighthouse before, but shouldn't there be a beacon of light visible for miles to warn ships away from the jagged rocks hidden by high tide? Wasn't that the point?

"We're here." Sloan leaned between the seats and grinned at her. "What's wrong? Did you think I'd get us lost?"

"I think we *are* lost." She squinted at the darkness and shook her head. "There can't be a lighthouse here."

"Well, there is. If you're looking for some kind of bright, shiny confirmation, you won't find it. The lighthouse has been shut down for years." He hunched forward and opened the toolbox behind him. Metal clinked and thumped. Then a *click* and a white glare filled the cab. "Good old Norton. I knew he'd have one. Let's go."

Red spotted her vision, and she blinked fast, rubbing her face with both hands. Tyler swore, and she heard him exit the cab. Turning, she shielded her face and frowned at Sloan.

"A warning would have been nice."

He aimed the flashlight at the floor and gave her a sinister smile. "I'm not nice."

Icy slivers of dread crawled up her spine. She dug her nails into her palm. "You can be."

"Perhaps." He inclined his head, and his whole bearing loosened up. When she let out a huff of relief, his hand snaked out to catch a handful of her hair. "But that's not what you want from me tonight."

A firm tug arched her neck, and sharp pain spiked from the roots of her hair. Her heart stuttered. Then she did. "Y-you said you'd g-give me what I n-need, n-not what I want."

"That I did." He released her hair and caressed her cheek with his calloused fingertips. "But tonight, your needs and wants happen to be the same. I've tolerated a lot of insolence from you, pet, more than with any other sub, but that ends now. Unless I'm wrong, you're acting out because you're frustrated. You have three Doms forcing you to lead the way, which feels unnatural, doesn't it?"

How did he know? Fine, she'd said the words once or twice—she'd even told Dominik she was done making choices, but this was the first time she really felt like she'd been heard.

But what exactly was she asking for? Wouldn't it be safer to immerse herself into this . . . lifestyle with Dominik or Max?

Yes. Only she was tired of playing it safe.

Ready to take the plunge, she mentally stepped up to the edge—then inched away. "I don't like you calling me 'pet.'"

"Do I look like I care?" Sloan took Tyler's abandoned seat and placed his hands on his knees. The muscles of his bare forearms tensed. "You can't have things both ways with me, Oriana. Either you surrender, or you don't. I thought I could carry on this way a little longer, but quite frankly, I'm tired of the teasing. If you're not ready, you better make it damn clear."

She was as ready as she'd ever be, but part of her needed to know all her options. Was it his way or nothing? "If I say I'm not ready, what happens? We just head home?"

"No. We'll check out the lighthouse and spend the night here. If all you want is some sweet vanilla sex, Tyler's perfectly capable of giving you that." His expression softened, as though to say he wouldn't hold the decision against her. "That's one of the benefits of having so many men at your disposal, love; you get to pick your flavor. Max can't really enjoy sex without indulging in his kink—and neither can I. But both Dominik and Tyler can give you that whenever you need it."

Still so many choices, but none too difficult to make. If she put herself in Sloan's hands, pain would follow. But he'd told her a certain level of trust was necessary for the extremes. They weren't there yet.

"Will I have a safe word?" *Lady in Charge* insisted on a safe word, but the concept frightened her. What if she couldn't get the word out? Then again, should she just assume he'd know when she'd had enough?

"Hey." His thumb brushed her bottom lip, and she realized it was trembling. The gentle touch brought her back to the present, back to where she still had the power to negotiate. "If you don't trust me enough to just tell me what you're okay with, maybe you're better off with Tyler. Or maybe I'm not being fair—I'd enjoy being with you if you want to keep things light—"

"No." She put her hand on his arm and dug her fingers into the taut muscles. "Please, don't lose your nerve now. I've been pushing, and I like that you're pushing back. I just don't know what my limits are, and I'm afraid I won't see them until it's too late."

"Jesus, Oriana, what exactly do you think I'm going to do to you?" He took her hands between his and gave them a light squeeze. "How's this? I swear there will be no permanent scarring."

She rolled her eyes. "That's reassuring."

"Good." The way his lips curved told her he'd caught her sarcasm and chosen to ignore it. *Jerk.* He tightened his grip on her hands. "This is a test run, so any variations of 'stop' will work. I'll also be watching you very carefully."

"O-kay . . ." She sighed, missing the initial anticipation, wishing all the talking hadn't been necessary. "And now—"

"Tyler can stand by as an extra bit of insurance."

Uck. She made a face as the last hint of danger vanished. Much as she lusted after Tyler, much as she'd enjoyed their time together, his presence would restrict rough play.

"Sure. Whatever." She tugged her hands free, then left the truck, slamming the door behind her. Who'd have thought Sloan would be the one to chicken out? Striking off toward the trees, she paused when neither Sloan nor Tyler followed. "You coming?"

"I'll be right with you, pet." Sloan tossed her the flashlight and waved her on. "Don't stray off the path."

Branches snapped underfoot as she stomped her way down the path. *Don't stray off the path? What am I, five?*

The wind rustled through the leaves, and ghostly white danced along the edges of her vision. Just the moon, filtering though the dense canopy above. Inhaling to steady her nerves, she soaked in the fresh scent of the ocean and wet cedar. Lovely—and peaceful. She'd never been much of a nature girl, but she could get used to this.

A raspy howl rose from somewhere to her left, sounding like it came from below. She froze, tucked her hands under her arms, and glanced over her shoulder. Sloan was certainly taking his sweet time.

Were he and Tyler having a heart-to-heart? Did he think he could talk his way around Tyler's issues?

"Arrogant." She mumbled to herself, glaring up as clouds spilled over the moon and pitched the forest into darkness. The circular beam of the flashlight bounced off a wall of trees and leaves. The path had disappeared. "And stupid if he thinks he can force Tyler to watch him beat me."

Swinging the beam from side to side, she tried to make out the path. To amuse herself, she went over what she'd say to Sloan when he finally caught up.

"I tried to see your point of view, Sloan, but I can't get my head that far up my own ass." She giggled, imagining the look on his face. He'd get all pissy Dom-like, but as usual, he wouldn't be able to do a thing about it. "If you can't get off without your 'kink,' what am I supposed to do with your limp dick?"

A few yards ahead, a narrow part between the trees revealed the white base of the lighthouse. No wonder Sloan had let her go alone. Despite being momentarily disoriented, she'd never been in any real danger.

"Ten?" She heard Tyler call out from somewhere behind her.

A shadow cut her off from the path to the lighthouse. Oriana spun and opened her mouth to scream. A hand covered her mouth, and a big arm locked across her chest.

"Ten!" Sloan clucked his tongue as she scraped his rough palm with her teeth. His deep, throaty tone made her shiver. "No biting, pet. You won't like the consequences."

Consequences? The word lodged in her throat. With wide eyes, she tipped her head to one side, trying to get a glimpse of Sloan's face. One look to see whether she should be afraid.

He held her still, and his lips brushed her ear. "In ten minutes, Tyler will join us. Unless you scream that is—I can't imagine him staying away then." He paused as though to let her absorb his words. "I'll move my hand if you promise to be very, very quiet."

Ten minutes. She closed her eyes as her pulse hammered inside her skull. Panic made her feel like a child, spinning around and around until she fell. The night sky, with its piercing stars and patches of thick grey clouds, swirled around her. Sloan could do anything to her in ten minutes.

But unless he took her far, Tyler could reach them in seconds if she screamed. Not that she didn't trust Sloan . . . somewhat. But she trusted Tyler more. And she had a feeling Sloan knew.

"So, what's it going to be?" Sloan asked. "Silence or a gag?"

As her skin turned cold, his palm became feverishly hot. The condensation of her breath on his skin wet her lips. Moisture below reminded her of the panties she'd been denied. One less barrier for Sloan to breach, not that a flimsy bit of fabric could stop him from taking whatever he wanted.

The idea thrilled her, terrified her. He'd left her a wide open window of opportunity to back out, and since she hadn't, he'd slammed it shut. Her nipples drew into hard little points of arousal, painfully squished under his arm. She made a plaintive sound, and he moved his hand.

"Well?" He ground his erection against the small of her back and laughed softly when she gasped. "Your answer?"

"Silence." She bit her lip as he released her and stepped away, giving her a cold look. "What?"

"I'm sure your little book instructed you on the proper way to address your Master or Mistress. I'm getting tired of reminding you." He folded his arms over his chest. "Say it, Oriana."

"For Christ's sake, we're wasting time!" His hand latched around her upper arm and she yelped. "Hey, you—" As his eyes narrowed, she swallowed the insult she'd almost spat at him. Very bad time to test him. "I'm sorry. I'll be quiet, Sir. I didn't mean—"

"I know." He smiled and gave her a little nudge in the direction of the lighthouse. "You have a lot to learn, but I'm a patient man." She took two small steps, and he came up behind her. "But if you don't hurry, we won't have time to play. Maybe I should just fuck you right here in the dirt so hard you feel like you'll break in half. You're probably wet enough for me to slide right in, aren't you, my little slut?"

Slut? Oh, God, is that what he thinks of me? Men don't take care of sluts; they use them. What if he'd been waiting to get her alone so he could— A rush of pure adrenaline spilled into her veins. *Run!* Her body screamed, but her knees buckled.

Sloan grabbed her arm and she whimpered.

"Shh." He stroked her hair and whispered. "A little fear, sweetheart, a little pain. Don't get so caught up that you forget what's real."

Air. Cold sweet air filled her lungs. Her head cleared and she peeked up at him. "What's real?"

"I take care of what's mine." He kissed her, a tender kiss that reminded her why she was here with him, alone. "And tonight, that's what you are. All mine."

All mine. Damn, that sounded nice. Not that she wanted the other men any less, but she had to admit, she enjoyed feeling like she belonged to someone.

She sighed into his mouth as he nibbled on her bottom lip, then drew back a little to look into his eyes. "So you won't try to break me?"

"Hell, no." He chuckled and set her away from him. Taking out a single key on a simple metal ring, he pressed it into her palm. "No breaking, just a few bruises." He pointed at the lighthouse. "Now get."

She took a step and his hand smacked her ass. Jumping, she glared back at him.

He arched a brow and reached down to undo his belt. "You have to the count of three." He slid the length of leather out and folded it in half. "One."

Letting out a strangled scream, she turned and ran.

Chapter Twenty Six

Sloan ducked under the cobwebs strung over the arched stairwell leading to the lantern room, going over in his mind how he'd handle Oriana with the same diligence he'd give positioning his men for a penalty kill. No verbal humiliation, at least until she felt a little more secure about their relationship. He stood for a moment to watch her lean over the railing on the lantern gallery, and a smile tugged at his lips. She bounced on the balls of her feet, looked back at him, then bit her lip. Eager and a little nervous. Perfect. Mind-numbing fear they'd explore together eventually, but anticipation would suffice for now.

But how to give her the edge she needed from him without overdoing it? Several times he'd found her limits and pushed enough to get a nice reaction, but when he eased off, she always seemed disappointed. Like she thought there should be . . . *more*.

Maybe he'd let her think too much.

Joining her on the gallery, he placed himself behind her and put hands over hers on the railing. "Next time, I expect you to wait for me on your knees."

Her spine went stiff. "Why—"

"To show you're well trained." He continued over her sputtering. "You'll also learn what's required from you in certain situations and obey my commands without question."

"I . . ." She straightened, and he trapped her hands on the bar. Her breaths came out in short little gasps. "But—"

"The answer you're looking for is 'Yes, Sir' or 'Yes, Master Sloan.'" He slid her hands on the railing until her arms were fully extended. Then he kicked her feet hip-width apart. "I don't want to have to punish you again, pet."

She squirmed, trying to pry her hands out from under his. He tightened his grip and felt the rigid muscles pressed against his chest go slack. "Yes, M—Sir."

Her body succumbed, but her mind wasn't there yet. The verbal slip told him she fought to retain some control.

Which just wouldn't do. He kissed her throat, then set his teeth in the quivering flesh. She went perfectly still.

"Don't move your hands." Reaching around her, he opened her jeans, then tugged them down to her knees. The smooth, pale globes of her exposed butt quivered, as did her thighs, but she didn't move. He glanced at her bowed head as he stroked her bottom, taking note of the stiff set of her shoulders. When he covered her bare pussy with his hand, moisture slicked his palm.

"Sloan—I mean, Sir—Oh!" Her back arched as he massaged her plump lower lips, then bucked as he prodded her gently with one finger. "Please!"

"Soon, bunny." The muscles of her cunt clenched around his finger, and he grinned at her tiny growl of irritation. "Get used to me calling you that, sweetheart; I rather enjoy the reaction it gets. You're *my* little puck bunny, aren't you?"

"No, I'm—" She hissed in a breath as he added another finger alongside the first and started pumping. "Just. . . just. . ."

"Yes." He traced a line with his wet fingers over her puckered anus. Her butt wiggled provocatively, and she shifted her thighs, trying to open them wider. His already rock-hard dick throbbed in response to the invitation, but another need had to be fulfilled first. "There won't be much warm-up, bunny, but when I have more time, we'll have a proper session."

"Session?" she whispered, then moaned when he squeezed both her ass cheeks.

"Mmmhmm." He withdrew his hand, waited until she wiggled again, then hauled back. *Whack*. Her butt blossomed in the shape of his hand. She yelped and threw her head back. "An hour of beating your ass until you're seeing stars. But Tyler will be with us any minute, so I'll have to cut this short."

Another two smacks, and he yanked his already open belt from his jeans and folded it in half. The scent of her sweet arousal drifted up on the cool sea breeze, and the light from the flashlight abandoned on the gallery floor made her slick juices glisten on her inner thighs.

She was ready.

The first strike cracked out loud, leather on flesh, a harsh contrast to nature's gentle melody. Oriana's cry joined the crash of distant waves, muffled so it played in tune with the rustle of leaves from below. Her butt rose up as though eager for the next blow, but he waited, drinking in the heady feeling of power. He rubbed the stark red welt he'd made—that she'd let him make. Not because he'd paid her to take whatever he dished out, not because he was one of the few real Doms in a club full of wannabes, but because he could fulfill a need inside her. One she hadn't even known she had.

He swung the belt again. *Crack!* The world became sharp, piercing into him as an acute awareness of his body and hers took over. Too fast, this level of control never hit him this fast. If Tyler weren't coming, he wouldn't stop until he made her come from pain warped into pleasure, but he could already hear the boy on the stairs.

Little whimpers escaped her, and she jutted her hips up at him in a way that said "take me now." He saw no reason to deny her.

But when he backed away to free himself from the confines of his jeans, she whined.

"More . . . please more."

More? More what?

"Please, Sir—Master . . . that felt amazing. The belt . . ."

He had to be dreaming. She actually wanted the pain enough that she was begging for it?

He backed into the door before Tyler could open it. Damn, the boy could see everything. Traumatizing the kid to indulge himself— and her—would be wrong.

"We can't, baby. Maybe next time—"

"Master, don't do this to me. I need . . ." She bucked her hips and he groaned.

She needed desperately, and he couldn't find it in him to say no. He turned and pressed his forehead against the door as his own desires blazed through him like his blood had become ignited gasoline.

"Five more minutes, Vanek." Pre-cum beaded on the tip of his dick, and he snarled. "I swear, I'll make it worth the wait."

The sound of Tyler hitting the door vibrated through the still air like the pounding of a metal drum. "What are you doing to her?"

"Giving her what she needs." He sucked in enough sea air to fill his lungs and turned back to the woman whose baser cravings only he could fulfill. "Don't watch. Your limits aren't hers."

Hauling off with the belt, he gave her everything he had, whipping her with the leather again and again until she screamed for him. Until she called him Master as though she meant it.

Chapter Twenty Seven

Oriana's pulse thudded under her blazing flesh, and each strike created a searing wave of pure sensation. She couldn't understand the way her body responded. Pain didn't register. The last few strikes were hard enough to bruise, some part of her mind knew that, but the heat spreading over her ass only caused blood to rush to her clit. One more solid smack, and she'd burst.

"Look at that." Sloan's hands covered her butt, rubbing in the heat. He bent down and bit into the fleshy part of one cheek. "You're so hot. I want to lick you." He spread her open and licked up the cleft of her ass. "Eat you." He bit her again, so hard the sensation stabbed right into her spine. Her back bowed as he molded his body against hers and pressed his dick between her thighs. "Fuck you."

"Yes." She rubbed against him, desperate for everything, anything he would give her. "Do it. I'm yours."

"Damn right, you are." He moved away, and she heard a wrapper rip. Then felt his cock, slipping and sliding in her juices. "All mine."

Her cunt pulsed and her insides rippled, prepared for him to fill her.

Instead, his fingers pushed inside her, then spread her moisture over her anus. The slick head of his dick followed, pressing hard. Jaw set, she pressed back, relaxing her muscles as he eased his way inside, panting at the insistent, painful pressure. Once he was fully sheathed, he pulled her away from the railing and wrapped his arms around her waist. The position brought him deeper, and she swallowed a cry as the stretching began to sting and burn.

"You're doing good, baby." He kissed her cheek and dragged his dick out a little. "Let me know when you're ready."

"I'm—" She hissed as he ground back in. The stinging had passed, but still, it seemed like there was too much inside her. With all the lube they'd used during her first two anal experiences, she'd only felt momentary discomfort before the slippery penetration became dark ecstasy. This was gritty, raw.

"It's okay; there's no rush." As though to prove his point, he palmed her breasts, kneading them gently. He nibbled on her earlobe, then grazed his teeth down her throat. She shifted restlessly as he tugged at her nipples, stretching them out until electric currents shot through her breasts. Then down into her pussy and her ass.

"Now." Her body shook, taking in everything, needing more. She clenched and relaxed, over and over, trying to draw him in. "Now, now!"

"Tyler!" Sloan's hands abandoned her breasts and fisted in her hair. "Come on!"

Tyler stumbled out onto the gallery and froze a step away from her. Licking his lips, he looked from her, to Sloan.

"Pull it out, boy." Sloan lowered her head until her face was level with Tyler's waist. "She'll need something to hold onto while I'm ramming her ass. And something stuffed in her mouth to keep her from screaming."

Oh, yes! Sloan in her ass, taking her hard while she sucked Tyler's dick—dirty, but perfect. She could already see the scene playing out in her head, and although it hardly seemed possible, her pussy got even wetter.

"Oriana?" Tyler's brow creased as he reached out to touch her cheek. "You'd tell me if you weren't okay with this, right?"

"Uh huh." She hooked her fingers to his belt, fingers shaking as she undid it. Sloan tugged her hair as he slid almost all the way out. "Oh! Hurry!"

Tonguing his upper lip, Tyler shucked his jeans and boxers. One hand aimed his dick at her lips. She flicked out her tongue to lick the bead of pre-cum off the tip.

Letting out a gruff chuckle, Tyler smoothed the sweaty hair away from her forehead. He looked at Sloan. "Why don't you hold her hips while she holds mine? Probably be easier."

Oh, good. Very good. She smiled up at Tyler as she latched onto his hips, curving her fingers around the hard ridge. Knowing he wasn't uncomfortable with what they were doing made it much easier to relax. He smiled back as though he understood. As Sloan's grip shifted to her hips, Tyler raked his hands into her hair and pressed the head of his dick against her lips.

"Open wide."

She giggled, then groaned as Sloan thrust in. Lips parted, she did her best to suck and swirl her tongue around Tyler's dick as Sloan pounded into her. Somehow the give-and-take heightened her pleasure, shooting her up to the apex of climax so fast her body shuddered with the effort to hang on long enough to enjoy it. The ledge she found herself on topped anything she'd experienced thus far. Her entire being felt like an instrument of rapture, being played in an epic heavenly chorus. Once she reached the pinnacle, there'd be nowhere to go but down.

Slurping, swallowing her saliva as she took Tyler as deep as she could—there, that pulled her away from the edge. As long as she divided her attention between the men, she could . . .

"Take over, Tyler," Sloan said.

What? She tried to lift her head, wondering if Sloan planned to pull out and change places with Tyler. Maybe that would be good. They would all last longer.

Instead, Tyler thrust in and out, faster and faster. There was no way to keep up with him. All she could do was keep her lips parted and receive him as he fucked her mouth. The grip on her hips kept her from thrusting back to receive Sloan, which forced her to brace and take him deeper and deeper.

Sloan curved over her, and the scruff of his jaw lightly scraped her throat as he spoke. "Let. Go."

Everything inside her coiled up. A hot wave of pleasure crashed into her, then another and another, like the black waves below frothing over the shore. She moaned around Tyler's dick, gulping down her screams.

"Oh, God!" Tyler grunted and pulled out. "I'm going to come. Let me come on those beautiful breasts."

Sloan bowed her back until her breasts jutted out. Hot spurts of cum spurted on them, making her feel dirty and wanton and pitching her right up to the verge of release. And she hadn't come down yet. Not even close.

"That's so fucking hot!" Tyler dropped to his knees and cupped her pussy. "Give it up, baby." His fingers slipped inside and he used his palm to rub her clit. "You've gotta know by now, we won't let you hold back."

Hold back? No, they'd already pushed her past the point where she'd even bother trying. She whimpered as Sloan pumped into her ass harder and harder, as Tyler's skilled fingers found the trigger within. A fierce orgasm tossed her up, pulled her under, until she drowned in the sensations.

"Breathe, sweetheart." Sloan's slack dick slipped out of her as Tyler withdrew his hand. He sat on the gallery and held her, whispering the same words over and over like a soft chant. "Breathe. Just breathe."

For a while, breathing was all she could do. Her body became solid in miniscule pieces. Then the world stopped looking fuzzy. Cuddled up in Sloan's lap, she let out a contented sigh.

"I think she's okay," Tyler said.

She rested her cheek against Sloan's chest and wrinkled her nose at Tyler. "I'm fine. Why wouldn't I be?"

"Because you were KO'd by a massive orgasm the other night." He leaned his elbows on the railing and puffed out his chest. "And we just gave you two."

Oh, boy. If he didn't have an ego before . . . "You're right." She curled her fingers over the collar of Sloan's T-shirt. "But what impresses me is that your endurance seems to be improving. I was worried for a bit."

"Ouch." Tyler smacked his hands over his heart as though he'd been shot. "You sure are mean."

"Not mean," she said, doing her best to smother a yawn under Sloan's arm. "Just trying to keep you in line."

"Better be careful, Vanek." Sloan wrapped her hair around his hand and pulled until she tipped her face up. He kissed her, his tongue as deep in her mouth as his dick had been in her body. After stealing all her oxygen, he grinned up at Tyler. "She might still want to try out that Domme stuff. And you're the perfect candidate. Keep it up, and she'll mail order a strap-on."

Tyler let out a huff and strode across the gallery. "So not happening." He raked his fingers through his curly hair. "Shoulda figured I'd get this after letting you take the lead. No points for an assist, eh, *Captain?*" His knuckles were white as he put his hand on the door handle. "I'll wait for you two in the truck."

The door slammed shut behind him.

Oriana stared at the dark glass and watched Tyler's slender form disappear. What the hell had just happened? He'd enjoyed himself, no doubt about it. Had the teasing really bothered him that much?

"Damn it." Sloan petted her hair and glared in the direction of the loud *thunk!* from below. "All right, up with you, pet."

Up? She dug her nails into her palms as she tried to stand and pain throbbed in her butt. Her second effort got her to her feet, but she didn't think she was ready for the stairs. And Tyler needed Sloan now. "Would you mind if I enjoyed the view for a bit? Tyler probably won't want to see me just yet—"

"I'm not leaving you here alone." Sloan's eyes narrowed. "Are you all right?"

She rolled her eyes. "I'm fine. He's not. Stop babying me and go make sure he doesn't get lost."

He dressed in a hurry and winced at another *thunk*. "I'm not babying you. I just beat your ass and—"

"And you hit like a girl." She laughed at his shocked stare. "I'm tougher than I look. Please, just check on him. I'll meet you at the trailer."

"You're both impossible." Sloan shook his head, then backed toward the door. "Are you sure—"

"Yes!"

"Fine." He scowled and yanked the door open. "Don't be long."

As soon as Sloan left, her thin mask shattered. The air around her became damp and chill, and she shivered. Bending down to pick up her clothes made her whole body ache. The bruises that had added to the thrill of the rough, wild sex hurt so bad she had a hard time standing straight. The pain made her eyes tear.

You liked it. You begged for it! She swallowed against the lump in her throat. For some reason, even though she'd insisted on Sloan going after Tyler, she felt . . . abandoned. The wonderful sensation of being taken hard became distorted, and she realized she'd just been used.

The idea of pulling jeans over her throbbing flesh made her

stomach turn, so she simply pulled on her shirt and bundled the rest of her clothes in her arms. Feeling like she'd aged twenty years since climbing up the lighthouse stairs, she descended, sobbing when she reached halfway and saw how far she had left to go.

"You're so fucking pathetic." She covered her face with her hands. "Why would anybody ever want you?"

Chapter Twenty Eight

I'm going to kill Sloan.

Dominik shook his head and climbed the steps up to Oriana's side quietly. He whispered her name so he wouldn't scare the hell out of her.

She still jumped, but when she looked up, relief spilled over the utter despair that had filled her eyes. "Dominik! How did you find us . . . I mean, me. Sloan went—" Her bottom lip quivered. "He went to find Tyler."

"Sloan mentioned a restaurant and a lighthouse he wanted to take you to. His father gave me the directions." His strained, neutral tone made Oriana frown, but he couldn't pull off anything better. Every ounce of his control went into not snarling. "You want to tell me why you're crying?"

The request seemed to shock her; she'd probably expected a command. She cleared her throat and dried her eyes with her sleeves. "Oh, I'm just being silly. We all had fun—me, Sloan, Tyler—but then I said something stupid and Tyler took off. Sloan went to talk to him."

Sounded so fucking reasonable. Still, he sensed she was leaving something out. Her voice sounded shallow—he took her hands, they were clammy and cold. Her eyes flicked nervously away from him. The "fun" hadn't just been sex. Sloan had done a scene with her.

"How long did Sloan stay with you after you had 'fun'?"

She looked at her hands. "Tyler needed him."

His eyes narrowed at her obvious evasion. "How. Long?"

"A couple of minutes."

"Jesus." *Stupid, lazy son of a bitch.* He knew Sloan wasn't big on aftercare—he usually left it to Dominik or Max when they played together, but neither of them had been here. He shouldn't have played with her if he wasn't going to take responsibility for her welfare. The scene had likely pushed Oriana too far, and she'd dropped once Sloan had left her.

"Don't be mad, Dominik. We didn't do anything I didn't want to do." She formed her lips into a superficial smile and squeezed his hand. "I wimped out a little, but I'm good now."

Bullshit. She'd probably convinced herself she'd gotten what she'd asked for. He had to fix this. *Before* they discussed why he'd come.

"I'm not mad, bunny." He smiled at her predictable little frown. "But we've got to have a chat." He stood and pulled her to her feet. At her wince, he froze. "Are you hurt?"

She gnashed her teeth together and shook her head. "Just a little sore."

Dead, Sloan. So dead you might as well pick yourself out a fucking tombstone. Out loud he said pleasantly, "Well, be that as it may, I missed you today. So you'll indulge me and let me carry you to my car."

Arms wrapped his neck, she held on tight while he cradled her in his arms. His forearm skimmed her butt, and she hissed in pain. Then tried to wiggle free. "I should—"

"Do what I say." He positioned her more comfortably and pressed her head against his chest. Her grip tightened as he carried her down the stairs. "Now, not another word unless it's 'Yes, Sir.'"

"Yes, Sir."

After he stepped off the last step, her whole body seemed to loosen up. Silly little thing. Sitting on those hard, cold steps had probably made her bruises hurt worse. Then again, she hadn't been clear-headed enough to have considered that. Which is why Sloan should have stayed. And why Dominik would.

Stop. Focus on Oriana. Plan Sloan's murder later.

"Close your eyes, sweetie. Close your eyes and listen to me, very carefully." He let his voice take on the gentle lull of the lapping waves, matching his slow strides. "When I met you, the first thing I thought after I caught you was 'God, why can't this woman be mine? Why do I have to let her go?', and once I let you go, I knew it wouldn't be long before I saw you again. I had a coffee before getting back on the ice because you made me crave the taste—you'd smelled like you'd rolled around in a mountain of coffee beans." He paused and listened to her steady inhales and exhales, getting slower and slower. "I decided when I saw you again, I'd tell you how beautiful you were. How special. Tell you that you were too good for

Paul. I knew I'd be repeating everything Max had already said, but I thought maybe you'd listen to me." He kissed her temple. She was almost asleep and wouldn't remember much when she woke, but he had to finish. "I don't need to tell you to leave Paul—that's a done deal. But I'll tell you this and you will listen."

She mumbled something that sounded like, "Yes, Sir."

"You deserve to be treated like you're precious, even when you're on your knees. Don't ever forget that." He laid her in the backseat of his Jeep, then fetched a blanket from the back to cover her with. Standing by the open door, he bowed his head and sighed. "How am I supposed to keep you safe, little one?" He rubbed his eyes and swallowed at the ache in his throat. "I'm no good to you as long as I don't know where I stand. I don't think any of us are. If you were mine, I wouldn't let you put yourself in situations like this." A shout in the distance brought his head up. Probably Sloan, still working on Tyler. Good. The captain was far more capable of getting through to the rookie than he was at handling a vulnerable sub. "You need things they can't give you. But I can." He shut the door firmly and strode around the Jeep. "And I will."

No more games. He refused to leave her to two fumbling, wannabe Doms. She needed a master. And now she had one.

* * * *

"You dumb ass!" Sloan grabbed Vanek's wrist before he could punch the tree again. The boy had stormed away when he first saw Sloan and tried to lose him in the woods. But Vanek was a city kid, so his efforts were pretty pathetic. He'd finally just given up and taken out his frustrations on an impervious oak. Thankfully, he only got two shots in before Sloan caught up with him.

Ignoring Vanek's struggles, Sloan dragged him to the truck, then forced him to sit so he could check the bloody mess the boy had made of his hand. "I broke my hand during a game in a fight I won and my career might be over. You gonna risk yours beating the shit out of a tree?"

Huffing in air like he'd just finished twenty laps around a rink, Vanek bowed his head and mumbled something Sloan couldn't make out.

"What?"

Vanek lifted his head and snarled. "I don't care! Fuck my career! Fuck the game! Do you think I want to end up like you ten years from now? I won't ever meet another woman like her, and I won't be a kinky toy to play with and discard. You're a phase she's going through, but me, I'm going to be more."

"Really?" Sloan nodded and took a few steps back. The sadist in him wanted to push until the kid snapped—or just get some quick satisfaction by cracking him in the jaw, but the Dom in him demanded a calmer approach. "Do you think dismissing her needs as 'a phase' will endear you to her? Max loves her—enough that he stayed away when she asked him to, then returned without one shred of judgment and found out what she needed from him. The things he can't provide, he sees that she gets them from us."

Raking his fingers into his hair, Vanek slumped forward. "Fine. But what does she need from me?"

"You're gonna have to figure that out with her, rookie." Sloan thumped Vanek on the shoulder. His phone rang and he plucked it out of his pocket. Mason's number flashed on the screen. "Hey, what's up?"

"I have Oriana," Mason said. The dial tone sounded.

What the fuck? Sloan shoved his phone in his pocket. How had Mason found them? Why had he come? The questions whirled through his mind as he sprinted to the trailer for a first-aid kit, then sprinted back to the truck. He dropped the metal box on Vanek's lap.

"Patch yourself up." He slammed the passenger's side door, then made his way to the driver's side. His grip made the steering wheel creak. "Something's wrong."

Chapter Twenty Nine

A bump jolted Oriana awake. She sat up, and pain rolled over her butt and down her thighs. *Ouch!*

Dominik leaned between the seats and touched her cheek. "Hey, sleepy. Sorry about that—I tried to ease over the bump, but the shocks on my Jeep are shot. You okay?"

"Uh huh." She rubbed her face with her fists and looked around. "Where are we?"

"About fifty miles from Dartmouth. We'll be home soon." Dominik shifted to one side and helped her climb over the front seats. "I stopped for a coffee. Would you like something?"

"Sure, a mochaccino would be . . ." Exactly what she had every time she went out with Max. God, she missed him. Silly, really, she'd been with him just that morning. She made her lips curve up. "Would be great. And maybe a cookie?"

Dominik chuckled. "A cookie? What kind of cookie?"

"White chocolate and macadamia nut."

"Excellent choice." He rolled down his window and leaned out to the place their order at the drive-through speaker. "Two mochaccinos and four macadamia nut cookies."

After handing her the tray of coffees and the paper bag of cookies, Dominik drove into the lot and parked. He left her the cookies, took both cups, then tested one before handing it to her. She gave him a questioning look.

"I won't have you burning yourself again," he said with a wink.

So unnecessary, but so sweet. She sipped at her coffee, feeling comfortable and content—despite her sore bottom. The ache would go away eventually. This . . .thing between her and Dominik . . . didn't seem like it ever would. She wanted to see where it would go. Maybe she should have a chat with Max and see if he'd mind her keeping Dominik around long term. She wouldn't know if she didn't ask, right?

"Open," Dominik said, then fed her a piece of cookie. "I hope you're okay with this taking the place of our date on Tuesday. I don't think we'll make it."

Oriana chewed the yummy nuttiness, then washed it down with a gulp of coffee. She was kinda happy she didn't have to wait to spend time alone with him, but . . .

"Why wouldn't we make it?"

"Ask me again later." He pressed another piece of cookie against her lips. "You need a bit of TLC at the moment. I plan to make you feel so cherished you won't ever doubt it again—"

"What makes you think I—"

He pressed a finger covered in cookie crumbs against her lips. "Interrupting is rude, pet. Now, as I was saying. You will be assured of your value. And you'll be taught how to properly get involved in a scene and learn safety precautions."

"I was fine with Sloan. Oh, shoot! He's gonna wonder where I took off to."

"I called him."

"Okay . . ." She licked her lips when his mouth drew into a thin line, but she refused to be a coward and let Dominik think badly of Sloan. "Like I said, we didn't do anything I didn't want to do. I kept begging for more and—"

"He gave you what you asked for."

"Exactly."

Dominik bit a cookie in half and chewed slowly. Then he gave her a blank look. "Wasn't he supposed to be in control?"

"Umm . . ."

"Oriana, listen to me. There's a reason I've insisted on deciding what you're ready for. I have the experience to push you just far enough that you'll enjoy yourself, but not so far that you'll regret it once we're done. Or for days after." He cleaned some crumbs off her chin with his thumb, then took her coffee and put it beside his in the cup holder. "If you need a bit of pain with your pleasure, I can give you that." His tone dropped to a tremble-inducing, core-clenching low. "I can hurt you in ways you've never dreamed of. But will dream of once I'm done with you, because you'll love every agonizing moment."

All her swollen bits slicked up and she moaned. So much for not being a nympho. Seemed like she'd never have enough. Every time she was alone with one of the men, her body responded in a way that screamed, "Sex! More sex!"

And as though he'd read her mind, Dominik grinned. "So what would you like to do now?"

Get naked! her insatiable self replied inwardly. She bit her inner cheek and reached for the glove compartment. "Got any good music?"

"Depends what you consider 'good.'" He clicked open the glove compartment when she couldn't find the stupid button. "Take a look."

She fished through the pile of CDs within. Not one of the artists' names was familiar. "Toby Keith? Trace Adkins? Who are they?"

He rubbed his knees and shrugged. "Country singers."

Was it just her, or had his cheeks gotten just a little red? His dark skin made it hard to tell, but she could have sworn he was blushing. She picked a CD and slipped it into the CD player. Then skipped to the song she was most curious about. Honey Bee.

The lyrics were cute.

"Aww, Dominik. This is nice." She touched his cheek. "I'd love to have a man thinking about me while he listens to this."

His big hands curved around her wrist. He brought her hands up to his mouth, then kissed her fingertips. "You have one."

And that means my world is perfect. What more could she possibly want? Her pulse sped up when she realized Dominik had tightened his grip on her wrists. A switch flicked inside her head. She knew what him taking control meant. "Show me what you were talking about before. Please, Sir."

He sighed. "What you need is a man to tell you when you've had enough. My job, unfortunately. Max and Sloan just aren't capable."

"But . . ." She tugged at her wrist. He didn't release her. Very confusing. "You're . . ."

"Ah. I see." He let out a throaty laugh, then leaned forward, forcing her back against her seat. "If I'm restraining you, or giving you orders, that must mean we're going to have sex."

She nodded.

He shook his head.

"That's not how I do things, love. I don't expect submission

24/7, but I retain the right to dominate you outside the bedroom when the mood strikes." He kissed her chin. Then the corner of her lips. Then moved out of reach before she could kiss him back. "Do you have a problem with that?"

Frustration almost got her saying "Yes!", but something about being denied heightened anticipation. And knowing he could command her anytime, anywhere . . . *intense.* To top it off, he was talking long-term, which gave her a nice, warm fuzzy feeling inside.

"I don't have a problem with that, Sir." She stayed perfectly still as he pressed one soft kiss, then another on her, eager for the moment he'd tell her to kiss him back. Amazing—under his control, even this became so much more. She could easily lose herself to this man. *Only* . . ."Would you mind if I speak to Max before committing to anything?"

"Not at all." He sucked on her bottom lip hard, then whispered against her lips. "Kiss me, Oriana."

She opened her mouth against his and gave him everything she had. His tongue thrust deep, circling hers, while his lips added just enough pressure to hold her in place. She nipped at his tongue, teased it, loving the feeling that the kiss would never end.

Dominik drew away much too soon, and she struggled against him, protesting until he hushed her with a stern look.

"I have something to tell you, but I wanted to make sure you were feeling comfortable and secure—" He rubbed his forehead and put his hand on her knee. "You're not going to like what I have to say."

The bottom was about to drop out of the pink, shiny bubble she'd been floating around in. She let out a resolved sigh. "What is it, Dominik?"

"Max got himself arrested."

Her bubble burst like a big blown glass bulb, shattering all around her.

＊ ＊ ＊ ＊

"Stop here," Oriana said, her hand already on the door handle. Dominik pulled the Jeep over at the curb and she hopped out.

Taking her wallet from her purse, she went into the bank and slipped her credit card into the instant teller.

"What are you doing?" Dominik asked from right behind her.

She jumped. Damn, the man was sneaky! When her heart settled back in her chest, she typed in her PIN and shrugged. "Getting the money to bail Max out."

How much? A thousand? Ten thousand? The instant teller wouldn't let her take more than two thousand.

Let's start with that.

The machine beeped. *Insufficient funds? What?*

"His bail hearing is set for tomorrow," Dominik said quietly, as though he hadn't just seen the glaring evidence of her screwup on the screen. "Max will be okay. Like I said, Max told me to tell you he'll be fine. He just didn't want you hearing this on the radio or reading it in the paper."

"I've just ruined his career." She felt around for something solid, feeling like the ground had turned to quicksand, like the world around her was caving in. "He never would have 'assaulted' Paul if not for me. At best, he'll be suspended, at worst, he'll do time."

Dominik pulled her into his arms and gave her the solidity she needed. "Don't be dramatic." He kissed her temple, then whispered. "Let's go back home and get some sleep. We'll figure this out in the morning."

Her hot breath dampened her face as she pressed it against his hard muscles. "He'll be in lock-up all night."

"Yes, but I'm sure he'll think you're worth every second of confinement. I know I would."

No one's worth it. Especially not me. But Dominik was right. She couldn't help Max now.

Tomorrow was a different story.

* * * *

Every vertebra in Max's spine creaked stiffly, as though connected by rusty hinges. He pushed off the cement bench, then went to the steel sink-toilet combo to splash some water on his face. He dried his face with his sleeve, then rested his hip on the sink and surveyed the small holding cell where he'd spent the night. After getting handcuffed and hauled to the station, being locked in here had been anticlimactic. There weren't any bars on the door. The cops hadn't roughed him up. Actually, getting arrested kind of reminded him of getting sent to the penalty box. Only there was stuff to do in the box, like chat with the fans or bitch at the refs. Here all he could do was sleep or stare at the pale blue cement walls.

Somehow, he had a feeling the local reporters would make him getting charged with aggravated assault sound as big as the trumped-up Gretzky debacle. Not that he cared. Media attention didn't bother him. This shit upsetting Oriana did, though. That and a possible suspension.

The small slot in the steel door slid open. "Wrists out, Perron. I've got to put the cuffs back on you. Your lawyer's here."

Max stuck his hands out. The cold metal cuffs snapped onto his wrists. As soon as the door swung open, he grinned at the short cop with the shiny bald head who'd booked him hours earlier. "I'm tellin' you—my lawyer's a genius. Keep your bets on the Cobras for the next game, Officer McCaige. The 'Catalyst' will perform his magic."

He's a cop, not a fan, Perron. He mentally kicked himself. Officer McCaige had joked about putting money on Minnesota when the teams met on Tuesday, but he didn't look like he was in the mood to kid around anymore.

"Hey, did something happen?" He glanced down as the cop's hand clamped around his upper arm. "My lawyer got me an after-hours hearing, right?"

"You're not eligible. Coach Stanton's doctor just sent in his report." The cop opened the interview room door and gestured for Max to go in. His tone was detached, like he didn't give a fuck, but he glared at Max as though he felt betrayed. "I almost bought the 'we scuffled and he fell.' Guess he 'fell' on your fist hard enough to break a few ribs, eh? You fucking pros think you're above the law, but I've got news for you, buddy. You might be looking at attempted murder."

And with that, Officer McCaige slammed the door in his face.

A queasy, too-much-beer-chased-by-a-bottle-of-tequila sensation spread through Max's gut. His skin felt hot, then cold.

Attempted murder?

"Max." The lawyer stood and held out his hand as Max approached the metal table. "Why don't you have a seat?"

Max didn't shake the man's hand. Or sit. His confidence in the slick man took a nosedive. Bernie King was the lawyer for the entire team. The coach charging a player with aggravated assault or worse . . . Well, wouldn't that be conflict of interest?

"I'd like to be assigned another lawyer. Can you arrange for someone impartial?" His voice sounded nice and level, like he'd just asked King to recommend a good restaurant.

King laughed and leaned across the table. "How am I not impartial? Max, I've got nothing to gain by keeping you here. The team pays me to take care of you, and that's what I'm going to do." His friendly smile faded when Max didn't move. "Tell me what happened, and I'll advise you on how to proceed."

Yeah, I'm right on that. "How 'bout you tell me what you know?"

"Fine." King sat stiffly, hands pressed to the table as though preparing to rise again in a hurry. "According to the security guard, you stormed into Coach Stanton's office, then locked the door behind you. He heard shouting, then heard things being smashed. He tried to get in the room and called the police when he couldn't. They found you holding the coach against the wall. He was bleeding profusely from a cut on his head. You claimed he grabbed you, and when you shook him off, he tripped and hit his head on the side of his desk. According to you, he—" King cleared his throat and imitated Max's southern drawl "—'keeled over, then laid there for a bit, real quiet-like. I done checked his pulse—he wasn't dead, which was good. Then, suddenly, he jumps up and starts yelling that he's gotta get out of there. I didn't want him to hurt himself no more, so I held him. And that's it.'"

Max seriously doubted he'd used those words—'course, he'd been pretty agitated, and his speech roughened up when he got stressed. Either way, King obviously didn't believe him innocent. Or smart enough to insist on another lawyer.

Lips curved in a cold smile, Max jerked his chin toward the door. "Thank you, Mr. King. You may leave. I find myself in need of legal counsel that won't treat me like a stupid redneck. I graduated from the University of Michigan with a bachelor's in engineering. So, you see, I've got the brains to know when I'm getting screwed."

King stared at Max for a moment. Then smirked. "Have it your way, Max. I might have been able to work out a deal for you." He picked up his briefcase and clucked his tongue as he made his way across the room. "You should have done what Stanton asked."

Slimy, manipulative bastard. Max should have guessed King would be in on something this dirty. "I play to win." He clenched his fist as his control slipped. "If Stanton wants to start rigging the games, he'll have to do it without me."

Letting out a snort, King walked out.

The glossy-headed cop stood in the open doorway. "Doesn't look like that went your way."

Max ignored his spelling out the fucking obvious and went over his odd conversation with King. The man's confidence irked him. The idea of another lawyer getting involved hadn't fazed the weasel at all.

But why? Like he said, he got nothing to gain by keeping me here. Unless—

Stanton had asked him to throw the next game. Which would put the Cobras five points out of the eighth spot in the Eastern Conference. With four games left, that wasn't an option. They didn't have a great shot at the playoffs, but for the first time, he considered the slim chance of them sliding in.

If you're not on the first line, they don't have to worry about you throwing the game.

He looked at the cop. "I'd like my one phone call now, please."

Chapter Thirty

D awn oozed into the living room, a sickly yellow light, like the sun itself was reluctant to rise. Sloan raised his fist to knock on Mason's door which had been locked all night. Several times Sloan approached the door and heard Mason whispering to Oriana while she sobbed.

Her pain chiseled Sloan's heart—odd, because he didn't do *empathy*—but he accepted Mason as the most capable of getting Oriana through this. Hopefully, he'd given her the strength for what came next.

He rapped on the door with his knuckles. "Oriana, Mason, we need to talk."

The door whooshed open. Mason's big body blocked the doorway. "You've got nothing to say to her, Callahan."

A small hand curled over Mason's shoulder, tugging him back. "Dominik, let him in."

Lips pressed together, Mason inclined his head, then spun around and went to sit on the bed.

Oriana held out her hand. "Come on."

Relief clocked him square in the chest. He gave her his hand and let her lead him across the room. She settled down by Mason and patted the mattress on her other side.

"Let's hear it."

The strain in her voice brought out every ounce of tenderness he possessed. He covered both her hands with his own. "Max called me." Her brow wrinkled, and she blinked fast. "Before I say anything else, he made me promise to tell you he was—"

"Okay. Yes, Dominik made the same promise right after Max was arrested. I've heard all that. I know the basics of what happened. What I want to know is how much is his bail set for? You'll pay it, right?" She tugged her hands loose when Sloan didn't immediately answer and hooked the fingers of one hand to his collar. "*Right?*"

If only it was that easy. He licked his lips, searching for the words that would make things okay for her. And found none. "There's no bail. Not yet. The charges were too serious for an after-hours settlement. But what's more important is—"

"Nothing's more important! God, Sloan. He's in *jail!*" She shot of the bed and let out a little scream. "He's your teammate. Your friend. How are you both so calm?"

Mason looked at him, then inclined his head in a way that said he would shelve their personal issues. For the moment. "Freaking out won't do him any good, pet."

"Don't call me that! Not now!" Her whole body trembled as though physically, mentally, this was all too much. "I was out playing with Tyler and Sloan while Max paid for my actions. I'm not stupid. I know this is my fault."

"Stop." Mason stood and snapped. "Sit."

Oriana sat, right there on the floor. Then scowled and almost bounced up again.

"Move and I'll chain you to the bed," Sloan said. He held up his hand when Oriana glared at him. "This isn't the time for games, but if you can't control yourself, the two of us are quite capable of doing it for you."

"I can control myself just fine, thank you very much." She gritted the words out through her teeth.

Sloan grinned at the feisty firecracker. "You're very welcome, love." He slid off the bed, onto the floor, putting them at equal level. "As I was saying, Max called me. He confirmed something we've all suspected for a long time, only it's worse than we thought." He paused to gather his thoughts. Part of him was still dumbstruck by the whole fucked-up situation. "A lot of people bet on the games. They use stats—player standings, ice conditions, et cetera. The bigger the odds, the bigger the payoff. There have been accusations in the past of player injuries being leaked—especially during playoffs when teams are really quiet about any exploitable weaknesses. We thought Paul might be giving out info to get a cut since he can't actually bet on games. But he's actually fixing the games. He told Max to throw the one tomorrow—as a condition to him leaving you alone. The man must be pretty desperate to show all his cards like that. Max thinks his 'partners' are putting pressure on him. We've been on a hot streak, so a lot of people are probably betting we'll win, what with the playoffs as motivation. For the first time in years, we might make it."

In a position almost identical to "the Thinker" statue, Oriana seemed to drift off for a bit, absorbing everything he'd said. Then she hopped to her feet. "Maybe Paul kept a record of the wagers or an account of his cut. If he doesn't know that I know, they might still be at the condo!"

She tore off her nightshirt, then dove for her suitcase. Her tits bounced as she flung random clothes around the room. Mason stared. Sloan did his best not to laugh. Much better. Once she set her mind on something, there was no stopping her, no matter how crazy the idea. Her energy sizzled into him, and he almost believed this one would pay off.

Mason didn't look so sure. "There's no guarantee, bunny." He bent over and started picking up the undergarments littering his floor. "I don't want you—"

"Shut up," Oriana said, pulling on a loose shirt, not bothering with a bra. Then she wiggled into a pair of tights, straightened, and put her hands on her hips. "Do you have a better idea, *Master?*"

Eyes narrow and black with ire, Mason fairly growled. "Yes."

Oriana's brows arched under her tousled bangs. "Unless it's a way to help Max or the team, I don't want to hear what you have to say. Punish me for my rudeness later."

"I plan to."

Focused as she was, Oriana still shuddered in response to the threat in Mason's tone. Sloan got a little hard, considering the ways he'd involve himself in disciplining her. Because he would. And with all those bruises he'd left . . . Mason wouldn't spank their mouthy little sub. Actually, Sloan would be surprised if Mason ever used spanking as a punishment unless he needed a spur-of-the-moment way to make a point. The girl had no idea what she'd gotten herself into.

* * * *

You might want to get your stuff out. Your dad sold the condo.

Oriana crumpled the note from Paul in her hand and took a deep breath. Bile rose in her throat. Her father had taken everything, which shouldn't have surprised her, but—

God, I really mean nothing to him.

Closing her account hadn't been enough. She'd been stupid enough to move here for him, to become dependent on him, giving him all the power. And in return, he'd tossed her away like so much trash.

I'm homeless and broke. This is what I get for trying to be the perfect daughter.

Of course, the "perfect daughter" wouldn't have resorted to blackmail.

What else was I supposed to do? Stay with Paul?

No. Maybe things hadn't gone as planned, but at least she was free. Whatever happened, she was finally worth something to someone. Several someones. She had everything she could ever want. Except Max's freedom. Which she was working on.

"This might take a little longer than planned." She tossed the words over her shoulder as she unlocked the door. "There are some things I need to get out of here. I have no idea how much longer this place will be mine."

She dropped the paper and went inside. A crinkle behind her told her one of the men had picked up the note. Didn't matter. She could stay with Max until she got a job and found a place. Despite her pride's protest, reason prevailed.

Once again, she needed evidence. If she found some, everything would work out.

"Where did Vanek go after you came back?" She heard Dominik ask Sloan from somewhere below while she scoured through the office off the bedroom upstairs. "I haven't seen him."

"He took off right after we pulled in," Sloan replied. "Probably went to stay with one of the other guys."

Her chest tightened. That was her fault too. She couldn't make amends with Tyler now, but as soon as she dealt with the mess she'd gotten Max into . . .

She flipped through all the account books on Paul's desk, frustrated when she realized she had no clue what to look for. None of the books would be labeled "Fucking Over My Team." One labeled "Stats" looked promising, but the numbers beside each player's name matched everything she already knew.

"Find anything?" Sloan asked as he stepped into the room.

There was no hope in his tone, only acceptance. He didn't believe they'd find anything here.

Please let him be wrong.

She opened a big black book without a label and ran her finger over the games listed by date. A discrepancy quickened her pulse.

"You won this game." She pointed at a date in March. "But this says loss. That's got to mean something?"

Please tell me I'm right?

Sloan took the book and propped his hip on the edge of the desk while he balanced the book on one hand. "We did win." He ran his finger down over the dates. "And look. There's a few other games, wins and losses, scribbled out." He flipped through the pages. "The last game he marked as a loss was scratched out so hard the page is ripped. This is it!"

She hopped up and hugged Sloan. "That's exactly what I wanted to hear!"

He hooked an arm around her waist and held her firmly in place. "Yes, but you do realize this won't stand up in court—or even under the scrutiny of the commissioner. But—" he cuffed her chin lightly with his fist when she let her disappointment show "—it should be enough for an investigation. We'll get Max a good lawyer. With his testimony and this, maybe the league will—"

"Let me see." Dominik took the book, pacing while he studied the pages as though memorizing every condemning detail. "We tied all these games, Callahan, then either won or lost in overtime. This proves nothing." He sighed. "Besides, even if you're right and Stanton 'predicted' the games ahead of time, how do we prove that now? We'll look like we're setting him up—and doing a lame ass job of it, too. All we have to go on is Perron's testimony. He's got a clean record, which should work in his favor. All he has to do is threaten to go public—if he did, the league would have to do an inquiry just to save face."

Oriana thunked her forehead against Sloan's chest. "So we did all this for nothing."

"Not for nothing." Dominik bent to kiss the exposed flesh

above the collar of her T-shirt. "We might have found something. In any case, Perron just called. He's got a new lawyer, one who might be able to get him out on bail by the end of the week. He sounds optimistic—and he wants to talk to you."

A starburst of happiness exploded in her chest. She looked over her shoulder at Dominik "He's on the phone? Now?"

"Yes." Dominik hooked a Bluetooth over her ear, hit a button on his cell, then motioned for her to "go ahead."

"Max?"

"Hello, darlin'. Are you all right?" His tone sounded gruff with concern. "Mason told me Sloan hurt you, then left you alone. I thought you were just going to meet his dad . . . shit, I don't mean you shouldn't have . . . well, you shouldn't have done anything extreme, but—"

Oriana moved away from the men, cupping her hand over her ear so she could hear Max better. She had to get herself a Bluetooth; she loved the way he sounded like he was right there with her. The only thing better would be if he really was.

"I told Sloan I was okay. Maybe I wasn't completely honest, but that's my fault. Besides, I would have gotten real bitchy if he hadn't gone after Tyler. He needed Sloan more than I did." She went to the bedroom, to her bed, and nestled into the pillows. "What about you? Dominik said you made him wait outside. You wouldn't be locked up if you'd had a witness."

Max was silent for what seemed like a very long time. Then he said quietly, "I needed to face Paul alone. Maybe it wasn't smart, but, you know, what's done is done. Forget that. I want you to do something for me."

She didn't even think twice before answering. "Name it."

"My lawyer got me half an hour of phone time. I want to spend it with you—picturing what the men are doing to you."

Two sets of footsteps dragged her attention from the pillow she was hugging to the door. Dominik went to her dresser and shuffled through the top drawer. Sloan crawled onto the bed behind her.

Air jammed in her throat. She stuttered. "W-what will they—"

"They'll do exactly what I've asked them to." Max's breath sounded ragged in her ear. "And I'll be here for a bit to make sure you're okay, then Mason will take over. Do you trust my judgment?"

Her body trembled with excitement, fear, and other feelings she had no words for. She hissed in a breath as Sloan pulled her hands behind her and positioned them at the base of her spine.

"Don't move," he said in a way that guaranteed she wouldn't.

Something rough, yet pliant, looped around her forearms. A rope. Slightly cool, and smooth, like satin. Like the curtain ties from her living room windows.

He wound the rope around and around, from just above her wrists to just below her elbows, tight enough to draw her shoulders back without putting any strain in her arms.

Sloan tugged the ropes. "Comfortable?"

She nodded. Then shook her head. The ropes felt odd, much more secure than hands or a belt.

"Oriana," Max said. "Trust? Answer?"

Oops. "I told you I trusted you. I always will." She meant it, but . . .

"Good girl." Max's approval made her all glowy from the inside out. "Dominik is going to blindfold you. Is he doing it?"

He was. One of the red and gold silk scarves from Oriana's collection—all gifts from her sister who didn't "get" her lack of fashion sense—slid over her eyes. Sunlight filtered through the sheer fabric, and she could just barely make out the shadowy shapes of her dressers, the bed frame, and . . . *Dominik?* Yes, had to be Dominik, Sloan was still behind her, testing the snugness of the ropes by running his fingers under them. Then he trailed his finger up her arms. The featherlight touch grazed a ticklish spot, and she jumped. The ropes seemed to tighten, like living things, snakes, inhibiting movement. She twisted her wrists. *I'm stuck.* Her heart hammered in her chest. *Oh, bad. Very bad.*

"You've got to play along for this to work, love. Talk to me. The way you're breathing, short and fast, makes me think you've been blindfolded—and perhaps bound as well?"

Max's casual question pulled her away from panic mode. His voice might not give her the carnal thrill Dominik's did, but it still affected her. Listening to him made her feel cozy, like shedding confining layers after a hard day, then curling up on the sofa with a favorite blanket and a mug of cocoa. Everything about Max made her feel like she was finally home.

"Did Sloan tie you up, babe? I asked him because he's got skill, and rope work relaxes him." Max paused. "He's admitted that tying a sub up is almost as erotic as the first slice of a whip on her flesh. The heightened anxiety as she forces herself not to struggle, the fear of what's to come . . . I'm not a sadist, but even I find that hot. Tell me, Oriana. Are you a little afraid?"

Her palms dampened. She hadn't been. He'd taken her fear.

Then handed it right back.

Answer. Max is waiting. "Yes. A little."

Max's voice soothed her. "Your safe word is Flora. You know the statue of the goddess near the bandstands I pointed out—she reminds me of you. Sensual. Beautiful. Can you remember that, precious?"

Her shirt was pulled off, left to hang over her bound wrists. She'd gotten somewhat used to being naked around these men, but not seeing where they were, not knowing what they'd do, made her feel much more exposed. She hunched over in an effort to hide her breasts. The pillow still in her lap covered her a little.

Until someone took it away.

"No hiding. Not today," Dominik said from right in front of her. "Sit up straight and put your feet flat on the floor."

She moved to obey.

"Wait," Max said in her ear. She froze. "Tell him your safe word."

She nodded, then tipped her head up. "Max wants me to tell you my safe word is Flora."

"Good. Use it whenever you need to, but I'll be paying very close attention to you, so I'll probably notice any discomfort before you even think to say the word." Dominik's fingers traced her lips. "You'll be including Max by giving him details. Otherwise, I'd want you silent. Since you have the advantage of speech, don't hesitate to let me know if you're overwhelmed. We can slow down, discuss any issues, and decide together whether or not to go on. Understand?"

She gave him a quick nod.

"If you're allowed to talk, 'Yes, Master Mason' might be a good idea right now," Max said. "You want to stay on his good side."

Max's warning kicked her anxiety up another notch. *Ugh, if you were here, I'd smack you.* "I understand, *Sir.*"

"Excellent, pet." Dominik's baritone deepened with disapproval. "Perron told us he wanted you to start using the title of Master during play. Did he fail to mention it?"

Should I lie? To Dominik? Not a good idea. "His exact words were, 'It might be a good idea.'"

"I see." Dominik didn't sound impressed with her honesty. "So you've no desire to please him. Or to truly submit."

"No! I do want to please him, I just . . ." *Just what? He's right. You ignored him 'cause you were annoyed.* But she did want to please Max. Very confusing. "I guess I took it more as a suggestion than an order."

Dominik's hand caught her chin firmly. "Yes, well, I suggest you stop using Max being nice as an excuse to deny yourself the experience of true submission. He's still learning, so you mistakenly believe you've got room to wiggle out of obedience. Sloan and I are here to rid you of that illusion."

Scarier and scarier. But this time, she let the fear trickle through her and stopped fighting how much it turned her on. Her pussy moistened, her nipples hardened. She was ready to do anything they asked.

Starting with doing as she'd been told. She placed her feet on the floor and said quietly. "I'm sorry, Master Mason. I'll be good."

Sloan roared out a laugh behind her. "This I've gotta see."

His disbelief made her even more determined. She remained perfectly still as something clunked on the floor near her feet. A ripping sound had her tensing up, but she didn't move when something flat and sticky was wrapped around one ankle. Then the other. Curious, she shifted her legs. They were restrained far apart.

"You've got some scissors for the rope I presume?" Dominik asked.

"Yeah." Sloan replied.

"Good. Cut her tights and panties off." Before she had a chance to react to Dominik's alarming instructions, he continued. "Max must be feeling left out, pet. Tell him what we're doing."

She wet her lips and nodded. "I can't see what they've used, but my legs are being held apart."

"Dominik used duct tape and a hockey stick," Sloan said. "Pretty creative."

Her eyes widened under the blindfold. *A hockey stick?* She relayed the information to Max.

He chuckled. "What a fucking visual. I'm gonna be thinking of this next time I get on the ice, darlin'. Your beautiful thighs open wide, restrained on my stick. Who needs a spreader bar?"

Obviously, anything Dominik "needed" he could improvise from whatever was handy. She hoped he wouldn't decide she needed some kind of gag. She'd rather not have a hockey puck jammed between her teeth.

That image made her giggle. Cold metal touched her hip, and she jumped.

"What's happening?" Max asked.

Snip, snip, snip. She felt her tights stretch away from where Sloan had cut.

She scrunched up her nose. "Sloan's hacking up my clothes. I don't know why they didn't take everything off before tying me up. Seems kinda stupid to me."

Max groaned. "Oh, Oriana."

"Tilt her back, Sloan." Dominik's tone had changed. He didn't sound annoyed or disappointed. Definitely not mad. The tone was more like . . . steel-edged control.

A firm grip on her shoulder tipped her until she was balancing on the roundest part of her butt. Her nerves buzzed as though every last one was on high alert. All her senses focused on Dominik.

The fresh, slightly musky scent of the shampoo he'd used the night before filled the air as it had when she'd slept in his arms. *Nice.* She smiled a little at the memory. The rough calluses on his palms slid up her calves, causing the muscles in her legs to jerk. He lifted her legs up high, then lowered them slowly. The scruff on his cheeks brushed her inner thighs. Little shivers of arousal traveled over her, and her toes curled. His shoulders forced her thighs open even more, causing her pussy lips to part. His breath teased her very wet folds.

Sloan let out a low laugh as he nuzzled her cheek. "Time to pay for being so naughty, bunny."

Pay? Oh! Dominik's tongue thrust right into her, pressing past the inner muscles that immediately clenched. The abrupt penetration drove heat up and up, until she felt like her climax was a spring, already coiled deep, ready to be released. She panted, amazed that he'd gotten the reaction so fast.

"Oriana?" Max prompted gently.

She shimmied her hips as the tip of Dominik's tongue wiggled. The bruises on her butt gave a throb of protest, but the pain merged with pleasure, heightening her awareness of everything he was doing to her. A little bit more . . . *Don't forget, Max.* She gasped and blurted out. "Dominik's got his tongue inside me. Oh! Mmm—Max, it's nice. So *fucking* nice . . ."

Dominik's wicked tongue eased in and out, torturously slow. He withdrew, swirled his tongue around her clit, then thrust. Withdrew, swirled, thrust. The rhythm brought her right to the precipice of what she knew would be one of the most intense orgasms she'd ever had. Her body shook. Her back bowed. Her eyes rolled back in her head.

And he stopped.

Every exquisite sensation abruptly died, leaving only the agonizing need for release. She clenched her fists and shook her head. "No! Dominik—Master—Please don't stop!"

"I already have, pet." Dominik lifted her legs up and off him. She saw his shadowy form through the blindfold, moving toward the window. "If you're very sorry and very good, I may eventually let you come. I haven't decided yet."

"Damn you, I'm sorry!"

"I'd try a different approach if I was you, darlin'," Max said with a hint of laughter in his tone. "Subs beg; they don't make demands."

She *hmphed,* then groaned as her core throbbed miserably. "Please, Master Mason, I'm sorry, honestly."

"I don't believe you," Dominik said. "Do you, Sloan?"

"Nope." Sloan gave her a light kiss on the cheek, then slid away from her. "She's desperate. Not sorry."

Dominik returned and knelt in front of her. Without a word, he slid a finger into her pussy and stirred it around until she squirmed, then pulled it out. "Not quite desperate yet, either. But very hot. Maybe we should find a way to cool her down a bit so we can start over."

She whined, pitifully. Shamelessly. She didn't want to cool down. Or start over. "Master—"

"Shh." Dominik pressed his wet finger over her lips. "Give Max something to dream about tonight. Tell him what you want."

"Yes, in detail," Max said, his tone husky and strained. "The guard just told me my time's up. I asked him for one more minute, so make it count."

Her head felt all light and airy, like her skull was stuffed full of big, fluffy cotton balls. But at Max's last words, the throbbing down below moved up to her chest. She tried not to think of him, locked up and out of reach. She pictured him there, in the room, watching Sloan and Dominik toy with her.

And did her best to make him feel like he was. "My pussy's so wet, Max, from being so aroused, from Dominik's tongue plunging deep inside me. The room smells like sex already and I can taste myself . . . Dominik slicked my lips with my own juices. I want him to fill me up with his big, hard cock and f-fuck me." Her throat tightened, making it difficult to speak. Talking dirty didn't feel natural. Missing Max made it worse. But she pressed on. "Then I want Sloan to fuck me. I want to come, then come again and again, picturing you with me." Her breath hitched and she sobbed. "I want to be used, and I want to forget that you're not here and that I don't know when I'll see you again."

"You listen to me." Max's gentle but firm command leveled her out, bringing her back from the brink of completely falling apart. He made it so she could breathe again. "Dominik is capable of taking you to a place where nothing but pleasure can touch you. Let him help you forget everything but what you're feeling. You'll be punished, then you'll be rewarded for taking your punishment like a good little sub. That's what you want, right?"

"Yes." At that moment, even punishment sounded like a good distraction. "Yes, Sir."

"That's my girl." His tenderness spread like the lovely burn of a strong shot of spirits. She heard his smile and forced her own even though he couldn't see. "Make me proud, love."

"I will." Silence. "Max?" The dial tone pierced her skull like a sharp spike of sound. All bound up, she couldn't get rid of it herself. But she tried anyway. She rubbed her shoulder against her ear to knock the Bluetooth loose. "He's gone. Take it out!"

Dominik unhooked the Bluetooth and stroked her cheek. "Hey. Relax. Give me a minute and I'll untie you. I don't think we should—"

No! We can't stop! I promised! She shook her head and latched on to the only way she could think of to force Dominik to keep going. "My *real* Master gave me an order I plan to obey. If you can't follow through with your part, Sloan will. Go away."

A chilling laugh from Dominik made goose bumps rise on her flesh. He kissed her lips, a firm, possessive kiss that told her he wasn't going anywhere. "You're sorely in need of discipline, my sweet. Unless you use your safe word, I shall be giving you exactly that."

Arousal spilled over sadness, coating it like sweet syrup. Not enough to drown the pain, but enough to distance her a little. She sucked her teeth. "I won't use my safe word, *Master.*"

"Good. I was hoping you'd say that." He paused. "Do you have the ice, Sloan?"

"Yeah," Sloan said, his voice rough. "She okay?"

Whoa, wait a second! Ice? Her lips moved, but her tongue refused to work.

"She'll be fine." A watery, sucking sound followed Dominik's words. He spoke like he had something in his mouth. "Hold her open for me."

Fingers settled on her pussy, parting her inner and outer labia. Lips covered her, then something cold was pushed inside her. Her muscles rippled, trying to push it out. "Ah! Cold!"

"Ice is, bunny." Dominik licked her clit, then chuckled. "My, my, you are hot. This one's almost melted already. I think you need more."

Another ice cube slipped in, followed by another, and another. Dominik sucked on her clit, and her entire body felt like it would melt right along with the ice. Then she heard a click and caught the scent of wax burning. Flames lapped over her belly and she screamed.

* * * *

Sloan poured a thin line of black wax across Oriana's stomach, smiling as she bucked against Mason's mouth, screaming. Mason brought her to the precipice of another climax, then stopped and gestured for more wax.

Another line, this time across her thigh. Her hips rose up as far as they could go, then dropped. Her thighs shook in little spasms. He let little drops fall between her breasts, and her nipples seemed to jut out, begging for their share.

Soon. He tipped the black candle, and wax spilled down the curve of one breast. Her breasts jiggled as she dropped her head back and stuck out her chest. More wax, on the other breast this time, long lines overlapping until he reached the pale pinkish-brown edge of one areola. Her whole body writhed—her concept of pain had morphed into intense pleasure. He loved how quickly she did that, looked forward to pushing her limits, making her balance the line between rapture and agony a little longer, just to see how high her pain threshold actually was. There were so many things he wanted to do to her . . .

"Pleasepleaseplease," she chanted, obviously so close another drop of wax would set her off.

But she wasn't where she needed to be. Not yet.

With one arm curved behind her back, Sloan tilted her and caught a very erect little nipple between his teeth. He tugged, and she jumped. Her responses thrilled him. His dick had been hard from the second he'd tied her arms behind her, but now he felt like he did just before a penalty shot. The clarity of his vision was razor sharp. Everything seemed magnified. He could see the tiny transparent hairs on the flesh of her breast sticking right up, feel the texture of her nipples on his tongue, smell the heady musk of her arousal. Her body seemed to speak to his, like her desires had been spelled out in the black splatters of wax.

He picked up the canvas bag he'd found in the kitchen pantry where Oriana stored her candles and other fun things. One last hard suck and he released her nipple.

"Brace yourself, bunny." He watched her tense, grinned, and fished a wooden clothespin out of the bag. He tapped her nipple twice with the end of the clothespin, then pinched the prongs, and clamped the hard little nub.

She yelped and jiggled around like she thought she could shake off the offending thing. "Sloan, what—"

"I prefer 'Sir' or 'Captain,' pet." He gave her other nipple a sharp tug, then snapped a clothespin on it.

Oriana's lips parted and she gasped. "Sir!"

Well aware that she'd enjoy the new sensations in a moment or two, Sloan turned his attention to adding more clothespins to the underside of both breasts. While he worked, Mason left the room, then returned with a fresh tray of ice, a hair brush, and some olive oil.

"What's the brush for?" Sloan asked, sure Mason didn't plan to style Oriana's hair.

"You'll see." Mason winked, then returned to his earlier position between Oriana's thighs. "You went through the ice very fast, sweetheart. I got you some more."

Rather than immediately stuffing more ice inside her, Mason began gliding a cube around her pussy, down one thigh, up the other, lapping up the trails of water as he went along. "No more ice for your pussy until you ask me nicely, pet."

Sloan grinned as he took a needle and some strong thread from his stash. He deftly threaded the needle, then glanced at Mason. "Do you think I'll finish with our sub's decorations before she starts begging for a cunt full of ice?"

Mason paused, holding what remained of the ice cube at the top of Oriana's mound to let the water drizzle down between her folds. "We haven't discussed hard limits with her. Are you sure she'll be okay with her flesh being pierced?"

Oriana's whole body went stiff. She shook her head. "Please, Sir! No piercing, no cutting! The pinching is almost more than I can take!"

Stroking her side to soothe her, Sloan murmured in his most

gentle tone. "I won't do any of that, little one. The pinching is just clothespins. I'm stringing them together to take them off."

The rigid muscles along her sides went soft, and she sighed her relief. "Oh. That's all right."

Brow arched, Mason watched him string the thread under and around the spring of each clothespin. "Aren't you supposed to drill holes for a zipper?"

"Usually, but one of the Dommes at the club taught me a different method that works in a cinch."

"Ah." Mason grinned and made a flicking motion with the finger and thumb of one hand.

Sloan dropped the lighter and a candle by Mason's knee.

Mason took a fresh piece of ice and drew it along the crease between Oriana's hip and thigh. "How are you feeling, Oriana? Any cramping in your arms or back? Any . . . *unpleasant* pain."

"No. I feel . . ." She purred like a content kitten. "Lovely. And I would like some more ice, please."

"Would you?" Mason waited until Sloan had the last clothespin strung up, then handed him an ice cube. After lighting the candle wick, he nodded at Sloan. "Well, since you asked so nicely."

Just as Sloan touched the exposed part of one clamped nipple with the ice, Mason let a drop of wax fall right on Oriana's clit. Her lips formed an O. A breathy cry escaped her, and then her face eased into an expression of pure wonder. Sloan pulled off the blindfold. The glaze in her golden eyes told him they'd gotten her in the right place.

A loud *Smack!* brought his gaze down to Mason. A bright red mark on Oriana's inner thigh showed where he'd hit her with the brush. Oriana didn't even jump. Instead, her lips curved in a smile of pure bliss. Another *Smack!* and her breathing sped up. Sloan eyed Mason as he gave her three more smacks on each thigh. Mason palmed an ice cube, positioned his hand over Oriana's mound, and inclined his head.

Sloan wound the thread attached to the clothespins around his fingers and tugged hard as Mason stuffed the ice into Oriana and then filled her with his fingers. Her lips parted in a soundless scream, and her whole body quivered as she came. Her body rocked like it did when he was deep inside her, as if she could feel him taking her hard. A light sheen of sweat coated her skin, and her head tossed from side to side as she helplessly rode the pleasure for what seemed like forever.

Exquisite. Sloan's dick twitched as he admired his work, as his heart and mind and fucking soul fist-thumped like they'd just scored the winning goal for the Stanley Cup. He grinned at Mason who grinned right back. Sharing this with one of his men—*No,* one of *her* men—he had to admit, felt pretty damn awesome. If only Perron could have been there too. His throat suddenly felt a little funny. Not like he'd get all emotional, but, hell, he enjoyed having his boy around. He couldn't recall the last time more than a day had gone by without them hanging out. And now he felt his friend's absence as much as he would on the ice.

Next time, Callahan. Definitely next time.

For now, he'd better man up. He and Mason had a spaced-out little sub to bring back down. Then he had a past carelessness to make up for.

Two tasks he would enjoy very much.

* * * *

Stretched out on some soft, cushy surface—clouds or a big marshmallow, Oriana couldn't decide—she felt her body slowly return. Every inch of skin, every nerve, every last hair on her head, seemed like it must be all glittery. She wouldn't say she'd been floating, but she'd certainly been somewhere else. Somewhere thoughts couldn't follow. Somewhere pain couldn't go. All she'd known was raw, carnal pleasure, as though her nipples and clit controlled every other part of her.

Reality came little by little. First, when her hands were unbound. The feeling of being suddenly free frightened her in a way she couldn't understand. But then the wonderful ropes returned, around her wrists and ankles, securing her. She didn't try to fight them. She didn't want them to let go.

Heat exploded from her nipples, and she arched off the bed. Firm hands held her down. Something hard and slick pressed between her thighs, stretching, filling. She cried out as it slammed in hard.

"Look at me, pet," a deep voice said. "Time to come back."

Her vision cleared a little. Golden specks surrounded a dark face. More golden specks filled beautiful brown eyes. She smiled. "Dominik."

"There we go. I want you with me while I make love to you, Oriana." He smoothed her sweat-slicked hair away from her cheeks and temples, then leaned down to kiss her lips. "Are you with me?"

"Mmm." She peered into his eyes and found herself slipping into the caves with the gold veins. *So pretty.* "I'm with you, Master."

Dominik chuckled, and the sound echoed off the walls of the caves. "Not quite. Sloan, undo her ankles."

The pleasant sensation of her legs being held went away. She whimpered. "No. I want—"

"Wrap your legs around my waist, Oriana," Dominik whispered before laying soft kisses on her cheeks. "You need to take back a little control of your body. Just a little. I've got you."

She did as she was told, and her limbs began to feel more real. The presence of Dominik's hard, pulsing dick came all at once as her core rippled into awareness around him. She moaned as he drew out slowly, then slid in, gradually increasing his pace. Her body felt drained, like she'd already come a thousand times. But deep within came the urge for yet another climax. If he reached just the right spot . . .

Her hips rose to meet him, and his pelvis ground down against her swollen clit. An orgasm hit her like wildfire barely extinguished, finding new fuel. She thrust up wildly, almost losing control once again.

With one last violent plunge, Dominik went still, and his dick twitched inside her. He didn't move again until his dick had softened. Then he slid out and took a seat on the bed at her side. When he rolled off the condom covering him and stood, she opened her mouth to protest. She didn't want to be left alone.

"I'm still here, sweetheart." Sloan settled on the bed at her other side and undid the rope holding one of her wrists to the headboard. "Just give me a minute to get you loose. I have a treat for you."

All her limbs being free seemed wrong, but she didn't have the energy to protest anymore. She just wanted to curl up in a little ball and go to sleep. Her body felt pleasantly used, but the lingering pleasure was shallow. Realizing how completely she'd lost control made her wonder what she'd said, or done, or let them do . . .

"Sit up for just a second, baby." Sloan helped her up as he spoke and cradled her against his chest. "Mason's brought you some water. Have a few sips."

She blinked as Dominik held out an uncapped bottle of water, then frowned when he brushed aside her fumbling hands and tipped the bottle against her lips. Turning her head, she reached for the bottle. She wasn't used to being taken care of like this. He frowned back at her until she dropped her hands to her lap.

The cool water was delicious. She gulped greedily and grabbed Dominik's wrists before he could take it away.

"Enough for now. Lie face down on the bed." Dominik's do-not-defy-me tone stole the urge to argue.

But as soon as she lay down, she wished she had the strength to say something. Every inch of her was sore, and Sloan hadn't had his turn yet. She didn't think she could take any more.

Sloan shifted on the bed and climbed over her. His weight rested on the back of her thighs. The scent of coconuts filled the air.

She glanced over her shoulder at him.

"Head down, sub," he said.

She pressed her forehead into her pillows. Her body tensed as he rubbed his hands up her back, then her bones liquefied as he pressed his very slick fingers into the muscles between her shoulder blades. The scent was suddenly familiar. A Christmas gift to herself, fractionated coconut oil, to go along with the couples' massage lessons she'd enrolled herself and Paul in—lessons he'd never found time for.

She'd also bought a bottle of almond oil for Paul. Had Sloan been able to tell which was hers, or was it just a good guess?

"My oil, but . . ." She blinked and tried to clear her head. "How did you know? There are others that I used for—"

"This is my body, bunny," he replied, pressing his knuckles into the rigid muscles of the small of her back. "I used the one I liked best."

Moaning as he continued to knead her body like dough, she decided she liked his answer. And liked him pampering her even more. She didn't feel weird or awkward or used anymore. She felt special.

Which probably explained the words that escaped her lips before she gave in to exhaustion. "I think I'm falling in love with you, Sloan. Almost as deeply as I've fallen for Max and Dominik."

Sloan stretched out beside her, then snuggled up against her in a way that made her sure she was dreaming. Snuggling just wasn't the captain's style.

"Tell me when you know for sure, Oriana. Be nice to know my feelings are shared."

Yep. Definitely a dream. Because that's exactly what you'd say in mine.

Chapter Thirty One

Thick foam slathered all over his cheeks and neck, Sloan sat on the edge of the bath and waited for Oriana to finish on the phone. They'd gotten back to Max's place early that morning. He'd just finished his pregame nap and started prepping to head to the forum when Oriana cornered him in the bathroom. Taking out a razor and a can of shaving gel, she'd informed him that he looked like shit, and, unless the Cobras made the playoffs, he had no reason not to shave.

And then the pushy little sub had *ordered* him to take a seat. *Told* him she intended to get rid of the stubble herself. His threats only made her smile in a way that said "You're going to hurt me? Promise?"

Mason definitely had better ideas for getting her in line than Sloan. Little Oriana enjoyed pain too much for it to be effective. A spanking for this brat would be like giving a naughty kid candy.

Not that he minded. Her masochistic side matched them perfectly. Besides, after seeing the sports headlines, he was pretty inclined to give Oriana her own way. Not only was Perron still in jail, but he'd been suspended for at least the remainder of the season, if not longer, pending an investigation. The commissioner refused to comment further on the situation.

This domestic stuff was likely something Oriana and Perron would have done if things were different. If using Sloan as a substitute made her feel better, then he'd put up with it.

Oriana paced the room, holding the phone against her ear with her shoulder, letting out a heavy sigh when she hung up. She hadn't spoken at all, so he guessed there'd been no answer.

She plastered a smile on her lips as she plucked the razor off the edge of the sink. "My father's not taking my calls. His secretary isn't answering either. Maybe everyone's busy . . . this game's pretty important . . ."

In other words, her father was pissed. He'd cut her off exactly as he'd promised. Until she crumpled under the pressure of managing on her own, her father would pretend she didn't exist.

Well, fuck him. Oriana wouldn't crumple; he and the men would get her through this with her pride intact.

But telling her so wouldn't help matters. Better revisit the matter of her fussing over a little bit of stubble. "This game *is* important. I should be with my men, not here getting primped. Who cares what I look like?"

"I do." And with that, she began scraping the razor up his jaw, cleaning away the hair with long, clean strokes. "And it's not just about how you look. Did you see the marks you left on my neck? I look like I've got rug burn."

"I'll give you rug burn." He growled, then smiled when she shivered. With one arm barred across the back of her thighs, he repositioned her between his knees. "You haven't seen my room yet. There's a nice thick rug on the floor in front of the fireplace. I've got a mind to drill some holes in the bricks for some chains."

She bit her bottom lip, her eyes sparkling with nervous anticipation. Then she cleared her throat. "You're making this difficult. I don't want to cut you."

"I trust you, sweetie." *Obviously, since you've got blades pressed against my throat.* An interesting thought occurred to him. "Speaking of which, how would you like me to use a knife next time we play?"

The answer in her hooded gaze was a definite "yes." But she shook her head. "I don't know if I'm ready for that yet."

Yet being the key word. They would both enjoy the added thrill. But she needed to feel safe. Maybe . . . "What if Perron—Max— what if he was there? Would you be ready then?"

"Yes." The razor went still. "No offense."

Tears painted a wet, black line beneath her lashes. His palm itched for a whip so he could self-flagellate. *I'm a fucking moron.* Mason forcing him to take over aftercare the day before might have bonded him and Oriana, but he was still emotionally inept. Never bothered him before, he didn't get that involved with his lovers. But he *was* that involved with Oriana. He cared about her happiness. He didn't want to hurt her . . . unintentionally, anyway.

He cupped her cheek. "He'll be out soon. His got a great lawyer who will get him a bail hearing. Focus on the positive."

"Yeah." She put on a brave front as she finished the job of

scraping his face, but he saw right through it.

He couldn't fix this for her, much as he wanted to. She needed Perron, which should make him feel a little insecure, but it didn't. He had his place with her, and he was sure, if he wasn't around, she'd miss him, too.

Once she'd wiped his face clean, she turned to leave. He caught her wrist and trapped her between his thighs.

"Sloan, I'm not in the mood for—"

"Quiet. Neither am I." He drew her to her knees in front of him and held her tight. "Just let me hold you for a minute, sweetie. Pretend it helps."

She rested her cheek on his forearm. "It does help, Captain."

Damn. He buried his face in her hair. *That's really nice to know.*

* * * *

The obnoxious ringing in Oriana's ear gave her a headache, but she kept trying to get through while waiting in Sloan's car for the men. Maybe her father would get fed up and finally answer. And once he heard what she had to say, he'd forget about being mad at her. No way did he know what Paul was doing—he wouldn't put up with it. He might suspect the money coming from Paul's partners was dirty, but the game itself was precious. Once he found out Paul was responsible for many of the team's losses, dreams of possessing "The Cup" would become his new obsession.

Her father's voice mail came on. She let her head fall against the back seat. Her eyes stung. "Daddy, please stop ignoring me! This is important!"

The car door opened. Sloan got behind the wheel.

Standing by the passenger side, Dominik leaned through the open window. "Why don't you sit in front, love?"

After pressing redial, she shook her head. "No, I'm good back here."

Of course, Dominik refused to leave it at that. He opened the back door. "I suppose making it a suggestion was a bad idea. You'll be alone during the game; we're not leaving you alone now."

Voice mail again. She pressed end. Then redial. "Does 'submissive' mean 'baby' in your language, Master Mason? Because I'll have you know—"

Dominik snatched the phone out of her hand, closed it, and stuffed it in his pocket. "No, but Dominant does mean lover, caretaker, disciplinarian, and whatever else the situation warrants. You're hurting yourself calling him again and again even though you know he won't answer. Why? Do you think you deserve him treating you like this because you went against his wishes?"

"No. I don't." *Do I?* She had to think that over for a minute. Truthfully, she wanted to make amends. "If I can help save the team, he'll be happy with me. And that's important. Maybe it shouldn't be, but it is. You hate him, and I get that, but he's still my father."

Knee braced on the seat beside her, Dominik leaned in and gave her a tight smile. "And I *get* that. But you will find a way to help the team that's more productive and less of an emotional mindfuck."

"Fine." She shifted over to give him space to sit. "So I guess I need to be disciplined again?"

The car door slammed and she jumped. Scooting all the way over to the other side of the car, she glanced up and tried to catch Sloan's eye through the rearview mirror.

His brow lifted as though to say "You asked for it."

Dominik's hand slipped behind her back and hooked around her waist. He slid her across the seat until she was practically glued to his side. His soft lips slipped down her earlobe. "You don't need discipline. You need a hug. Come here."

Oh! Well, she couldn't argue with that. She threw her arms around his neck and shoved herself into his embrace, smiling when he chuckled. The man was infuriating sometimes—especially when he was right.

This was exactly what she needed. Hugs. Lots and lots of hugs.

"Eventually, we will have to address you sassing me though, pet," Dominik said, tone light, but holding a note of seriousness. "I believe, once the bruises on your butt fade, I'll introduce you to a cane. What do you say?"

The very idea of him using a cane on her, considering the cutting impact her little pink book described, made her sore bottom clench and her panties damp. Her response was muffled by his jacket. "Yes,

Sir."

A peek at the rearview mirror, and she caught Sloan's grin. And wink. He'd likely guessed her reaction. Which made sense, since she'd begged him to hurt her.

Because, sometimes, I need that, too.

* * * *

Humming the chorus of a country song, Dominik taped his stick blade and rocked his skates in time to the beat. He'd expected nothing when he'd climbed in the backseat of the car with Oriana, but getting stuck in traffic had brought out her inner tease. And she'd paid for her teasing without a word of complaint. Then again, her sweet, soft lips gliding up and down his stiff cock didn't allow for many words.

It's good to be the Dom. His humming gave way to whistling.

Sloan whipped a puck at his head. The puck missed and clucked against the wooden back of his stall.

"Stop whistling, or I'm gonna make you swallow the next one." Sloan stood and adjusted his jock. "I should have let you drive."

T.J. stepped into the locker room wearing nothing but black Under Armor. The skintight polyester one piece was custom made and gave him the look of a really tall batman—missing just a mask and cape. He usually got to the locker room first because he preferred getting suited up before the horde came in. Actually, Dominik could only think of once when T.J. hadn't. The day after his daughter broke her leg.

He gave Sloan and Dominik an unreadable look, then shuffled over to his stall. Something was up.

Before Dominik could question him, Sloan blurted out, with his usual tact, "What the fuck's your problem, T.J.? You run over a puppy on your way here?"

If the captain's direct approach wasn't so effective, Dominik would have decked him. But since the men usually toughened up or spilled, he simply sat back and waited to see which T.J. would choose.

"My daughter got some bad news from her doctor, but she'll be all right. I found a specialist to take care of her." He hunched over and shrugged. "I had a rough couple of days."

"Shit, man, why are you here?" Sloan wrapped his right wrist and tore the athletic tape with his teeth. "Go be with your kid."

T.J. shook his head a bit too fast. He spoke while he pulled his shoulder pads over his head. "I'm playing." His gaze skirted away from Dominik's. "I promised her I would."

Nodding slowly, Sloan taped his other wrist. Then he gave T.J. a toothy grin. "Gotta respect that."

Dominik ran his tongue over his teeth and shook his head. T.J. was lying. But he wouldn't call him out—not until he figured out what the big man was trying to hide.

He didn't get a chance to pry. The rest of the team came in from the player's lounge, hollering like a bunch of drunk asses. Vanek was the loudest of them all.

"This is the year, boys! I can taste fucking Stanley!"

"So is that your new boyfriend's name, Vanek?" Carter, a third-line center, called out. "Mouthwash, my girlfriend says it gets rid of the aftertaste."

Sloan laughed. "She wouldn't have that problem if you'd wash your balls before she sucks on them."

"Hey, did you guys see the lineup?" Ingerslov, the backup goaltender, asked. "I thought Callahan was the one fucking the coach's girlfriend. Why'd he dump Vanek on the fourth line?"

The locker room went dead quiet. Both Sloan and Vanek looked like they'd been gut-checked. Vanek darted across the room and squinted at the whiteboard. He dug his fingers into his curly hair and silently read over the lineup.

"I—" He blinked at Sloan as the captain stepped up beside him. "But—"

"I thought that asshole was still in the hospital." Sloan punched the wall beside the whiteboard, and every man in the room winced.

The last thing they needed was their captain injured again. Fine, their odds weren't good, and they'd managed to cruise through a quarter of the season without him, but at the last leg of the race to the playoffs, none of them was ready to give up.

In the forum and on the road, Sloan usually kept his temper in check. But once he lost it, there were only two men who could rein him in.

Thankfully, Dominik was one of them.

"I've got an idea of how to deal with the Wild when they cork up the neutral zone. You wanna get the last game up on the screen?" Dominik waited, watching Sloan glare at the board, praying to the hockey gods that shop talk would get through to him.

Finally, Sloan inclined his head and went to the back room to set up the video system.

Dominik dropped a heavy hand on Vanek's shoulder and leaned in, speaking low so no one else could hear. "Go find Oriana and give her a heads up."

"But—"

"No." Without meaning to, Dominik had used the same tone he'd use on a defiant sub. And that shut Vanek right up. *Interesting.* He filed the information for later use and continued. "I don't care what happened between you. If nothing else, you're friends."

Vanek squared his shoulders. "We're a bit more than friends, Mason. I'm just surprised you'd send me instead of going yourself. Are you that confident that you'd give me a head start?"

A head start? The boy thought they were in some kind of competition for Oriana? Did he really believe he could make her forget the rest of them? Was he that delusional?

Rather than waste his time getting in a pissing contest with the kid, Dominik simply shrugged. "Give it your best shot. Just warn her that Paul is here."

"Gotcha." Vanek gave him a mock salute, then headed out. Halfway out the door, he paused and looked back. "No hard feelings, buddy. I still got you on the ice."

Dominik stared after him long after the door swung shut. Then he shook his head and grinned. The rookie had become like a little brother to him during the two seasons they'd played together. If Oriana was any other girl, he'd step aside and wish him luck. But Oriana wasn't just any girl. She was . . .

Mine. A primal part of his brain snarled. The controlled part amended. *Partially.*

Might not work for some, but it worked for him. And her. And them.

Them didn't include Vanek. Not long term. But, with the new revelation, he had some ideas for Vanek when they brought Oriana to the club. Which got his mind on ideas for her.

He resumed his whistling as he joined Sloan by the big screen.

* * * *

Oriana picked up the pay phone and fished some change out of her pocket. Her cell phone being confiscated wouldn't stop her from trying to reach her father one last time. Besides, he wouldn't recognize the number, so he might answer.

"If I get jumped by a fan, you're so gonna pay."

Her heart flipped in her chest, and she dropped the phone. It clanged against the wall as she looked up into Tyler's smiling face.

"Did I scare you?" He leaned his elbow on the wall over her head, his expression showing that he really hoped she'd say "yes."

"A little." She dropped her gaze to his snug, dark blue shorts, drew them up over his chiseled chest, nicely outlined by his skintight T-shirt, and felt . . . nothing. He was still sexy as hell, but her body didn't react to his the way it did to Max or Sloan or Dominik.

He cupped her cheek and studied her face. Then his eyes turned cold. "I don't measure up to them, do I?"

Oh no! Was she that easy to read? She really didn't want to hurt him, but she couldn't pretend . . . *Damn it, he's gonna think I used him. Which I basically did.*

She put her hand on his chest, pleading with her eyes for him to understand. "You must think I'm so selfish. I didn't mean—"

He silenced her with a kiss, then whispered. "I don't think you're selfish. I think you're confused because you've never really been loved before." He kissed her again. "How does it feel?"

"Wonderful." She bit her bottom lip. How freakin' messed up was this? She cared about him. A lot. Only not in the same way he cared about her. "But I'm not in lo—"

"Don't. Don't say something you'll regret later," he said, softly. "The other men overwhelm you with the whole dominance thing. You're mistaking that for something deeper, but it's too soon to know for sure. All I ask is a chance to prove I can be the man for you. You don't have to decide now. No pressure. All right?"

No pressure. That was the best thing she'd heard all night. There'd be other opportunities to make him see he *wasn't* the man for her. She gave him a shaky smile. "All right."

"Go up to the press box and watch the game. I'm winning this one for you." He traced her bottom lip with his thumb. "Can I have a good luck kiss?"

She nodded and let him claim her mouth, enjoying the warmth, the tenderness, even though the kiss felt like the end of all they'd shared. She could only hope she'd left him with some fond memories, that maybe, just maybe, they could still be friends once he accepted this was really over.

"We'll go out sometime—maybe catch a movie, just the two of us." He didn't wait for her answer before he continued. "Oh, and Dominik asked me to let you know Paul's around. You should be fine if you head right upstairs, but keep your eye out."

Lovely. She sighed and followed Tyler to the elevator. A group of men in suits got off. Near the stadium entrance, a gang of teenage girls mingled, all wearing Cobra's jerseys. Most with Tyler's number on their backs.

One turned and let out a piercing scream.

Tyler bolted.

Well, whatever happened, Tyler would never lack for attention. And he'd eventually find the woman for him. He deserved more than she had left to give.

She got on the elevator.

Just as the elevator doors were about to close, a man in a big black Cobra's sweatshirt slipped in. The hood of the jersey covered his face, and her blood chilled as he crowded her against the wall. With her luck, Paul had found her. But the man was too tall to be Paul. Maybe another player who'd decided to take a shot at the team's resident slut?

Her lashes clung together as her eyes watered. She'd certainly earned *that* title.

"Tears, Oriana?" His hands smacked the wall on either side of her head. Inside the shadows of the hood, Max's ocean eyes sparkled. "And here I was, thinking you'd be happy to see me."

One look at his face parted the dark clouds smothering her soul. Laughter broke free, and she latched on to the back of his neck, pulling him down so she could kiss his eyelids, his cheeks, his lips.

"I *am* happy to see you!" She forced herself to keep talking before she started blubbering. "What are you doing here? Did you get a bail hearing? Why didn't you call me?"

The elevator chimed, and the doors slid open. Max drew his hood up and touched a finger to his lips. Tim got on the elevator with a man who looked so militant Oriana half expected to see a gun strapped to his back. His white shirt and tie made him appear as tame as a wolf wearing sheepskin. Eyes the color of oak bark after a downpour locked on her, making her feel like a little bunny who'd make a nice snack.

Dean Richter, the general manager. She hadn't seen him since the night she'd found out Paul was cheating on her. And she'd never spoken to him. Had never wanted to, either. He got along well with both Paul and her father and treated her and her sister with barely tolerant disdain.

She huddled against Max, hoping Richter wouldn't notice him and would ignore her.

"Miss Delgado, what an unexpected . . ." Richter's lips twisted, as though tasting his next word. "Pleasure."

Screw being polite. Seeing him was unexpected but definitely not a pleasure. She felt around for Max's hand and let out a sigh of relief when his fingers laced with hers and squeezed.

Richter glanced at their clasped hands, then up at Max. He frowned. "Sloan? Shouldn't you be—"

Max flipped his hood off. "Sloan's getting ready. And I shouldn't be here at all."

"No." Richter stepped toward them and braced his elbow on the wall beside Oriana's head. "You shouldn't." He gave her a wolfish smile. "But I'm glad you decided to stop by. I've been meaning to ask you about your . . . unique relationship with Delgado's daughter. Are you planning to let her distract the whole team or just our best players?"

"Delgado's daughter." Like she didn't have an identity of her own.

No wonder he gets along with Paul.

"You fu—" She choked back the insult as Max clamped his hand around the nape of her neck.

"Saturday was our best game this season." Max stroked the length of her throat with his thumb. "Maybe she's just the distraction we needed."

"Maybe." Richter reached out and plucked a strand of hair off her shoulder. He wound it around his finger, his expression thoughtful. "I could use that kind of distraction myself."

Oriana twisted away from Max, shoved him back as he made a grab for Richter, and snatched her hair from the man's grasp. "Tough. Max doesn't share me with just anyone."

"But you admit he shares you?"

I should have kept my mouth shut. "I didn't say that."

"That is exactly what you said." He shook his head and went on before she could come up with any more lame-assed objections. "Don't misunderstand me, Oriana. I don't care who he and his buddies fuck. I only wish they'd avoided the drama that came with fucking *you*. Both Paul and your father claimed you were nothing like your sister. They claimed you were quiet, obedient, and—according to Paul— too plain to attract the kind attention Silver does. Up until now, I believed them." He used his finger to tip up her chin, and she smacked Max's chest when he lunged forward. "But somehow, without Silver's beauty or natural charm, you managed to attract all kinds of attention. And you've done more damage in one weekend than she managed to do in the months she spent publicly humiliating your father."

The elevator shuddered to a stop. Oriana sucked in a breath, ready to scream at him in defense of herself and her sister. But instead, she stepped off the elevator and squared her shoulders. Screaming at him would only prove his point.

So she tried a different approach. Silver might have all the family "charm," but Oriana had the brains. And it was about time she used them. "You're right. Mr. Richter."

Tim, who'd seemed perfectly happy to stand back and observe the passive-aggressive confrontation, slipped around his brother and touched Oriana's shoulder, shaking his head. "He's not right. You didn't want any of this."

"I wanted the same thing as Silver. Freedom. I was angry and afraid, and I didn't think of the consequences of my actions." She smiled at Max before turning to Richter. "But more good than bad came from what I did. You should thank me for 'fucking' your best players, Mr. Richter."

"Really?" He sounded amused and intrigued. "And why's that?"

"Because it gave me the motivation and the means to save your team."

Chapter Thirty Two

The girl should be in law school.

Max hooked his thumbs in his pockets and leaned on the wall behind Oriana, pride swelling in his chest, his dick swelling in his jeans. He'd always admired the way she trudged on despite Coach and her father's efforts to drag her down, but her strength had gone into simply putting one foot in front of the other.

Freedom looked fucking good on her.

Richter's expression was that of a man being told his faiths were based on fairy tales. Not convinced, but he'd hear her out. "How exactly do you plan to 'save' my team?"

"The fans are loyal, right? They proved that when the bid was made for the team five years ago. But attendance has been going down because the team's shown no consistency. You have some of the best players in the league, you should be Cup contenders, but you always fall short of making the playoffs." Her tongue darted over her lips, and she leaned closer to Richter, dropping her tone as though afraid to be overheard by the wrong person. "Haven't you ever wondered why you lose against some of the top teams by just a couple of goals? I'm sure you've heard the rumors."

"There are plenty of rumors, Oriana. If you're planning to use the one where Paul's defensive system is killing the team, I don't want to hear it. He's a damn good coach, and if the men followed his plays, they'd have the consistency they need. The problem is he's working with too many fucking egos, and I plan to change that." He sighed and shook his head. "Callahan is done here. Mason has one more year left to his contract, and if he doesn't fall in line, I'll trade him too. Perron—" He paused. "I'll be straight with you; I haven't decided whether or not I should renew your contract—"

Max scowled. "You're a fucking idiot, Richter. You'd rather tear the team apart than consider—"

Oriana elbowed him in the gut, knocking all the wind out of him. Then she pressed her hand over his mouth and jabbed her finger into Richter's chest. "Put Ingerslov in nets tonight. If I'm wrong, the Cobras might lose tonight, but if I'm right and you don't put him in, they don't have a chance. They've won two games in a row, and they've never been closer to making the playoffs. There's gonna be a lot of money on this game."

"You think the games are rigged?" Richter laughed. "That's insane. If Paul was fixing the games—which I assume is what you're implying—someone would have caught on by now."

"Not if he was smart about it," Oriana said. "He only needs one player to control the results. Unless the rest of the team starts playing a little too good, which they have been. Your defense is strong, and you have one exceptional line. You're lacking depth, but I think that's mostly because the rest of the team has given up. Why not show them you haven't?"

Head bowed, Richter paced away from Oriana, then returned and pulled his brother aside. "What do you think?"

Tim shrugged. "I think you should listen to the girl." He shot Oriana a wink. "Besides, *if* we're making a run for the playoffs, it makes sense to rest our starter. We do this real casual-like, and there shouldn't be any trouble."

"But you believe Paul's capable of . . ." Richter rubbed his lips with his fist. Then he nodded slowly. "Go tell Ingerslov he's up tonight. Let me know how Paul reacts."

"I'm on it." Tim pressed the button to call the elevator, then turned to Max. "Paul screwed up the attempted murder charges by calling another doctor in to clear him to leave the hospital. But he's got a restraining order on you, so stay out of sight."

Obviously. Max draped an arm around Oriana's shoulders. "I got that, but I thought you wanted to talk to me?"

"*I* asked to speak with you." Richter waved his brother on and led the way to his office. "I've heard Paul's side of what happened in his office. I need yours."

Taking a seat in the big, leather chair across from Richter's huge desk, Max pulled Oriana into his lap, needing her close. She blushed and tried to stand, but he simply tightened his grip on her waist. When she squirmed, he pinched her inner thigh.

She let out a high-pitched squeak and glared at him.

He caught her wrist and placed her hand over his erection. "The GM is a busy man, honey, but I do believe he'll give me a moment to discipline you if you don't behave. I missed you, and I want to hold you while me and him chat. Is that really too much to ask?"

For a second, the fiery glow in her eyes looked ready to ignite; he'd fueled an argument. But then her lips curved in a contented smile, and her whole body softened up. She snuggled into his chest. "No, Sir."

"That's my good little love." He kissed the top of her head, then looked at Richter who sat behind his desk, watching them with a closed-off expression.

Which slowly darkened to rage as Max recounted the events that led to his imprisonment and suspension. Richter had stood by his coach, despite the rumors, despite the grumbling of the players and fans. With good reason—a lot of coaches took heat when a team had a bad season. But he'd finally grasped the truth. He'd been betrayed.

Thankfully, he'd taken off his blinders in time to prevent any permanent damage.

* * * *

Oriana let the men talk over her head, perfectly happy to be left out of the conversation now that she'd had her say. Putting herself out there was not fun. She'd been afraid Richter would laugh at her and tell her she didn't know what she was talking about. Okay, he *had* laughed, but then he'd listened.

She tugged down the collar of Max's shirt a little to expose the pale gold dusting of hair at the top of his chest, then absently toyed with the curls. Her body had reacted almost instantly to his command and the brief bite of pain, the damp heat between her thighs made it hard to remember—or care—where they were. A naughty little voice in her head told her Max would enjoy having Richter watch them, but her chest tightened at the thought. She didn't want Richter to watch. The intimacy she'd shared with Max when she was with the other men . . . she couldn't say why, but it was special.

There were only two other men she wanted seeing her at her most vulnerable. Her nipples drew into sensitive peaks of need, and she shifted so they weren't squished between her arm and Max's chest.

Richter's gruff laugh made her jump. He gave her a toothy grin when she looked at him. "I'm heading to the box. Feel free to join me once you're done, Oriana. Your man will need updates on the game since he has to stay here, and I don't have a TV in my office."

"Thank you, Sir." Oriana's whole body felt so feverish she was sure only a dunk in a bath full of ice would cool her down. And thinking of ice only got her hotter. She was about to spontaneously combust in Max's lap.

"We appreciate the offer." Max's hand cupped her pussy as he spoke, making her wiggle uncontrollably. "I'd ask you to stay, but I'm feeling a little selfish right now."

"I completely understand." Richter stood and circled the desk, pausing at her side to skim his knuckles down her cheek. "Make it up to me by bringing her to the club some time. I'd like to see how Sloan's progressed with the whip. He's one of my best students, but his methods lack . . . passion when he's doing a scene with the subs who volunteer. I have a feeling things would be different with this one."

Her mind painted a lusty visual of Sloan in some dark, dungeon-like room, wielding a whip while she was chained to a wall. She could almost smell the sweat that would bead his bare chest. Her muscles twitched as though preparing for the lick of the whip. Would it be like fire? Like the kiss of a blade?

The wet throb between her thighs made her whimper. Max cleared his throat, snapping her from her painfully erotic fantasies.

"Stand up."

Oriana scrambled to her feet, then looked around the room, confused. Richter was gone? When had he left?

"Pay attention, darlin'." He covered her butt with both hands, digging his fingers into bruised flesh hard enough to make her gasp. "I thought so. And I do believe you've been punished enough by Callahan and Mason to have learned your lesson?" He waited for less than a beat before twisting her hair in one hand and jerking her head back. "Your answer?"

Her eyes teared at the sharp pain in her skull, but the sensation of being completely under Max's control made her knees weak. She whispered. "Yes, Master." Then braced her hands on the desk as he unzipped her jeans and jerked them down to her knees.

"Just look at the color of that beautiful ass." His fingers brushed over tender flesh, gently, simply tracing the lines of welts left by Sloan's belt. Then he dropped to his knees behind her and sank his teeth into one cheek.

Sharp pain speared up, coiling around her spine, flaring up into her core. She cried out and her hips jerked. His fingers drove up into her, curving forward to rub against the one spot that made her insides burn with pleasure. Another bite and she could feel herself melting into his palm. His fingers slid in and out, in and out, then slipped over her clit. He spread her pussy lips wide with the fingers of one hand, then used the fingers of the other to pinch her clit. The pressure increased until she couldn't bear it anymore. She lifted her hips to escape and he bit her again.

"Stay still." His nibbled on her flesh, his breath adding moisture to the sweat slicking her skin. "And do not come."

Panting, Oriana did her best to obey, but she wanted to curse at him for teasing and torturing her. With how worked up she'd been before he'd touched her, foreplay really wasn't necessary. And *this* kind of foreplay was almost too much.

He pinched a bit harder and she moaned.

"Try not to scream." He kissed the base of her spine, then released her.

White fire rolled up from her clit and the nub pulsed like a tiny, heart. She bit her tongue and kicked at her jeans, wanting them off, wanting her legs wide apart so Max could slam into her without any resistance. Not that there'd be much with how wet she was.

Max shoved her against the desk. "Leave them on." She heard the distinctive sound of him putting on a condom. "Brace yourself, love."

One violent thrust and he filled her so abruptly she felt like she was being formed around him. Every single steel-hard ridge seemed to stretch her until he fit perfectly, deep within. When he didn't move, she shimmied her hips.

He slapped her thigh. "You haven't been trained very well, have you? I'm disappointed."

If Dominik heard that, she'd so pay. Hooking her hands to the edge of the desk, she locked her arms and forced her body to still. "I'm sorry, M-Master, but this is the first time it's just the two of us."

"Mmhmm." He curved his chest over her back and murmured into her hair. "But that doesn't mean you have any control. I'll take you as slow—" he drew out of her, inch by inch, until her inner muscles were clenching just to hold him in "—or as hard—" his pelvis slammed into her ass and his dick drove in even deeper than before "—as I want."

"Yes." Her breathless whisper was drowned out by the hammering of her pulse, by the wet smack of flesh on flesh as he began to pound into her. "Yes, oh, yes."

The desk groaned as she leaned all her weight on it, desperate to keep still. Max fucked her passionately, viciously, and her body absorbed the impact, mindlessly clawing for release no matter how hard she fought.

He gripped her hips, raising her up on her tiptoes. "Not yet, baby. Just a little more."

She whined, and her nails scraped the varnished wood of the desk as she resisted yet another insistent climax. She felt like she would drown in the pleasure and gasped as Max pressed her face down on the desk and pulled on leg free of her jeans. He spread her thighs apart as he pistoned in and out of her. His fingers slid down the cleft of her butt, and he pressed the tip of one against her back hole.

"Not yet," he said as he worked his finger inside.

"Ah!" She moaned, then smothered herself with her arm. Her insides rippled with tiny spasms. Dormant nerves sparked. She tensed up, feeling herself losing her last bit of restraint. *No more! No more!*

Max grunted. "Now!"

Her body imploded with raw ecstasy. A torrent of pleasure bowled over, and she threw her head back, lips parted, but no sound escaped. Hands fisted, toes curled, she felt like her entire being would come apart. She sensed Max coming with her, and the way he jerked deep within brought on an aftershock of climax. Not one orgasm—maybe a hundred, a thousand. If not for the desk and

Max's hands on her hips, she would have crumpled like a rag doll. None of her limbs seemed solid.

After easing out of her with a tenderness that contradicted the brutal way he'd just fucked her, Max picked her up and slumped into the closest leather chair. He dried her sweat- and tear-soaked face with his sleeve, then kissed her brow.

"Do you know how much I love you, Oriana?" He hugged her and bowed his head to her shoulder. "When I was locked up, all I could think of was you—just you—and how much I wanted . . . I don't know, the opportunity to have you all to myself."

His admission was sweetness and bitterness all at once. Exactly how was she supposed to react? Happy that she could make him feel that way? Or scared that he'd had a change of heart and would force her to make a very hard choice?

It was bound to happen. "So where do we go from here?"

"Go?" He sat back and frowned at her. "What do you mean? I thought you were happy."

"I am, but . . ." No point in prolonging things and hurting anyone else. "I figured you'd eventually decide you were done sharing."

"Do you want that?" His brow creased when she shook her head. "Is it Sloan? I don't see you being tired of Dominik, but maybe Sloan's a bit much for you to—"

"Sloan's fine. To tell you the truth, the only one I'm ready to let go of is Tyler." She covered her mouth with her hand, then shook her head. "I mean, unless . . ."

"I see." He stretched his arm across the back of the chair, then drummed his fingers on the leather. "You've finally come to terms with the fact that your feelings for Tyler aren't as deep as your feelings for the rest of us. The guilt is eating you up. You're waiting for some karmic backlash, and you thought this was it."

"Kinda." She smiled, relieved that he knew her well enough that she didn't have to spell things out. "It would serve me right having to choose between the three men I love."

His brow arched. "Love?"

Her heart stuttered. *I've gone too far.*

Then he laughed. "I'm shocked. Not so much with Dominik,

but Sloan . . . I thought me and his dad were the only ones who'd ever love him. Does he know? Have you told him?"

Amazed, Oriana shook her head. This man was incredible. Unbelievable. And most of all, wonderful. She giggled and smacked his chest. "You've got to stop scaring me like that! I'm never sure where I stand with you. Any normal guy would get pissed off if his girlfriend told him she loved another man."

"Since when am I normal?" He wiggled his eyebrows and grinned. "As long as Sloan doesn't steal you away from me, it's all good. Now, answer me. Have you told him?"

"Not yet."

"Good. I want to see the look on his face when you do." After patting her thigh, he helped her to her feet. "Now, go check the score. We just screwed right through first period."

"Must you be so crude?" She put her hands on her hips, pretending to be mad.

He slid his hand under her jersey and ran his thumb over one very sensitive nipple. "Mind your manners, or I'll fuck you until there's only five minutes left of the game."

Much as she'd enjoyed herself, she didn't think she'd survive another round with him. She darted across the room and hurried into her jeans before he decided to follow through with his threat. And before she decided she wanted him to.

"I won't be long." She promised, kissing him so quick she missed his lips and scraped her lips on his chin. "Stay out of trouble."

"I should say the same to you." He gave her a level look, suddenly very serious. "Richter has as much experience as Mason, and he's a stickler for discipline. If you get mouthy with him, he's liable to drag you back here and take out a switch. And you won't like it."

Like I'd be stupid enough to mouth off to that guy? Of course, she was stupid enough to mouth off to Dominik and Sloan, but that was different. And anyway, they were *her* Doms. "You'd let him do that?"

"If you embarrassed me by acting out in front of a Master like Richter?" His jaw hardened. "Absolutely."

Note to self. Do not embarrass Doms. "I'll be good." She bit her lip.

"Are you going to tell Dominik about before?"

A grin lit up Max's face. He rubbed his chin as though he really had to think about it. "What will you give for my silence?"

"Anything," she said, and she really, truly meant *anything*. She'd had enough of Dominik's brand of punishment to last her quite a while. Maybe forever.

"Anything? How about this? Tell me why you don't want him to know."

"Because he'll punish—" She caught herself and shook her head. That wasn't why. The actual reason made her smile. "I don't want to disappoint him." Her nose wrinkled. She'd *so* regret this. "Or you."

"Good girl." His lip curved. Strolling across the room, he seemed to dismiss her. But then he rested his hip on the corner of Richter's desk and folded his arms over his chest. "So you'll speak to Dominik yourself?"

Uck, no. Yes? "Maybe. *Probably.*" She smirked as a mischievous little sprite sprang up inside her mind. "But if I get spanked, you don't get to watch."

His bark of laughter followed her down the hall. If she hadn't felt so blissfully beaten, she might have skipped, or danced. Her thighs and butt were sore, yet her steps seemed light. Having Max back made the world bright and cheery and perfect.

All we need now is a win.

Chapter Thirty Three

Salty rivulets spilled from Sloan's hair like he'd dunked his head, helmet and all, in the ocean. Third period, tied at one, and the Cobras led in shots on net. Didn't mean much, as far as he was concerned, but the time they spent in control of the puck certainly did. Well, that and the way Coach Stanton paled a little every time they came close to scoring. They barraged shots at the Wild goaltender, picking up sloppy rebounds, turning the game into target practice as the Wild defense floundered.

Sloan grinned at the Wild center as he waved his left winger over to cover the wide open slot in front of the net. The man snarled a curse under his breath as the player gave him a blank look. The Wild had considered the game in the bag, and their arrogance had cost them.

Too bad only half of you showed up to play, eh, boys?

The Cobra's tenacious play would have made the score one-sided if the net minder hadn't morphed into a wall after the first goal, but he appeared less and less solid after every attack. He'd slowed slightly on the glove side, but not enough for them to take advantage. There was only one way to get through him. They needed a fucking screen.

Five minutes and the game would go into overtime. The Wild stats in overtime made the Cobras a joke. If they couldn't score within the next ten minutes, they might as well go home. Perron was the only player they had who could take a shootout. Vanek got too nervous, and Sloan's aim was still off.

On his second straight shift, Sloan's thigh muscles cramped up. He ignored the dull pain and took the face-off. He'd get the puck out of their zone and head to the bench. A few minutes rest and he'd be ready for the final stretch.

The puck hit the ice. He surged forward, skimmed over the puck with his stick, then swiveled to retrieve it from a Wild defenseman. Mason barged past him and checked the man into the boards. The defenseman pinched just long enough for Sloan to safely leave the ice.

Coach Stanton made a lackluster gesture for a fresh line. Vanek hopped over the boards and Sloan scowled. The rookie had been shuffled from line to line sporadically throughout the game, as though Stanton hoped the kid wouldn't do as well without the chemistry he'd developed with the first line, then brought to the fourth. The coach didn't seem to realize Vanek could adapt to any situation and make it work for him. He was a goddamn chameleon, able to play right, left, or center. In front of his own net, he was almost suicidal when blocking pucks.

If Coach wanted to lose this game, he'd have to bench Vanek. Which he couldn't do without people getting suspicious. Sloan grinned over his shoulder at Tim who was muttering something into his headset. Tim grinned back and gave him a thumbs-up. Someone higher up was keeping an eye on Stanton; that much had been made obvious when the assistant coach *suggested* they rest the starting goalie, Giroux.

Carter nudged Sloan and jutted his chin toward the ice. "Stanton's really got it in for that kid. He's logged in more ice time than most of the defensemen."

Unfortunately, Sloan knew *that* couldn't be blamed on Stanton. "Someone lit a fire under the kid. The second his shift ends, he's begging to get back on. Tim's been letting him—all Stanton is doing is fucking around with the lines, making sure we're never on the ice together."

"Hell, man, even you couldn't keep up with him. Besides, he's forcing the rest of us to up our game, you know? It's good for the team."

"Yeah, as long as either T.J. or Mason are with him. He's pissing people off."

The whistle blew, and the crowd laughed. Sloan and Carter leaned forward to watch Vanek pantomiming boxing in front of the Wild's bench. Mason blocked a player who lunged at Vanek, then made a "wanna go?" motion with his hand. The other guy backed off.

As Vanek sidestepped to take a seat on the bench, Tim leaned over and grabbed a handful of his jersey. "What the fuck is up with you? You're too good for that kind of bullshit."

"I'm just having some fun, Timmy boy." Vanek spit out his mouth guard, then chewed on the end like a cocky calf. "Chill out!"

'Timmy boy?' What the hell? Sloan motioned Carter back, picked up a water bottle, and tossed it at Vanek. The bottle hit Vanek's chin and he jumped.

"Do that again, and I'll make sure you sit out the rest of the game," Sloan shouted before heading onto the ice. "You looked like an asshole out there."

"Fuck you, Callahan." Vanek gave him a one-finger salute, which showed on the scoreboard as Sloan rushed into play.

He glanced up just long enough to get nailed. His knee hit the ice, and he vaulted forward, sweeping his stick out after the puck. The blade of his stick nicked the back of a player's skate, and the man dove like he was an Olympic swimmer going for distance.

A shrill whistle. The ref swung one arm down and pointed from Sloan to the box.

"Tripping? Are you fucking cross-eyed?" Sloan groaned when the ref pointed again, doing the usual "deaf official" thing. Not like he really expected the guy to change the call, but he couldn't go quietly to the sin bin when he hadn't done anything. "Hang up your whistle and go paint some water lilies, Monet."

Skating backward, the ref came to his side and patted his arm. "You're a smart guy, Callahan. How about you use those brains and shut up before I toss you?"

Good idea. Sloan nodded and ducked into the penalty box. Two minutes—he'd still have about fifty seconds to score once he got out.

From behind the thick glass, he watched as play carried on. Vanek was on with Carter, T.J., and Mason. Good thing the rookie had the team's giants as backup, because they were facing the Wild's biggest line. Vanek won the face off, but T.J. missed the pass, forcing Mason to circle behind the net to retrieve it. He made a risky cross ice pass to Carter who surged forward, Vanek on his heel. Vanek picked up his pace and tapped his stick on the ice. Carter snapped the puck to him at the blue line, then crossed just on side. He swiveled around a lone defenseman. The Wild scrambled to catch up. Vanek delivered a perfect saucer pass and got pummeled by the second defenseman.

Thornton.

Play seemed to switch to slow motion as Vanek left his feet. His helmet flew, and he dropped like gravity had suddenly kicked in. His head bounced off the ice.

The horn sounded, and the crowd erupted in cheers. Then the cheers died.

Vanek didn't move.

Carter's skates made a slashing sound as he raced to Vanek's side. The ref shouted for the trainers. Sloan stood, his brain going over what happened, like a recap could make it less real.

A puddle of blood formed a halo around Vanek's head.

"You bastard! I'll kill you!"

Mason's roar tore Sloan out of numb oblivion. The big man had Thornton down and didn't seem to notice the two officials trying to pull him off as he jackhammered punches into the Thornton's face.

T.J. stood to the side, staring at Vanek. Trainers and doctors crowded onto the ice. One of the linemen opened the door to the penalty box.

Sloan flew from the bin, and the rink blurred around him as he tackled Mason. He got an elbow in the jaw for his efforts. Mason wasn't seeing him. By the haze in Mason's eyes, he saw only blood. Rage had him in a lockjaw and wouldn't let go.

Blocking a punch, Sloan bodily hauled Mason around until he lay on his back. Mason snarled and took another swing, throwing his whole body into the motion. Sloan evaded, then fisted his hand into the collar of Mason's jersey and backhanded him hard enough to snap his head back.

"If I don't get to help the guys lift up Vanek on that stretcher, I swear to God I'll stay here and beat on you until they need to cart you out on another one." Saliva and blood spilled over his lip. He sucked it in and spit over his shoulder. "Pull yourself together."

Mason nodded. Sloan stood and helped him up. They both went to watch the medics tend to Vanek.

His stomach clenched as the doctor spoke right in Vanek's ear, trying to get a response. Minutes felt like hours, and an eternity passed before the trainers carefully rolled Vanek onto the dark blue board and secured him with straps. Huge orange blocks were placed at either side of his head, and another strap went across his forehead. The doctor let Sloan, Mason, Carter, and T.J. heft the board up. The crowd, still standing, clapped and cheered as they gently laid the board on the stretcher.

Vanek still hadn't moved. His long lashes rested on his cheeks. He looked like a little boy, fast asleep. Bloody blond curls matted to his head ruined the image. And sleeping boys' chests rose and fell with deep breaths.

Sloan watched Vanek's chest, preying as he followed the stretcher, whispering to whatever higher power there might be for just one breath. *Just one.* He swallowed as he reached the end of the ice and the stretcher was rolled out of sight. The rookie's chest remained still.

No rising. No falling. Nothing.

* * * *

The raw sound of Oriana's scream echoed off the walls of the press box long after the medics took Tyler away. Or maybe they only echoed in her head. She couldn't really say because she wasn't quite *there* anymore. Hands under her elbows supported her as though her body couldn't manage to stand upright on its own. Someone led her into the hall. Each step was automatic, her legs on remote control. A wash of cold coated her insides, and she felt like she might vomit coolant. She choked on a sob as a door opened in front of her.

Max's smile froze on his face and melted away. "What's wrong?"

"T-Tyler . . ." Violent tremors stole her voice, stole her breath, and silver-specked darkness almost stole everything else. She gorged her palms with her nails. "He's hurt."

Wrapping her up in a solid embrace, Max half-carried her into the office and forced her to sit. He thanked someone, then handed her a bottle of water.

A tiny sip and her stomach lurched. Max held her hair back, and a trash can was held out. After her stomach emptied, Max dabbed her lips with a gray handkerchief.

"Tell me what happened."

She looked up. He wasn't talking to her.

Richter took a knee at her side and patted her hand. "Vanek took a bad hit and cracked his head on the ice. He was rushed to the hospital."

Max's color dropped several shades. He swayed a little on his feet. One fist clenched at his side. He thumped it into his thigh again and again. Finally, he gave a jerky nod and crouched in front of her.

"We need to go, Oriana." His tone sharpened a bit more with every word. He took her hands and eased her nails from her palms. "Please. We need to go. When he wakes up, we should be there."

"Yes." She inhaled and closed her eyes to find her center. Then she pushed to her feet. "My God, I'm sorry, Max. You're wasting time here with me when—"

"Don't start that. I know what it's like to see a man down on the ice, not moving. It's fucking scary, especially when it's one of your own." He didn't rise from his crouch right away. Rubbing his hands briskly against his knees as though his palms were cold, he stared at the floor between her feet, nodding to some voice only he could hear. "Damn kid, I told him not to wear his helmet strap so loose. He never listens . . ."

Seeing Max struggling to pull himself together, Oriana was disgusted by her own weakness. Max cared about Tyler, on a much deeper level than she possibly could after such a short time. And her falling apart forced him to focus on her pain rather than his own. Rather than siphoning off his strength, she should be lending him hers.

She bent down and cupped his face in her hands. "Max, let's go see him. He'll learn his lesson after this, even if we have to tie him up and beat it into him."

Max straightened with her, brushed a soft kiss over her lips, then gave her a tentative smile. "He'll be okay."

Brave mask glued on, she pulled Max's hood up, then wrapped her arm around his waist. "Of course he will."

Outside the forum, Oriana hesitated by the passenger side of Max's car and gazed up at the slice of moon, surrounded by dirty, snow-colored clouds. She could only find one pinprick of light in the hazy sky and couldn't tell if it was a star, a satellite, or a plane, but, whatever it was, she made a wish on it.

Please let him be okay. Let me have been overreacting.

No wishes could change the facts they got at the hospital. Tyler wasn't okay.

But he was alive.

Chapter Thirty Four

The small waiting room was crammed full of sweaty bodies. Cozy in beige and brown tones, with three blocky sofas, a coffee table full of magazines, a tiny TV up in one corner replaying the game and big windows shrouded by thick curtains. A hush fell over the room as The Hit came on screen. Oriana winced as Thornton's elbow connecting with the back of Tyler's neck played out in slow motion. The ref hadn't made a call because at first it looked like a clean hit. But the NHL board of governors would review the hit and probably suspend Thornton.

Unless they had their heads up their asses. Which sometimes happened.

Carter, who hadn't stopped pacing since he'd arrived, punched the stack of magazines and jabbed his thumb over his shoulder at the screen. "He didn't even have the fucking puck anymore! Don't tell me that wasn't intentional. Thornton had it out for the kid."

Across the room, Ingerslov braced his forearms on the window ledge, parting the heavy curtains to reveal the dark pitch of night. "The puck left Vanek's stick a millionth of a second before Thornton hit him. Doesn't even count as interference." Grumbles from the other men had him turning and taking an "I surrender!" pose. "I'm not saying I think it was an accident; I'm just not holding my breath on Thornton getting penalized."

Dominik's thigh flexed under her hand. He moved as though to stand, and she pressed her hand into his rock-hard stomach. Then she looked at Max.

He inclined his head. Good, they were on the same page. Screw appearances.

She straddled Dominik and clucked her tongue as she checked the cut at the edge of his lip where Sloan had hit him. "I don't like seeing you guys fight one another."

Rubbing up and down her legs, Dominik glanced around the room, then shook his head. "I'm not surprised that you're disappointed. I'm the most experienced of the bunch, and I lost it. Why should you trust me not to do that with you?"

"I'm sorry, I missed the memo about Doms being completely infallible," she said in a hushed voice. "If you were in control all the time, I'd start questioning your humanity. You did what I wanted to, Master." She leaned close to whisper the last in his ear. "Whether the league punishes him or not, Thornton's hurting. You beating him to a pulp was fucking sexy."

"Bloodthirsty bunny." Dominik chuckled, then smoothed his hands over her hair. "You know how hot I get hearing you get all passionate about the game? I don't feel like I have to justify the time or energy I put into all this. You fit." He curved his hands around her waist and tugged her close so she could feel him nice and hard between her thighs. "Perfectly."

"I think so, too." And despite feeling him ready for her, she made sure her eyes told him the words went beyond amazing sex. She slid her lips over his and whispered. "You know what I mean, right?"

"I do," he said. "But I think you'll be more comfortable telling me when we're alone."

Carter made a strangled sound behind her. "I'm so confused. No offense, Oriana, but am I getting my turn too?"

Leaning all her weight on Dominik so he couldn't get up and rip Carter to shreds, she peeked up at the man and smiled. "Sorry. My roster's full."

The waiting room door swung open, revealing Sloan.

"Two skull fractures." Sloan lightly scratched the bottom of the scar on his face, bone white against his pale skin. "They had to do some kind of surgery to relieve the pressure on his brain. He's in stable condition, but they've got to observe him for a couple of days." He glanced up at the TV, shook his head as The Hit played again from a different angle. He grabbed the remote off the table and clicked the power button. "They'll let me know when he wakes up. The rest of you might as well go home. I'll keep you all updated."

Most of the men mumbled agreements and trudged from the room. Max and Dominik stayed where they were. Carter lingered in the doorway for a moment.

"Can he still play? Do they know?"

"It's too soon to tell, buddy. From what I know, with this kind of injury, takes at least a year before the doctors will even consider clearing him for contact. If there are no complications."

"Damn." The shadows already around Carter's eyes darkened, stealing the youth from his face. "He crashed at my place last night, and all he could talk about was making the playoffs. He said it would be tough without Perron, but he thought we could do it."

"We can. And we will." Sloan gave Carter a carved stone smile. "That's one of the first things I'm telling him when he wakes up. We're doing this for him. And Perron just might be able to help us."

Max shot off the sofa as though propelled by a loose spring. "How? I'm suspended."

"That might change. Another player has come forward, willing to testify that Coach talked him into making sure we lost—"

"Who?" Dominik asked in a dangerously low tone.

Sloan continued as though he hadn't heard the question. "And your lawyer got the cops to question the hospital staff. The report from a triage nurse conflicted with the doctor's findings. Another nurse said Paul had a couple of visitors while he was waiting for treatment. And the doctor who treated Paul agreed that he could have gotten the cut on his head exactly like you said. This case is messy, but your lawyer seems pretty damn confident that he can get all charges dropped and get your suspension revoked so you can play Friday."

"I'm glad you got a new lawyer, babe." Oriana rose and slipped behind Max to hug his waist. "This one is awesome."

"Asher is the best." The quiet, familiar voice came from behind Sloan.

Not possible. Oriana covered her mouth with her hands as Sloan rolled his eyes and stepped aside.

Dressed in a pale pink trench with a thick, black belt, Silver stepped into the room with the same detached poise she used on the red carpet. Her updo gave her hair the appearance of a short, sweeping pixie cut, but Oriana knew the fine golden strands were hip length. Silver was vain about her hair. With her stance and "you've been graced with my presence" air, she came across as vain about everything. Pretty decent performance, but Oriana had reading her sister down to an art.

She strode across the room and dragged her sister into the hall. "What are you doing here?"

"No 'thank you'?" Silver's painted red lips formed a pretty pout. "After I sent Asher to save your man?"

"Your boyfriend is a lawyer?" *How did I miss that?* Okay, sometimes she mentally logged out when her sister's stories got downright crude, but she wouldn't have missed her sister trading in her bad boy fetish and settling for a stable, normal man.

Not that I'm one to talk.

"Yeah, he got me out of a parking ticket, and we fell in love." Silver batted her eyelashes. "His boyfriend is a lawyer, too."

Sloan snorted behind Oriana. She spun around and scowled at him. "Can we have a minute?"

"Yes, ma'am." The waiting room door closed. Hard.

Rudeness? Punishable offense? She couldn't find it in her to care, although her pulse sped up a little because her body wasn't interested in where her mind was at.

Regardless, she put her hands on her hips and faced Silver, continuing as though they hadn't been interrupted. "You never answered me. Why are you here?"

With no one around to catch her being less than the renowned Silver Delgado, her sister's shield of perfection shattered like a fine coating of crystal. Her face crumpled up, and tears spilled down her cheeks in black streaks.

"It's Daddy. He had a heart attack."

* * * *

Beep, beep, beep. The monitors filled the room with rhythmic medical sounds. Oriana sat on the edge of the bed, holding her father's hand. Silver had told her he'd woken up a couple of times, long enough to tell her to get her gay boyfriends out of the room. And that the doctor said he was stable.

Stable. She kept hearing that word, but it had lost all meaning. Tyler was stable. Her father was stable. And neither would ever be the same.

Apparently, her father had the first attack on Sunday, but when

Anne, his secretary, checked on him, he said he was fine. After watching him struggle with simple tasks like eating and getting dressed, Anne insisted he see a doctor. He refused. Said he was feeling a little off. No reason to panic.

He lost consciousness watching the game at home, and Anne called for an ambulance.

Stubborn man. Oriana used a tissue to wipe some drool off her father's chin.

His lashes fluttered, and his eyes opened.

"Daddy." She bent down to kiss his hollow cheek. "I'm here."

His hand twitched. He shook his head. Then mumbled something.

She put her ear close to his lips to hear him better. "What? Try again, Daddy; I didn't hear you."

"Out." His voice was a raspy croak, and every word seemed grated out of his throat. "Get out."

Stroking his hand, she shook her head. "You have to stay here. The doctors are doing everything they can to make you better."

He shook his head again. The heart monitor screamed as his pulse became erratic. "You. Get out! Get out! Silver! Silver!"

Her chest felt like it had been cracked open, like her heart was exposed, hammering cold, hard beats. She let her father's hand fall to his side and retreated, one step at a time, until the wall wouldn't let her go any further.

Not a wall. A solid body.

"He's not thinking straight, love." Max rubbed the back of her neck and drew her out of the room. "Look, the nurse is here. Let her deal with him. Tyler's been asking for you."

Tyler. Yes. Tyler wants me. Needs me. She grabbed Max's hand and clung to him, because she wasn't sure her legs, which didn't feel like part of her anymore, would take her anywhere.

"Bring me to him."

* * * *

Max watched Oriana, curled up next to Vanek, holding him as though he was a delicate teddy bear. She laughed and chatted and scolded the boy in a way that made the hospital a cozy place, like they were at his house, just hanging out.

She was giving the rookie all the love and support she couldn't give her father. Which had Max a little worried. It wouldn't be good for either her or Vanek if she kept him on as a lover out of some warped sense of obligation.

Vanek kissed her forehead, then her nose, then her lips. Weak, sloppy kisses, like he'd had trouble finding her mouth. "I didn't score the winning goal, but I came close. Is that good enough?"

"Good enough?" Oriana let out a tense, high pitched giggle. "You almost got dead for that assist! Yeah, it's good enough!"

One arm flopped across Oriana's ribs, Vanek closed his eyes and sighed. "As long as you think so, works for me. Just . . . just promise me something?"

"All you have to do is ask."

"Stay with me." Vanek gave her a lost little boy look Max couldn't write off as fake. "I'm a little freaked out here."

Without hesitating for a second, Oriana snuggled closer and whispered, "I'm not going anywhere until we can take you home."

Vanek fell asleep, and, not long after, so did Oriana.

Max pulled out the sole chair, which doubled as a stiff, single bed. He got a pillow and blanket from the attending nurse and settled in for the night after sending both Dominik and Sloan home for a change of clothes for them all. He knew he couldn't keep them away for longer.

But if Oriana was hanging around, so was he.

Chapter Thirty Five

Four months later

The aroma of grilled steak filled the kitchen as the patio door swung open. Sloan added the last touches to his potato salad and glanced over his shoulder as Oriana's laughter lit across the room. Vanek followed, dragging the garden hose behind him.

"Spray that in my kitchen, and I'll crack the other side of your skull."

Oriana slapped his arm and he jumped. "That wasn't nice." She reached for the spoon he'd dropped in the bowl, licking her lips. "Oh, this looks good."

Rapping her knuckles lightly with a big wooden spoon, Sloan snapped. "Wait for supper, bunny." He grinned when she glared at him. "Actually, you can do so right there." He pointed at the floor by his feet.

She shook her head.

He pressed his lips together. "On your knees."

She knelt gracefully, eyes down. He knew she hated submitting where others could see her, which made her doing so that much more special.

Smoothing a strand of hair behind her ear, Sloan said softly, "Good girl." Then, as a treat, he fed her a bit of salad. "Tell me what you think."

Her cheeks flushed. "I think you were born with an unfair advantage. A pro athlete, an amazing cook, a . . ."

"Yes?" Sloan held out another spoonful for her.

Vanek made a disgusted sound as he slammed around inside the fridge. "Why must you treat her like a dog?"

The screen door snicked shut. "Tyler, honey, what's taking so long?"

Oriana almost scrambled to her feet as Chicklet sauntered across the kitchen, but Sloan kept her in place with a heavy hand on her shoulder.

Chicklet gave Oriana a sympathetic smile, then winked at Sloan.

Tyler came out from behind the fridge door with a couple of beers and a winning smile. "On my way, babe. Me and Oriana were just playing around. Sloan got all anal."

"Oh, yeah?" Chicklet's expression hadn't changed, but disappointment seeped into her tone. "I thought we'd discussed this. Their relationship is none of your business."

A stubborn look on his face, Tyler set the beers on the counter beside him. "She's still my friend."

"Yes, she is. And I'm sure if she needs your help, she'll ask for it." She tapped her fingers on her hip. "I'm not hearing a reason for you to keep me waiting."

Idly petting Oriana's head, Sloan watched as Chicklet exerted her own brand of control, and Tyler, without even knowing he was doing so, surrendered to her.

Had to give Dominik credit, he'd read the boy well. Sloan never would have considered Chicklet a good match for Vanek, but they'd . . . clicked. The night after they were eliminated from the second round of the playoffs, they'd seen Max and Oriana off on their delayed trip, then taken a drive down to Darby. And stopped off at Chicklet's bar for an early morning drink. Chicklet struck up a conversation with the boy and coaxed him out of his sour mood. She'd gotten him to let out his frustrations. About everything.

Oriana wouldn't be thrilled with how much Chicklet actually knew, but Vanek should have someone outside their "group" who understood his needs.

Chicklet understood. And even though Vanek might never kneel to her, she had him pretty well trained.

Vanek inched closer to Chicklet, then brought his hand up as though to caress her cheek. He didn't touch her until, with a regal nod, she let him know he could.

"Are you jealous?" Vanek sounded like that would please him, which proved how young he still was.

"I'm not jealous." Chicklet's smile was serene and unassuming. "I just won't come second."

"You don't." Vanek leaned forward and kissed her. His look held something close to worship. "Can I give you a foot rub to make up for it? You've been on your feet all day."

"You may." Chicklet drew her index finger down his chest, then hooked it to his belt. "And if you're good, I might let you watch me and Laura make out."

"Yes, ma'am."

Sloan chuckled as Vanek trailed Chicklet out into the yard. *Boy's got it made, so long as he doesn't mind being treated like a dog. Or a treasured, loyal pet . . .*

He reached down and tugged Oriana's hair to get her attention. She tipped her head back and gave him a happy smile.

"Get up here." He patted the counter and waited until she hopped up before holding out his hand. "You still haven't shown me your ring."

A light, glowing blush spread across her cheeks. She'd been a little shy with him ever since she'd returned from her travels with Perron. This was as good a time as ever to find out why.

She displayed her ring as though it was a jewel-encrusted bomb she'd hang onto until it blew her hand off.

"Max said he proposed in the sanctuary gardens."

"Uh-huh."

"Then Dominik showed up and asked you to wear his collar."

"Yeah." She touched her naked throat. "The ceremony will be the same day as the wedding. But . . ."

"But?" He took out a fancy glass bowl, distracting himself by transferring the salad so she wouldn't feel pressured.

"I'll be connected to both of them in some way. What about you?"

So that's what's been bothering her. Well, he'd fix that soon enough.

"We'll discuss that later. So, about Silver. Is she hanging around?"

Oriana groaned. "Yes. Daddy gave her power of attorney. And her boyfriends helped her make a case for taking over ownership of the team. But . . ."

"Why didn't he give it to you?"

"Because he didn't!"

Her lips quivered. Time to change the subject.

"Did Max tell you about T.J.?"

She shook her head.

"Well, Richter is trying to cover up the whole scandal, so he bought out his contract. The traitor's gonna retire without anyone knowing he tried to throw a game for a lousy ten grand."

"The ten grand was a down payment. He would have gotten more if you'd lost." She fiddled with the hem of her skirt, keeping her thighs together in a way that told him she'd been denied panties. Again. She crossed her legs when she caught his eyes on her thighs. "His daughter's been living with a nonunion in her tibia for a while. If he hadn't brought her to the States to see a specialist, she'd still be waiting for treatment. She has diabetes. She—"

"I would have loaned T.J. the money. But whatever. It's over. You wanna play nurse tonight?"

Letting out a *pff* between her lips, she slid off the counter. "No, thank you, Sir. I've had enough of hospitals to last me awhile. Didn't Max tell you I'm changing my major?"

"Nope, Max won't stop going on and on about plans for the wedding. If he says the words 'flowers' or 'cake' to me one more time, I'm gonna get medieval on his ass."

"You've been watching too much TV."

"Yes, well I've gotta keep my material fresh." He gave her the sly grin he knew creeped her out and slid a butcher knife from the cutting block case beside his bowls. "You get so wet when I use the right threats."

The way she was looking at him, she was probably pretty wet already. "Are you planning to use a sharp knife this time?"

"Not yet. You still twitch too much." But he would ice the blade next time they did knife play to give the illusion of a sharper edge. "Bring the salad out and ask Mason to serve the steaks. They should be ready."

"Okay." She picked up the tray with the potato, pasta, and Greek salads. Then she bit her lip. "You never answered me. I'm getting married to Max and collared by Dominik. What about you? Do you feel left out?"

"Why should I? I have my own unique way to claim you." He prowled around her, eyeing her breasts, then her flanks, running his tongue over his teeth. "I just haven't decided where I'm going to leave my mark."

"Your mark?" She squeaked. "Umm . . . what kind of mark?"

"I was thinking branding." He ran his hand down her thigh, enjoying the way she shivered, the same way she did whenever he suggested something new and potentially painful. They were taking baby-steps with most forms of pain play because she had some "squeamishes" and limits they both still had to learn, but he constantly found new things for them to try. Branding would be one of those things, once he found someone he trusted enough to do it to him. And once Oriana was comfortable with something so permanent. For now . . . "In a few years, we'll discuss it. Until then, there's a procedure called body etching. It's not as permanent, but it hurts more."

"Etching? As in cutting?" She shuddered. "I'll take the branding, thanks. Extreme heat kills nerves. I'd only feel it for a few seconds."

"You will not 'take the branding.' The etching is just like a tattoo, without the ink. Picture a needle, piercing your skin a thousand times, the endless vibration buzzing right through you. A man from the club does it, so he'll let me strap you down first." He grazed his knuckles over her pert nipples. "Then I can toy with you, maybe even fuck you nice and slow so as not to disturb him. How does that sound?"

Her legs shifted, and the salad bowls rattled on the tray. She inhaled then gave him a glazed eye look that made him want to drag her away for the exotic scarring that very moment. Her dazzling smile etched poetic tripe all over his heart as she whispered "Sounds just right for us."

"Just right for us." Damn straight. The Cup would have been an awesome achievement, but this woman was worth more than any trophy he could share. There'd never come a season when he'd lose her. Because even though he couldn't do it alone, he'd give her everything she needed.

And that was a fucking win in his books.

THE END

DEFENSIVE ZONE

The Dartmouth Cobras

Sneak Peek

Dean rubbed his hands on his knees and sat up straight. Aside from the bride walking down the aisle in a dress that had several of the players adjusting themselves in their seats, the ceremony was as long and dull as he'd expected. It reminded him of an ex-girlfriend who'd been into soaps. She'd be sitting there, all teary-eyed, mumbling about how *finally* the current super-couple was getting their dream wedding. And he'd be forced to sit there, feigning interest while the priest went on and on for three episodes. Sappy personal vows would be exchanged, and the couple would rush out while the cast cheered and blew bubbles at them because rice was bad for the stupid birds.

Unless something interesting happened. Like the bride getting shot or someone in the crowd stood up and claimed to be having the groom's baby.

No such luck. Not that he wanted Oriana to get shot, but the minister . . .

Hell, is he reading the extended version?

The wedding ended. The collaring began. A bit more to the point, but Dominik seemed determined to cover everything. He included Max and Sloan in the ceremony, having Sloan cuff Oriana while Max held her hair out of the way as she knelt and the collar was placed around her throat and locked.

"You belong to us, love," Sloan said, loud enough for everyone to hear. "Tonight you submit to our pleasure. Do you consent?"

Oriana's cheeks glistened as she tipped her head back. "Yes. But—"

Dominik frowned. "But?"

Well, this just got interesting. Dean leaned forward.

"I don't want to wait for your mark, Sloan." Oriana took a deep breath. "I want something tonight."

"Are you sure?" Sloan laid his hands over her cheeks, using his thumb to swipe away her tears. "I'm happy to oblige, bunny, but I don't want you to regret it tomorrow when you're not all emotional. People will see it. We're taking our honeymoon somewhere warm."

"I don't care—let them see." Oriana closed her eyes and touched her collar. "I need you to be part of this."

"I am." Sloan straightened. "And I will be. Dominik and Max will chain you for me, babe. Is that okay?"

Oriana shuddered. "That's perfect."

The foursome moved to a playroom, and the crowd followed as one without being invited. Dean stood in the doorway and glanced over at his brother as he and his wife approached.

"Was my wedding this long?"

Tim made a face. "Your divorce was longer. I think the four of them will make it work, don't you?"

Despite being bored out of his mind, Dean had to admit he could see the men really loved Oriana. And she loved them back without restraint. His wife had never been like that. She'd taken his ring and his collar, but she'd always held part of herself back. As soon as their daughter had grown up enough for her to gain some independence, his wife had decided she wanted the same. For years he'd told her to find her own interests, to be more than a stay-at-home mother—which she obviously hated being—and his sub. She'd insisted that was what she wanted, then suddenly decided she wanted none of it. She met a man who could give her a cozy, carefree life and ditched her daughter because, as she'd said, she'd never really wanted to be a mother. In front of their daughter.

Seeing the utterly crushed look on his daughter's face, he'd hardened his heart and signed the divorce papers. But that hadn't been enough. His wife wanted his money. He made more than her new man and she wanted alimony. He'd resisted at first, but the long court battles had taken their toll on his daughter and he'd finally given in. Let the bitch have the money. His daughter needed to know someone still wanted her.

He'd been blind when it came to his wife, but he didn't think Oriana's men had that problem with her. She was as open and honest as they came.

"They'll work." Dean adjusted his leathers. Damn, just thinking about the next part of the ceremony had him wanting to find a willing sub. "Not what I'd want, but I've never met a woman like Oriana. It's hard to believe she's Delgado's kid."

"Can't argue that." Tim pressed a light kiss on his wife's brow. "But some of us get lucky and find the pick of the litter. My baby has a messed up family too, but she rose above it. You wouldn't want to know her siblings or her parents. But coming from them made her the strong woman you can't help but admire."

This was true. Tim didn't tell him much, but he'd done enough scenes with Tim's wife, enough aftercare before Tim took her away for the sexual stuff, to have learned a bit.

For the past two years, he'd kept scenes nice and impersonal. Platonic with Tim's wife, exploring a bit of pain, and purely sexual with the subs that came to the club not wanting a commitment. Maybe one day he'd find a woman he'd want more with, but he was happy with what he had now. He wasn't ready for anything deeper. Granted, his daughter was eighteen and getting past the family drama, but she and the team were his focus. He didn't need more.

Not yet.

Then again, he was open to the possibilities. The woman in pink, for example. He hadn't seen her since he and Landon had watched her filling in the forms, but if she proved to be available as he thought she was . . .

Well, he might make an exception for her. A brief glimpse of what she had convinced him he could give her more. Even if only tonight.

＊ ＊ ＊ ＊

Silver swallowed convulsively, fighting not to jump every time Sloan's whip hit her sister's bare flesh. Her cheeks had reddened slightly when Oriana had been stripped, and she hadn't wanted to look at first, but as each sharp *Crack!* got louder, she couldn't stop herself from staring at the long, red welts on her sister's back, butt, and thighs.

So far, so good. After all, Silver had been to plenty of BDSM and fetish clubs, she'd seen people whipped before. Of course, all the places she'd gone to had been more glamorous than Blades & Ice. The few men that had used a flogger or a paddle on her ass before fucking her knew better than to leave marks. She always had a list of limits a mile long when she played.

Looks like Oriana has a shorter list. A mocking voice said as she watched Sloan pause and kneel to kiss an unmarked spot on Oriana's hip. He stroked up her thigh and tipped his head back to say something only Oriana could hear.

Oriana nodded.

As Sloan straightened, a sick feeling of dread pooled in Silver's gut. She dug her nails into her palm and glanced over at Asher—who was kissing Cedric and completely oblivious to everyone else in the room. A few other people were making out or . . . more. Apparently watching the scene had gotten a few people hot.

But these people didn't know Oriana. Oriana always put other's needs before her own. She would let Sloan push her further and further, never asking him to stop if she thought it was what he wanted. And Sloan was just the type of asshole to take advantage of her passive nature.

Oriana's not stupid. Maybe this is what she wants.

Silver fumbled with her purse and took out a lollipop.

The whip snaked out over Sloan's head, came down in a black blur, and curled around Oriana's hip. Oriana gasped. A thin line of blood trickled.

Silver dropped the lollipop and rushed forward. "You son of a bitch!"

Sloan froze and stared at Silver. "What—"

Smack! Her palm went numb and she watched her handprint on his face darken to a bright red with satisfaction. The crowd went silent.

"Get away from her!" When Sloan didn't move, Silver snatched the whip from his hand and tossed it across the room. "She trusts you! How could you do that to her?"

His dark eyes narrowed. "Silver—"

"Don't 'Silver' me! You don't fucking scare me, Sloan." She

strode up and poked him in the center of his bare chest. "The worst thing is, I was willing to give you the benefit of the doubt. But you're the same arrogant bastard you've always been. I think we both know exactly why you enjoy beating on women, don't we? Does Oriana know you're an impotent freak? Is that why she needs Max and Dominik?"

The area around the handprint on Sloan's face turned a darker shade of red. When he didn't say anything, she looked over at Max, who was standing in front of Oriana, speaking softly, and Dominik, who was watching the crowd expectantly.

"Dominik, are you seriously going to put up with him treating her like this?"

The big black man ignored her.

Rage bubbled up inside and she moved to get his attention.

Suddenly, Sloan's hand shot out. He hooked a finger to her collar. "Who are you here with?"

"Excuse me?" She pried at his fingers in an effort to get free, but his hand seemed like one solid piece of iron. "Why does it matter?"

"Subs in this club don't disrespect Doms and get away with it." He jerked her collar. "Don't. Move."

All the blood left her face. She went still.

"Where's your Master?"

"He's there." She pointed at Asher, pleading with her eyes for him to come get her away from Sloan. *Fuck not being scared. This guy's crazy!*

Asher's eyes went big and round. He shook his head "Look, man. We're not like . . . I can't . . . damn, she was just worried about her sister. Give her a break."

"Are you refusing to punish her?" Sloan threw his head back and laughed at Asher's nod. "Why am I not surprised? You treat BDSM like you do everything else, Silver? Like it's one big fucking game? Was coming here as a sub just your idea of playing dress up?"

"You better watch it Sloan," Silver said, doing her best to sound brave and strong even though, for the first time in her life, she was the center of attention and really just wanted to disappear. Everyone was staring at her like *she'd* done something wrong. "I'm your boss."

"And I give a shit?" Sloan caught someone's eye, and Silver tried to twist her head to see who. "You dealing with this or are we just kicking her out?"

"That's entirely up to her." The man's voice was deep, just gruff enough to be sexy, but it was the edge, the way he spoke, as though obedience was a given, that made goose bumps rise all over her flesh. "I'll give you a choice, Silver. Sloan, you can let her go."

As soon as she was released, Silver shuffled away from Sloan, careful not to get too close to—*shitshitshit*—Dean Richter. Even over the phone, the man intimidated her, but it had been easy to come off as unimpressed without his sharp, hazel eyes locked on her, seeing everything she tried to hide.

"Are you listening to me?"

Silver evaded his steady gaze and tried to see around him. "Oriana?"

Dean glanced over his shoulder. "She's fine. Perron, Mason, would you please take Oriana to another room to come down?" He smiled. "It looks like she managed to stay in a good place."

Neither Max nor Dominik said anything, but moments later, a door at the other side of the room opened and closed.

"I want to go with them." Silver hiked her chin up and finally managed to look Dean in the eye. Her pulse quickened. "Please. Just let me see if she's all right."

"So polite now." Dean circled her slowly, close enough that his leather pants brushed her thighs and his breath stirred her hair. "You're used to getting your own way, aren't you, Silver?"

As if that's a bad thing? "You said you were giving me a choice."

"I am." Dean stopped at her side. "Your choices are leave my club and don't ever come back, or accept whatever punishment I choose to give you."

"Punishment for what?"

"You're dating two lawyers and you don't know better than to sign something without reading it?" One brow arched, tone light, he seemed to be laughing at her.

A few people in the crowd did.

Deep, deep breaths and an eyeroll kept the tears back. "I wasn't planning to do a scene tonight; I didn't think it was all that important."

"What you signed applies to every time you come here."

"Then I won't come back."

"Very well." He stepped aside. "You may leave."

For some reason, everything inside her rebelled against the very idea of walking out. And she couldn't quite figure out why.

Oriana. You're just worried about Oriana.

"I'm not going anywhere until I see my sister." She put her hands on her hips. "Things will be very unpleasant at work if you won't be reasonable."

"Don't threaten me, Silver."

"You should call me Miss Delgado."

Dean let out a gruff laugh. "I don't think so, pet. But while you're still here, I suggest you refer to me as either Master or Sir."

"Why should I?" She sniffed and gave him a swift, detached once-over. "Like Sloan said, I'm not a real sub."

"Aren't you?" He took a step forward and she took two quick steps back. He closed the distance between them and put his finger under her chin before she could move again. "Stop."

Her knees locked and she made a small sound in her throat as tiny fluttery things danced inside her belly at his command. She struggled against the clenching down low, but she couldn't stop herself from leaning, just slightly, toward him.

"There are things you could learn about yourself here, Silver. Things I and other Masters with experience could teach you. Have you ever been restrained?"

"Yes."

His eyes narrowed. "Respectfully, Silver."

She sighed. "Yes, Sir."

"Ropes or cuffs?"

"I hardly see why I would tell you—"

"You will tell me." His hand framed her jaw in a firm but not painful hold. "And you will not question me again."

Her mouth went dry. Her eyes wide. She was almost panting. "Cuffs. Handcuffs."

"What else have you done?"

Mind racing, she went over her considerable experience and tried to figure out a way to answer that wouldn't make her sound like a slut. His dark look didn't give her the impression she could make something up so she went with vague. "Everything. I've tried a bit of everything."

"Everything?" His brow shot up. "How old are you?"

"Twenty-two."

People were laughing at her again. She wanted to scream, to throw something—but she had a feeling that would only get her in more trouble. Tears of frustration blinded her. One spilled down her cheek.

"Stay with me, pet. I'm the one you need to impress, not them." Dean used his thumb to wipe the tear away. "I've been in this lifestyle for about fifteen years, and *I* haven't done everything. You've barely had a taste."

"Fine." She wet her lips with her tongue. "But that doesn't mean I *want* to do more."

Dean let his hand fall to his side. "Then the choice is clear, isn't it?"

Yeah. Clear as fucking mud. Seriously, why even discuss all this with him? If she stayed, he would punish her. And it wouldn't be all fun and games. She could walk out with her pride barely bruised—impressing him didn't matter.

Shouldn't matter.

But it did.

"If I stay—"

"Silver," Asher called, warily eying Sloan, who still hadn't moved. "Let's just get out of here. There are other clubs."

"He's right, you know," Sloan said, his tone clipped. "This obviously isn't the place for you."

Several murmurs of accord came from the dwindling crowd. They were getting bored of her. No one wanted her here and the entertainment value had passed.

"If you stay?" Dean prompted, as though he hadn't heard anything but her words. He put his hands on her shoulders, and suddenly it seemed like they were the only two people in the room. Like his opinion *was* all that mattered. "Hear me now, Silver. I will be very disappointed if you take the easy way out. I think you're stronger than that. But I won't force you. You can go home with your boyfriends and have a pleasant evening."

She winced. Sure, going home with Asher and Cedric would be . . . pleasant. All she had to do was make sure they didn't forget she was there. Getting punished would be better.

She gulped as she resolved herself to her decision. *Maybe.*

"All right." She took a deep breath and rushed through the rest. "So long as it doesn't get too . . . personal." She forced a smile. "I'm not available."

"That remains to be seen." Dean muttered before he squared his shoulder and glanced over at Asher. "You may stay if you'd like. But I warn you, don't come here again playing the Dom if you won't follow through."

Asher nodded slowly. "Well, you see, things aren't really that way between Silver and me. If I decide to get involved in things with Cedric here, it will be different."

Wow. Thanks for completely abandoning me. Silver let out a strained, but light, laugh. "Glad you made that clear, Asher."

"Silver—"

"You can go. I'll be fine."

Apparently, that was exactly what he'd wanted to hear. Because he left without looking back, Cedric following demurely on his heel.

"Give me your wrists." Dean slid his hands down her arms and forced her to focus on him as he undid a pair of cuffs from his belt. "I don't give safewords for punishments, but I won't push you any further than what you can take."

Oh, that's reassuring. She ground her teeth and let him secure the cuffs. "I take it asshole gets to watch?"

"You will refer to him as Master Sloan in the club, pet."

"Like hell, I will!"

"If you don't, your punishment will be even more severe." Dean's tone softened. "And you don't want that. Kneel. Tell Master Sloan how sorry you are for interrupting his scene."

Her knees bent a little, as though her body had already decided to obey. But then she caught Sloan's smirk and her pride snapped back into place. This fucktard had hurt her sister. He might get the satisfaction of watching her suffer, but he'd never get her respect.

She folded her arms over her chest and sneered. "What will it be, ten lashes? Twenty? Bring it on. I'm not apologizing to that sorry excuse for a man."

The expression on Sloan's face—damn, she wished she had a camera. Any amount of pain Dean could dish out would be worth that souvenir.

"You're going to wish you didn't say that, pet." Dean sighed and took hold of her upper arm, towing her with him out to the main room. "Ten is a good number."

"I'm glad you agree."

He drew her in front of a large, throne like chair and folded his arms over his chest. "Now strip."

"Strip?" She rubbed her arms and nodded. Fine, there was a crowd, but she had nothing to hide. All those women giggling and pointing could eat their fucking hearts out. She peeled off her top and shorts and faced Dean before letting out a flippant "So what are you going to use?"

"My hand."

Aw, fuck.

* * * *

Dean struggled to keep his eyes on the mouthy little sub's face. Not that the pink number had left much to the imagination, but somehow she hid more in the swatch of cloth than most women could in a muumuu. Even naked, her posture and icy smile disguised the vulnerable woman he'd gotten a glimpse of earlier.

Why did the woman in pink have to be Silver Delgado? Why couldn't she have been someone a little easier to handle? Like . . . that Paris Hilton chick.

Not that high maintenance women appealed to him at all, but hell, maybe Silver wasn't at all what she pretended to be.

He pulled off his suit jacket, draped it over the high back of the large, oak throne. Then he pushed the padded, velvet arms out of the way. The piece was custom made, used most often for spankings because it was damn comfortable, but the seat split down the middle to spread a bound subs' thighs wide for a good fucking. He glanced down at the seat and shook his head.

Not this time, Richter. She needs something else from you tonight.

Settling himself into the chair, Dean patted his thigh. "Come on, Silver. Let's get this over with."

She looked over her shoulder at the small gathering and inched closer. "Can't we do this somewhere a little more private?"

"No." He reached out and caught the short chain between her cuffs to pull her to him. "You had no problem disrespecting Master Sloan in front of an audience."

"He fucking deserved it."

Tired of arguing with her, he hooked an arm around her waist and dropped her over his left knee. As expected, she immediately kicked and tried to roll off his lap. So he pushed her knees down and held them in place with his right leg, all the while firmly gripping the nape of her neck to restrain her. "No. But *you* deserve this."

Without a breath of warning, he hauled back and laid a solid smack on her tight little ass. His hand was big enough to cover both cheeks, and a bright red mark blossomed over her pale flesh. She let out a screech which he cut off with two quick slaps, one on each cheek.

"Damn you!" She bucked her hips and screamed when he responded with a resounding smack on her upper thigh. "You're hurting me!"

"That's the point, my dear." One more *crack!* and he decided to give her a little break. He petted her colorful bottom, speaking in a low, soothing tone. "There are rules here. You will learn to obey them."

"You think this will turn me into a good little sub?" She tossed her hair away from her face and glared at him. "Are you really that stupid, shithead?"

He had to clench his jaw to keep from laughing. *Shithead? I think you're ready for more.*

"You." *Smack!* "Will not." *Crack!* "Swear." *Slap!* "At me or any other member of this club."

"Fuck you!" She choked on a sob as his hand connected with the soft undercurve of her ass. "Stop! Stop!"

"One more if you promise to behave," he said.

"I promise!"

Finally. For a minute there, he'd wondered if she'd ever back down. He really didn't want to have to prolong her punishment, being that this was obviously the first time she'd ever been disciplined. Much as he enjoyed having her laid out, naked and available, she needed to know that accepting that she'd been in the wrong came with its own reward. He had a feeling a "good girl" would go a long way with her.

"Brace yourself, pet." He felt her tense up and waited. A bit of a head game, but he couldn't help pushing her, just a little, to see how she'd react.

A few shaky inhales and she let her body go slack.

He gave her a solid *whack!* and set his hand on the small of her back as she absorbed the impact with a quiet dignity he had to admire. Gently stroking her tender bottom, he let his approval deepen his tone. "You did very well, Silver. I'm proud of you."

She went perfectly still. Abruptly her whole body stiffened up, and he had to tighten his grip to keep her from tossing herself to the floor. "As if I care? That's some ego you've got, Richter."

Well . . . he had to admit, that wasn't at all what he'd expected from her. He gave a curt nod and patted her butt. "In any case, your punishment is served. After you apologize to Sloan—"

Her laugh cut through his dwindling sympathy. "You've got to be kidding me. Did you miss the 'I'd rather take twenty lashes'?"

Stubborn didn't cover it. She had to be hurting! What was up with the continued defiance? "Silver—"

"Let me up." She hissed, squirming. "You got your kink on. I'm done."

"You're done when I say so."

"As if! You know, I could use you as a blueprint to build an idiot."

"Is that so?" He fisted his hand in her hair. "You've just earned yourself ten more. Sad thing is, I'd originally intended five because of your lack of experience."

"Oh yeah?" She wrenched her hair free and turned her head to curl her lips at him. "Well, experience this, asshole."

Bending down, she set her teeth into his thigh.

His pants were thin enough for her to latch onto a nice chunk of skin. But the pain didn't reach the part of his mind that had locked on to the task at hand. He couldn't be angry at her, not when she was practically begging for more.

"Twenty it is."

* * * *

Defensive Zone

THE DARTMOUTH COBRAS #2

Silver Delgado has gained control of The Dartmouth Cobras—and lost control of her life.

Hockey might be the family business, but it's never interested Silver. Until her father's health decline thrusts responsibility for the team he owns straight into her hands. Now she has to find a way to get the team more fans, and establish herself as the new owner. Which means standing up to Dean Richter, the general manager and the advisor her father has forced on her. The fact that their 'business relationship' started with her over his lap at his BDSM club shouldn't be too much of a problem. Their hot one night stand meant nothing! But how can she earn his respect when he sees her as submissive? Can they separate work and the lifestyle she's curious to explore?

Balancing her new life away from Hollywood, living among people who see her as the selfish Delgado princess, has her feeling lost and alone until Landon Bower, the Cobras new Goalie slips into her life and becomes her best—and only—friend. The time they spend together makes everything else bearable, but before long his eyes meet hers with more than friendship, reflecting what she feels. Which could ruin everything.

Two Dominant men who see past her pretty mask and the shallow image she portrayed to the flashing cameras. A gentle attack from both sides that she can't hope to block unless she learns how to play.

But she's getting the hang of the game.

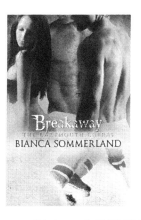

Breakaway
THE DARTMOUTH COBRAS

Against some attacks, the only hope is to come out and meet the play.

Last year, Jami Richter had no plans, no goals, no future. But that's all changed. First step, make up for putting her father through hell by supporting the hockey team he manages and becoming an Ice Girl. But a photo shoot puts her right in the arms of Sebastian Ramos, a Dartmouth Cobra defenseman with a reputation for getting any woman—or, as the rumors imply, man—he desires. And the powerful dominant wants her...and Luke. Getting involved in Seb's lifestyle gives her a new understanding of the game and the bonds between players. But can she handle being caught between two men who want her, while struggling with their attraction to one another?

Luke Carter's life is about as messed up as his scarred face. His mother is sick. His girlfriend dumps him. When he goes to his favorite BDSM club to blow off some steam, his Dom status is turned upside down when a therapeutic beating puts him in a good place. He flatly denies being submissive—or, even worse, being attracted to another man. He wants Jami but can't have her without getting involved with Sebastian. Can he overcome his own prejudices long enough to admit he wants them both?

Caught between Luke and Jami, Sebastian Ramos does everything in his power to fulfill their needs. His two new submissives willingly share their bodies, but not their secrets. When his own past comes back to haunt him, the fragile foundation of their relationship is ripped apart. As he works to salvage the damage done by doubt and insecurity, he discovers that Jami is hiding something dangerous. But it may already be too late.

Visit the Dartmouth Cobras

www.TheDartmouthCobras.com

About the Author

Tell you about me? Hmm, well there's not much to say. I love hockey and cars and my kids…not in that order of course! Lol! When I'm not writing—which isn't often—I'm usually watching a game or a car show while networking. Going out with my kids is my only downtime. I get to clear my head and forget everything.

As for when and why I first started writing, I guess I thought I'd get extra cookies if I was quiet for awhile—that's how young I was. I used to bring my grandmother barely legible pages filled with tales of evil unicorns. She told me then that I would be a famous author.

I hope one day to prove her right.

For more of my work, please visit: www.ImNoAngel.com

PRAISE FOR BIANCA SOMMERLAND'S BOOKS

"I just have to start by saying that this book is not for the faint of heart or the easily offended. Secondly, I have to say to the author, **Bianca Sommerland**, I give you a standing ovation. *Deadly Captive* was dark, sinister, erotic, intense, sexy and dangerous. Wow!"

-Karyl
Dark Diva Review of Deadly Captive

"My heart broke a little for Shawna. The entire set up made sense and from a personal note, I've been in the same situation. That's when I completely connected to the story and I was moved to tears."

-BookAddict
The Romance Reviews review of The Trip

Made in the USA
Lexington, KY
03 December 2014